Master Guns

A Novel

Raymond Hunter Pyle

This story is a work of fiction. Names, characters, places, and incidents either are the product of the author's imagination or are used fictitiously, and any resemblance to actual persons, living or dead, business establishments, events, or locations is unintended and entirely coincidental.

then watched the crew-chief standing at the port-side machine gun with a headset on and talking to the pilots. The other gunner moved to his gun on the starboard side. The helicopter began to flare and the crew chief held up one finger. One minute out.

Kelly checked his M-16 and told his team to lock and load. Lance Corporal Hoover and Private Moore loaded a round. Doc Anderson, the corpsman, moved his selector to safe. The UH-34 was approaching the LZ, and the pilot was going in fast. The LZ was small with a lot of obstructions on the periphery of the clearing and the chopper had to come down in just the right position with the tail held in a slot-like area between two large trees. Slipping to either side was not an option. The floor of the clearing was overgrown with scrub trees and elephant grass about seven feet high in places. The pilots would flatten the grass as best they could with the rotor wash.

He knelt near the door holding the frame of the net seats that lined the side. He felt the pain in his stomach he always got on insertions like this one and squeezed tight on his bladder. Every time, damn it. He almost lost control of his bladder every time he inserted.

In just seconds he would know what they were facing. The team was ready to clear the chopper fast and prepared to fight as soon as they hit the ground. The door gunners were ready and on edge. They were just seconds from the critical time when the helicopter would settle into the clearing in a slowly descending

hover, the time when they would make the best target, the time when they were almost stationary, a perfect target for an RPG.

The grass began to flatten from rotor wash and Kelly scanned the tree line with his eyes. He hated this part of the insertion. With limited LZs available the enemy would know where the Americans had to come in to land a helicopter, and helicopters were about the most prized targets a North Vietnamese soldier could bag. Anything could be waiting for them and there was no way to tell what was out there until the shooting started—or didn't. The odds were good they could exit the helicopter without a problem and move away from the LZ before VC or NVA could get organized and converge on the LZ. Then they just had to get to an observation point and stay hidden for a couple of days and make it to the extraction LZ. Piece of cake. Right. Five Marines alone in the grass with God only knew how many VC/NVA looking for them. This wasn't the way an insertion was supposed to be done. Recon Marines depended on stealth and avoiding contact to stay alive.

If you had to go in by air, stealth began with dummy insertions followed by a fast, unobserved real insertion and a quick move to harbor. This one should have been planned for a covert insertion from an infantry patrol, not by air. From the ground, they could have dropped out of a patrol unobserved and moved away while the infantry held the enemy's attention. But G2 wanted intelligence now and pairing up with an infantry patrol took time and planning, so the bird had

been scheduled.

He watched the whipping grass get closer to the door and stood up. His team stood up behind him. They would clear the helicopter in ten seconds so the pilot could immediately transition to lift and get out of there. He would be lifting even as they exited the aircraft, and he would take the helicopter about a half mile away and wait for Kelly's call to make sure the team was safe and moving away from the LZ.

The elephant grass bent under the helicopter and Kelly looked over his shoulder at the crew chief. The chief talked on his headset while keeping his eyes on the tree line and then gave the sign to exit. Kelly didn't have to tell his team anything. They were watching him and ready to go. He jumped off the helicopter and dropped almost four feet into the bent grass, the rotor wash beating against him and slicing the edges of the grass across his arms and legs. When he hit, the sixty pounds of gear he was carrying buckled his knees and sent shock waves up his spine and into his head. The rest of the team hit around him and they immediately formed a wheel flat on the ground, each man facing outward in a 360-degree circle, feet touching.

At first he thought they had a good insertion and began thinking about his route out of the LZ. Noise from the helicopter adding power and lifting was so loud he didn't even hear the helicopter's door gunners start firing, but the shock of a bad insertion quickly became apparent. Incoming small arms began hitting

around the team. More small arms rounds ricocheted off the helicopter and zinged around and above the teams' heads.

The helicopter lifted slowly, spooling up its power. Soon Kelly and the team could hear the guns firing. He lifted his head slowly to see what was going on and immediately dropped back prone on the ground. Muzzle flashes could be seen in the trees all around the LZ. The grass around the team began to shred with the volume of incoming tearing it apart. They were caught in a shower of flying vegetation and rounds cracking overhead with sonic pops. Kelly pulled the radioman close and grabbed the handset. The radio was preset to the insertion frequency and was ready.

"Lifter Three this is Boatload," he screamed into the mouthpiece "We are compromised and under fire. Get us the hell out of here."

"Hold on Boatload. We're taking heavy fire."

The helicopter continued to rise and then veered away from the LZ and out of sight over the trees.

Without the sound of the bird, the gunfire from the trees became one massive roar of incoming from every direction. The only reason the team was still alive was the concealment the grass gave them and the tempting target the helicopter made diverting some of the enemy fire. He signaled the team to move away from their current location. The enemy knew where they were and small arms incoming was hitting all around them.

They bellied through the grass and vines trying

to find anything that would give them some cover or at least get them below dirt a little bit. He ordered the team to hold their fire and not give their position away. He unfolded his map.

The LZ was a fixed set of coordinates that Kelly had an accurate fix on from the helicopter's navigation equipment. He made a circle on the map around the LZ and calculated his first artillery call. He grabbed the handset and called the Ca Lu 105mm battery. He called for one round of HE to be adjusted. It had to happen fast or the VC would begin moving in too close. Ca Lu called the first round in the air. Several moments later Kelly heard the ripping, howling sound of incoming. It hit in the canopy where he expected it to and shook the earth under the team. He began walking artillery around the edge of the LZ in the trees.

"Boatload this is Avenger Six, what is your status?"

Avenger was a Marine Huey gunship squadron based in Danang.

"Avenger Six this is Boatload. We are surrounded and still taking incoming. We need you about as quick as you can get here. Over."

"Roger, Boatload. We are two minutes out. Mark your position with smoke."

"This is Boatload. Roger. Marking position with yellow smoke. Hit everything as close as you can."

"Roger, keep your heads down."

Kelly immediately turned his attention back to the insertion bird.

"Lifter Three this is Boatload. We need to get the hell out of here right now."

"Boatload this is Lifter Three. Coming in behind Avenger. Move your asses when I get there."

"This is Boatload. Roger, out."

Small arms continued hitting around them and shredding the elephant grass. A round made a splat sound between Kelly's legs. No sense in moving. Incoming was hitting randomly around and between the team members. One place was as good, or as bad, as any other. Then a mass of concentrated fire saturated their position.

He heard a scream and looked to his left. Lance Corporal Hoover grabbed his thigh and curled up in a fetal position. A random round had found him. Doc Anderson immediately crawled to Hoover and began working on his leg. Then another massive roar of incoming slashed the grass around the team and Private Moore was literally flipped over by the impact of a round penetrating his shoulder and driving through to his chest. Kelly grabbed the radio handset. Calm was gone. He was close to panic.

"Lifter Three this is Boatload. I've got two Whiskey India Alpha. We need help right now."

"Boatload this is Avenger Six. Stay down. LZ in sight. I've got two yellow smokes in two locations. Mark your location with another color."

Apparently, the enemy was listening in on the radio transmissions and had duplicated Kelly's smoke.

"Roger, Avenger. Tossing smoke now. Tell me

what you see."

Kelly waited for the reply and wished the flyboys would speed it up.

"Boatload, I see red smoke."

"That's us, Avenger."

"Roger. Where are you in relation to your smoke?"

"This is Boatload," Kelly screamed. "Smoke is ten feet from team. Kill anything outside a ten-foot circle around the smoke."

"This is Avenger Six. Roger, out."

The next thing he saw was a Marine Huey gunship hovering near the north edge of the LZ. Light flashed on both sides of the helicopter and explosions started erupting in the tree line. The Huey turned slowly and then more flashes followed by more explosions in the trees. The Huey continue to rotate and put rockets into the trees all around the LZ. Then he started moving forward slowly and his guns started working the grass in the LZ. Avenger was taking fire from the ground the whole time. Then another Huey gunship appeared and began working the tree line with guns.

"Boatload this is Lifter Three. I'm two minutes out. Get ready."

"Roger, Lifter. We are moving now. Same LZ. I repeat. Same LZ."

Doc Anderson lifted Hoover, and Mendes grabbed Moore's arms. They started moving back to the original insertion point, the only point where the UH-34 could get low enough for loading. The gunships

continued working the grass and trees with their machineguns keeping enemy heads down.

Kelly heard the UH-34 coming and waved the team down. When he saw the bird hover and begin to descend with its tail positioned over the slot between the trees, he helped Mendes with Moore. Doc acted as a crutch for Hoover, and they moved under the rotor wash of Lifter Three, not wanting to waste even a second getting on the bird.

The big helicopter hovered, paused, and descended further. Kelly could see inside the bird and the crew chief leaning out of the door watching the ground below the bird and talking on his headset. The helicopter dropped further and Kelly stood, pulling Moore's shoulder up, wanting to be out of there. Mendes started forward with Moore's other shoulder. Doc Anderson and Hoover followed them to the cargo door. They stepped up to the deck and carried their loads into the troop compartment with small arms incoming hitting the helicopter around them. As the helicopter began lifting, several rounds of incoming small arms clanked against the skin of the bird, some punching all the way through and exiting through the skin on the other side.

Kelly sat on the floor and rolled Moore over. Doc knelt next to him and checked the wound. He looked up at Kelly and shook his head no. Kelly stretched out on the deck and rubbed his forehead with both hands. The patrol never even got under way. They were waiting. Fuck!

CONTENTS

Raymond Hunter Pyle

CHAPTER 2

Dong Ha Marine Base, Sector Five
3rd Reconnaissance Battalion HQ

Sergeant Major Cullahan met Master Gunnery Sergeant
Dick Rhodes at the LZ when Rhodes landed at Dong Ha.
The Sergeant Major looked like he had just come off the
parade deck at Parris Island. His utilities were tailored,
starched, and pressed; his eight-point cover was
starched and blocked; his jungle boots looked new with
spit shined heels and toes. The nylon mesh of the boot
sides was still colored green and when walking, the
soles still gave a crinkling vibration from the steel mesh
inside designed to guard against punji stakes, pointed
wooden stakes made by the VC and smeared with feces,
a danger the Sergeant Major was unlikely to approach
within five miles at any time. Even the Jeep looked like

it had been shined. He took a handkerchief out of his back pocket and lightly wiped the dust off the toes of his boots while he waited for Rhodes to get his bags off the chopper.

"How're ya doing, Dave? Rhodes said and put out his hand. "Looks like you found a mama-san to handle your laundry and clean your pipes. You old dog."

Sergeant Major Dave Cullahan jerked his thumb at the back of the jeep and tried to keep his anger in check.

"Put your bags in the back, Master Gunnery Sergeant. You know better. I'm the senior NCO in the battalion and I try set a good example."

Senior NCO my ass, Rhodes thought, but didn't get to reply before Cullahan continued.

"Your uniforms could use some attention. When's the last time those boots felt a brush?"

"About the last time I felt a shower," Rhodes said. "When's the last time your shoulder felt the recoil of an M-14?"

Cullahan started the jeep and put it in gear. Rhodes could see the red creeping up Cullahan's neck. Cullahan started to reply, but apparently decided not to go there.

"Master Gunnery Sergeant, I expect you to set a good example for our Marines and I expect you help me keep this battalion squared away. As the battalion's senior NCOs, number one and two, so to speak, we have the colonel's trust and he has high expectations of us. I know I can depend on your support."

"Of course, you can, Dave," Rhodes said. "But I'm sure you and the First Sergeant have the shitter burning details under control, so I'll stay focused on operations. How did I rate the Battalion Sergeant Major as my driver?"

Rhodes knew Cullahan wasn't used to anyone addressing him as anything but Sergeant Major and knew he didn't like it. He waited for Cullahan to say something about the use of his first name, but Cullahan took a different track.

"The Colonel felt it was appropriate to have the battalion's senior enlisted man meet the battalion's number two senior enlisted man, so to speak, and I thought it would be a good opportunity for us to talk."

"So, you already heard about me making Master Guns?"

"When the list came out, of course," Cullahan said. "By the way, congratulations."

"Yeah, thanks. So, you knew I was coming back?"

"Major Slaughter made us all painfully aware of that, Master Gunnery Sergeant. Let's get together and let me brief you in over a beer. I've got a few things I'd like to make you aware of."

"Yeah, sure, Dave. Right after I get checked in."

Cullahan visibly grimaced at the use of his first name again. Master Guns Rhodes and Sergeant Major Cullahan had a history that had soured after Cullahan made First Sergeant. Cullahan had worked for Rhodes when Cullahan was a staff sergeant and Rhodes was a company gunny in the Fourth Marines. Cullahan hadn't taken direction well. He also held a grudge.

There are two paths into the top two enlisted ranks in the Marine Corps and a Gunny Sergeant (E7) must indicate which path he wants to follow when he is recommended for the E8 selection board. One path can be called command advice and administration and points selection to E8 First Sergeant and then E9 Sergeant Major. The other path allows the Marine to remain in his MOS and points selection to E8 Master Sergeant and E9 Master Gunnery Sergeant.

Rhodes decided to stay with his infantry MOS and moved up to Master Sergeant and then Master Gunnery Sergeant. Cullahan made Gunny and then decided to go the route of First Sergeant and then Sergeant Major. Cullahan ended up advancing faster than Rhodes simply because there were more First Sergeant and Sergeant Major slots generally than there were Master Sergeant and Master Gunnery Sergeant slots in the 03 MOS. Fact is, Rhodes wouldn't have made Master Guns when he did if an existing Master Guns hadn't bought the farm in Danang by a rocket, opening a slot the selection board could fill.

Along the way, Rhodes and Cullahan's careers seemed to pull them together in the same commands, and a certain amount of friction had developed. Cullahan thought Rhodes was too lax with military bearing and too familiar with his Marines. Rhodes thought Cullahan had a broom handle up his ass and never missed a chance to let Cullahan know. And

Rhodes always seemed to be the CO's fair haired boy, which did not go down well with Cullahan.

Rhodes making Master Gunny was not a happy event for the Sergeant Major. After chaffing under Rhodes's Company Gunny leadership for two years and then making Gunny himself, Cullahan enjoyed his peer status. When he made First Sergeant ahead of Rhodes's Master Sergeant he never missed a chance to stick his diamond in Rhodes's face. Then when he was selected for Sergeant Major while Rhodes was still a Master Sergeant and likely to stay that way, Cullahan had been ecstatic. Hearing Rhodes had received his fourth rocker and pineapple patch had ruined Cullahan's day, and then Slaughter had announced that Rhodes was coming to 3rd Recon Battalion. Life just wasn't fair.

When they got to the Operations shack, Rhodes pulled his bags from the back of the Jeep and dropped them on the dirt. Cullahan didn't waste his breath with a good bye and just drove away. Rhodes took a deep breath smelling the familiar and unwelcome odors of the DMZ again. It hadn't been nearly long enough since he had smelled them the last time. Thirty days leave in Hong Kong had been everything he'd hoped for and went a long way toward getting his nerves settled down after his last tour in-country, an extended eighteen-month tour with the infantry and combined action teams. Major Slaughter, now Third Recon Battalion's S3 and Rhodes's ex-company commander, a captain then, had sent Rhodes to the states for training after his leave. It had been a good and needed break, but three months away from the sound of incoming hadn't been nearly enough.

Master Guns Rhodes had done well in the Corps from the start. Some men just seem born to be Marines. Enlisting in the middle of the Korean war when he was twenty-one, three or four years older than most recruits, and after three years of college, three or more years better educated than most recruits, Rhodes took to the Corps like the proverbial duck to water. After a lackluster attempt at civilian academic success and unable to find anything that interested him in civilian life, the college kid called professor, and not kindly by the DIs, had found a home and a calling.

He only put eighteen months in Korea, but he came home a sergeant with a silver star, a purple heart, and a whole lot of combat experience. He reenlisted and did a tour as a DI at Parris Island. With his combat tour, DI tour, and superior ratings, Rhodes had all the punches in his ticket he needed to move up.

Over the next five years he finished his senior year for his history degree in a Navy Department sponsored extension program for military people with the University of Maryland. Rhodes was encouraged to apply for OCS, but he liked being an enlisted man just fine. He refused OCS two more times. He liked being a rarity, an enlisted man with a degree. It had a way of disconcerting junior officers and punching a hole in their arrogance. Of course, now with the pineapple patch in the center of his stripes, he didn't need much else to deflate junior officers. Nobody screwed with the Master Gunny. The only enlisted rank senior to his was Sergeant Major, but that was only a formality. They were both E9s, the top enlisted grade.

Slaughter was expecting him and greeted him with a smile and outstretched hand.

"Good to see you, Dick. Damn, it's good to have you back. Congratulations, Master Guns."

"Thanks, Major. I won't bullshit you and say it's good to be back. What's going on up north?"

"Con Thien is taking some incoming today. Harassment mostly. Are you squared away with berthing yet?"

"No, sir. I came straight here."

"Why don't you go ahead and get checked in and issued. Come back here before chow and I'll brief you in."

"Yes, sir. What have you got in mind for me?"

"Operations Chief, but I want you to get some operational experience with the teams first. We'll talk about it after you get checked in."

Rhodes turned his records in at Personnel, Finance, and Medical, and then got his hooch assignment from the housing officer. With more SNCO hooches available than SNCOs he made sure he didn't have to share a hooch with anyone, not even the Sergeant Major, especially not the Sergeant Major. Dave was a good man and a good Marine, but when he was selected for E8 First Sergeant he had changed. Probably had to, to move up on that track. Selection to Sergeant Major had just made him more chicken-shit, in Rhodes's opinion. Rhodes was promoted to Master Sergeant a year after Cullahan made First Sergeant. Cullahan made Sergeant Major two years before Rhodes made Master Gunny so he really was senior to Rhodes by date of rank and by TO&E, but they were both E9s. Hell, even in the Corps some pigs are more equal than others.

Rhodes, having his own private hooch, would cause a little hate and discontent among the lieutenants who had to share two to a hooch, but it was good for them. It let them know what the pecking order was. He was a Master Marine. They were trainees. He saved the armory for last and the weapons corporal wasn't being cooperative.

"Standard issue is an M-16, Master Guns," the Armory Corporal said.

"Do you have a good M-14 back there, Corporal?"

"We have twenty, but they're for special weapons issue to the teams."

"Looks like I'm going to spend some time with the teams. I want an M-14."

"Master Guns, I don't have the . . ."

"Look, numb-nuts . . .," Rhodes began, but cut it off. The Corporal was just doing his job. "Who's the armorer?"

"Staff Sergeant Tucker."

"Amos Tucker?"

"That's him, Master Guns."

"Christ, he was a corporal the last time I saw him, and that wasn't very long ago. Tell Tucker I said to get off his ass and get out here."

The corporal grinned and shrugged his shoulders. He went deeper into the armory and came back in short order.

"He's coming, Master Guns."

Soon Tucker moseyed through the opening between weapons racks wearing thick glasses and inspecting the trigger group of an M-16 he was carrying. He had a plug of tobacco stuffed in his cheek. He didn't look up until he was in front of Rhodes.

"Corporal Tucker, if you don't get some fire in your ass I'm going to have you burning shitters until you rotate back to the states," Rhodes said.

The armory corporal grinned and backed away. Tucker looked up slowly squinting through his coke bottle glasses. Neither NCOs nor officers bothered him. He knew he was the best damn armorer in the Third Marine Division and had a home anywhere he wanted to go.

"Hello, Master Gunny. Where the hell did you come from? I thought you rotated out last fall."

"I did. Who the hell was stupid enough to give you staff stripes? The last I heard you were having trouble hanging on to corporal stripes."

"Says you. Congrats on the pineapple patch."

"Yeah, thanks. The boss says I need some operational experience. That means I'm going to be in the grass for a while. I want an M-fourteen."

"The Sixteen is standard issue."

"Tucker, we can play games all day long if you want, but in the end, I'm going to have an M-fourteen for my personal weapon. What's it going to take?"

Tucker turned the trigger mechanism over and studied it for a moment while he thought.

"Well, let's see," he said. "I do have a really nice fourteen I've been keeping back as my own weapon, but I don't go out and I don't have to stand perimeter duty. I might be able to see my way clear to . . ."

"Tucker, knock it off. What do you need?"

Tucker studied the trigger housing he was working on some more.

"It's a damn nice rifle," he said and studied the trigger some more.

"You already said that. What do you need?"

"I put in for R&R in Hong Kong, but the quota is full," he said. "Openings happen sometimes, you know, guys get hurt and a quota opens up, but someone else's Gunny always seems to get to the First Sergeant ahead of me and if . . ."

"Let me see the rifle."

Tucker went to the back of the armory and returned with a mint M-14.

"I've been over this rifle myself and I'd say it's match grade with the modifications I made. If you can't fire a two-inch group with it at a hundred meters you can't shoot."

Rhodes broke it down and inspected the parts. Tucker had floated the barrel and said he did some work on the trigger. He put it back together and tested the action. Sweet and crisp. Four or five-pound pull. The rifle looked like it had never been issued except that it was clean and oiled.

"Consider it done," Rhodes said. "I'll talk to the Sergeant Major. How is it on full rock and roll?"

"Like any fourteen. If you can handle it, it will get the job done. I'd leave the bipod on it if I were you."

"I can handle it. Magazines?"

"I can give you two bandoleers. Load them yourself."

"Make sure you give me a couple extra boxes of tracers. Did Slaughter bring you along with him, too?"

"Yeah. He's a persuasive guy."

"Tell me about it. How about a forty-five?"

"You get one. Want to pick it out yourself?"

"You do it. You know more about them then I'll ever know."

Tucker held his hands up in mock amazement. "My God. I am in the presence of an intelligent Master Gunnery Sergeant. Corporal Fisher, bring me one of the forty-fives from the rack next to my work bench."

Then Tucker was reminded of who he was mocking.

Very quietly Rhodes said, "Tucker, one of these days you are going to cross the line and we're going to do the tango." Quietly, but there was no mistaking the menace.

Tucker spat tobacco juice in a C-Rats can. "Yeah. Bad joke. No disrespect intended, Master Guns."

The forty-five looked brand new, but was clean and oiled.

"Staff Sergeant Tucker," Rhodes said, "with a little time and a whole lot of supervision from a real NCO you might turn into a half-assed staff sergeant yet."

"Take care of that rifle, Master Guns." Tucker said. "If you leave before I do, I want it back. Corporal, get the serial numbers and sign him out."

When Rhodes left the armory carrying his M-14, he noticed again his left-hand shaking. He held it up and made a fist. The slight tremor was still there. It had started near the end of his last tour. He put his hand down and ignored the tremor. He knew what it meant.

Slaughter was ready for him when Rhodes returned to the HQ bunker.

"Dick, you might as well get right into it. You've got two days to get settled in and then you're going out on your first recon patrol. Go over this Ops Order and I'll be right back."

Rhodes had some of the training, but he had never been on a real recon patrol. He sat at Slaughter's field desk and picked up the order. It described a mission like the ones he had reviewed in Okinawa. Small team behind enemy lines. Determine size, location, disposition, of VC/NVA units in area of operations. He focused on the Shackle grid at the end of the order.

A shackle grid was a means for authenticating transmissions and encoding coordinates for fire missions and unit location. It consisted of a row of numbers, one through zero, across the top and the 26 letters of the alphabet distributed in columns below the numbers. For authentication, a station would challenge with any letter in any column. The answering station would authenticate with any other letter in the same column. Encoding numbers for coordinates was done by picking a letter from the column under the number you wanted. The receiving station found the letter and read the number at the top of the column. Simple, handy, and reasonably secure for short periods. The grid was changed frequently so the enemy wouldn't have time to break the code.

Rhodes sat back and thought about the mission. Looked like pure observation. Stay out of sight and report what you find. But the operations order included artillery instructions, so the team would probably be authorized to call in a fire mission on concentrations of enemy. Slaughter walked in and sat on the edge of the desk.

"Just tag along, Dick. Get a feel for the area and the teams. Staff Sergeant Kelly is team leader and he's Force Recon. He's as good as they get. I want you to take a radio. You are Striker Three. As Ops Chief, you'll have that call sign permanently."

"How big is the team?"

"Four enlisted Marines and a corpsman plus

you. They're used to working together so you may get some resentment. Work your way through it. Those guys hate to have a new guy with them no matter what his rank is."

"I can handle it."

"No doubt in my mind," Slaughter said. "Go on and get settled in and go meet Kelly in the morning. He'll be planning the patrol."

In 1967, the Marines that came to the 3rd Marine Division's 3rd Reconnaissance Battalion were not handpicked. They were assigned from a pool of replacements or volunteers just like any infantry unit. Therefore, Slaughter wanted Rhodes and other experienced infantry SNCOs in the Recon Battalion. Early in the Vietnam conflict, Recon assets including Force Recon had been used for almost anything in Vietnam but recon. Slaughter called it the super grunt syndrome. Some commanders wanting an elite group around them were even using Recon as security for their HQs, an incredible waste of talent.

To solve the problem of misuse, General Walt, a WWII Raider Marine himself with a strong grasp of Recon value and use, folded First Force Recon Company into the Division's Recon Battalion for tighter control and required any request for Recon missions to come through the Division G2 (Intelligence). Some of 1st Force Recon Company had been split up and scattered throughout the platoons of Third Recon Battalion to put experience and training in the battalion teams. This consolidation and approval process worked to curb the misuse of Recon assets by commanders, but it also blurred the role of Division Recon and Force Recon and created a kind of misuse of its own.

Traditionally, Force Recon was responsible and had the training for pre-assault and deep penetration post assault recon and special skill insertions such as submarine and parachute. The Division's Recon Battalions went ashore with the division and served the division commander within the division's artillery fan, the area where the commander had the assets to do something with the intelligence they developed. But the roles were no longer clear with Force and Battalion assets mixed together, and Third Battalion's teams were used for every type of recon mission.

Recon indoctrination training and some in-country recon training sometimes supplemented with jump and jungle warfare training in Okinawa was slowly being added to battalion recon training, but getting it on-line was taking time. New and raw replacements were broken in on the job with the teams. Recon is probably not a set of skills you want to learn on the job, but there it is.

Many of the new-order recon troops did not have the esprit de corps of the men who went through Force Recon training in Lejeune, jungle warfare training in Panama, submarine training in the Caribbean, scuba training in San Diego, jump training at Fort Benning, and often specialized training in mountain warfare, EOD, communications, Forward Observer training with artillery, etc. Neither were they trained by experienced Force Recon Marines who had served in Force Recon and Raiders in WWII and Recon in Korea, as Force Recon troops were. They needed confidence and a way to find their own identity, but like FNGs everywhere they were hardly tolerated.

Rhodes, even though a Master Gunnery Sergeant, was a new guy to the Recon Battalion. He had to earn his way out of the newbie status just like every FNG. No matter what your rank, if you screwed up a small patrol miles behind enemy lines, you could get the patrol killed.

CHAPTER 3

Rhodes found the Sergeant Major at the Battalion HQ bunker complex. To avoid any further antagonism, he stopped by his hooch and put on a fresh set of utilities and applied a coat of Kiwi black to his boots and gave them a good brushing. There was no way he would spit shine them. They're boots for crying out loud. His utilities were tailored and had good creases from the way he folded them, and his cover was starched and blocked by the laundry mama-sans in Danang. The utilities were faded, but after an eighteen-month tour in-country they were supposed to be faded. He had no intention of walking around in new utilities looking like some FNG pogue. He felt his face and had a quick shave. He didn't shine like the Sergeant Major, but even from a football field away he was every inch a Master Guns.

The Sergeant Major was in the Executive Officer's office when Rhodes stepped into the command bunker. Major Rockwell, the Exec, was one of Rhodes's least favorite people. He was more chicken shit than the SarMajor and he and Rhodes had had run-ins before when the Exec was a chicken shit Lieutenant at Parris Island and again when he was a chicken-shit captain in Bravo Company 1/4. In Rhodes's opinion, Rockwell was born a pogue and would die a pogue. There are warriors and there are pogues. A warrior runs toward the sound of guns. A pogue finds an excuse to inventory the O-Club liquor supply.

"In here, Master Gunnery Sergeant," Cullahan yelled when he spotted Rhodes.

Rhodes removed his cover and entered the Exec's office. He came to attention six inches from the center of the Exec's desk and reported.

"At ease, Master Guns," Rockwell said. "Glad to see you had a chance to get squared away. Have a seat."

So, you've already had a little chat with the Exec, did you? He thought as he looked sideways at Cullahan. Screw it. You are two of a kind. It was obvious Rockwell's utilities had never seen the insult of dirt or sweat and he wore gold oak leaves. Shiny gold oak leaves. That said a lot about his plans. He had no intention of going anywhere his rank insignia could single him out as a target.

"Yes, sir," he said. "The chopper ride up here plays hell with a military appearance, but the senior NCO has to find the time to set an example, sir"

He was pleased to see Cullahan's head snap

around at the mention of senior NCO. Rockwell smiled and shook his head vigorously in agreement. The senior NCO crack went right over his head.

"Yes, yes. I'm glad to hear that from you, Master Guns. It is so difficult to keep the Marines squared away here. They go out on patrol and come back looking like they've been in a brawl in the mud. And then they think they can just stay that way. Their leaders must set a good example. You are exactly right. We must find the time. Sergeant Major, I think we have an ally."

Cullahan was not happy at all and his displeasure showed on his face. He just grunted in response to the major's comment.

"Well, let's see what we have you slotted for, Master Guns," Rockwell said. "Looks like you are to be the new Operations Chief. An excellent place for you to exert some influence on the teams. Let me welcome you aboard. I'll be looking for good things from you, Master Guns."

"Thank you, sir. I'm sure this is going to be a learning experience for me. Sergeant Major, do you have time now to brief me in, or should I come back later?"

"Now is fine," Cullahan grunted. "By your leave, sir."

"Good, good," Rockwell said. "Go on and get the Master Guns squared away. Welcome aboard, Top. My door is always open."

The meeting with Cullahan was quick and consisted of Cullahan making every effort to be sure Rhodes knew the Sergeant Major was the senior NCO in the command. Rhodes called Cullahan by his first name and Cullahan called him Master Gunnery Sergeant. He knew he would have to have a word with the First Sergeant about Tucker's Hong Kong Quota. Cullahan would probably deep six it just out of spite. He returned to his hooch and got a good night's sleep.

Kelly was working over three maps when Rhodes got to the team hooch at 0700. He looked up when Rhodes knocked on the screen door. The hooch belonged to the team and Master Gunny or not, he was an outsider until he was invited in.

"Staff Sergeant Kelly?"

"Yeah, who you?"

"Rhodes. I wanted to meet your team."

"Oh! Come on in Master Guns. Captain Turner said you'd be coming by. You're going out with us?"

"Well, that's the plan. Major Slaughter wants me to work with several of the teams before I start in the Three shop. Are you working on the patrol plan?"

"Yeah. Come on over. I'll show you the patrol route. We've been in there before and didn't see much activity, but that doesn't mean it'll be quiet this time. Our patrol area is north of Khe Sanh along these hills."

Kelly was a solid looking NCO. Maybe five-ten, one-eighty, squared away appearance. His easy-going manner would give his Marines confidence.

"Where are they going to insert us?" he asked.

"We'll do decoy insertions along the slopes below hill 861 northwest of Khe Sanh and then insert here," Kelly said with his finger on a point near hill 558 west of what was left of Route 9 and west of the Rao Quan River. "We'll patrol along this small ridge toward 861 and extract here."

Rhodes studied the map for a moment getting a feel for the terrain based on the contour lines that indicated the hills. It wouldn't be fun humping a full pack over that steep ground. The length of a recon patrol was pretty much determined by what the Marines could carry. The three big operational priorities were water, batteries for the radios, and ammunition, all of them heavy. Without water the patrol was over in a matter of hours. Before the last battery was exhausted, the team had to call for extraction while it could. Without ammunition, the patrol couldn't defend itself. That was just the big three. Then there were food, weapons, med supplies, lights, signaling and marking munitions, grenades, binoculars, web gear, ponchos, personal items, etc. The longer the patrol, the more had to be carried. Even Recon Marines have a limit.

"Okay. It's two days," he said. "How do you want me to pack? I'll be carrying an M-fourteen with twenty mags, four frags, and a PRC-25."

"Two days if we're lucky," Kelly said. "Something to keep in mind on every patrol, Master Guns. The departure date is fixed. The return date is estimated and can be changed by the weather and the enemy. Take at least four canteens. We still have some of the Northeast monsoon left, but water is scarce out there."

"Dress?"

"The days are pretty good now, but it gets cold at night. Up to you if you want to take a field jacket. Could get heavy and uncomfortable in the day though."

"How are you going to do it?"

"I wear a long sleeve cammie bush jacket and pack my poncho. The liner will keep you warm enough at night."

"Okay. I'll do the same. Look, Kelly, it's your team and you're the boss. I'm along for the ride. Use me any way you want to."

Kelly seemed to relax a bit.

"That's good to hear. I take some staff officers now and then. They don't always understand it's my team."

"I do. I mean it when I say put me where you want me. I have a lot to learn."

"Can you relieve my tail-end-Charlie to give him a rest if I need you?"

"Yeah, I can do that. I can also call in a fire mission if you need me. But I'm the new guy here. I'll do what I'm told."

"Do you speak any Vietnamese?"

"Some. I spent some time in a Combined Action Company back in sixty-five."

"That could be helpful. Hell, maybe you won't be dead weight after all, Master Guns."

Kelly grinned and put out his hand. "Come back at sixteen-hundred and I'll introduce you to the team."

He shook Kelly's hand. "Forget ranks on patrol. Can we just use my call sign?"

"Sure. The team too?"

"Yeah. It would help. On patrol just call me Striker. The Major said that would be my permanent call sign."

"Sounds good, Master Guns. On patrol, it's Striker."

"Done," he said and got up. "See you at sixteen-hundred."

He met the team at sixteen hundred and sat in on the pre-patrol briefing. The team consisted of Kelly as team leader, Corporal Stephen Masters – assistant team leader, Lance Corporal Pete Chambers – primary radioman, Lance Corporal Tex Mendes, and HM3 Doc Anderson. Doc doubled as secondary radioman.

During the briefing, Kelly decided to take only the primary radio since Rhodes would be carrying a radio. Doc Anderson grinned real big when he heard that. The PRC-25 was a heavy mother with the battery attached.

Kelly, and Masters would carry M-14s with M-76 rifle grenade launchers for the White Phosphorus (Willie-Pete) rifle grenades. They might not use the WP grenades during the patrol, but if they had to, Kelly wanted those weapons in the hands of the most experienced men. Willie-Pete was not only good for marking targets with a thick white smoke, but if you had to disengage from an enemy with superior numbers and terrain, Willie-Pete made a much better smoke screen than smoke grenades, and when that white-hot crap was flying the enemy was keeping their heads down— or burning—sometimes both.

Firing the M-76 took a couple of extra steps and could confuse an inexperienced shooter under fire. A spindle valve had to be turned and a crimped cartridge had to be loaded to launch the grenade. Then the rifle had to be set back to normal magazine fire. SOP was to fire the grenade, reset the spindle valve and then immediately fire a magazine of 7.62 into the target area so the rest of the patrol could dial in on the tracers and saturate the target with directed fire. Firing the M-76 effectively, especially with incoming hitting around you, took a calm hand and a cool head. The four WP grenades would be distributed throughout the team.

Chambers, Mendes, and Doc Anderson would carry M-16s, and Chambers would also sling an M-79 grenade launcher. Everyone packed some of the M-79 frag and smoke rounds. Three men packed a few pinions for getting up rock faces, and two men carried fifty foot lengths of rope. All members of the team carried at least four frag M-26 hand grenades along with two bandoleers of personal ammunition, and a claymore. Kelly packed colored smoke for marking an LZ.

Since this was his first patrol, he decided to stuff extra magazines into his pack also. His previous tour with an infantry company had given Rhodes a set of priorities for the field. Food you could do without for a few days, water for a couple of days, ammunition you could not do without for even one fight. Rhodes watched the team members while Kelly briefed them, watched them with a growing sense of dread he was almost used to. Another operation he might not come back from. It was hard to keep that out of his mind after eighteen months of combat.

The briefing was quick, no questions. Recon teams don't say much on or off patrol. On patrol, they never talked above a whisper and avoided even that when they could, preferring hand signals. Each team developed their own form of sign language along with standard hand signals. After a while together they knew each other so well they didn't even need signals. Usually just a glance and a movement of the eyes would do. Off patrol the habit of silence tended to continue.

The team was used to each other and trusted Kelly. Rhodes got a few sideways glances when Kelly introduced him, and a couple of nods, but otherwise the team ignored him. He knew that would change in the grass. Until he proved he could be trusted, he would be watched. If he proved quickly he could move quietly with the team and not do stupid FNG stuff, the patrol would settle into normal patrol behavior. If he screwed up, he would be a burden and treated like a burden, subtly, but for sure. Kelly wrapped up the briefing before chow.

"Okay, that's it. We've been in there before, but

let's not relax. While we're out, Master Gunny Rhodes is Striker. Calls for Striker Three are for him. To keep it simple just call him Striker between us. Any words for the team, Striker?"

"Yeah, thanks. Look, I'm the FNG here. I've had the training, and I've been in the crap in Phu Bai and at the Rock Pile, but I'm a Recon cherry. Don't be afraid to treat me like a cherry. I expect Staff Sergeant Kelly to direct me like any other member of the team. Nuff said."

A few shoulders relaxed slightly and he got a couple grins. He had passed a small test, but he still had to prove he wouldn't do something stupid that would get the team killed.

That evening Rhodes checked his pack, cleaned his weapon, and took a shower that would have to last a few days. The shower water smelled like diesel. The queasy feeling in his gut came back and he chewed a couple of stale C-rats Chiclets to settle it down. The tremor in his hand had settled down until it was hardly noticeable. Tomorrow he would face the unknown—and the known. With eighteen months of Combined Action duty and infantry behind him, maybe the known was worse than the unknown, the memories worse than the fears. He had a lot of demons from the past to conjure up. He tried to keep them at bay.

Physically he was as good as most twenty-year-old Marines. It was a point of pride he worked at, but he had to admit it took longer for the joints to warm up in the morning now, and a cold, wet night in the grass left his body aching for a lot longer than it ever had before. And he also had to admit, too many beers had started a gut on his six foot one inch 200-pound frame he was having trouble getting rid of. Could he keep up with the young men, or would he be just one more old pogue along for the ride? Mid-thirties wasn't old, but the Marines on the teams were in their late teens. They could drink all night, get up and go on a three-day patrol, come back, get one night's rest and do it all over again. Old is relative. So is in shape.

CHAPTER 4

The team was trucked to the airstrip at 0700. A UH-34 landed at 0750 and the team lifted off at 0800. Kelly sat between the pilots with his maps and coordinated the dummy insertions and the final approach to the insertion LZ. They made a dummy insertion, a spiral down and hover for a few seconds, then the helicopter flew at tree-top level to the insertion point. The pilots did an over-flight and allowed Kelly to get a good look at the LZ, then did a long curve back with another dummy insertion along the way and spiraled down quickly, stopped the spiral abruptly, and settled into a hover with the rotors beating the elephant grass down.

The team exited the helicopter with only a two-foot drop. With the weight they each carried, the small drop was welcome. The helicopter was down for only fifteen seconds and lifted off as soon as the crew chief saw Rhodes, the last man, disappear from the door. The pilots flew to another location and did another dummy insertion and then stood off in the distance in case the team had to be extracted from a bad (read hot) LZ.

As soon as the helicopter departed, the elephant grass sprang back up and the team was concealed in seven-foot high grass mixed with vines and scrub trees. The February heat wasn't too bad and overcast skies helped. Kelly formed the team in a perimeter and waited to see if the insertion had attracted any attention. The quiet time had two purposes. First, it let their nerves settle down from the landing. Second, it let Kelly orient the team with compass and map while listening for movement near the LZ. But they couldn't wait long. Eventually each of the dummy locations and the real LZ would be checked out by the VC one way or another.

After replacing the tape antenna on the radio with the whip, Chambers did a radio check and notified the helicopter and Striker Six through one of the hill top radio relay stations that team Boatload was on the ground and moving. Rhodes saved the batteries on his radio and wondered what the hell had been in Slaughter's mind to make him want Rhodes to carry the damn thing.

As he looked around and tried to penetrate the grass with his eyes, he felt more alone than he had ever felt in his life. Just him and five Marines alone in the VCs backyard. If anything happened there wasn't an American within miles to help. He listened hard with his heart beating in his ears. He gripped his rifle tightly to still the tremor in his hand. The enemy could be anywhere. Maybe just feet away.

Not hearing any activity, Kelly led the team out of the LZ with Mendes on point and Doc Anderson as tail-end Charlie. They struggled forward. Getting through the elephant grass and vines had them all sweating inside of a hundred yards. They were on the side of a small hill that started the low ridgeline the team would generally follow, if possible. Rhodes could see only Chambers in front of him and Doc Anderson behind him. The team moved slowly and quietly, spreading the grass when they could, cutting it slowly and quietly when it wouldn't spread. Spreading was preferable because the grass would spring back up and hide their trail, but the grass and vines were so thick spreading wasn't always possible. Vines were handled in the same manner. Push them down or aside if possible. Cut them if not. Thinking they had only moved a hundred feet at most, he was surprised when Kelly stopped the team and formed a perimeter.

They were at the crest of the hill, a good two hundred meters from the LZ. Kelly took Mendes forward to see what they could see. Not a word was spoken. Soon Kelly and Mendes returned to the perimeter and with hand signals moved the team out and along the ridgeline. Rhodes wanted to know what was going on, but he kept his mouth shut and trusted Kelly to lead the team. Depending on someone else to lead was a hard lesson for him. You didn't get to Master

Guns without becoming at least a bit of a control freak. Holding back and waiting for another enlisted man else to make the decisions went totally against his nature.

The ridgeline got steeper and higher and the team maneuvered for two hours in the grass and scrub trees below the military crest to a point where Kelly could observe the valley below them from concealment. Kelly circled his hand above his head and the team assembled around him. After quick whispered instructions, he spread the team out in a wide perimeter, each man essentially a listening post, and began the day's work. He kept Rhodes and Chambers with him.

In a low whisper, Kelly began Rhodes's orientation. "The sun is behind us. That's a good thing. No reflection off the lenses to give us away. There's a trail about a klick out running east to west. See if you can find it."

He put his 7X50s to his eyes and scanned slowly from the base of the hills out to what he figured was a kilometer. He saw only grass and low jungle.

"Give me a marker," he whispered.

Kelly pointed to get Rhodes in the general area and then said, "Look for the copse of trees standing alone in the grass. Move your glasses up slowly from the trees and look for a red strip in the grass."

He followed instructions and after a few slow sweeps said, "Okay, I've got it."

"Keep your eyes on the trail," Kelly whispered.

He nodded and balanced his binoculars with his

elbows on his knees. Kelly began a slow methodical section sweep with his glasses. The quiet of the jungle was almost oppressive, yet somehow comforting. As the Marines quieted and became part of the environment the normal sounds of insects and animals returned. Rhodes could hear the quiet buzz of a small observer's plane flying off in the distance and soon the sharp but faint sound of jets passing so high overhead they couldn't be seen. Faint *wumps* of artillery in the north hardly disturbed the quiet of the day. A rock ape grunted somewhere on the side of the ridge.

Soon Kelly stopped his binoculars on one spot and watched for a few moments. He made a mark on his map and entered a note in his small journal. He resumed his sweep. Rhodes, continuing his watch, stiffened and glanced sideways at Kelly. Kelly noticed and raised his eyebrows. Rhodes raised three fingers and pointed at the trail. Kelly moved his glasses and watched.

Rhodes put his elbows back on his knees and steadied the glasses. Three Vietnamese in pajama like garments, black bottoms and white tops, were walking along the trail to the east. They were talking and gesturing with their hands, not a care in the world. Kelly made a note and a mark on the map.

Later, faint sounds of chopping or hammering could be heard coming from a copse of trees not far from the base of the ridgeline a few hundred meters to the west. Kelly made a note in his journal and a mark on his map.

Two hours later, without additional sightings, Kelly had the team saddle-up and move west along the ridge. Rhodes was getting the feel of patrolling quietly and the team seemed to be relaxing with his presence. They covered about an additional two klicks before Kelly called a halt and pointed toward a stand of bamboo near the crest. It was 1730 and time to find a safe night harbor. Kelly called for a reference round on a set of known coordinates out in the valley from the Khe Sanh 105s. The reference round allowed him to orient his map to the reality of the terrain and provided a known point he could adjust artillery from. A single round wouldn't cause any alarm with the VC/NVA because the fire bases fired random H&I all the time. Then Kelly set up on-call artillery around the harbor position. The team moved into the bamboo carefully sliding between the pole like bamboo stalks in the thick stand.

Well inside of the bamboo Kelly called a halt and told the team to set up for chow. Three men watching, three men eating. Two rings. The outer ring watched. The inner ring ate. The men watching faced inward to the eaters, but were watching across them to cover a sector of the perimeter on the other side. That way they could also watch the face of the man across from them and could react to a change in expression from the man on the on the other side watching the area behind them. Rhodes liked that. It was like having eyes in the back of your head. Soon the watchers and the eaters switched roles.

When everyone had eaten, the team buried the trash quietly and as it was getting dark, got in their wagon wheel night positions. Each man formed the spokes of a wheel facing out with their feet touching in the center. Since they hadn't seen much activity and the bamboo provided good concealment, Kelly put them on one hour watches, one man awake. Rhodes followed the team's example and spread his poncho under him. Maybe it would help keep the leeches away. Fat chance.

The watch shook him awake at 0300 for his watch and he had to stretch quietly for a few minutes to get the aches out of his muscles. He was pleased the man he relieved went straight to sleep, trusting him to stay awake and provide a good security watch. He guessed he had passed another small test. At 0400 he woke his relief up and quickly fell asleep.

He woke up with light in his eyes and blood suckers buzzing around his ears. His mouth was gummy and his body ached and itched. A day's growth of beard fouled with sweat and dirt added to his discomfort. He knew that soon he wouldn't even notice it. He had to pry one eye open due to gunk from irritation setting in on his eyelid. His gut rumbled and complained about its empty state.

Day two. They would extract at their planned extraction LZ at 0830 the next morning if everything went right. He was anticipating that event a little more than he wanted to admit. The team quickly got breakfast behind them, buried trash, and formed up to move out. Kelly checked-in on the radio to give a status and then briefed the team for the day's march. He pointed out the day's objective and route of march on the map and moved the team out. With the route and objective understood by every member of the team, they had a rally point if the team got split up for any reason.

A major north/south trail, almost a road, ran close to the ridgeline they were on for a short distance about two klicks further to the west. Kelly wanted to see if there were any signs of use on the trail, or if they were lucky, see what was using the trail, especially in the south-bound direction toward Khe Sanh. Two klicks were going to be a slow, hard trek in the scrub and elephant grass on the side of the ridge. Kelly moved the team down the side of the ridge opposite the side facing the trail they were looking for. He had a good land mark to guide him. A basalt outcropping identified by previous patrols near the crest marked the point where the trail ran closest to the ridgeline. The outcropping would also make a good observation post and provide some cover.

Later, with self-imposed thirst biting at his throat and sweat dripping in his eyes, Rhodes looked at his watch. Eleven hundred. They had been slogging, pushing, cutting, quietly cussing, and aching with effort for five hours. He had developed blisters on the downhill side of his feet and his ankles felt like someone was sticking hot pokers in them from walking on a slant. On two occasions, they had heard noises below them, but hadn't seen any movement through the canopy in the valley on that side of the ridgeline.

Finally, he saw the outcropping. Basalt rock jutted up about ten feet high in a band that fit over the ridgeline like a horseshoe. With the goal in sight, his energy seemed to rebound. Soon they could settle into a harbor, drink some water, and spend the rest of the day observing.

Kelly brought the team to a halt and broke out his binoculars. He watched the outcropping for several minutes and motioned Corporal Masters over to his position. They conferred quietly for a few moments. Kelly passed the word the team would approach the outcropping in column with fifteen meters spacing. He put Masters on point.

They moved up the ridge slowly and in short fifteen or twenty foot movements, only one man moving at a time so each man could stay in contact with the man in front of him and stay concealed and quiet. Masters was the first to enter the rocks. Kelly held the rest of the team in concealment until Masters signaled for them to come in.

The outcropping provided good concealment and cover, but it also stuck out like a sore thumb on the ridge. It was obviously a good observation point, obvious to the team and to any VC in the valley. It would also be very easy to put mortars or artillery on. The team stayed low, moved slowly, and once settled in position, ceased all movement.

A wide jungle valley was spread before them. The disorienting feeling of familiar and foreign mixed together made Rhodes uneasy again. You don't belong here, the feeling said. The view was familiar in the greens and yellows that faded to blue and gray in the distance almost like colors blended and faded in the mountains of Pennsylvania or West Virginia through summer humidity. But the shapes of the hills, particularly the sharpness of the ridges and the jungle covered sentinel peaks that poked straight up like a monument, told you, this isn't Kansas, Toto. And, of course, hundreds of NVA/VC weren't hiding in the greens and yellows of Pennsylvania.

Although the outcropping provided plenty of cover it was also a prominent landmark and would draw the eyes of any watchers out there. It was like lying in ambush. You couldn't move, not even to wipe sweat out of your eyes or to swat a bug or squash a fire ant. Someone could be watching from out in the valley. Lying still, the team would be hard to spot in the shadows of the rocks, but movement could be detected from a long distance. Although in his concealed position he was probably exaggerating the need for absolute stillness, he didn't dare move. This kind of patrolling was all new to him. He held his binoculars steady with his elbows on the ground and watched one sector of the trail. No sound. No movement. Hardly breathing.

Soon his arms cramped and the back of his neck started burning with muscle strain. Sweat dripped into his eyes. A bloodsucker sank his proboscis into Rhodes's cheek, and another did the same on the edge of one ear. Something crawled along the back of his neck. The outside of the binoculars was wet with sweat and getting slippery. He thought, I could be sitting in a clean office on the Island right now, in a clean, starched uniform, a cold beer waiting at the SNCO club. And no one would die there. Some recruits would wish they could, but the danger would be imagined. Not like here. He quickly got control of those thoughts, but the tremor in his left hand returned and made it difficult to hold the binoculars steady.

He heard Kelly grunt and turned his eyes that way. Kelly had a death grip on his binoculars and was looking at the north end of the visible trail. Rhodes moved his binoculars slowly, just a fraction of an inch at a time. Soon he saw what Kelly had reacted to. A single NVA soldier in green uniform and khaki pith helmet moved south on the road, his head moving side to side, his eyes moving up and down the ridge, his AK-47 at port arms. He moved down the trail about a hundred meters and stopped. His head did a hundred and eighty-degree sweep in front of him and then he scanned the ridgeline slowly. He looked right at the outcropping for several moments. Rhodes held his breath. The soldier was looking right into Rhodes's lenses.

After another scan all around, and a search of the sky, the NVA point man signaled with his arm and a platoon of uniformed men moved down the trail towards him. Kelly slid down in the rocks, cupped his hand around the handset and called the sighting in and asked if an AO was in the area. He continued talking trying to find air asset to bring in. He didn't want artillery because the NVA would know a recon patrol was within sight of their position if artillery came screaming in out of nowhere, and there was only one good place in sight that made a good OP.

Rhodes continued to watch the NVA and kicked Kelly's leg when a squad detached from the platoon of NVA and started climbing the ridge towards the outcropping. Kelly put his eyes over his rock and dropped back quickly. He signaled Masters to take point and indicated the direction down a rocky ravine on the back side of the ridgeline. It was time to di-di

Giving up the high ground and the solid cover of the outcropping bugged Rhodes at first, but he kept his mouth shut and let Kelly do his job. This was a Keyhole patrol and their instructions were to avoid contact if possible. Their job was to develop intelligence on terrain, enemy movement, composition, concentrations, and potential LZs for future operations. In any case, six men should not take on a platoon of NVA regulars with an unknown number behind them. Still, it rankled. And yet, he felt uncomfortably relieved as they moved away from enemy contact.

Masters led the team northeast down a rock cluttered mini-ravine without leaving a trail. They made it through the rocks and into a stand of bamboo, good old thick growing bamboo that hardly let even light in, and went to ground. If the NVA came looking for them the team wouldn't have much cover, but the concealment was complete.

The team remained in the bamboo stand for two hours and then moved cautiously back to the rocks after careful observation for movement. The NVA had moved on and the trail was empty.

The team remained in the outcropping until near dark and Kelly decided to make it their night harbor. It had good cover and concealment, had an excellent route for retreat, and had already been checked out by the NVA. The outcropping was probably as good a harbor as they were going to find by dark and they were close enough to their planned extraction point to make it by 0830 if they left at first light. And it had one big advantage: there weren't any leeches in the rocks. Kelly set the team up for chow and set the watch. He put the team on fifty percent alert with one man watching the trail, one man watching the other side of the ridge, and one man watching the ridgeline.

They'd had a little excitement, but nothing to write home about. Rhodes wondered if most of the patrols were like this one. The recon's ways were hard to get used to for an old infantryman. The jobs were completely different. In the infantry, you tried to make contact and always moved toward the enemy and tried to initiate a fight. For that reason, infantry had to travel in large numbers. Recon teams were too small to survive contact with very many enemy and their job was to collect intelligence not fight, so they put as much effort into avoiding direct enemy contact as the infantry put into finding the enemy. Two different missions. Two different skill sets. Both valuable. Both necessary.

Around 2300 his sleep was interrupted with a kick to his left foot. He came completely awake but didn't move. Kelly put his mouth next to his ear and whispered, "Movement in the rocks below us."

Rhodes stifled a groan and slipped silently up a rock and looked at the side of the ridge below him. The night wasn't completely dark, but neither was it light enough to make out any details. Then he saw movement in a shadow about thirty meters below his position. He moved his eyes slightly to the side of where he saw movement and waited. Soon he heard metal on rock. Then he heard a voice. The sing-song of Vietnamese drifted up from the rocks below him and an answer called out not far from the first voice. Then more movement and more voices. A spark lit up the rocks in one spot and was quickly covered with something leaving just a soft glow. More voices sounded below the fire.

Kelly put his mouth next to his ear. "Setting up camp. Don't know how many. We're going to di-di. Slowly, quietly. You take rear guard."

Rhodes just nodded his head.

"Got that?" Kelly asked quietly.

Rhodes was reminded how much he had to learn. A nod wasn't enough in the dark. He squeezed Kelly's arm.

They put on their gear without a sound. Just before the team was ready to move out, Kelly held his hand up. The sound of someone climbing toward their position was clear. Kelly tapped Masters on the shoulder. Masters led and each team member fell in behind him, hand on the shoulder of the man in front of him. Rhodes fell in last and kept his head swiveling to watch the back trail and to avoid kicking a rock and making noise. Fifty feet down the ravine they went to ground and got still, just six more lumps to blend in with the rocks and boulders.

A voice called out from the outcropping. Another, fainter voice answered from the other side of the ridge. The man in their old position laughed and then the sound of rocks being dislodged tracked his progress as he scrambled back down his side of the ridge. Masters stood and took the team down the ravine to the bamboo stand.

The rest of the night was quiet and the team was happy to let it remain that way, but no one slept much. They set out early in the morning and moved straight to the extraction LZ. There seemed to be a lot of enemy movement in the area and Kelly wanted to observe the extraction LZ location before the extraction bird came in.

Rhodes hadn't spoken thirty words since the patrol started and didn't see any lessening of the team's reticence as the extraction approached. They observed the LZ for an hour and only moved to the edge of the clearing after the bird made radio contact. The extraction went off without a hitch and thirty minutes later the team landed at Dong Ha. That patrol met the definition of a good recon patrol. Definition: A good patrol is any one you walk away from.

CHAPTER 5

After debriefing, Rhodes went to the Three Shop to talk to Major Slaughter. They went over the details of the patrol and slaughter asked for Rhodes's impressions.

"Kelly's a good leader and his team knows what they're doing," he said. "I'll tell you this though. Recon is a young man's game, Major. Two of them were eighteen-year-olds and impressed the hell out of me. Not sure I made much of an impression on them though."

"Really? I think you're wrong. They referred to you as Striker during the debriefing. You already have a handle. I think that says a lot."

"I told them to call me by my call sign in the field to keep things simple."

"Still, they usually refer to augments as just 'the master sergeant,' or 'the Lieutenant.' Or 'the pogue we took along.'" Slaughter laughed. "I think you've been accepted."

"Maybe I passed a couple of their tests. It was hard holding off with those targets in front of us, but Kelly was team lead and I kept my mouth shut."

"He mentioned that. I think the word will get out and you'll be made welcome on your next patrol."

"You've got one in mind, sir?"

"I do. A couple of important things have happened in Recon over the last year. General Walt recognized the unique ability of the teams to locate concentrations of enemy and the opportunity they have to call in supporting fire to make Charlie's life miserable. You went on a Keyhole patrol this time, pure recon. I want to put you on a strike team next to get a feel for their capabilities. The strike teams go deeper, stay longer, are bigger, more heavily armed, and engaging the enemy is part of their mission."

"Firefights?"

"Not if they can avoid it—maybe, if it's a small unit that can be ambushed. Their real value is calling in artillery and airpower. These guys are hard-corps recon.

"When do I go out?"

Slaughter shuffled through some papers and found the one he wanted. He used his finger to find the line he wanted.

"Next week. I'll keep you in the shop for a few days so you can get a feel for what you're going to be doing. I want you to meet the colonel and I've got you scheduled to do the G2 briefing and some other things so people can get to know you."

He worked with the assistant S3 on operations orders for the rest of the week, including the Op-order for the patrol he would be on the following week. The work was interesting and challenging, and he had to admit, he liked being in the S3 bunker a whole lot better than being on patrol. He liked it a whole lot better than infantry patrolling too. In the infantry, you just stayed out there for weeks on end.

Two evenings after his first patrol, Rhodes was passing through the team hooches to get back to his own hooch when he passed a tent with music from AFRS escaping through the screen door and accompanied by several Marines. He looked in as he passed and saw six Marines inside. All of them were swaying with the music and joining in. Sounded like pussy music to him, but what the hell. The Marines were just kids. Some of them only shaved because they were required to.

Just before he reached his hooch, he heard a voice calling.

"Striker! Master Guns! Wait."

He spotted the clerk from the HQ complex double timing to catch up.

"What do you need, Corporal?"

"The Sergeant Major wants to see you, Master Guns."

"Now?"

"That's what he said, Master Guns."

"Where is he?"

"In his office. He sent me to find you."

"Okay, you found me. I'll find him soon as I can."

"Master Guns . . .uh . . .he said right now."

What now? Rhodes thought.

"Okay. Have you had chow yet?"

"No, Master Guns. I've been looking for you."

"Go on and get some chow. I'll see what he needs."

Cullahan was fixing a cup of coffee when Rhodes got to the HQ bunker. He saw Rhodes enter and pointed at his field desk. Then he took his time fixing the coffee. Finally, he walked slowly to his desk.

"What do you need, Dave?" Rhodes said.

"The proper way to address a senior NCO is by his rank, his full rank. That's more than just a reminder. You are addressing the Battalion Sergeant Major. It has come to my attention our Marines are starting to call you Striker. What's that all about?"

"It's my call sign. It saves confusion and time in the field, Dave."

"Your rank is Master Gunnery Sergeant and you are the second ranking NCO in the battalion. Don't you think that kind of familiarity risks contempt and poor discipline?"

"No, I don't, Dave."

"That's it? Just no you don't? I'd like an explanation for this breach of good order."

"Fuck you, Dave."

Rhodes turned on his heel and left the HQ bunker. He knew he had to get out of there before he did something that would really be a breach of good order. Who the hell did that pogue son of a . . .

"Master Sergeant Rhodes. Hey, Dick."

He looked over his shoulder and spotted a dirty Marine in full infantry combat kit double-timing toward him. When the Marine got closer, he recognized him. Mike Marowski. They'd served together in 3/4 before Marowski was transferred to 1/9. Mike had been a good squad leader. He was a buck sergeant the last time Rhodes saw him, but now he had a rocker under his stripes.

"Hey, numb-nuts. What are you doing here?"

"What's this shit I've been hearing?" Marowski said. "Master Guns? Well damn, Master Guns, congratulations?"

"Thanks. How about you? I see you made staff."

"Yeah, just after you left the company. Hell, I made the Gunny boards this time too. High sequence number though. Probably July or August before it happens."

"That's great. You were a good sergeant. So, what are you doing here? Where's One-Nine?"

"We're out on Operation Prairie Two. The company is resting at Cam Lo right now. I brought a six-by in for ammo and rations. You got any beer?"

"Hell, yes. Come on in. It ain't cold, but it's wet."

Rhodes and Marowski drank beer and caught

up on what had been happening to old friends and who was no longer with them. There seemed to be a lot of friends missing now. They reminisced about old screw-ups and Marines who should never have been Marines. They were laughing over one particularly memorable screw-up when Rhodes heard a knock on his hooch door.

"Yeah," Rhodes yelled.

"Striker? It's Kelly."

"Striker?" Marowski said.

"It's a long story," Rhodes said quietly. "Come on in, Kelly."

Kelly opened the door and started to come in and then stopped.

"Oh, sorry, Master Guns. I didn't know anyone else was here."

"No problem. Come on in. This is an old friend, Mike Marowski. Mike this is Staff Sergeant Kelly, Team leader for recon team Boatload."

"How ya doing, Kelly?"

"Good. Damn, Marowski, you smell like you just came out of the grass."

"That I did. Delta Company, One-Nine, winning hearts and minds and kicking ass."

Kelly laughed. "Is that all the beer? I can get some more."

"Na, grab one out of that box." Rhodes said. "It's warm."

"Ain't it all?" Kelly said. "I've forgotten what cold beer tastes like. I have a delicate problem I wanted to get some advice on, but I can catch you later. Don't want to ruin a celebration."

"Let's hear it. Mike's been around. It will be good practice for his new Gunny stripes. You don't mind, do you, Mike? Kelly is one of the good ones."

"Hell, I've got nothing else to do. Let'er rip."

You made the list? Kelly said. "Congrats. Look . . . I'm not sure how to put this. I picked up a replacement, a Lance Corporal, and he's . . .well, he's . . . well, I'm not sure how to handle it or even if I should."

"He's what?" Rhodes said.

"Well, he's . . .what's the word? Effeminate. Yeah, that it. The guy reminds me of a girl."

"How do you mean?" Marowski asked. "Is he queer?"

Kelly shrugged. "Hell, I don't know. He sure acts like it. The rest of the platoon is talking. Nobody wants to have him on a patrol."

"How the hell did he get through recruit training?" Rhodes said. "I can tell you the DIs look close for that kind of thing."

"That's what makes me hesitate," Kelly said. "He got through so his drill instructors must have thought he was okay. I can't even imagine a queer getting through Parris Island. Hell, even the Hollywood Marines (west coast) would catch that. But that doesn't solve my problem. No one will even sleep close to him. It's fucking up the team and its messing him up too. He didn't ask to come to Recon."

"How is he otherwise?"

"Seems like a good Marine. He's right there when something needs to be done. He has radio training. I'm afraid to talk to anyone else. If I'm wrong it could fuck up his whole life. You know what they'll do if they think he's queer."

"Shit!" Rhodes said. "Damned if you do. Damned if you don't. Who is it?"

"Lennon. You didn't meet him. He came in two days ago."

"We could see about having him moved to something in camp and keep him off the teams until people get to know him."

"Can you do that? It would help. If it's just mannerisms, maybe the teams will get used to him. He ought to be a clerk anyway."

"Okay, let me talk to Slaughter in private. I'll see . . . "

The door slammed open scaring Kelly into dropping his beer. Slaughter rushed in out of breath.

"Master Guns! Get your gear on and report to the Operations Center. Carry all the ammo you can handle. We're putting together a reaction force to reinforce a striker team in trouble. Staff Sergeant Kelly, get a move on. Second Platoon is going out. Who are you?"

"Staff Sergeant Marowski, sir, Delta, One-Nine."

"One-Nine? What . . .No time now. Get a move on, Dick."

Slaughter spun and hurried out of the hooch. Kelly followed Slaughter, and Rhodes started putting his gear on.

"I better get out of your way, Master Guns. I'll catch you later. One-Nine is moving to Con Thien in May so I'll see you then."

"Right," Rhodes said. "Catch you later, Mike. I've got to go."

Rhodes ran to the Ops Center in full kit and was briefed by Slaughter. The center was full of officers and SNCOs. A strike team was surrounded on a hill top near Ca Lu by what they thought was a full company of NVA regulars. So far, artillery was keeping them from being overrun, but the NVA was getting closer and the artillery would soon have to stop to avoid hitting the team. Spooky was on station and dropping flares. If the team didn't get reinforcements soon they would be slaughtered. It was going to be a hot insertion—if they could get in at all.

Rhodes had been selected to lead the reaction force because of his infantry command experience. Another platoon was being readied to follow the reaction team in. He looked at the maps and aerial photos. He glanced through the radio log. Nothing the Ops Center had gave him any reassurance. The team on the hill was in big trouble and it looked like the reaction team would be too little and too late. The tremor in his left hand returned. It's too damn soon to go out again, he thought.

The reaction team was already at the air-strip when Rhodes got there. He and Kelly did a quick inspection of the platoon's gear and weapons and got a head count while they waited for the UH-34s that would take them to the fight.

CHAPTER 6

Kelly stopped Rhodes after the platoon was inspected and pointed at a short, thin Marine standing nonchalantly looking at the sky with his hand on his hip and his hip cocked out to one side.

"Lennon," Kelly said.

Rhodes glanced at the young Marine and shook his head. What Kelly meant by mannerisms was obvious, but hell, the toughest Marine he had ever known had a lisp and would have pounded you into the ground if you mentioned it.

"Well, he got everything right with his weapon and gear," he said. "Let's see how he handles himself."

He began to go over how he wanted the teams dispersed when they landed, but the sound of rotors interrupted their talk.

"Listen up," he yelled. "Saddle up and get on the birds as soon as they touch down. Teams six and seven with me. Teams eight and nine with Staff Sergeant Kelly. We're going into a hot LZ so be ready to fight as soon as you leave the bird. Do not lock and load until Staff Sergeant Kelly and I give the word. Is that clear?"

The whole platoon indicated it was clear in loud voices.

He was worried about this operation. Inserting a normal sized infantry platoon with forty-eight Marines would be risky when facing a company of NVA, but a Recon platoon was half that size. Inserting in a hot LZ at night with only the light of flares complicated and increased the risk. He had to get his force on the ground and oriented quickly to bring maximum suppressing firepower on the enemy so the platoon could move to the besieged team already there. Rhodes hoped the team on the hill had the ammunition and presence of mind to give it everything they had left to help the helicopters get in.

When the choppers landed at Dong Ha, Rhodes counted his team as they ran on board and watched for Kelly's thumbs up before he boarded. He felt the bite of the rotors increase while he was still in the door and the bird lifted as soon as he was onboard.

Inside, he did another survey of his team and weapons, working out tactics and contingencies as they flew through the night. What if the second bird couldn't get in? Kelly would be considering the same contingency. What if Rhodes's bird was hit? Both insertion teams had two M-60s. Both had four M-79s. Every man was loaded with extra ammunition and grenades. Every man carried extra M-79 rounds. Personal weapons were almost evenly divided between M-16s and M-14s.

He made his way forward and sat between the pilots watching for the glow on the horizon that would mark the hot LZ. The Co-pilot spoke on the radio and turned to face Rhodes.

"We're going straight in. They've got three dead and the remaining five are wounded. They know we're close. When we hover, the remaining Marines will do what they can with what they have left. Get to them fast, Master Guns."

"Just get us on the ground in one piece," Rhodes said.

Soon he could see a bright spot on the horizon. The bright spot quickly grew until he could make out tracers. It seemed like the tracers were all coming from either the air or were moving one way towards the top of the hill. He couldn't see much going out from the hill top. Time to move back and get the teams ready.

He moved to the rear of the bird and took the seat closest to the open door.

The crew chief yelled, "Two minutes!"

Rhodes stood up and grabbed a hand hold by the door. He cupped his hands to focus his voice and yelled, "Lock and load. Safe your weapons."

Rhodes knew from the briefing they were going into a small, marginal LZ near the crest of the hill. Only one helicopter could get in at a time. The strike team was under siege in a cluster of rock formations on the highest peak about a hundred meters from the spot chosen for the LZ. The reaction force would have to fight their way across that 100 meters to get to the besieged Marines, if the reaction team could get on the ground at all. The fight would be up hill and across relatively open ground.

Two Huey gunships would work the LZ over hard before the first bird attempted its insertion. Rhodes's bird had to unload fast so Kelly's bird could get in. The time available to get both birds in and unloaded would be counted in seconds. Every additional second the insertion took gave the enemy a second to recover and bring fire on the helicopters.

The pilot of the lead helicopter did a fly-over and gave Rhodes a good view of the LZ and the situation on the ground. The tracers he could see told him there would be enemy between the LZ and the Marines he was there to help. Christ, could it get any worse? Kelly's bird followed and gave him the same view.

The helicopters started down in a fast, steep spiral. Rhodes spotted the second bird behind his bird. The helicopter tilted almost sideways, but centrifugal force held the Marines in their seats. The bird righted and the nose lifted, slowing the descent so quickly the Marines sank into the net seats and then the door gunners opened-up sweeping the brush at the edge of the LZ. Rhodes stood up.

"Get ready!" he shouted.

As he crouched and readied his muscles for the exit, the bird shuddered as three hard incoming hits rang along the fuselage and pieces of aluminum flew across the overhead.

"Go! Go! Go!" the crew chief yelled.

Rhodes left the door in a dive. Incoming small arms tracers were peppering the helicopter and zinging into the open door where Marines were running and diving off the side to find cover. As he watched and counted his teams, one of his Marines was hit in the door and tumbled head first into the dirt below the bird. The helicopter lifted even while the last man was still exiting. He had to jump five or six feet down to the ground. His sixty-pound load collapsed his legs when he hit.

Rhodes quickly put his team in a perimeter to protect the LZ with the M-60s laying down a base of fire. Every man on all four teams carried multiple 100-round M-60 7.62mm belts around their necks. They wouldn't have to carry them far so they had loaded up. The guns were well provided for.

His radioman anticipated his next move and handed him the handset before Rhodes asked for it.

"Devil guns this is Striker Three, What's your situation? Over"

"Striker this is Guns. I can see you. Get up here fast. We're bingo ammo. I'm throwing fucking rocks."

"How close is contact?"

"They're on top of us. Don't fuck around,

Striker. I need you now."

Rhodes saw a hand waving marking the strike-team's location in some rocks.

"Devil Guns, how are you spread out?"

"We're all together in a tight circle."

"Get your heads down, Guns. I'm putting fire right over your heads."

"Don't talk, fucking do it."

Rhodes put one M-60 in place and had them begin firing short bursts inches over the strike team's position and into the areas on Devil Gun's flanks where muzzle flashes could be seen. The other M-60 covered their rear and the LZ. Kelly's bird had cleared the LZ and Kelly was putting his team in place to cover both flanks and the rear. Rhodes formed his teams in a wedge and waited for the opportunity to move forward. He sensed someone sliding up next to him.

"I can put a grenade right on the other side of their position," a voice said next to Rhodes.

Rhodes looked to see who it was. Lennon grinned at him. "I can reach it, Mr. Striker."

"That's a long throw," he said.

"I used to play deep outfield. I could hit the pitcher mound from the fence."

Christ, Lennon looked like he was having fun. Rhodes thought for a moment.

"Okay, put one over their position but to the side. If you make it, just keep tossing them."

Lennon pulled the pin on an M-26, let the spoon fly, and with an overhand throw from a kneeling position threw the grenade in a long arching flight that ended a few feet past the striker team and over the rise. Two incoming small arms rounds buzzed by his head, but Lennon was more interested in the results of his throw. Rhodes had to pull him down.

"Dead on," the voice from the radio said. "Keep them coming."

With Lennon's grenades dropping and exploding just on the other side of the strike team's position and Kelly's teams covering the rear, Rhodes put his thirteen Marines on line and moved forward to clear the area between him and Devil Guns. Resistance was surprisingly light and got lighter as they moved forward, but they were still taking heavy fire from the flanks. The NVA had pulled their troops from in front of the Marines and reinforced the flanks to enfilade the teams as they moved forward. The gooks were masters at using wounded or dead Marines to draw other Marines into their traps. With the way forward relatively clear, Rhodes called for his guns.

"Take extra rifle ammo with you for Devil Guns. We're going to give you covering fire. When you get there, get into the rocks with Devil Guns and start laying down covering fire into those flanks for us. We'll come up under your fire." Go!"

He heard Kelly's voice giving orders behind them as they started taking heavier fire from the rear and both flanks. The hill top was surrounded and Rhodes had to move the teams into a tighter perimeter at the top with the strike team before the enemy decided to cut them off again.

"Kelly, form a wedge. Cover us. Keep your sixties quiet and protect them."

Kelly waved acknowledgement. They were all on their faces now. Incoming small arms fire was increasing and you could hardly hear yourself think. It took a moment to get organized. Tracers were buzzing over their heads and mortars were walking in towards both groups of Marines. Rhodes checked the placement of his teams and got ready.

"On my signal," Rhodes yelled. "Give them a mad minute of fire."

Selector switches immediately went to full automatic.

"Ready . . . Now!"

The machine gun teams moved out toward the hill top on their bellies.

The entire team opened-up on the flanks and rear on full automatic. Red outgoing tracers looked like the tail lights of heavy traffic on a night highway. He let it go on until he was satisfied the gooks had their heads down and the sixties had made it to the rocks. As soon as the sixties in the rocks started laying down a base of fire, he moved his line forward with Kelly's line following and fighting.

Two teams with Rhodes leading, bellied forward in a wedge and two more teams followed Kelly in a reverse wedge bringing up the rear and keeping up heavy defending fire on the rear and both flanks.

Rhodes yelled to his teams, "Form a perimeter

around Devil Guns and cover Kelly's teams. Drop your M-sixty belts with the guns."

Kelly's teams moved forward close to the ground under heavy covering fire. As soon as they began coming through the perimeter, Rhodes had the M-60 gunners stop firing and moved them to new cover to avoid having their positions compromised by mortars. The reaction force had made it to the strike team with only one additional casualty, but they had used a lot of ammunition doing it.

One by one the platoon moved into the rocks with the strike team and filled in the perimeter. Rhodes now had four M-60s on line and able to cover 360 degrees of the perimeter. Marines began unloading grenades on the ground in front of them. Grenadiers began dropping M-79 rounds from fifty to a hundred feet out and along the flanks and walking them closer as they got a feel for the wind. Kelly moved around the perimeter, directing fire and calming Marines.

Rhodes crawled past Lennon to get to the strike team leader who was wounded and bleeding but still fighting.

"Give me your grenades, Mr. Striker," Lennon said.

"Knock off the Mr. Striker shit, numb nuts," Rhodes said as he dropped eight grenades next to Lennon and crawled on to the strike team leader.

"How ya doing, Devil Guns?"

"You got any water?"

"Yeah, here." Rhodes said loosening his canteen. "Corpsman up," he yelled.

"Where's your officer?" Devil Guns asked.

"I'm commanding," Rhodes said. "What's your status?"

"Three KIA, the rest wounded. Maybe four effective."

"I have two KIA on the way in. That gives us twenty-eight left who can still fight."

"Better than five. I'm really glad you guys got here."

"Yeah me too. Stay down and let the corpsman fix you up. I've got it."

"It ain't over yet. There's at least a company out there. They're regulars too. Who are you?"

"Striker Three. Master Gunny Rhodes."

"I'm Frank Minnick, Staff Sergeant, Devil Guns team leader. Kelly told me about you. Said you're okay. Take care of my Marines, Striker."

"I got it." He noted that Minnick had an M-14 and lifted a bandoleer of 7.62 over his head and dropped it next to the team leader. "Hang in there," he said as he moved to intercept Kelly. Minnick immediately loaded a magazine. There was blood on the magazine when he was done.

"Kelly, over here," Rhodes yelled and took the radio handset. He told the spooky on station to keep the illumination rounds coming. Two gunships were standing off and waiting their turn when they had enough light to place fire. The NVA were trying to get right on top of the team. It was a standard tactic to nullify supporting fire. If they got close enough, artillery and gunships had to hold off for fear of hitting the team.

Rhodes ducked as a mortar exploded on the hillside just over the rim. Kelly bellied up close and pulled his helmet down on his head.

"Keep those damn sixties quiet," Rhodes said. "I don't want them compromised. We'll only use them if we're about to be overrun. I want half the platoon ready to move out and see if we can push the gooks back away from the perimeter. We need some room to spread out. Those damn mortars are going to wipe us out the way we are."

"How do you want to do it?"

"Every other man around the perimeter move out ten feet and hold. As soon as they are set, move the rest out to fill in. Spread the perimeter as we move. See if we can get over the rim and push them back down the hill. You take the first wave. I'll move the second wave."

"Give me a minute to get them set."

As Kelly moved away to organize the Marines, a lull set in. Incoming slacked up and the Marines naturally responded with less firing of their own. With relative quiet, Rhodes found time to think instead of just reacting. In their current tight perimeter, the machine guns ended up with almost zero field of fire except to the rear where the LZ had been. The Marines were taking some fire from that direction, but the NVA knew the dangers of that open space as well as the Marines did.

The real problem was the slope in front of the Marine's position and the flanks. Forward was only forward because that was where the NVA were massed and that was where the chicom grenades, automatic weapons fire, and mortars were coming from.

After assessing the situation, Rhodes decided that instead of expanding the circle, he would expand the flanks out into an arch perimeter facing the concentration of enemy and let two of the M-60s cover the rear where they had a good field of fire. He could always contract the perimeter and close-up the circle if he needed to. He had to call Kelly back and change the plan. Well hell, no plan survives contact with the enemy anyway. There really isn't a lot of doctrine or options when you are surrounded and about to be overrun. The tremor in his left hand turned into twitching.

He discussed the change with Kelly and then Kelly took the left flank out and Rhodes took the right flank out. With the new configuration, the whole team had a better view and better fields of fire and all downhill, but Rhodes lost two more men in the process. It was a good move, though.

The move took the NVA by surprise. They weren't expecting aggression from the small band of Marines on the hill, not after beating the hell out of the original team. But they were facing Marines. The Germans called them Devil Dogs in the first war. The

Japanese called them demons in the second war. The Vietnamese just called them Marines and knew what that meant.

One of the military's dirty little secrets is, in most battles and in most armies only about half of the infantry tried to killed their enemy. Half fired high or wide, some not wanting to kill, some out of panic. Killing deliberately goes against human nature for most people, even for soldiers. That's why Marine infantry can be so devastating. They are trained for one thing only. Killing. One hundred percent of Rhodes's Marines were shooting to kill, seeking targets, trying to get some, trying to destroy what was in front of them. Their concentrated, disciplined fire was as deadly as a company of most infantry.

The sudden increase in disciplined fire from the arch drove the enemy back down the hill a good fifty feet all along the line. Rhodes used the advantage quickly and called in artillery as close to the line as he dared, and then called artillery in on the LZ behind them. As the first rounds came in the team found as much cover as they could. Shrapnel screamed over their heads and NVA screamed below them. A red strobe was already out at the top of the perimeter. Rhodes ordered an orange air panel out at each end of the perimeter, hoped they could be seen in the flare-light, and called in the gunships.

The NVA were tough little bastards and disciplined as

hell. He had to give them that. Even with the pounding they were taking, the incoming from the enemy began again and never let up. A bugle sounded and two lines of infantry moved up the slope on an angle from two directions supported by mortars and supporting each other. The gunships cut them up, but the amazing bastards kept coming.

Thank God the sides of the hill were steep. Rhodes revised his estimate of enemy strength upwards from company size. Two companies, maybe more. And he now had twenty-two Marines facing them, about ten of them wounded. It was beginning to get hairy. Hairy, shit! It was getting impossible. He moved two of his M-60s up to the line to slow the advance and keep the NVA from getting too close again. They had a commanding view of the slopes below them, but the NVA had a lot of cover.

After a few minutes of heavy fighting and not slowing the enemy much, Rhodes was tempted to move his other two sixties to the line, but just as he was about to give the order, the team started taking heavy fire from the rear and the last two sixties opened-up on the area around the LZ. The sixties suppressed the incoming and movement from the rear, but very quickly 60mm mortars began walking toward the machine gun positions. Rhodes yelled for the sixties to cease fire and move. Both machine gun teams made it to new cover before the mortars reached their old position.

The incoming was heavy, but the Marines were holding

and Rhodes was beginning to feel like they had a good chance of making it to first light when supporting arms could really pound the hell out of the opposition and reinforcements could get in. With burning in his throat, he realized he hadn't had any water since the teams inserted on the hill. He sat down next to the radioman and gulped half a canteen of water and tried to calm his mind.

The water helped and he began thinking about putting out listening posts over the rim. They had a few claymores and he needed Kelly to get them set. He needed to get a status on the ammunition. They were going through a lot of ammunition. The needs of command took over and his mind began to calm down.

Then the radio spoke and he received some bad news. Spooky was out of illumination rounds, out of ammo, and bingo on fuel. The relief spooky wouldn't arrive on station for twenty minutes. Twenty minutes of dark. Twenty minutes with no support from the air. Twenty minutes for the NVA to move in so close supporting arms wouldn't help. He notified Kelly and pulled his panels in and his perimeter back into a tighter circle near the top of the hill and doubled up on the forward slope. He put out one strobe in the middle of the perimeter and hoped light from the new spooky would arrive soon.

He needed to keep pressure on the opposition, but without light he didn't have a lot to work with. Artillery coordinates were already plotted. On-call fire missions were ready. Rhodes called for continuous fire at the base and on the sides of the hill to keep reinforcements from coming up the hill. He talked with one 155mm crew at Cam Lo and walked rounds up the slope and then across the slope. By that time the only light he had was the light from the rounds exploding. He lost three more Marines seriously wounded by mortars. He needed medevac, but he needed light to get the slicks in.

While Kelly directed placement of claymores in the dark and moved a few Marines over the rim into listening posts, the senior corpsman bellied up to Rhodes and gave him a new status on the dead and wounded. Ten dead including three from Devil Guns. Six seriously wounded and not able to return to the fight. Eleven minor wounds treated and the Marines returned to the fight. Twenty Marines left to fight and half of them wounded to some extent.

Just a reinforced squad to face God only knew how many NVA regulars who were getting desperate as dawn approached. And the Marines were getting low on ammunition, except for M-60 7.62mm belts. They didn't have a lot, but they weren't critical yet. Rhodes was glad he had conserved the sixties.

They could hear the NVA moving closer on the slope. Lennon bellied close to Rhodes and said, "Watch this, Mr. Striker."

Lennon stretched out on his side and pulled the pin on an M-26. He listened for a moment and stretched his arm out down his side. He listened some more to the sound of NVA moving on the slope and then let the spoon fly. He counted, "One, two, three," and with a side launch of his arm tossed the grenade over the side of the hill. Two seconds later the grenade exploded in the air resulting in several screams

"Air burst," Lennon said and giggled. Lennon crawled to another position on the perimeter and asked for a grenade.

"Don't call me mister, numb nuts!" Rhodes yelled and then laughed. He fucking giggled, Rhodes thought. He fucking giggled. The laugh went as quickly as it came, but the moment had eased Rhodes's panic back to just high stress.

Lennon continued to move around the perimeter and did his trick over and over. He could think spatially and his muscle control was amazing. Virtually every grenade he threw drew screams from the hill side. Of course, with the number of enemy out there, hitting them wasn't hard. Tossing a grenade in almost any direction for almost any distance was bound to get some results—as long as the grenades lasted.

Marines began calling to him and holding out a grenade for him to launch—except for one big, mean looking grunt from the strike team. When Lennon crawled next to the big Marine, Rhodes saw the big guy knock Lennon over on his side with a fist. His voice was loud enough to hear over the sound of incoming.

"Stay away from me, you fucking fairy."

Lennon visibly cringed, but he crawled away and took a grenade from another Marine. He looked back at the big Marine and shouted, "I'm not a fairy." Then he ran into the rocks on the perimeter. Oh shit! Rhodes thought and was up and running bent over after Lennon.

He crawled into the rocks and saw Lennon bellying between rocks down the side of the hill. He started after Lennon, but had to stop when several rounds of small arms began hitting close to him. Lennon stopped about fifteen feet below the perimeter rocks and listened for a moment. He pulled the pin on his grenade and listened some more. He turned his head slowly side to side and then stopped, facing an outcropping with basalt fingers jutting in several directions. Lennon stared at the rocks for a few moments and then raised up on his knees. Several small arms rounds hit the rocks around him, but Lennon ignored them and slowly reached his arm back.

Rhodes heard the ping as the spoon released and then Lennon's arm flew forward and launched his grenade. Rhodes started firing short bursts at muzzle flashes and yelling for Lennon to get back to the perimeter. The grenade landed in the rocks and a moment later blew. High pitched screaming started in the rocks.

Three Marines joined Rhodes and began laying down a base of fire to cover Lennon. He yelled for Lennon to get back right then. Lennon started back up the hill with small arms hitting all around him. He made it back to the perimeter huffing and giggling.

"Just what the fuck did you think you were

doing?" Rhodes yelled, getting more pissed every second.

"I am not a fairy!" Lennon shouted back.

"Don't ever do that again," Rhodes yelled back. "Get the hell out of my sight."

It was all Rhodes could do to keep his hand still. His heart was pounding in his chest so hard it hurt. He almost lost that fairy son of a bitch.

The firing picked up and Rhodes and Kelly had to move around the team and force them to conserve ammunition. Everyone was down to one or two magazines. The sixties had a couple of hundred-round belts apiece. Grenades were getting scarce and Rhodes began collecting them and giving them to Lennon. They were holding on, but hope was getting slim.

Then the NVA launched a massive mortar attack that kept the Marines down and caused more casualties. Rhodes thought about the claymores, but didn't want to waste them. He needed a better idea of how close the enemy was getting. He got that indication a moment later.

A chicom landed not far from Rhodes and the blast rocked him sideways. On his side and still in shock, he saw the man next to him suddenly go slack and gore splatter from his head. At first, he couldn't understand what he was seeing, but as his vision cleared, he was treated to the full horror of the hit. The back of the Marine's head was gone. He wiped at gore splattered on his arm and leg and almost lost it.

While Rhodes pulled himself together, Kelly dragged another man to the Doc. The reaction force was down to a squad. Sixteen effectives. The NVA moved in closer behind the mortars and more chicoms began hitting inside of the perimeter. Rhodes had to force himself to think. Kelly bellied over to Rhodes and held up two Willie-Pete rifle grenades.

"Can you put them about fifty feet down the slope?" Rhodes asked.

"Yeah, but this shit can splatter a long way."

"Do it. We need the light and we need to slow those fuckers down."

Kelly fitted the grenade to his M-14 and loaded a crimped round. He moved the angle of the barrel back and forth until he was satisfied and then fired the grenade. He immediately loaded the next one and fired it to a different area. The side of the hill lit up with a bright white flash that dimmed slowly.

Kelly reset his rifle to magazine fire and crawled back to the edge of the rocks. The screams from burning NVA on the side of the hill began spreading and getting louder. The white-hot phosphorus shot up and out in glowing fingers that burned everything it touched. The splatters from the explosions reached out forty to fifty feet in all directions. Once it touched flesh it was fueled by the moisture and oxygen in the flesh and burned until it burned all the way through whatever it was on. They could scream; they could cry; they could invoke the name of whatever god or committee they worshiped, but they couldn't put it out.

After the WP strike the NVA doubled their efforts. Time was running out for them. Two NVA sappers made it to the rocks, but were quickly dispatched with K-bars by Marines who were waiting for them. Hearing scrambling in the rocks below the rim, Kelly blew one of the claymores and was rewarded with one anguished scream. Two more claymores were blown by panicked Marines and probably wasted. With NVA soldier calling out to the Marines from just over the rim, the situation on the hill was desperate and Rhodes was close to panic himself.

Finally, spooky came up on the net and Rhodes requested immediate illumination and asked the gunships to standby. The gunships had also been relieved with fresh birds that had full loads of rockets and ammo.

As soon as the illumination started Rhodes called for medevac for his wounded and dead. He got good news with the acknowledgement. A company from 1/9 was being flown in to the base of the hill to reinforce the Recons. Then things got very serious.

A soft glow could be seen on the horizon. Dawn was about to break and the NVA had to move. The mortars became more frequent and probes on the perimeter became constant. Rhodes held the sixties back. It wasn't quite time yet and the fields of fire would be very tight and very close. The machine gunners, big guys, held their M-60s at the hip and prepared to repel sappers penetrating the perimeter.

Two riflemen guarded each machine gunner.

Ammunition was critically low and hand to hand fighting broke out at two points on the forward side of the perimeter. The NVA were right on top of them. This was it. The NVA were making their push to overrun the Marines.

Rhodes pulled the remaining Marines into a tighter perimeter so they could cover each other's back and prepared for hand to hand fights all around the perimeter. The ammunition was almost gone. He saw Lennon pick up his M-16, dump an empty magazine and load a fresh one. Lennon had been focusing on grenades and still had six magazines left no one knew about. Rhodes left Lennon one mag and distributed the rest to Marines who were completely out.

Then a sound in the distance. A beautiful sound. Rotors. Many rotors. The UH-34s and Frogs spiraled in at the base of the hill, too far away to be of much help, but they would keep reinforcements from coming up the hill. They also put pressure on the rear of the unit already on the hill. That was good news and bad news. The Marines were coming, but the artillery had to stop.

Then as the troop transports began dropping down at the base of the hill, three Huey slicks came in behind them and circled the hill to come in at the LZ behind the team. Help was on the way.

He ran bent over behind the perimeter and told the Marines to throw rocks over the hill hoping the NVA would think they were grenades and keep their heads down. He had one M-26 left in his bush jacket lower pocket and gave it to Lennon. "Make it count" he said. Lennon giggled. Rhodes didn't have time, or the desire, to laugh. Of course, that wasn't a problem right then. He was close to panic and holding hard to his sanity.

NVA were moving around just over the rim deliberately making noise and shouting, "Marines, you die." Rhodes ran behind the Marines and checked ammunition. All but two Marines had some ammunition left in their last magazine. He threatened to kill the first Marine that fired more than one shot at a time and rip the arms off anyone that missed his shot. He could hear the panic in his own voice and forced himself to slow down and talk slower.

The first slick got down and unloaded a fire team of infantry under heavy fire. The bird got off, but it was smoking as it disappeared over the hill picking up air speed.

He told the sixties to use their ammo to suppress fire around the LZ. The second bird landed and another eight grunts moved out of the LZ and toward the Marine's perimeter.

Another slick flew straight to the perimeter and hovered taking hits all along its fuselage. A crewman pushed ammunition boxes out and the boxes crashed and shattered inside the perimeter. Fortunately, no Marines were under the boxes.

Rhodes and Kelly started running loaded magazines to the perimeter. Rhodes found a can of grenades and dumped it next to Lennon. Lennon giggled and started pulling pins and letting spoons fly. Four grunts ran into the perimeter and flopped down next to recon Marines.

The volume of fire from the perimeter increased and Marines started moving closer to the rim and forcing NVA back down the slope. More reinforcements reached the teams and the volume of outgoing increased again. With grenades, automatic weapons, and a fresh supply of ammunition, the Marines shattered the pressure on their perimeter.

Suddenly the whole momentum of the battle shifted. A company of Marines was moving up the slope and now a resupplied platoon with fresh grunts fought from the top. The incoming mortars stopped as gunships found their marks. The NVA already retreating and scattering when they heard the helicopters in the distance became more focused on surviving than attacking.

Marines began extending their perimeter and tending to the wounded. As the expanding action moved away from him, Rhodes dropped down behind a rock and squeezed his eyes shut where no one could see him. Slowly and deliberately he loaded a fresh magazine in his M-14, letting the familiar task calm his mind and shaking hands. He took a deep breath forcing the panic down and moved back to his Marines. They needed a leader who was in control. It was his job to give it to them—or at least the appearance of control.

The sun came up slowly. With a company commander

and four lieutenants on the hill taking the fight to the NVA, Rhodes pulled his teams back and began the task of tending to the wounded and identifying the dead and preparing them for evacuation.

The fighting died down as the NVA tried to evade marauding Marines. More slicks got in and brought water and supplies. The teams received some water and C-rats from the incoming slicks. A few Marines were smoking the stale cigarettes from the C-rats, even a few who didn't smoke.

Finally, the firing died down to just sniping from the enemy. Alpha Company skipper from the 1/9 reinforcements had squads searching out NVA holdouts and getting a body count. Rhodes had done his own count around the crest of the hill and counted forty-four with several clusters of three and four dead NVA in one place. Their wounds were made by small wire fragments from M-26 frag grenades. He figured they were Lennon's grenade kills. He'd give him credit for them, but he wasn't going to tell him. The pansy fucker would probably giggle and Rhodes was afraid he would smack the shit out of him if he giggled or called him Mr. Striker one more time.

A medevac slick circled and Rhodes assigned men to get the wounded to the LZ first and then the dead. A short time later three UH-34s came in and lifted the teams out and flew them back to Dong Ha.

CHAPTER 7

Rhodes was jumpy when he got off the helicopter in Dong Ha. His nerves were strung out and he had a slow anger burning inside of him. Staff work slaughter had said. Bullshit! The previous night had been as bad as any action he could remember.

After the debriefing and after reviewing the rough drafts of the interviews, he walked through the team area. He wanted to see how the teams were coping. He didn't stop at any of the hooches but he looked in at Boatload's hooch. The team was doing what they had been doing before the reaction force battle, listening to AFRS, playing cards, and shooting the bull. The First Sergeant would have them burning shitters soon, but for now they could rest and unwind.

He saw one promising change though. Lennon was in the middle of the team and telling as many lies as any of them. Adrenalin flowed from the bloodstream and out the mouth as excited words. The quiet time would come later after they filed away their demons. Rhodes watched and listened for a moment at the screened entrance to Boatload's hooch.

"I told Mr. Striker to watch this and tossed a grenade dead onto some gooks."

"Lennon, you fairy, you don't call sergeants mister, not even Master Gunnery Sergeants. You only call warrant officers and junior officers mister. Were you sleeping in recruit training?"

"I'm not a fairy. Mama says I just have gentle ways." Lennon said,

"Gentle? You blasted more gooks with those lemons than the rest of the team put together."

"That's different. Anyway, there I was and Mr. Striker was cussing and . . ."

It was good to see Lennon fitting in, but he worried Rhodes. Praise for the stunt he pulled slipping out through the perimeter to prove himself wasn't the kind of reinforcement Rhodes wanted to see. He liked his Marines aggressive, but with discipline. He should have kicked Lennon's ass. What would he do next? He didn't want to see Lennon stuffed into a body bag after trying to prove he wasn't a fairy. He really should discipline the kid, as an example to the rest of the team if nothing else, but he couldn't bring himself to do it. Rhodes was just so relieved to have the kid alive and safe he couldn't think about a good solid punishment for stupidity. He was just relieved to be alive himself, he admitted.

He moved down hooch row and looked for the strike team's hooch. Devil Guns was a First Force team. Staff Sergeant Minnick was at Delta Med or maybe back in Danang by then. He was hit bad more than once. With three KIA and three serious wounds in the team the rest of the team would be split up and put with other teams. There wasn't much of the team left.

That kind of disaster in the teams was a rare event, strangely enough. You'd think that small five to eight man teams working alone would be more vulnerable than full platoons of infantry. But the stats didn't bear that out. The small highly trained recon teams suffered a much lower casualty rate than the infantry. Supporting arms were a lot of the reason for that, but mission and training played a big part too. Infantry missions were designed to find and engage the enemy. Recon missions were designed to find the enemy while avoiding detection. If you came to Recon, you faced a much scarier daily life and a faster pace of life, but you stood a much higher chance of finishing your tour alive.

Rhodes found the hooch and knocked on the broken screen door. The door still had its screen intact, but the frame was broken and it was just stuffed into the door frame. Someone's anger or frustration probably. He asked if he could enter. The teams didn't have much to call their own, not even their own time, and very little privacy. If they kept it squared away they deserved the relative privacy of their hooch. Knocking and asking permission didn't cost anything, and even though no Marine would dare deny a Master Guns permission, it was a small show of respect that went a long way.

The three remaining team members were packing when Rhodes entered the hooch. They weren't talking.

"Is it alright to come in?" Rhodes said.

Corporal Lane, the assistant team leader looked up from his pack.

"Sure, Master Guns. Any word on Staff Sergeant Minnick yet?"

"I spoke to the corpsman before they put Minnick on the bird. He said Minnick was hurting, but he was going to make it. He'll be in Japan before you go on your next patrol. You guys doing okay? You need anything?"

"How about Tolly and Ski?" Lane said. The other two Marines just watched silently.

"They're on the Repose (hospital ship) by now. We should get a report tomorrow. I'll let you know. Look, if you want, I can talk to the First Sergeant and get you guys a couple of days down in Freedom City."

"Thanks, but we're good," Lane said. "It's like getting thrown from a horse, Master Guns. You need to get back on right away."

"You're sure?"

"Yeah."

"Can I ask you something about the patrol, just between you and me?"

"We were already debriefed," Lane said and

looked away quickly.

"I know. I read your comments. Look, I'm new. I've got a lot to learn. For my ears only, how did you guys get caught like that?"

Lane looked at his team mates. One man shrugged and looked away.

"Master Guns, I'll just give you some advice about recon. Not saying it has anything to do with our patrol, just saying. Okay?"

Rhodes nodded.

"When you are deep, never stay in one place more than a few hours no matter how secure you think it is. If you call in a fire mission assume you are compromised and move to a new harbor immediately no matter what the pogues in S2 want. Pick a harbor that has zero value for observation. The gooks aren't dumb. If you can pick a good OP, so can they. They will know where to look for you. They know if you can see them they can see you or at least your position. You may not be compromised, but assume it and di-di to a safe harbor. And never, ever, harbor overnight at an OP your team has occupied for any length of time, especially if you called a fire mission from there. That's my advice."

Rhodes thought about it for a few moments, locked it in his mind for later thought, and held out his hand.

"Regardless," he said, "you guys did a hell of a job out there. Thanks for the advice. I won't forget."

After shaking each of their hands, he returned

to the operations center and went back through the debriefing interviews seeing what else he could glean. By 1600 he was exhausted from too many hours awake, too much adrenalin in his blood, and too little food in his stomach.

In the morning, Rhodes was given his next assignment. He would participate on a recon strike patrol with a team of eight. They would be patrolling within the Khe Sanh artillery fan and could expect constant and fast support from supporting arms. He had two days in the operations center before the patrol, and Slaughter put him with an experienced Captain to prepare the Ops Order for the patrol. Rhodes could hardly believe it. Christ, he was still shaking from the damn rescue mission. Two days wouldn't be enough to get his bowels moving again.

Slaughter took him aside for a private word.

"Dick, this mission is a touchy one. I want you along for two reason. First to continue your field orientation. Gunny Hopkins who will be leading the patrol is one of our best deep recon leaders. Second, I want you there to . . . well, to be a witness if the patrol doesn't get what it needs from Khe Sanh."

"Trouble, sir?"

"Pogues and politics. Technically, we shouldn't even be doing this recon. A detachment of Third Force Recon Company is working out of Khe Sanh. The detachment commander and I had a long talk a few days ago. The base commander at Khe Sanh won't believe Third Force recon reports indicating large concentrations of NVA north of the base near hill 881 South. Third Force patrols have had company sized concentrations of enemy under observation and have called for artillery. The base commander refused the artillery coverage telling the recon team they were seeing small VC units."

"How long has this been going on, sir?"

"Too long. Recons have been refused artillery several times. The Colonel won't even attend intelligence briefings. Something is going on out there and we need to know what it is."

"What about that colonel if we need artillery?"

"I'll make damn sure you have air assets available. Look, it's a complex patrol for artillery coverage anyway. You have an artillery shadow problem from the north or south depending where you are on the hill."

"Yeah, I can see that," Rhodes said. "If we're on the north side, the hill will create an artillery coverage shadow for artillery firing from Khe Sanh. But calling fire missions on a hill that steep is tricky as hell anyway."

"You got it. If you need help to get out of trouble while you're on the hill, it's going to be tricky getting it on target."

"That colonel wouldn't deny that kind of mission, would he?"

"I doubt it, but you'll have gunships on call and an Air observer in an OV-10 nearby to assist."

He wanted to remind Slaughter he was being

brought in for the S3 shop not for patrols. But what the hell, if anyone should, Slaughter ought to know the score. No plan ever survives enemy contact. Not even a plan to keep Rhodes in the Ops Center. He could only hope Slaughter would be satisfied with his field experience soon. He was getting just too damn jumpy. Coming to recon after eighteen months in the grass with the infantry probably wasn't his best career move.

The complexity of getting a patrol ready for launch was amazing. Just the number of notifications that had to be made boggled the mind. Artillery batteries with scheduled H&I (Harassment and Interdiction) missions had to be aware of the patrol route and time table. H&I was random and could wipe out a patrol without any warning. Supporting artillery had to be given a heads-up to provide supporting fire missions and on-call missions to protect night harbors. Artillery blocks had to be recorded in the ops-order. Air Wings had to be notified. Infantry operations in the RAO had to be notified. Coordination with Air Observers had to be set up. A single failure to notify the right people could result in a friendly fire incident that would wipe out a patrol.

He laughed when he heard the patrols described as secret missions. It seemed like the only people who weren't notified about the patrol were the NVA, and they probably got it through their own channels.

For the teams, life ground on. Shitters had to be burned, perimeter watches had to be stood, sandbags had to be filled, and all of that in addition to a full patrol schedule. The Sergeant Major and the First Sergeant did their best to make Sector Five look like Parris Island. Patrols away from the First Sergeant were preferred to staying in base camp. On patrol, you were a bear. You shat in the woods, slept on the ground, and found cover where nature provided it. But you were a Marine, a warrior, not brute labor.

Rhodes tried to stay in the operations shack and away from the Sergeant Major and the Exec, but that wasn't working out. Cullahan was going out of his way to make trouble for Rhodes and the Exec was backing him by bad-mouthing Rhodes to Slaughter. Telling the Battalion Sergeant Major to screw himself probably wasn't the smartest thing Rhodes had ever done. They were both E9s and there wasn't much Cullahan could do to Rhodes, but Cullahan was the Battalion Sergeant Major. He was the enlisted advisor to the Battalion Commander. He had real power and he was beginning to take it out on the teams through the First Sergeant. Rhodes knew he had to find a way to make peace with the Sergeant Major. That wasn't a task he looked forward to. Cullahan held a grudge for a long time. Getting your own ass almost blown away didn't seem to be enough. Kissing Cullahan's ass was probably going to be necessary.

CHAPTER 8

On Saturday morning, early, Rhodes checked-in at the Ops Center. The Sergeant Major was leaving just as Rhodes showed up. Slaughter waved Rhodes into his office after he got a cup of coffee.

"What the hell did you do to piss off the Sergeant Major, Dick?"

"Is he pissed at something, sir?"

"You know damn well he is. He's got the Exec on a war path too. Now what did you do?"

"Nothing much, sir. I just told him to go fuck himself. But just between the two of us though. There wasn't anyone around. Hell, it wasn't anything to get pissed off about."

"You told the Sergeant Major to fuck himself? You're shitting me."

"Well, I think the exact words were, fuck you, Dave. I said it nicely though. He had his panties in a twist over the teams calling me Striker and wanted me to explain my lapse in discipline like I was some damn PFC. I don't know who the hell he thinks he is, but if he thinks he can stand me tall and chew me out he has another think coming."

"That's it?" Slaughter said. "That's all you did?"

"Yeah. Except I left him standing there in his spit shined boots with his mouth open."

Slaughter grinned and then barked a laugh. "Damn if I wouldn't have loved to see that. I'll talk to the Colonel and advise him he probably shouldn't get involved in a matter between the two tops in the battalion. He'll sit on the Exec. Dick, do me a favor. Don't piss off the Sergeant Major and the Exec again. A favor to me? Please? There's things going on you don't know about and I don't want you to screw it up. Okay?"

"Well, sir, I won't deliberately piss him off, or at least I won't go out of my way to do it. But that pogue has a broom handle up his ass. What's going on?"

"Just do me a favor, okay? You'll find out when it's time."

Rhodes's eyebrows slowly dipped down as he looked at slaughter. Slaughter was up to something, and it was probably something that was going to bite Rhodes right in the ass. Screw it. He didn't have time to worry about it right then.

"Jeep's here, Major. I've got to get out to the LZ.

"Go. Just remember what I said."

"Aye, aye, sir."

Rhodes in full kit was driven to the air strip in a jeep. The Patrol he was augmenting was planned for four days in the hills northwest of Khe Sanh but could be extended to five or six days. The division wanted intelligence on enemy concentration, armament, terrain, and access to the high ground, especially around hills 881 south and 881 North. That was the mission concept that was passed on to Khe Sanh Commander to get the artillery blocks put in place. Fearing a situation like the French faced at Dien Bien Phu, Division G2 was beginning the planning for an operation to take the high ground that made the combat base at Khe Sanh vulnerable. Hills 881 north and south, and 861 looked down on the combat base from about five miles away and would make perfect artillery points—either for bombarding the base or defending it.

Gunnery Sergeant (Tank) Hopkins was inspecting the Team's weapons and gear. Tank and Rhodes had spent two hours and several beers the previous night discussing the patrol. He was an interesting guy. He was built like a fullback and smart as a math teacher. He had turned down a Company Gunny slot to stay with the recon teams. He liked working deep behind enemy lines with small teams.

Tank had only one loose end to tie up at that time. One of his team members had been shipped to Danang with malaria and he needed a volunteer to fill out the roster. The first person Rhodes saw when the

Jeep stopped at the assembly area was Lennon with a shit-eating grin on his face. Rhodes lugged his gear to the LZ and stopped next to Lennon.

"Lennon, what are you doing here?"

"I heard you were going on this one so I volunteered, Mr. Striker."

"Don't call me Mister, damn it. Didn't you get enough excitement with Boatload?"

"That was scary," Lennon said.

"You didn't look scared. You giggled every time you tossed a grenade."

"I can't help it, Mr. Striker. I always giggle when I'm scared."

"Well, get control of it, Lennon. You sound like a girl. It's embarrassing."

"I'll try, Mr. Striker."

"Damn it, I told you not to . . ."

"Sorry, Master Guns."

"Lennon, how the hell did you ever make it through recruit training?"

Lennon clenched his fists and glared with his eyes straight ahead. He made a *Grrrr* sound that made Rhodes laugh, but he wasn't trying to be funny.

"Tough, was it?" Rhodes said.

"I'd like to play catch with that sadistic monster," Lennon hissed.

"Who? Your drill instructor?"

"Yes, the sadistic monster."

"What do you mean, play catch?"

"With a lemon with a two second fuse."

The M-26 grenade is shaped like a lemon. Rhodes grinned and shook his head.

"I guess we've all felt that way at times," Rhodes said.

"Even you, Mr. Striker?"

"Look, numb-nuts, I told you not to call me . . ." Rhodes was interrupted before he could get into a good chewing out.

"Welcome aboard, Striker. I want you second from the end right in front of Doc Bannon. Lennon, I want you in fifth position, right in the middle. Did you bring plenty of grenades?"

Gunny Hopkins slapped Lennon's pack. The word had apparently gotten out.

"I brought a dozen, Gunny Hopkins."

A dozen grenades might not seem like much, but they each weighed about a pound. A dozen grenades added twelve pounds to Lennon's load and he wasn't a big kid.

"All right!" Hopkins said. "The bird is on the way in. Load up as soon as he touches down." Hopkins turned and yelled, "Saddle up, damn it. I want that bird off the ground ten seconds after he touches down. You will NOT lock and load until I give the word."

Rhodes didn't feel any of the reserve he expected from the team on the way to the insertion LZ. At first he was surprised, but after he thought about it, not so much. Having two new guys with the team would normally make a team nervous until they determined if the newbies could be trusted. But the word had gotten out on Lennon, and apparently, the word had gotten out on Striker. After the relief team battle, he found more and more of the teams were calling him Striker. Hesitantly at first, but when he didn't react negatively, with enthusiasm. The unique moniker didn't really encourage familiarity—hell, a company commander was called the skipper—and it made communications in the bush easier. And, what the hell, it was an ice breaker.

Rhodes was second from the tail-end-Charlie in the patrol, so he was loaded second on the helicopter. Gunny Hopkins came forward and sat next to Rhodes and pointed out each of his team members. Rhodes didn't try to remember all the names, but he did remember the three important ones. Lance Corporal Harris, the point man. PFC Lakin, the radioman. Doc Bannon, the corpsman. Along with Hopkins they formed the four corners of the team's mission box.

Hopkins broke out his maps. Understanding him over the sound of the rotors was difficult, but Rhodes got the gist of it. The patrol route would take the team up and down steep hillsides. Carrying five canteens, extra ammo, a radio, and a full pack up those hills was going to be a bitch. Thank God some of the monsoon season was still going on. They expected overcast skies, some rain, and temps in the mid-seventies during the day. The nights would be cool and wet. Four days of misery and then extract—if they weren't compromised before then.

Compromise was a good possibility and

extraction sites were limited on the hillsides. If they had to run for it, the run would be slow and uphill. The planned extraction LZ was on top of a high flat finger ridge off hill 881 North. And they had to get a look at the top of 881S first. Eight hundred and eighty-one meters, about 3000 feet, up a steep, thickly jungled slope. This crap was young men's work.

The HC-34 did a dummy insertion near Hill 861, another one on the valley floor and then did a long arching flight to the base of 881S and did another dummy insertion.

"Get a grip on something," Hopkins yelled from his seat between the pilots. "We're going in on the next one."

The insertion LZ was the rounded top of a finger ridge that poked up 300 feet from the valley floor. The pilot and Hopkins had done an over-flight and picked the site the previous day. They also had an alternative site picked out that would do, but was less desirable due to terrain features. Earlier artillery missions had blasted an open place in low jungle single canopy just large enough for one helicopter to get in.

The site had been identified by a previous recon patrol as a potential LZ and Hopkins and the pilot liked it when they did the fly-over the previous day. It had a big plus and a big negative. On the plus side, it was surrounded by thirty-foot high single canopy mixed with grass and bamboo. The helicopter would be below the canopy when the Marines unloaded so watchers wouldn't be able to tell if it was a dummy or real insertion. Potentially, that would give the team time to put some distance between them and the LZ before anyone could get to them.

On the negative side, the surrounding canopy provided plenty of concealment from which the NVA could spring an ambush if they were waiting. But the plus outweighed the small odds of the negative. The NVA/VC had to be somewhere, but they couldn't be everywhere all the time.

The helicopter started its spiral. Hopkins moved to the door, knelt, and held on. The bird dropped like a rock and then slowed the descent with a suddenness that felt like a touchdown.

"Go, Go, Go," the crew chief yelled.

Hopkins slapped the backs of each Marine as they jumped from the door. When Rhodes passed him, Gunny Hopkins followed him off the bird. Ten seconds, that's all it took. Before Rhodes could even get his breath and recover from the shock of hitting the ground from three feet with sixty pounds of kit on his back, the bird lifted off and disappeared over the canopy.

Hopkins grabbed Harris and oriented him in the right direction. Each man fell-in in his proper position as the column moved out of the LZ. They traveled what Rhodes estimated to be about two hundred meters, formed a tight perimeter and got silent.

A rifle fired nearby, just a single shot. Hopkins whispered, "Shit!" That's a signal shot. They suspect we're here."

"Are we compromised?" Doc Bannon said.

"Maybe not. Let's wait and see."

Hopkins oriented his map with the compass, studied the map for a few moments and then folded it and put it in the thigh pocket of his cammie trousers. The team settled in. They knew the gunny and they knew what to expect. No words were necessary. Lennon put two grenades on the ground in front of him. Lakin nudged Doc Bannon and nodded his head at Lennon and his grenades. They both grinned.

Rhodes felt his stomach tightening. This was the bad time. They were on the ground and the helicopter was gone. If the enemy decided to hit now all they could do was call for extraction and then hope they could hold out long enough to get out. And the LZ was small, so small the helicopter would make a massive target. The tremor started in his left hand.

His wedding ring rattled against his rifle stock from the tremor. Rhodes looked at the ring and tightened his hand on the wood. He looked around the team to see if anyone had noticed. Why am I still wearing it? he thought. It's done and over. The marriage isn't going to get fixed. He reached for the ring slowly with his other hand, pulled it off and squeezed it for a moment feeling the coolness of the gold. He opened his hand and let the ring slide into the grass, another piece of his life claimed by Vietnam dirt.

For the first two minutes, there was just silence. No further signals by the VC. They probably didn't know for sure if a team inserted or not. Then normal jungle sounds resumed gradually. A bird calling at first. Then a quick, darting sound of movement in the trees. Then mixed chattering, birds and who knew what else. For the next five minutes the team heard movement and chattering in the trees, a good sign since the animals would normally get very quiet if anyone were moving in the general area. Finally, Hopkins, his eyes moving side to side, seemed satisfied and moved the patrol out.

They were out of harbor only five minutes when the first mortars hit the LZ behind them. Rhodes counted the explosions. Five. Then silence returned. The gooks had the LZ dialed in, but the incoming seemed to be just H&I. Recon by fire. The rest of the team didn't seem concerned and kept moving forward behind the point man. Neither mortars or troops followed the team.

They had to get along the small ridge, find a route up 881S and then move slowly up the hill. If they could make the peak without contact, they could establish an OP and visually command the entire area all the way to Khe Sanh. Two of their objectives would be completed with one climb. Hopkins moved them along the ridge under the low canopy, thick vegetation, vines, and thorns. Harris put on bush gloves and moved carefully. Thorns ripped holes in utilities and left slices and punctures on hands and arms. Before they had gone another hundred meters most of the team had blood drying on several cuts and punctures.

A klick closer to the hill the low canopy ran out. The trees got smaller and fewer, but the elephant grass got higher and thicker. As the trees disappeared, the elephant grass and vines mixed together, tangled, and made progress frustratingly slow. Hopkins took them down the side of the ridgeline and continued to move through tall elephant grass. He kept looking up at the jungled slopes of 881S. Rhodes knew what was going through Hopkins's mind. *We might not be able to see them, but if they're up there they may be able to see us.*

CHAPTER 9

After moving slowly along the side of the ridge, no more than seventy-five meters in an hour, often less, disturbing as little as possible, Harris stopped the team. He found a trail that came up from the valley floor, turned, and ran along the ridge below the crest toward 881S. It appeared to have been used regularly with visible tire-tread like footprints all along the dirt. It wasn't shown on the map and hadn't been covered in the briefing. Hopkins marked his map for correction and noted the trail.

Hopkins signaled Rhodes forward and waved the team down in the grass for a break.

"We need to cover some ground," Hopkins said quietly. "If we keep going at this pace we're going to be stuck down here without a good harbor site when the light goes. I'm thinking take a chance on the trail, real cautious, but make up some time."

"I don't like moving on gook trails, Gunny, but it's your patrol." Rhodes said.

"I'm not asking you to decide. Just want to know what your gut is telling you."

"My gut is telling me I screwed up when I let Slaughter talk me into this crap," he whispered. "How good is your point man?"

"As good as they get."

"Okay. If you're going to do it, let me take the rear guard."

"You got it. Fifteen meter intervals."

Hopkins pulled the team together and gave them direction. Harris stepped out onto the red dirt trail and moved forward, watching for sign, watching for wires, listening for the enemy.

It was no wonder the trail wasn't on any maps. It was well concealed by high elephant grass, bamboo stands, and in many places, was covered by overhead vines that spread from foliage on one side of the trail to trees and tall plants on the other. In places the team had to bend double to pass under the covering foliage. The team found sticks that had been placed to extend vines from one side of the trail so they would eventually connect with anchor points on the other side. The overhead vine cover was man made. Walking the trail was like walking through a green tunnel in many spots. The few pieces of trail visible from the air or to distant OPs would just look like small disconnected bare places in the jungle, not a trail. The VC were masters at using nature to conceal their presence. With American air power ruling the skies, they had to be.

The first sign of trouble came from behind. The nine team members were spread out along the trail by almost a football field in length, keeping intervals, moving silently and as quickly as the point man felt safe in moving. Rhodes was moving in the awkward tail-end-Charlie dance of a few steps forward, turn and few steps backward, watch both flanks, watch over your shoulder, listen, rub the kink in the back of your neck. He was an infantryman and knew the dance well. The stress was building and he was hyper-alert.

The trail, as most mountain trails do, followed the terrain and was developed along a route that offered the path of least resistance. It had frequent bends, curves, and dips as it wound along the contours of the ridge.

After being on the trail for fifteen or twenty minutes, Rhodes thought he heard or perhaps sensed something behind him, an easy feeling to have when you are the last man. The mind can play tricks on you in the grass, but he had learned to trust his instincts. As he came around a bend that hid the back trail from the trail ahead, he hurried forward and sent the next man in line forward at double time to warn the rest of the patrol. He let the interval between him and the patrol increase, slowing, walking the inner edge of the trail, facing the back trail to see if anything was catching up with him.

The team closed intervals and passed the word. When word reached Hopkins, he moved them into the grass and moved back to find Rhodes. He waved him forward double-time and moved back up the trail toward the team. When Rhodes caught up with him, Hopkins waved him into the grass with the team.

They moved further down the ridge in the grass, moving around foliage and bending blades aside so they would spring back and not create a visible trail. When Hopkins was happy with their distance from the trail he waved the team down and hugged the ground, waiting quietly. They waited ten minutes before they heard the first sound, sweating, letting the bugs bite, knowing leeches were sinking their suckers and searching out orifices. Rhodes let the sweat run into his eyes and blinked it away. He ignored the pounding in his chest. Fear is just a feeling. Fear is just a feeling.

At first it was just a rattle of gear as someone moved, just a tinkling sound of metal on metal. Every eye tried to penetrate the jungle in front of them, but the eyes were the only thing that moved. Marines froze in place, breathing with shallow, silent breaths.

Then came the sound of sliding footsteps on the trail. Many sliding footsteps. Then a quiet singsong call and a short, quiet answer. The footsteps stopped. Silence. What the hell were they doing? Rhodes slid his selector to full automatic. Hopkins turned his head and glared at him. Rhodes acknowledged the warning with a shake of his head.

Lennon was on the other side of the man next

to Rhodes. He noticed Lennon's pack shaking. Oh crap! Lennon had his mouth buried in his hands and his face pressed into the grass below him. His chest shook, but no sound escaped his mouth. *I can't help it, Mr. Striker. I giggle when I'm scared.* At least he was smothering it.

More quiet voices came from the trail. They were conversational in tone, not excited or cautious. Everyone spoke quietly in the bush, even Charlie. More sounds of metal clinking and gear hitting the ground. A soft girlish laugh and then singsong chatting between several people. Taking a break.

That was reassuring in a way, but how long were they going to sit there? They obviously didn't know the Marines were there. Would they notice the Marines' footprints in the red dirt of the trail? The VC knew the tread pattern of Marine jungle boots as well as they knew the Goodyear tread pattern of their own truck tire sandals. Rhodes couldn't stop the speculation from churning over and over in his mind. He couldn't stop his heart from racing.

The enemy unit, whatever it was, stayed for almost twenty minutes and then packed up and continued its march toward the hill. The Marines remained in their hide for several minutes after the unit left. Hopkins moved close to Rhodes.

"I didn't want us compromised," he whispered. "That's why I brought you in. How many do you think there were?"

"I'd say eight or ten."

"Yeah, I agree. You did a good job back there.

I'm going to stay on the trail a while longer. We've got to find a harbor site high enough to see something. We'll move back into the grass soon and look for a route up the hill. You still okay with rear guard?"

"Sure. It's your patrol, Gunny."

"Yeah and you're Striker Three, Slaughter's boy. Let's move out."

Rhodes knew he had been naive to think he could tag along without effecting the team. He had the Operations Officer's ear and the Operation's Officer had the CO's ear. Team leaders were going to be conscious of that. The proof was in Hopkins taking the time and risk to explain his motives. The grunts didn't seem to care, because Rhodes wasn't a threat to them and he had proved himself capable in the grass. Their team leader was the big cheese in their lives. But the team leaders were SNCOs, career men, and they would be worried about what Rhodes might say to Slaughter or the Sergeant Major. They were going to be uncomfortable with a Master Gunny looking over their shoulders and assessing every decision they made, and no matter what Rhodes said or did, that's the way they would feel.

The team moved out with Rhodes in the tail-end-Charlie position. Hopkins tightened-up the intervals this time. Harris moved slow and cautious, taking his time at every turn and bend. The trail seemed to be used a lot so the probability of booby-traps on the trail was low, but the point man watched closely anyway. On a trail the VC often marked their booby-traps with a pattern of stones in the dirt or sticks placed in a way that other VC could spot them. Harris knew the patterns as well as anyone.

As the trail tilted upwards toward the heights of hill 881 South, Hopkins moved the team back into the grass and looked for a place to observe the upslope to find a route to the top. He found a ravine, more of a wash for run-off, that was steep, but it had a lot of foliage and scrub trees for concealment and handholds. It would take them up 200 feet and held the promise of safe harbor near the top where a thick stand of bamboo covered the hillside.

The trip up the ravine was pure misery. The rocks were slippery and full of snakes and fire ants. The climb was steep, full of snags to catch their gear, and treacherous to ankles. But the team had a lot of low canopy to conceal their progress. Hopkins had chosen well.

The climb was slow, but no one complained about that. Half-way up the ravine Rhodes saw his first King Cobra. Thankfully it slithered back into the rocks. He also took his first fall and bruised his knee. One more agony to add to the heat and fatigue.

He dug the toe of his boot in between two rocks and pushed his aching body up another two feet. He looked up at the man in front of him and blinked sweat out of his eyes. More sweat dripped off his nose onto his lips. He grabbed the base of a small tree and pulled with his arms to ease the strain on his bruised knees.

His sixty-pound pack felt like it weighed a couple hundred pounds. He pulled once again and his pack snagged on the branch of a scrub tree. His temper flared and he wanted to cuss at the top of his lungs. Fatigue was setting in and his nerves were getting raw. He got control of his temper and let his weight drop back a foot freeing his pack from the snag and then started up again.

After a two hour climb they reached the top of the ravine and moved into the bamboo. Hopkins checked-in by radio and set the team up for chow.

Since the patrol was a four-day effort they had been provisioned with LRRPs, freeze dried rations, to save some weight. LRRPs, or lurps, as they were called, were a new and scarce item in the supply chain, but they were quickly gaining favor with the teams. The LRRP package was flat, light, and took up very little room in the ruck while C-rats were heavy, bulky, and didn't offer any taste or nutrition advantage to compensate for their weight. But, as with most other items, the Army had more LRRPs than they could use and the Marine Corps had to beg for them and still couldn't get enough for just deep recon patrols. After chow Hopkins moved the team back to a position where they could observe the trail until it got dark.

Rhodes watched Lennon squirt a leech with bug juice and then flick it off his arm with a fingernail. He shivered and checked his other arm. Christ, the kid acted like a girl. Lennon had taken a fall too, but he didn't complain. He might act like a fairy, but the kid was all right. Just a kid with mannerisms developed from his childhood, probably from parents and home life. Rhodes couldn't show favoritism, but he liked the kid's grit.

The team observed two more small groups of Vietnamese on the trail. One of them moved down the trail toward the finger ridge. The other came from somewhere below and moved up the trial and disappeared in the thick jungle on the slopes of 881S. The uniforms were mixed. Some were in green uniforms with pith helmets and web gear led by one or two officers in khaki uniforms and pith helmets. Others, mixed in with the green uniforms, were a combination of PJ type bottoms with green or black tops. Some had web gear and weapons and some had only weapons. A few were apparently mules and carried large packs on their backs, but without weapons. They were amazingly strong little men. Hopkins didn't attempt to call in artillery, hoping for a larger concentration before risking compromise. He did call the sightings in and wrote in his journal. There seemed to be a lot of foot traffic going up and down hill 881S.

When Hopkins did his Check-in before moving the team into night harbor, he was directed to move up the hill the following day and attempt to assess the top for LZs and artillery placement. The team moved way back into the bamboo and set up their night perimeter. After setting out claymores, Hopkins put the team on fifty percent alert.

CHAPTER 10

The night passed without incident and the team got about five hours sleep each. All the watches reported hearing movement and even distant voices, but nothing close to the harbor. Hopkins took some time to scan the hill with his 7x50s looking for another route to the peak. The problem was, now that they were on the hill, observing it was difficult. Most of the slope provided good concealment and a lot of cover in the form of outcroppings and small ravines, but the concealment also concealed features of the land beneath. Hopkins picked a likely route and moved the team out of harbor.

The team climbed for three hours and at the top of what was almost a cliff, discovered a shelf of rock under a rock overhang. Better yet, the overhang was mostly one big boulder and blocked the view from above. The view of the finger ridges jutting out from 881S and the jungled plain at the base of the hill was spectacular making the spot a perfect observation post. Rhodes got his 7x50s out and scanned the rolling plain all the way to Khe Sanh's perimeter.

At that time Khe Sanh's perimeter wasn't much to brag about. Army Special Forces, ARVNs, and Bru Civilian Irregular Defense Group (CIDG) occupied most of the base with a company of Marine infantry and a detachment of Recon occupying one sector. He watched as dust from roads showed men and vehicles moving around the compound. Man, put one 105mm or 155mm up here and you could sure make life interesting on the combat base.

Rhodes knew the area had a bad fog problem at certain times of the year but that day was bright and clear. He could pick out all the structures. Even the ammo dump was obvious, possibly because he had seen a sketch of the base, but if he could find the dump so could the NVA. Khe Sanh had been strictly an Army Special Forces camp until recently, but the Marines were taking over. From where he sat, it sure didn't look like it would be a hard task to take Khe Sanh away from them, and all the high ground around it was up for grabs.

Hopkins deployed his team for defense and set up to begin the day's observation. They had to finish with 881S that day and move back down to the ridge and toward 881N in the morning. It would take most of the next day to get there and find the extraction LZ.

At 0950 Hopkins spotted his first movement. A platoon sized NVA unit with two hand-pulled carts moved along a trail out in a valley between 881S and 861. It was a known trail and already noted on the map giving Hopkins a known grid coordinate to use for a fire mission. Since the carts were probably used for ammunition, he decided to go for it. He called for an HE mission from the 105s at Khe Sanh and was told to stand-by.

"Stand-by?" Hopkins whispered looking at Rhodes. "I've got enemy in sight."

Rhodes nodded his understanding, but wasn't happy. Hopkins tried again and emphasized he had enemy in sight. He was told to stand-by again. A minute later he was told the fire mission was denied.

"Son of a bitch!" he whispered.

"Just roger and tell them denial is logged," Rhodes whispered back. "Believe me, the artillery gunners are as pissed-off as you are."

Hopkins made the call and handed the handset back to the radioman in disgust.

Hopkins stuck with the OP for two more hours, requesting two more fire missions both of which were denied, and then began moving the team up the hill. Since they hadn't called in any artillery, or at least hadn't had any approved, the OP was good for several hours. The NVA had no reason to suspect a recon team was in the area—unless the team was being tracked and set up for an ambush, and that wasn't worth thinking about. But staying there wasn't doing the team any good. It was obvious that Khe Sanh wasn't going to honor any artillery requests unless it was a team defense call. At least the team was getting a fair amount of intelligence on troops, how they were armed, trails, and potential LZs for future missions. But the Marines wanted to see something blow up.

Rhodes hoped they could get to the top soon and move back down to the ridgelines. The team was going through their water quickly on the climb. They had about 300 feet to go, all of it almost vertical, but at least they had a lot of tangled foliage to give them some concealment. He looked up and dreaded what he saw. Boulders and sharp outcroppings covered with vines formed an almost vertical cliff face nearly two hundred feet high, but it had a few natural ledges to provide some relief. Getting up the mess between the ledges was going to be a problem. Well, he only had to worry about the next one. One at a time. Don't make grief for yourself.

"Doc," he said quietly, "Let me get braced and you use my back to step up and get a hand hold. Once you get a hold on the top of that ledge I'll get under you and push you up."

"Okay. Ready?"

"Wait. Take your gear off. I'll hand it up."

Doc stepped on a small boulder and then on Rhodes's back and got his hands on the ledge doing a pull up so Rhodes could get his shoulders under his feet. When Rhodes straightened up with a groan, Doc pulled himself up onto the ledge.

"Take you gear off and hand it up," Doc said.

With Rhodes's gear off, Doc could pull him up enough to get his elbows on the ledge. Rhodes pulled himself up the rest of the way, cussing quietly and groaning.

"Same thing again," he said.

The rest of the climb involved one man acting as a ladder for another and boosting a partner over rocks and boulders. Arms ached and thighs burned. Upward movement began to be measured in feet per hour.

Later, the team was stymied by an outcropping that covered the width of the ravine. There were only a few obvious handholds, and pinions wouldn't hold in the ancient basalt. Somebody had to find a route up the rock. Harris gave it a try.

Harris was moving horizontally across the face of the outcropping looking for hand holds when a foothold gave way and left him hanging ten feet above the team by one hand. His M-16 dropped straight down as he swung his loose arm to grab a second handhold and his feet kicked at the basalt trying to find purchase. Even with two hands he wouldn't be able to hold long with sixty pounds on his back. Hopkins dove and caught the rifle before it went clattering down the side of the hill. Lennon pushed the radioman out of the way and scrambled four feet up the rock getting good foot holds and pushed his shoulders up under the point man's feet. He grabbed one foot and put it on his shoulder. Harris found the other shoulder. Shit, Rhodes thought, let them try to call him a fairy now.

Stabilized again Harris could feel around for a new foot hold and found one by stretching his leg far to the right. He continued his sideways climb gaining a little height with each movement. When he was twenty feet above the team he looked down and shook his head no. He started moving down the rock. They had good concealment on the face of the rock from branches of a large tree growing out of the rocks below and shading the outcropping. The team would be hard to see from below. Harris had enough cover to move up without being discovered, but he couldn't continue the steep climb with his pack on his back.

He explained the situation to Hopkins and said he thought he could make it to the top without his pack. If he carried one of the ropes he could pull his gear up and then help the next man up with the rope. Hopkins thought it was worth the try especially since they were running out of day and they needed to start back down the hill soon or find a safe harbor. But the top of hill was only fifty feet above them and they needed to achieve that objective that day.

Harris started back up the rock with just a fifty-foot line slung over his shoulder. The climb went quickly with the weight removed from his back and Harris already knowing where the handholds were for the first twenty feet up. Ten minutes later he dropped the end of the line over the side of the rock and hauled his gear and rifle up. Then it was Lakin, the primary radioman's, turn. Without his gear and radio, he went up quickly also. The route up the rock was well marked now and the rest of the team made it to the top over the next thirty minutes, but they didn't have much reserve energy left when they got there.

Rhodes sent his gear up on the rope and then followed the team to the top. They had not only climbed thirty of the remaining fifty feet, but they had done it quietly. Now they were at the critical moment. They had to go up the final twenty feet through tangled vines and scrub brush, do it quietly, and crest the hill to see what they were facing on top.

Hopkins pulled the team together under the brush with the top of the outcropping as a base. Harris was the best climber and had the best point skills. It fell to him to make the twenty-foot climb and report back what was waiting on the top. He had plenty of hand holds this time, but getting through the tangle of vines and brush was going to take time. Hopkins wanted him to tunnel under the foliage if he could, bore a hole the others could follow, and stay concealed as much as possible.

They weren't hearing any sounds of movement from the top, but that didn't mean there wasn't a platoon up there waiting silently for them to poke their heads up. NVA on top paying close attention could have heard something. The team could have been spotted on the assent and a radio message sent to the top too. The possibilities were many and scary.

Harris started through the vines close to the side of the hill. The going was excruciatingly slow. To move silently, he had to cut each vine, stuff it back into the rest of the tangle, and then cut the next vine or plant silently. Jerking a vine or tugging on it could cause a rattle in the brush, or possibly dislodge a rock and send it clattering down the slope. Small tree trunks too thick to cut with his K-bar, he just had to squirm around. He took all the time he needed to do it silently; it was his head that had to poke above the crest and look around.

Forty-five minutes passed before Harris poked his head back out of the foliage tunnel and waved the team to follow. Hopkins went second, Lakin the radioman, third, then a team mate, then Lennon, two more team mates, then the Doc, then Rhodes. When Rhodes got to the top, Hopkins had the team spread out against a wall of red dirt left where a section of the hill had caved from the rain, probably during the worst of the monsoon. The crest was right above their heads.

Harris stood on Lennon's shoulders and went over the top on his belly. The rest of the team followed and pulled Rhodes up by his hands.

They were on a slightly rounded peak, one of two that defined the top of hill 881S. A slight saddle connected the two rounded peaks. The one they were on was slightly higher and had a general slope to the saddle. The top of the hill was shaped sort of like a lengthwise half peanut shell laid open-side down and covered in thick jungle. Hopkins moved the team into the foliage silently and put them in an arch perimeter facing the peaks, ten feet apart. They went still and silent listening for movement.

Rhodes went over his view of the hill top in his mind considering what it would take to turn the hill top into a fire base for artillery. It would take a team of engineers with explosives on top of the hill to clear an LZ. Wouldn't hurt to lay some artillery on the area first to do some initial demolition and clear some jungle. In any case, the hill would make a very good fire base and provide open fields of fire all the way to Khe Sanh once it was cleared of jungle on top. It would be easy to defend also. A company of Marines could hold off a regiment of NVA from those heights. Of course, if the Marines didn't take the hill and set up their own fire base first, the NVA would have the same advantages over the Marines.

Hopkins gave it thirty minutes and signaled Harris to move out. They searched the peak until the light started to fade and Hopkins made notes in his journal describing what was under the foliage. Helicopters could see the top of the jungled covered hill, but the jungle hid terrain features that would be important to the planners.

As far as the team could tell, they were alone on top of the Hill. Hopkins took them deep in the grass and trees covering a slight slope on the side facing Khe Sanh and set up for chow. They were stuck on the hill until morning. He called in directly to the relay and passed his intelligence to Dong Ha. After a LRRP meal, which took a lot of their remaining water, they went into listening mode. Two faint lights from Khe Sanh were visible twinkling off in the distance, but the position in the foliage didn't offer a view of much else. Hopkins moved the team closer to the edge of the foliage and put them on fifty percent alert.

The first part of the night was quiet. Rhodes watched the two lights twinkle at Khe Sanh and quietly squashed bugs crawling inside his trousers. He slept for an hour until he was shaken awake for his watch.

In the middle of the night and shortly after he had finished his watch and drifted off to sleep, Rhodes was shaken out of his sleep again with an insistent nudging to his arm. He opened his eyes and pushed back at the hand that was shaking him, signaling he understood. Everything was silent, at first. Then he heard the soft voices—and not far away. They were faint at first, but then grew louder as men in the night moved closer to the team's harbor.

He moved his head slowly and scanned the foliage around him. Slowly, dim detail began to resolve out of the dark of the night. There was some moonlight from a cloudy sky that was breaking up, enough to see movement and large shapes. He could make out the shapes of his team mates on both sides of him because he knew where they were. Hopkins had picked a harbor that also allowed some visibility toward Khe Sanh through the foliage. Through the low elephant grass and brush in front of him he could see over the edge of the hill and the two distant lights at Khe Sanh. Why in the hell would they have lights on out there? Did they want to become a target? What the hell were the sergeants doing?"

Then a shadow crossed in front of one of the lights. Movement. A human form in the dark. Looking slightly to the side of the form, he saw more detail. Arms lifting from the sides to the head. Then the form squatted and disappeared. Quiet talking, calm, routine passing of information. Then a quiet laugh and a return laugh close to the first. Rhodes could hear more than one on the hill in front of him.

Over the next fifteen minutes he thought he identified five different people out there, but no more. It wasn't even a full squad unless there were more of them somewhere else on the hill. The rest of the night was spent listening for more movement. By first light the faces of every member of the team were covered with fresh bites, and leeches were setting up colonies on necks, arms, under shirts, and even in hair. Still they couldn't move. He could feel a leech inside of his ear. He refused to think about what was inside of his trousers.

They had a perfect ambush. The enemy soldiers were so close the Marines could listen in on the conversation. Rhodes could imagine the indecision in Hopkins's mind. The ambush might work, if they were alone on the hill, but disengaging would be hell and every VC/NVA in the area would be alerted.

As the sky lightened the figures near the edge

of the drop-off resolved into people in tan uniforms. There were seven of them. Four wore web gear with ammo pouches and canteens and carried AK-47s. Three wore higher quality uniforms, pistol belts, and had binoculars. They were watching Khe Sanh.

Now that he could see them clearly, he realized how exposed the team was. He wanted to squirm back into the undergrowth, but movement or sound of any kind could be disastrous. The team could take out the seven they could see without a problem, but how many others were supporting them? And then with the enemy alerted, how would the team get off the hill and to the extraction LZ? They had to tough it out and hope the NVA would move on.

Chapter 11

As the sun rose in the sky his stomach growled. Rhodes thought every NVA soldier between them and Khe Sanh had to have heard it. Hopkins glared at him and Lennon buried his face in his hands. Rhodes slowly stretched, bending his sides as much as he could without moving his body overall. The stretch seemed to help. The NVA in front of them didn't seem to be in any hurry and obviously didn't have any idea they were being observed while they observed Khe Sanh.

A small plane landed at Khe Sanh. Probably a Beaver. One of the NVA officers used a hand-held radio like a walkie-talkie for a moment. Soon Rhodes saw a puff of smoke near the runway. A few moments later he heard the soft, distant report of an explosion. The officer had called a fire mission from a mortar. There was nothing the team could do about it, though. Without knowing how many other NVA were on the hill, Hopkins couldn't use the radio or move.

The radio toting officer called in two more shots, neither of them doing any damage, marking his map each time, and then, finally, jabbered at his team and started walking away towards the other side of the hill. Hopkins raised his hand slightly telling the team to get ready. He pointed Harris at the point on the lip where their foliage tunnel started and then gave it another two minutes. Finally, Hopkins waved Harris on and held everyone else up. When Harris disappeared over the lip, Hopkins sent the radioman. He turned to Rhodes and whispered, "Same way for the rest of the team. You last."

"Got it," Rhodes said.

Hopkins ran bent over to the lip and slid out of sight. Rhodes sent the rest of the men one at a time until it was his turn. He listened for a moment and then started through the grass and brush for the side of the hill. He was almost there when he heard the sound behind him.

He dropped straight down and hugged the ground. Sounds of brush being cut and pushed aside came from behind. He turned so his head was facing the noise. He started squirming backwards toward the lip.

He made it to the lip before he saw the first Vietnamese. His feet were hanging over the broken edge of the hill, so close to safety, but he had to stop moving. The NVA soldier was looking right at his position. The soldier hacked at another bush absently keeping his eyes on Rhodes. At least that's what it felt like. Then the soldier looked over his shoulder and jabbered something. Rhodes took the opportunity to slip over the lip and moved quickly into the tunnel below the brush.

He was only a few feet down the tunnel when he heard voices above him. He stopped moving. He was sure the team could hear the voices and therefore knew what was going on and why he was delayed. Lying still against the sharp cut-off stalks remaining on the bottom of the tunnel started a new agony. Sharp points, sliced on a bias, cut into his utilities and a hundred little points poked him in tender places. With his body still, he began noticing the things crawling on his skin underneath his clothes. And then he noticed the things crawling in the brush next to him, specifically, one long, multi-colored thing coiled next to his hand on the dirt above his head.

Now Rhodes wasn't a snake expert, but he did know that snakes that had triangular shaped heads with blunt noses were vipers and deadly. This one seemed to have a triangular head—or sort of triangular. He stayed very still. He had a deep-seated phobia about snakes. He hated the damn things. If it had been a VC he would have reached out and rung his neck. But this was a snake. He froze.

The snake was right next to his left hand which was above his head and flat on the ground. It wasn't a big snake, not like the cobra. But coral snakes and bamboo vipers are small and they are as deadly as the cobra, maybe more so. It didn't matter. It was a damn snake.

He watched the snake. The snake was motionless and watched Rhodes. Can snakes blink? This one didn't. Rhodes didn't either. Would it strike if he jerked his hand back? The NVA above were completely forgotten.

The talking above him ceased and Rhodes heard movement away from the lip of the crest. Sweat and grease-paint dripped into his eyes, burning, no way to wipe it. The more he watched the snake's eyes, the less everything else mattered. Just the snake and his left hand. Silence.

Then a tap on his heel. A whisper.

"What's the hold up?" It was Hopkins.

"Snake," Rhodes whispered back without turning or taking his eyes off the snake.

"Where?"

"Next to my left hand, above my head."

"Jerk you hand back."

"No way."

Silence.

"Don't move."

"Yeah," he whispered.

Suddenly he was yanked back two feet by his ankles. He didn't have to be encouraged further. He jerked his hands back and pushed backwards kicking Hopkins in the face.

"Fuck!" Hopkins whispered

"Move," Rhodes hissed. "I ain't stopping."

They moved down the tunnel making way too much noise and finally emerged on top of the basalt outcropping that had served as the previous day's base.

Hopkins put his mouth next to Rhodes ear. "The rest of the team are already down. Go down the rope. I'll toss the rope and climb down. Send your gear down first."

"On my way."

Rhodes tied his pack, radio, and rifle and lowered them to the team. He left the rope hanging down and started down the rock. He made the bottom in less than five minutes. Hopkins tossed the rope over and started down. His gear was already down.

Hopkins took a full ten minutes climbing to the bottom. Once on the bottom, he unfolded his map and motioned Rhodes to join him.

"Did that snake hold you up all that time?" Hopkins said quietly.

"No. A squad of Vietnamese almost tripped over me. I had to wait on top until I had a chance to get over the edge."

"Do you think they saw you?"

"I doubt it," Rhodes said.

Hopkins studied the map for a few moments.

"It's a long, hard slog to the LZ. I don't think we're going to make it in time. Not with all the enemy we've been seeing."

"We better find some water then. I have maybe one more gulp. I doubt anyone else has any more."

"We'll go for the LZ and look for alternate sites. I'm going to put Doc on point and give Jenkins a break."

"Want me to stay in back?"

"You up to it?"

"Yeah."

"Okay, I'm going to check in and give them our status. Then move out."

The team moved down the hill slowly reversing the steep climb. Going down was harder than the climb up. They couldn't use each other as ladders. Hopkins avoided the trail this time. By the time they reached the finger ridge on which they had inserted, everyone's water was gone. That was double trouble because they needed water for the freeze dried LRRPs as well as for drinking. They wouldn't get chow until they found water, and it hadn't rained since their first night in harbor. Water was going to be hard to find.

While the team rested, Rhodes looked them over. They were a ragged bunch. Eyes were sunken with fatigue. No one had shaved or washed in three days. Faces and hands were filthy with red dirt from the climbs up and down ridges and hills. Their bodies were covered with scratches and cuts from the grass, vines, and thorns. Utilities were filthy and torn with flaps of cloth hanging loosely from major tears. The side seam of Hopkins trousers left leg was torn open with his hairy leg showing through. Everything on the Marines was soaked with sweat.

Hopkins took them down the side of the finger and began moving toward 881N. The elephant grass was taller and the vines thicker in the valley at the base of the hills. To make it worse, the valley wasn't flat. They had to cross smaller finger ridges and go around vine covered Basalt and dirt formations that jutted up randomly. Without water, body fluids disappeared quickly and heat exhaustion began to set in. Finding water became a higher priority than reaching the LZ.

Moving up a small finger ridge no more than fifty feet high with a gentle slope, Doc Bannon, walking point now, stopped the team with a raised fist. Everyone squatted down and Hopkins went forward on his belly. Soon Hopkins gave the sign to get flat on the ground and move forward. Doc had found a small pool of stagnant, scum covered water in a cluster of rock formations at the top of the rise.

Each man moved to the pool and with a grimace dunked and filled one canteen. The water stank and tiny things slithered in it. Doc watched and made sure each of them put halazone tabs in the canteen and made them shake the canteen to mix it up. All sorts of nasty microscopic creatures found that little pool to be a lovely home. They would find the human gut even more lovely.

Most of the team had the experience and good sense to bring a few packs of Kool Aid to dilute the taste of the nasty water and halazone, but Lennon hadn't. Rhodes gave him a half pack to empty into his canteen. Probably would have been better to let him learn his lesson, but the kid made such a terrible face when he took his first drink Rhodes couldn't help himself. Lennon seemed so damn helpless sometimes—until it was time to toss grenades. The Kool Aid helped, but even with the Kool Aid you had to hold your nose to get the canteen to your mouth.

Having good concealment and solid cover in rock formations around the pool, Hopkins gave the team a break to cool down. The place was like a naturally formed miniature Stonehenge.

With a few minutes available, Doc began doing his job. After finding two leeches in the crack of his own ass, Doc made everyone drop their trousers and look each other over for leeches in tender places. When the leeches are full of blood you can feel them on you, but they start out tiny and are easy to miss until they have some blood in them. Not only that, but they had to be backed out with bug juice, not dislodged roughly or they could regurgitate and infect the bite. You didn't want infected leech bites in the crack of your butt while you were sweating and trying to hump a few miles through the jungle. That truly smarts.

Looking at someone else's asshole wasn't really a Marine thing to, but it was necessary. You check my asshole, I'll check your asshole. The damn leeches loved any orifice they could get to. If they got inside, well . . .

Lennon didn't want to drop his trousers, but Doc wasn't taking any crap from anyone. Lennon was made to drop-trou and bend over. Lennon shivered when Doc checked him. The image of a scared, wounded animal came to Rhodes's mind. Lennon had two leeches lodged inside the crack of his ass too, and Doc backed them off with a shot of bug juice. Before they finished, 25 leeches were backed off legs, assholes, penises, and ball sacks, but none had slithered or slid into any orifices—as far as anyone could tell. Hopkins waited a few minutes to let the smell of the repellant diminish and then moved the team out of the rock formations one at a time with Harris back on point and Rhodes left behind to bring up the rear.

Chapter 12

Rhodes was still in the rocks by the pool waiting for the last two members of the team to move out when the first rifle shot rang out from further down the side of the small ridge. He was still inside of several basalt outcroppings that jutted up through the ground about five feet high forming a fort like cluster that had made the spot a good harbor.

When the first shot sounded, Rhodes and Doc, who was falling in second from the end this time, bellied forward to see what was happening and to give the team covering fire. The shot they heard had been from an AK-47, a distinctive sound.

The elephant grass, about seven feet high, came right up to the rock cluster and made it hard to see anything. Only the seventh man could be seen backing toward the rocks. Weed crunching sounds from the others could be heard getting closer though. The seventh man made a final dash into the rocks.

"Harris has been hit," he said.

Doc moved into the grass toward the sound of the team, pulling his unit-one around to his side. Rhode's moved his selector to full automatic and prepared to give the team a base of fire to keep the enemies heads down. He set three grenades on the rock in front of him. The sounds of movement got louder and Hopkins and the radioman appeared through the wall of grass carrying Harris. The rest of the team followed them in with Lennon bringing up the rear walking backwards and giggling quietly.

Doc began cutting Harris's shirt open and Hopkins deployed his team.

"Lennon, set out claymores. Striker, show him where. Lakin, report contact and tell Khe Sanh to stand by for a fire mission. The rest of you get your claymores out."

Hopkins deployed his perimeter and dropped down next to Rhodes. Sweat beaded on his face and further depleted his bodily fluids.

"What's out there?" Rhodes said.

"Don't know. Never even saw the fuckers. Harris walked into something, we got him, and moved back. There's a lot of grass, but no cover out there at all. Lakin, have you got Khe Sanh yet?"

"On the hook, Gunny."

"Give me the handset." Hopkins folded his map

into a small square and called the coordinates for an on-call mission. Khe Sanh's 105mm battery didn't give him a stand-by this time. With artillery set up, Hopkins reported contact and one WIA and requested extraction. A gun ship was diverted from another mission near Cam Lo and Hopkins was given an ETA. He was told to stand-by on the extraction. Lennon walked backwards into the rocks unspooling the det-wires for the claymores. Rhodes connected the clackers and set them in front of him. Other team members were doing the same thing. With a semicircle of nine claymores deployed on the outer side of the rocks, grenades set out in front of the Marines, and weapons ready, Hopkins unfolded an orange air identification panel over a jutting rock in the center of the cluster. The Marines got quiet and waited.

Call the fucking fire mission, Rhodes thought, but he kept it to himself. It may have been just one or it may have been a hundred out there. But letting them get close was stupid. That's what the VC liked. Get close, grab us by the belt, nullify supporting arms and air power.

As if he had read Rhodes's mind, Hopkins grasped the handset and called the mission. The team got down in the rocks. The first whooshing round screamed in a hundred meters from the harbor. Hopkins gave adjustments and walked the artillery around the position. Rhodes, lying next to Hopkins, scribbled the coordinates and noted where the rounds hit, readying to take over if Hopkins was hit. Hopkins walked the artillery until he was satisfied and then called a halt.

The team listened for movement, no open field of fire, dependent on their ears for a warning, knowing the enemy was too close for the artillery to have done any good. An OV-10 arrived overhead and circled. Hopkins talked to the observer and got a report of what he was facing. The observer could see the yellow panel and reported a platoon sized movement not more than twenty-five meters west of the panel. The enemy was approaching the Marines on line. Too close for artillery support and soon, too close for the gunships to help. Nine men facing a platoon of NVA. They weren't VC. They weren't running away. They were trained regular soldiers. Not the odds Rhodes hoped for.

The OV-10 had rockets, but the approaching NVA were too close even for him to help. He did a wider loop to see what was behind the platoon. Happily, he couldn't find any reinforcements coming up from any direction—at least not yet. The Observer dropped down to almost tree top level and did a pass over the area. He reported the Vietnamese were spread out on both sides of a trail of crushed vegetation.

"They're following our trail right to us," Hopkins said quietly. "They probably don't know how many we have here. Maybe they don't know about these rocks."

"This might be the only LZ were going to get," Rhodes said. "The bird can't land, but we can probably get in if he can hover low."

"We have to deal with what's coming first."

The gunship contacted Hopkins and gave him an ETA of five minutes. Then the extraction bird contacted him and gave him an ETA of fifteen minutes. They just had to hold out for fifteen minutes—and deal with what was coming.

The pilot of the OV-10 called and said the Vietnamese were closing on the Marines position. Hopkins moved behind five of his Marines on that side of the rocks and told them to open-up at knee level when he blew the claymores. He returned to his position and took two clackers in his hands. Rhodes did the same. Lennon straightened the pins on four grenades and kept one in one hand and a finger of the other hand in the pin loop.

They heard movement in the grass. Hopkins and Rhodes rose with their eyes just over their cover rocks and watched. As soon as Hopkins saw movement in the brush he dropped down and looked at Rhodes. Silently he mouthed, "One, two . . .Now!" They both squeezed the clackers hard twice. Two of the claymore fired on the first squeeze. Two more fired on the second squeeze but the delay between the two was so small it just sounded like one rolling blast. Rhodes and Hopkins dropped the clackers and grabbed their rifles. Thousands of metal-balls the size of .22 caliber bullets blasted through the elephant grass and were followed by four M-14s and two M-16s on full automatic. For good measure, Lennon tossed grenades at four points spread across the NVA front. As soon as his first magazine was empty, Hopkins ceased the firing.

Rhodes had been ready to explode, but now he was ecstatic. The Vietnamese hadn't even fired their weapons. It had been total surprise and devastation. His ecstasy was short lived. An Ak-47 on full automatic opened-up on the rocks and then another joined in. Then another. Soon six weapons were firing on the team through the shredded grass in front of their position. Then two chicoms fell and exploded just outside of the rocks. The firing was wild and the grenades were off target. The NVA didn't know exactly where their opponents were. Hopkins asked the Observer to see if he could see the shooters.

The OV-10 did a low pass and took small arms fire. He reported six Vietnamese, grouping and moving away from the Marines' position. He also reported several bodies, but didn't have time to count them. He told the Marines to keep their heads down. He was going to put rockets on the Vietnamese.

On his first pass, he came in from behind and the rockets screamed low over the team's position. Hopkins received a call from the gunship. He was one minute out and told the Marines to stay down. Hopkins let the Observer vector the gunship in. The *fluka-fluka* of rotors could already be heard. The team resumed their deep cover.

The gunship worked the area over with his guns and then stood off in a hover. He was joined by a second gunship five minutes later. Both war birds circled the harbor. While the war birds watched, the extraction bird contacted Hopkins and told him he was two minutes out and asked for the status of the LZ.

"Reacher One this is Delta Crow. Lima Zulu is on top of twenty-meter rise, has high rocks and is surrounded by seven-foot-high elephant grass. Suggest you hover the grass on the south side. We have one Whiskey India Alpha. Lima Zulu is quiet now, over."

"Roger, Delta Crow. Mount up. We are one minute out."

The birds began coordinating with each other and the gunships began working the grass with their guns. The Observer in the OV-10 climbed for a better look.

"Delta Crow this is Angel Two. You have movement to your south. Estimate platoon or greater size force."

"Roger. How long have we got?"

"A few minutes, but they are within rifle range of the Lima Zulu. As soon as your greyhound clears the airspace, I'm calling in artillery."

"Roger. Delta Crow out."

"Delta Crow this is Reacher One. Move your asses. I'm coming in."

The HC-34 dropped like a rock and at the last instant the engines screamed and the descent stopped. He hovered, turned his tail away from the rocks, and dropped further until a wheel touched the ground just feet outside of the rocks. The rotor wash began beating the grass down and beating the Marines up. The pilot held his hover with just one wheel touching the slope.

Doc and the radioman were first on carrying

Harris. Lennon and the rest of the team followed with Rhodes following and then Hopkins. Hopkins did a fast count, signaled the crew chief, and the bird lifted fast. The sound of the screaming engines and straining rotors was so loud the men inside couldn't even hear metal on metal as small holes appeared in the aluminum skin letting little beams of light shine through. The bird banked and picked up speed.

Lennon started giggling. That started a chain reaction and soon the whole team was laughing. The crew chief grinned and shook his head in wonder.

Rhodes wasn't laughing. He was trying to keep his cool. They weren't a bunch of super grunts laughing in the face of death. It was adrenalin, relief, and terror, all escaping at the same time. The patrol was over and they were safe. Until the next time. How many more times could he manage to make it out? Jesus, that had been close. He folded his hands in his lap and leaned forward hiding the tremors he couldn't control.

Chapter 13

Slaughter made the team stand down for an hour to rehydrate and get some chow before he started the debriefings. After they started, the debriefings went on for the rest of the evening and well into the night. Every team member was asked about the enemy sightings and if he heard the artillery call denied. Four including Rhodes and Hopkins witnessed the denial. Rhodes never did find out what happened with that information or who wanted it, but a change of command took place at Khe Sanh not long after those incidents.

After the debriefings, Slaughter, Captain Lang the assistant S3, and Rhodes sipped some beer and discussed the patrol. Rhodes needed something to distract his mind from the thoughts that swirled through his head. He needed something to distract his mind from thinking about the next patrol. Somehow, they got into a discussion of how long, distance wise, the ideal recon patrol should be. As they talked about distances, Slaughter interrupted the conversation to ask a question.

"You know," he said. "I've used and heard the term thousands of times. Been using it since the platoon leaders course in college. But I never wondered before where that term comes from." Slaughter grinned. "Everyone knows Master Gunnery Sergeants know everything, so here's my question, Dick. Just where did the term klick, spelled either way, C or K . . .Where did it come from? Why is a grid square on a map a click?"

Rhodes didn't give a shit about clicks or klicks and he wasn't in anything even resembling a jolly mood, but he was good at covering and he didn't want Slaughter and Lang to see how close he was to slamming something on the table just to let off some steam. He put on a happy face and toughed it out.

"Well, sir, you are a wise commander, an unusual thing for a field grade . . ."

"Watch it."

Rhodes grinned, feeling a little better. "I just happen to hold that bit of lore. Or at least I have a good story that makes sense. First, a klick, K, or a click, C, are essentially the same thing. Both stand for a kilometer, a thousand meters. You see it written both ways, but when you see it with a C, it is generally referring to a map. One click is one grid square. Since a grid square is a square kilometer, if you move a click on the map, you move a kilometer. Transportation types and grunts will often write klick with a K as shorthand for a kilometer. So essentially they mean the same thing."

"I know all that," Slaughter said. "But where did the term come from? A klim or a klom I could see, but not a klick. That's not even close to sounding like kilometer"

"As I understand it, and, mind you, I got this from a Sergeant Major, so it must be true. The term "click" probably came from the Aussies. You didn't hear it used before Vietnam. Or, at least, I didn't. Of course, I'm not as old as you, sir. . ."

"Watch it."

Now that he was into the explanation, he started feeling a little better. The smell of explosives receded and memories of screaming men in the grass quieted—or maybe he was just glad for anything that would distract his mind.

"Anyway, do you remember how we counted and kept track of distance in the land navigation course?"

"Sure," Slaughter said. "One man on the patrol would keep track of distance traveled by counting out a hundred meters based on his pace. Usually around 100 paces on level ground. A little less downhill, a little more uphill. The counter tied a knot in a string every hundred meters. You could tell how far you had gone by counting the knots."

"Right," Rhodes said, getting into the story. "But

the Aussies had a different idea, same concept but different method. They use the L1A1 rifle, or SLR, self-loading rifle as it's known, as their standard battle rifle. It's a gas operated, semi or full auto, seven point six two NATO round, with an external gas regulator. Damn fine rifle too. I wish we had a few. They put these damn mickey mouse M-16s to . . ."

"Dick, get on with it, will you?" Slaughter said, rubbing his temples with his fingers.

"Right. Anyway, the gas regulator on the SLR has ten setting marks. An Aussie patrol uses one member to count distance too, but he uses the gas regulator on his rifle to record hundred meter blocks by advancing it one mark for each hundred meters. When he sets the regulator to the last mark—ten—the regulator makes a loud click. It only clicks on the last setting. They've traveled one click of the regulator, or ten times a hundred meters, a kilometer."

"You're shitting me," Slaughter said. "Did you know that, Pete?"

"No, sir, can't say I ever thought about it. The Striker is a fount of wondrous and arcane knowledge."

"Dick, you better not be shitting me. I'm going to tell that story at staff meeting. If you're making that up, you better tell me now."

"No, sir, That's the straight poop. A history major would not shit you. Besides, it's straight from the Sergeant Major and he is absolutely a no-shit Marine."

Slaughter watched Rhodes closely for a few moments but Rhodes was a picture of innocence.

"Damn," Slaughter said. "I wasn't expecting it to be that, but it makes sense. Dick, I need to talk to you in private for a few minutes. Pete, will you excuse us?"

"Of course, sir. I'm up to my ass in mission planning anyway. Check with me in the morning, Striker. I'm planning a new one for you I think you will find absolutely fascinating."

Rhodes's stress level went way back up.

"Yes, sir. I'll be in at 0700."

"See me at 1300 and sleep in. Christ, you just got back."

"Aye, aye, sir."

Slaughter went to the fridge and took out two more cans of beer. He set one in front of Rhodes and then propped his feet on the table.

"Dick, I want you to listen to my whole spiel before you say anything. Hear me out before you go into denial. Okay?"

The pre-mission flutters tickled at Rhodes's stomach. The last time Slaughter did this kind of thing was at the airport when Rhodes was departing from his first tour and a new tour of combat had resulted, a tour Rhodes should have been smart enough to turn down. The odds don't reset just because you get new orders.

"Okay, sir," he said. "I think"

"Dick, the Colonel and I have been talking about the enlisted to commissioned officer direct commission program. I'd like to recommend you for direct commissioning."

"Major, you know how I . . ."

"I asked you to hear me out. Okay?"

"Yes, sir," he said, feeling not at all like listening further. He had Master Gunnery Sergeant stripes, E9, top of the heap. He didn't want some damn butter bar commission to be ordered around by some half-assed Captain or First Lieutenant. Besides, when the war was over a reserve direct commission would be just one desk closer to the door. The Corps always got cut deeper than the other services when the hostilities stopped. RIFs would be the order of the day and no matter what it felt like right then, Vietnam would become history sooner or later.

"Look, I know you always wanted make Master Gunny. You got it, but, Dick, I'm talking about command. You have the experience, you have the talent. You could do so much more."

"Major, can you really see me as a Second Lieutenant? I can't. Master Guns means something in the Corps. It means a lot. Christ, second lieutenants make coffee for me, sir."

"I'm not talking Second or even First Lieutenant, Dick. The Colonel and I want to make you a Captain."

"Captain, sir? But that's a company commander."

"If you're lucky. Commanding a company is the best damn job in the Corps. I can't promise you that, but you'd make one hell of an assistant S3. Captain Lang is ready to rotate. I want you as my assistant S3."

"Major, maybe you've had too many of those

beers. You can't promote an enlisted man straight to Captain."

"Yes, we can. It's already been done. Under the new guidelines, senior NCOs in the top two grades can be direct commissioned to Captain. Your AFQT scores are in the top 1%. That alone would put you in OCS if you had listened to me on your last tour. You've already commanded a platoon and did an outstanding job. You've already served as company exec as a Master Sergeant. There's no way we can promote you to even First Lieutenant without a pay cut, and serving as an O-1 or O-2 wouldn't do you or the Corps any good. You've already got more experience in what they do than most senior First Lieutenants in the Corps. And you have a degree. The colonel can make it happen. Can you handle it?"

He just stared at Slaughter for a few moments. He needed time to think.

"Jesus, Major. I can't answer you right now. I've got to think about it."

"Dick, I've spent a lot of time and used up a lot of favors getting the Colonel and his boss on your side. Don't make me look bad."

Rhodes felt the heat rise in his face. He hadn't asked for Slaughter's interference in his career.

"That's a low blow, Major. Why didn't you talk to me?"

"I wanted your mind on the job, not on this. And I needed you showing what you are capable of. Why do you think I've had you in the S2 meetings, briefing the G2, and going around meeting our supporting units? What's holding you back?"

He wasn't sure if he should explain. It sounded kind of selfish. Slaughter was trying to do a good thing. But Captain's bars. Jeeze, he never even considered that.

"Major, the Corps is my career. Hell, it's my life. I don't have a wife now or family. I don't have any interests outside of the Corps. What happens after this war is over if I get a reserve commission? You know what. The same thing that happened after the Second war. Same thing that happened after Korea. The reserves will be the first to go."

"That's not the way it works, Dick. At worst, you would be offered the opportunity to reenlist at your highest enlisted grade. So, you'd be a Master Gunny again. You've already got sixteen years in, so you'll get your twenty in. And your retirement pay would be based on your highest commissioned rank. But I doubt that you'd get RIF'd. Do a good job and request to go regular in a couple years. You've got a degree. Put two outstanding fitness reports with it and you'll get it. I've checked all this out. Now, any other problems?"

"Christ, a Captain? Major, I wouldn't know how to act in the officer's mess. Who's going to teach me how to hold my pinky out when I sip a martini with the General?"

"Did you notice any stiff pinkies when you were in Third Battalion with me?"

"No, sir, but there's so damn much I don't know

about that world."

"You know all you need to know. Believe me, you have good instincts. You'll pick it up fast."

Rhodes rocked back in his chair and sipped at his beer to gain a little time to think. Battle stress was gone now, or at least it was submerged below a new kind of stress. Captain's bars. Railroad tracks. Probably not any better than being a Master Gunny Sergeant. Maybe not as good. Nobody fooled with a Master Gunny. But hell, it was an interesting thought. Maybe he could make Major down the road. Field grade. Field grade perks. Could he even imagine himself as a light colonel? Scrambled eggs on his hat. Shit. He laughed.

"What?" Slaughter said.

"I was just thinking . . .possibilities . . . scrambled eggs." he laughed again.

"Who knows. You've got the talent. Major before you retire for sure. Now you're thinking right."

He hesitated. The last time he let Slaughter talk him into . . .But he's talking captain bars this time. Is it possible? Hell, why not?

"Well, sir, if you are crazy enough to recommend me, I guess I'm crazy enough to go along with it."

Slaughter just stared at Rhodes for a moment.

"Dick. A word of advice and a favor. To me, please? Don't ever say anything like that again especially around the Colonel. You are excited, honored, amazed the Corps thinks enough of you to give you this fantastic opportunity to lead and serve."

He rocked back in his chair and chuckled.

"Aye, aye, sir. I am duly honored and amazed. And that's no shit."

Chapter 14

Rhodes spent a lot of time thinking that night. Not only a commissioned officer, he thought, but a captain to boot. He wished his dad and mom had lived to see it. They had been proud of him when he graduated from Parris Island and even more proud when he made sergeant. What would they have thought about Captain? It would have made them happy.

Rhodes had been adopted when he was six by an older couple in their fifties. They had given him a childhood and a loving home. His mother died during his first tour in Vietnam and his father died a week later before Rhodes could get home on emergency leave for his mother's funeral. He never really got any closure even with the double funeral. The last time he had seen them they were happy and well. Then they were gone.

At least he had that memory.

To make matters worse, while he was home he found out his second wife was screwing around with a state cop. He was lucky in some ways. There were no kids from either of the marriages, and both wives left him for civilians while he was overseas. That hurt, the civilian part, but not having to pay alimony or child support eased the pain. And he also had to admit, he'd let either of them share a sleeping bag with him again if he ever got the chance. He couldn't say the no-fault divorce had affected him all that much. The marriage had been a weak one from the start, and probably a foolish one. She was too young to handle the separations. Hell, he had trouble getting her into bars sometimes. But all three losses took away any reason he had for returning to the states and was the major reason he let Slaughter talk him into signing a waver on his return to combat date and signing up for another tour in-country.

Getting a commission might make him happy too if he still had his parents to share it with. As it was, he wasn't sure how he felt about it. It didn't scare him, but then it didn't excite him all that much either. He was still enjoying the glow of making Master Gunny. He went to sleep a little overwhelmed with everything that was piling up on him and wondering where this new development would take him. Hell, maybe it wouldn't happen at all.

He was up at 0600 as was his habit, but he decided to

use the extra time Captain Lang had given him to check on the teams. He was pulling on his boots when Staff Sergeant Kelly knocked on the hooch door.

"Come."

"Striker, I need your help. Can you come down to the hooch?"

"Sure, what's up?"

"It's Lennon. You'll see."

Rhode's followed Kelly to Boatload's hooch at double time. Kelly wasn't talking so he wondered what all the hurry was about. He found out when he stepped inside of the hooch. Lennon was on his rack and he looked like a truck had run over him.

"What the hell happened to him?" he asked.

"Nobody knows," Kelly said. "But he was UA (unauthorized absence) when it happened."

"Why isn't he in sickbay?"

"Master Guns, he was UA. That's why I needed your help."

"Where's your corpsman?"

"I didn't want to get him involved until I talked to you."

"Get the corpsman down here and get Lennon to sickbay. What the fuck were you thinking, Kelly?" You can't cover up shit like this."

"I'm taking care of my team. It looks to me like he was worked over. I don't want the Skipper to work him over too. That's my job."

Rhodes thought for a moment. Kelly was a good leader and probably right. He'd see that Lennon learned his lesson. There was no sense letting the situation get out of the team. Sometimes you have to know what not to see. And then there's the First Sergeant. Christ, that's all I need. Cullahan will figure out a way to use this.

"All right. We'll talk about it later. Get the corpsman down here."

"I'm okay, Mr. Striker," Lennon said through swelled lips.

Lennon had his eyes closed. They were almost swelled closed.

"No, you are not okay. For one thing, you went UA. For another, while UA you sustained injuries that left you unable to perform your duties. Finally, you are not okay physically and you need medical attention. Now what happened to you, Lennon?"

"I don't want to talk about it, Mr. Striker."

"Don't call me mister, damn it. Lennon, I can't help you if I don't know what happened. What happened to you?"

Lennon was quiet for a few moments. Then tears leaked from his eyes.

"They beat me up, Mr. Striker. They called me a faggot and beat me up."

"Who beat you up?"

"Four. . . four Marines. They had a sergeant with them."

"Come on, Lennon. Just tell me all of it. Where did this happen?"

"At the club, over in the grunt sector. Three of them tried to start a fight with me in the club but they got thrown out. When I left, they were waiting for me with a sergeant."

"What were you doing over there? You know that's off-limits for Recon."

"I have a . . . friend. I mean, from my home town. I just wanted to see him and talk about back home for a while. We went to the same high school. I didn't plan on getting in trouble, Mr. Striker."

Rhodes looked at the bruised and swollen face. The rest of Lennon was about the same. They had really worked him over. Who the hell would do that to a kid like Lennon? Hell, that wasn't hard to answer. Half the Marines in the Corps would do it if they thought he was queer. Especially if they had a few beers in them and had never seen the kid in combat.

"Okay, Lennon. I'll take care of the UA with your platoon commander, but you won't be going out with your team for a while, and as soon as you are able you're going to be burning shitters. I'm not going to ask you now, but you *are* going to identify the people that did this to you."

Lennon didn't say anything and Rhodes let it go. No one wanted to be known as a rat. Even after what happened to him, Lennon wouldn't identify his attackers. Rhodes signaled Kelly to follow him outside.

"See if you can find out who did that. I want names."

"Shit, Striker. The team will know before noon."

"Sit on them, Kelly. I don't want somebody on Boatload facing a court martial. Get the names to me.

Tell the team I'll see that it's taken care of. You got my word. Those bastards will wish they never heard of Lennon."

"I'll do what I can, but I'm going to need a light duty assignment for Lennon. Can you help me keep him out of the First Sergeant's hands?"

"Yeah. See me later today."

On the way to the Ops Center, he thought about Lennon and men like him. He was a good Marine, a little swishy in his manner, and that gave people the wrong idea, but when the incoming started he fought as well as anyone on his team. He had the best damn grenade arm Rhodes had ever seen. The little fucker could put a grenade in a three-foot circle at fifty feet. No way was he queer. Of course, Rhodes didn't think he'd ever known any queers, but still, he was sure he'd recognize a real one, and Lennon was not one of them.

Captain Lang was laying out maps and aerial photos for a new mission when Rhodes arrived at the Ops Center. He discussed the patrol area with Lang and then went to the debriefing files. The files were set up with cross references for information relating to any patrol area in the Third Battalion area of operations. He began putting the intelligence package together for the mission. Before the team went out, the team leader would have an opportunity to review everything known about the area assigned to his team and have time to study aerial photos of the terrain. With that information covered, the team leader would do a fly over with the pilot who was going to insert them and identify potential LZs.

On his upcoming mission, Rhodes would be embedded with a five-man Force Recon Keyhole team. The patrol area was a stretch of piedmont along the DMZ north of Gio Linh, the northeast corner of leatherneck square. The DMZ and North Vietnam were the only things north of there. Covert insertion by helicopter was impossible in the rolling piedmont that characterized that whole area. The helicopter would signal every NVA and VC within ten miles that an insertion was underway. The team would have to go out with a grunt patrol, drop off in the bush, and hope they weren't noticed. A flyover would be done, but not to find an insertion LZ. Emergency extraction LZ sites were the priority. The team would be trucked out to Con Thien and then embedded with a platoon on patrol until they reached their jump-off point.

The area north of Con Thien and Gio Linh was mostly coastal plain and ancient river bed piedmont. The patrol would be moving right up to the banks of the Ben Hai river to see what the enemy was doing in the DMZ on the south side of the river. The DMZ overlapped the river by two klicks on both sides. The only concealment in the area was hedgerows that had grown up along abandoned rice paddy dikes, dense vegetation near streams and anywhere water was found, and a dense tree line on the banks of the Ben Hai river. Except for a few scattered abandoned rubber plantations with stands of old rubber trees, everything else was elephant grass, tall cane, reeds, vines, and scrub trees.

The area was a frequent target for B52 Arclight strikes and artillery duels, so bomb and artillery craters also provided the possibility of some cover, but that worked both ways, for the Marines and for the NVA. The team would have to do its traveling at night and harbor during daylight. It was going to be a hairy mission and not one Rhodes looked forward to. He had three days to get prepared.

Later, Rhodes arranged with Kelly to have Lennon assigned to the Ops Center as a clerk for light duty. When Rhodes checked with the First Sergeant to let him know what he was doing with Lennon, the First Sergeant wasn't at all happy. Word had gotten to him through one of his snitches about Lennon's UA. The First Sergeant wanted to write Lennon up.

"He works for me," Rhodes said. "I'll handle it."

"He was UA. He's due a mast."

"First Sergeant, I said I'll handle it. Now leave it alone."

"Master Guns, are you trying to tell me how to do my job?"

"No," Rhodes said. "I'm telling you to let me do my job. Lennon is my Marine. I'll handle it."

The First Sergeant, usually a Flexible guy, with a Master Guns at least, had gotten stubborn for some reason.

"Your recons are getting sloppy. They need an

example."

"I said I'll handle it," Rhodes said.

"I'll see what the Sergeant Major has to say about that."

"You do that, First Sergeant. In the meantime, Lennon is working for me.

Lennon reported to Rhodes in the morning. He was walking and talking, but he looked like the walking dead.

"Can you get around, okay?"

"I'm just bruised up, Mr. Striker. They didn't break anything,"

"Why the sling on your left arm?"

"It's just a strain. My throwing arm is good though."

"Maybe so," Rhodes said. "But your face looks like somebody did a cha-cha on it."

"More like a flamenco," Lennon said and did a little flip with his right hand. He tried to smile, but the smile turned into a grimace and a groan.

He watched Lennon for a few moments, wondering. Nah, he thought. It's just his way.

"Can you do filing and stuff like that?" he asked.

"Sure. I'm pretty good with paperwork."

"Okay. Let me show you how the debriefing file cross reference works. I've got a stack you can work on."

Lennon caught on quick and seemed to understand the cross-reference system intuitively.

Rhodes watched him for any signs of injury, but Lennon just winced occasionally and kept on working. After a while Rhodes ignored him and got on with his own planning.

He let Lennon work for a couple of hours until he looked like he was dragging.

"Lennon, there's a cot back there in the ready room. Go lie down for an hour."

"I'm good to go, Mr. Striker. I'll have these files done in a few minutes."

"Just do what I say. Go lie down."

"Yes, sir, Mr. Striker."

"Don't call me mister, damn it."

The response had become almost habitual and lacked any force. Rhodes didn't even realize he said it.

He left Lennon on the cot when the planning day was done and returned to his own hooch. He had a couple of warm beers and relaxed back on his rack to think. The thinking part didn't work out. He fell asleep in just a few minutes. He woke up with a hard knock on his door.

"Master Guns, are you in there?"

It was Slaughter.

"Come on in, sir. I was just catching some Zs."

Slaughter came in and sat on Rhodes's foot locker.

"Dick, I asked you not to piss off the Sergeant Major or the Exec. Now you got them and the First Sergeant pissed off at you and they're complaining to the Colonel. What happened now?"

"Nothing that I know of. What are they pissed off about now?"

"The Sergeant Major says you are interfering with the First Sergeant's duties and the Exec says discipline has gone to hell in the teams since you got here. What'd you do?"

"Major, I don't know. The only thing I can think of is Lennon."

"What about Lennon?"

"He's one of my Marines. Well, he's not really mine. He's in Kelly's team. He got himself into some trouble and I told the First Sergeant I was handling it and to leave it alone. He wanted to write Lennon up. Between me and Kelly, we'll see that Lennon gets all of the additional duty and instruction he needs."

"Christ, Dick. Couldn't you have just walked away from it? We don't need this shit right now."

"Major, it was you that taught me to keep things unofficial as much as I could. Remember? You were a pretty good Skipper, sir, and you took care of your Marines. You want me to be different?"

Slaughter didn't answer right away. He stood up and walked toward the door. Then he stopped and tuned around.

"Aw hell, no. But damn it, the Exec sits right there next to the Colonel and he's all too happy to make you look as bad as he can. He is not in favor of seeing you commissioned. What's with that? Do you two have a history?"

Rhodes rubbed the back of his neck. Pogues and

politics, he thought. Do I really want to be a captain?

"Yeah, we go back a way," he said. "He's always been a chicken shit pogue. We've had a few run-ins over the years."

"All right. I'll do what I can with the Colonel. Please stay the hell away from the pogues. Will you?"

"I don't go looking for them, Major. I'll try to keep my head down."

Late that night the alert sirens went off and Marines poured out of their hooches and into bunkers. Rhodes woke up cussing the sirens and ran to the Combat Operations Center (COC). The Marines manning the watch appeared totally confused as they darted from radio to radio and carried messages in and out of the watch commander's office. He got a cup of coffee and stood against a sandbagged wall to stay out of the way. Thirty minutes later the all-clear sounded.

"What was it?" He asked the COC Gunny.

"They thought it was a mortar attack in the grunt sector at first," the Gunny said. "But they're thinking a fragging now."

"Yeah? Who got fragged?"

"Weird. Just some grunt tent. Nobody was hurt, but the back of the hooch was blown in. They figure somebody tossed a grenade. The guys inside heard it hit the back of the hooch before it blew."

"What a crazy damn war," Rhodes said. "Well, I'll get out of your hair."

As he opened the door to his hooch, Kelly came down the row at a run.

"Striker, have you seen Lennon?"

"No. I left him at the Ops Center. He was getting ready to go back to the team hooch. What's the problem?"

"Nobody can find him. I did a head count when the alert went off, but Lennon wasn't there. We've searched the sector and no Lennon."

"Let's try the Ops Center. Maybe he stayed there."

They double-timed to the Ops Center and rushed in the door. No one was in the office. Rhodes ran to the ready room and pulled the door open. Lennon was lying on the cot.

"Lennon! Wake up. Where the hell have you been?"

Lennon opened his eyes and looked around.

"Hi, Mr. Striker. I guess I've been right here."

"You're a mess. How'd your utilities get so dirty?"

The knees in Lennon's utilities were muddy and one was torn. The entire front of his utility shirt was smeared with mud and his face and hands were dirty.

Lennon looked down at his utilities and then stared at Rhodes and Kelly.

"I think I fell," he said. "I was going back to the hooch and I got dizzy. I remember that. I had to crawl back to here. I think I got on the cot and then . . .I guess I fell asleep . . . and then you came in. I'm feeling better now."

"You didn't go anywhere else?"

"No, Mr. Striker. I could hardly walk."

Rhodes let his eyes bore into Lennon's eyes.

"You're sure of that?"

"Yes, sir. I was really tired."

He watched Lennon's face for a few moments hoping the silence would make him nervous, but Lennon just stared back.

"Did I do something wrong, Mr. Striker?"

"How's your throwing arm, Lennon?"

"My throwing arm is really good, Mr. Striker," and then Lennon grinned with cracked lips. "Real good," he said again.

Nobody got hurt, Rhodes thought. Do I really want to know?

"Do you feel up to walking back to your hooch?"

"If Staff Sergeant Kelly can help me, I think I'll be all right, Mr. Striker."

"Okay, di-di. And stop calling me mister!"

Chapter 15

The patrol mounted up on a six-by at 0600 in the morning. Staff Sergeant Akins was leading. Akins was a small man with excess energy and quick movements. He was obviously respected by his team. Lance Corporal Hood was primary radioman. Two rifleman, Lance Corporal Pulson and PFC Shaffer followed Hood, and Doc Blankenship HM2, brought up the rear. Doc was a big lumbering guy. His eyes never stopped moving. They all knew about Striker and were glad to have him along—well, that might be a little strong—they didn't mind having his M-14 along. The Marines were armed with M-16s and one M79. Everyone carried grenades and M-79 rounds. It was noisy and wet in the truck, but Striker and Akins had plenty of time to talk on the way to Con Thien.

After the mission briefing the previous day, Akins had visited with his primary artillery support battery at Gio Linh and briefed the battery officer and shooters. Coordination and communications problems were getting so complex that Third Battalion made it SOP for team leaders to meet with artillery and when possible forward air control officers before a mission into areas of frequent activity and this patrol area was subject to constant aircraft flyovers and multiple fire missions.

The weather was clearing during the first week of March and Akins didn't expect a lot of rain during the patrol. The whole week had been dry except that morning, and the day time temperature was getting into the upper eighties. Akins explained they were going to move fast and quiet at night and harbor during daylight. If they got into trouble they'd call for extraction and move to an LZ. Then he confided another little piece of information.

"Striker, we're going to take care of another piece of business on this patrol. Are you up for a little bit of ritual?"

"Like what?"

"You and Pulson are new guys and need to be baptized."

"I have two hairy patrols, a reaction team, and eighteen months of infantry in I Corps under my belt," Rhodes said. "I'm not new."

"Don't matter. You won't be Third Recon until you've been baptized."

"What the hell are you talking about, Akins?"

"I'm taking a chance here, Okay?" Akins said.

"On what?"

"That you're not a chicken-shit Master Guns. You could get my ass in a lot of trouble. This shit is definitely not sanctioned activity."

"What?"

"Baptism. If you want to be considered an old hand by the teams you've got to be baptized."

"Akins, will you get to the point? What the fuck are you talking about?"

"In the Ben Hai River. You will be a newbie until you've touched the water in the Ben Hai River, as close to North Vietnam as you can get. It's dangerous and it's probably stupid, but there it is. There are Recons who have touched the water and there are the others. Are you up for it?"

"The mission comes first," Rhodes said.

"Of course, but our patrol route will take us into the tree line along the river anyway."

He thought about the risks and benefits. Like any elite military unit, the troops often had their own code, a code that went beyond what their service laid down. Hell, even college fraternities had initiations. You could order them stopped, write regulations, scream, threaten, punish, but in some things, the troops made their own rules, and often, it was better to look the other way. Good leadership often involved knowing what not to see. But there was a big difference between not seeing and active participation.

"What's the risks?" he said.

"You could get shot. But then, there's a pretty good chance some of us are going to get shot anyway." Akins grinned and punched Rhodes's shoulder.

A small shot of anger flashed in Rhodes's eyes as he looked at his arm and then at Akins's eyes. That was just a little too much familiarity for Rhodes, but he suppressed it. The look had been all Akins needed.

"If the opportunity presents itself while we are carrying out our mission," he said. "Pulson and I will get out feet wet, but we will not go out of our way to tip-toe in the Ben Hai."

Damn if that didn't sound like some tight-assed pogue, he thought and continued.

"But, if you as the patrol leader feel that a quick look across the Ben Hai into North Vietnam is necessary and worthwhile, I certainly would not question your judgment, now or later."

Akins grinned and nodded his head. There would be a couple of baptisms before the patrol ended.

Con Thien was destined to become a major story in Marine Corps history and one of the bloodiest fire bases ever occupied by Marines, but in early 1967 it was mostly a thorn in the NVA's side and just a target for harassment. That's not to say it was a pleasant place to be. Harassment included artillery, rockets, mortars, and small arms, but not in the quantity that would come later. Still, even just one 122mm rocket on top of you can be pretty miserable. Rhodes and the team stayed in bunkers for the rest of the day and experienced some of the H&I incoming from the NVA.

The platoon with Easy Money recon team embedded got off on time. Walking the edge of an old dirt trail next to what was going to be the Trace, a cleared area that would stretch from Con Thien to Gio Linh when the jungle was bulldozed up, was easy going compared to moving in elephant grass and low brush. Three klicks toward Gio Linh Akins took the team into the grass and quickly found a harbor in thick brush. He put the team in a night harbor wheel. Only a few minutes of light remained.

The team had moved into cover one at a time along a stretch of higher than normal elephant grass where seeing the patrol from any distance would be impossible. Unless an observer had counted the Marines as they left Con Thien and counted again when they returned, Easy Money should have an unobserved path north. Nothing was certain, of course, but the insertion was as good as they could have hoped for.

Doc Blankenship took the point followed by Pulson, Akins, Hood the radioman, Rhodes, and Shaffer on tail-end-Charlie. Rhodes no longer carried his own radio. Shaffer carried the team's second PRC-25 radio. Rhodes would relieve him on tail-end-Charlie when Akins was ready to relieve his point and tail.

Moving silently at night through low grass, brush, and wait-a-minute vines that snagged ankles and packs was a new and unwelcome experience for Rhodes. Even going out on night ambush in the infantry didn't compare to this. You had to depend on the point man to keep you out of trouble because you couldn't see what your feet were stepping on or in. The team members kept their intervals close, but since they had a small amount of light from the partly cloudy sky, enough to see the faint outline of the man in front of them, they didn't have to maintain physical contact.

Doc found a narrow trail that was growing over with weeds and vines, and he led the team up the trail. Following a gook trail in daylight was a no-no, but at night it was about the only way to make any real progress. But Doc had to be super cautious. VC and NVA liked to camp close to trails at night and they also liked to cut shooting alleys in the grass, narrow fields of fire from their night position that led right to the trail. The shooting alleys were often cut on a thirty or forty-five-degree angle to the trail making them hard to detect in the dark. Sometimes they were just a tunnel through the vines about knee level. And then there were booby-traps and punji pits. Walking point was a very scary profession. Rhodes didn't want to be on patrol at all, but he was especially glad he wasn't on point.

Easy Money had been moving slow but steady for three hours without finding much but bomb and artillery craters when Rhodes saw the figure in front of him kneel suddenly. At the same time, he heard a loud hissing sound and saw sparks rising into the sky only three or four hundred meters away. The team got prone and Akins went forward to kneel next to Doc. Akins covered himself with his poncho and reached his hand out. Hood put the radio handset in his hand and the handset disappeared under the poncho.

Rhodes belly-crawled to Akins and put his ear close to the poncho. Akins called for a ranging round from Gio Linh.

"Red Horse this is Easy Money six. I have a Rocket launch site. Fire mission. One round HE. . ." He gave the coordinates and told Red Horse he would adjust.

They waited for two minutes and then from the sky over their position came a sound like ripping cloth. Akins raised up and watched the impact. It's hard to estimate distance at night, but Akins had a good estimation of his own position and called a correction in immediately. He was speaking so softly Rhodes could only hear portions of the call.

". . . Left One hundred . . . "

The next round came in. Akins corrected again.

". . . Left one hundred, add one hundred. . . "

The next round must have satisfied Akins because he called a five-round fire for effect and immediately sent Doc on point on a different route away from the fire mission. Doc took the team to the west for thirty minutes and Akins brought the team to a halt and conferred with Doc again. He had a new fix on their current position confirmed by the artillery impacts. The poncho came out, Akins ducked under with his red light and map, and soon Doc had a new compass heading taking them back to the east and north. The rest of the night consisted of slow, careful movement and quiet waits listening for movement. Other than the rockets, the night passed quietly.

Chapter 16

Sergeant Major Cullahan knocked on Major Rockwell's door and entered his office. The Sergeant Major looked like he was ready for command inspection as usual. Rockwell liked Cullahan's starched appearance. In his mind, Cullahan was everything a Marine should be. Top Rhodes could learn a few lessons from Cullahan if he wasn't constantly trying to suck up to the lower ranks.

"Good evening, Sergeant Major. What's the problem?"

"Well, sir, I'm not sure there's a problem, but I would like to discuss something with you off the record, so to speak."

"My door's always open for you, Sergeant Major. Fire away."

"Yes, sir," Cullahan said. "Look, this is kind of

sensitive with Master Gunnery Sergeant Rhodes and I being the top two NCOs in the Battalion."

"Rhodes again? What now?"

"This is hard for me, sir. The Master Gunny and I go back a long way and . . .well, I don't like to bad mouth a senior NCO."

"It's off the record, Sergeant Major. Let me decide if it's bad mouthing. Spit it out."

"Well, sir, I just think it's really inappropriate for a leader to sit back and take credit for things people subordinate to him did. That kind of behavior is bad for morale."

"I agree. That would be more than inappropriate. It's despicable. You are speaking about Master Guns Rhodes, I presume."

"Yes, sir. That rescue operation. I don't want to say Rhodes is actively taking credit where it isn't due, but the men can tell when something isn't quite right. Rhodes is getting all kinds of credit for leading the reaction force and rescuing the Devil Guns recon team. Now, sir, I'm sure Master Gunnery Sergeant Rhodes performed adequately, but my understanding is that the real leadership was provided by the team leader, Staff Sergeant Minick. In fact, the word I got is Minnick continued leading the team and the reaction force even after he was wounded."

"What was the Master Guns doing?"

"Oh, I'm sure he was . . .I don't think I should say anymore, sir."

Rockwell watched Cullahan closely for a few

moments. There wasn't any sense in pressing the Sergeant Major. It was amazing he even opened-up as much as he did. A good leader should fill in the blanks himself. Knowing Rhodes, Rockwell wouldn't have a hard time filling in the blanks. Cullahan was confiding in him and he respected that.

"Sergeant Major Cullahan, I think I understand. Why don't you let me handle this and just forget about it? I appreciate the position you are in. After I check around a bit, I think a quiet word in the right ears would be appropriate here."

"Thank you, Major. I was sure you would understand. I know Master Gunnery Sergeant Rhodes was recommended for a medal for that action. I'm sure a medal is in order, but perhaps someone should think about who should really get it."

"Let me handle it. Thank you for your trust Sergeant Major."

"Thank you for your understanding and discretion, sir."

Cullahan waited until he was out of sight before he shot a bird at the ceiling. "And fuck you right back, Dick Rhodes," he said quietly.

Chapter 17

Easy Money reached their first night's objective at 0435. Doc led the team into an old abandoned rubber plantation. Moving the team was almost impossible in the old tangled tree stands, but the same would apply for the VC/NVA. They struggled through about a hundred feet of the mess and set up for chow. When chow was out of the way and the trash buried, Akins put the team in a night wheel to wait for enough light to find a good observation point along the edge of the tangled mess of old scrub rubber trees, bamboo, cane, vines, and elephant grass. All the foliage seemed to be grown together. It was great concealment, but a bitch to get through.

With silence all around them, and no hint of anyone but them having ever been there, the team started tunneling through the undergrowth as soon as they could see some detail at a couple of feet. It was bright daylight when they reached the edge of the tangled plantation jungle and could see out on the plain. Akins set two hour watches, one man on duty alternating until noon, and let the rest of the team get some sleep. Hood called in and confirmed they had reached objective one then called Red Horse, the Gio Linh forward observer, and set up on-call artillery for their position with shackled coordinates. Rhodes took the first watch.

The day turned out to be a bust. Either the NVA were taking the day off or they had picked a different part of Vietnam to play in. Most of the team managed to get a few hours' sleep in the heat and everyone had time to remove leeches and let sweaty feet dry out in the air. Snuff dippers and tobacco chewers indulged, but smokers just had to tough it out.

Easy Money harbored for the rest of the day and moved north at sunset. In the twilight, they could occasionally see the tree line along the Ben Hai river, now less than a klick away. The grass was mixed with reeds and closer to the river was taller, and movement was more difficult.

The night was ink black with overcast skies and no moon. The team had to maintain physical contact in order not to lose anyone. Movement slowed to a crawl. In places the low jungle became so thick and tangled forward movement was impossible. Pulson, now on point, had to cast around for less dense jungle.

Around midnight and not having progressed much toward the river, Pulson stopped abruptly and knelt. The rest of the team, each with a hand on the pack in front, stopped and knelt with Pulson. The man in front of Rhodes reached back and squeezed his arm, pulling downward. He wanted Rhodes flat on the ground. Rhodes felt a chill of fear. No one had done that before on any patrol he had been on. Something was going on he didn't understand. He stayed as still and quiet as he could.

Artillery could be heard hitting to the west. Occasional small arms popped through the silence from the direction of Gio Linh. Closer in, things moved through the jungle, things that liked the sounds and smells of humans, occasional grunts or snorts, no way to tell what, didn't want to know. Flying things bit, sucked blood, and were content. Marines let them bite and remained quiet.

Then other sounds revealed the presence of danger. Human sounds. Soldier sounds. He heard a voice, deliberately suppressed to nearly a whisper, very close. As the team lay quietly without their own sounds of movement masking the sound around them, other human sounds could be heard. Another voice speaking quietly and steadily as though giving a lecture. Vietnamese sing-song. Then a clank of metal and a grunt. Then on both sides and in front of the team the sound of men grunting and the rustle of brush.

A shrill whistle shattered the near silence and

suddenly small hand-held lights came on and to the team, it seemed like a full company of Vietnamese began moving forward through the tangled low jungle. In the dark, Easy Money had penetrated the perimeter of an NVA unit and neither the Marines nor the NVA had known.

Rhodes lay quietly with the team and prayed none of the moving soldiers would walk right through their position or shine a light near them. There was a lot of crashing into brush going on. The NVA had trail-breakers throwing themselves onto the reeds and grass and pushing it down so the men behind them could move a few feet forward. They weren't making any faster progress south than Easy Money was making north. Fortunately, Easy Money came in on a northeast angle to the NVA's line of march. The NVA probably wouldn't cross the trail left by Easy Money.

It took a while, but finally the sound of crashing and NVA chatter and laughing moved far enough away for Akins to feel comfortable in moving the team again. This time he pointed Pulson in the direction the NVA had come from. Easy Money eased through the brush until they reached the crushed trail made by the passing enemy company. Hood called the sighting in. That call would not bring happiness to the fire bases. With a company of NVA moving south, Gio Linh and Con Thien would be put on 100% alert and no one would get any sleep that night.

The path of crushed grass and reeds went in the right direction so Akins decided to keep the team on it to make up some time

Due to the trace left by the NVA, the rest of the patrol to the river went more quickly than anticipated. Akins called a halt a hundred meters from the trees at about 0300 to observe for a few minutes before moving out of the heavy low jungle into the trees. He had moved the team off the NVA trail earlier, but the brush and grass wasn't as thick or as high in the flood-plain of the river, and the team could move quickly even in the dark. Thirty minutes of watching and listening didn't reveal anything to cause any alarm so Akins moved the team forward cautiously. It took the team thirty minutes more to reach the trees.

Inside of the low canopy tree line the grass thinned and the reeds grew thicker. Akins had time for a quick recon to find a daytime harbor and OP, but he had some unfinished business to take care of first. He gathered the team close and put them in a wheel. He waited another thirty minutes giving any undesirables time to reveal their presence.

0430. When he was satisfied their area was quiet, he motioned Rhodes and Pulson to drop their packs and follow him and told Doc to stay with Hood and Shaffer and remain where they were.

Akins, Pulson, and Rhodes moved cautiously north through thickening reeds until they heard soft lapping water sounds. They squatted and listened. After a few moments, Akins moved them forward again. Gradually the reeds got thicker and taller and the ground got wetter. Soon they were in ankle deep water and then they were up to their knees.

"Welcome to the Ben Hai river," Akins said softly. "You have walked in the Ben Hai and are no longer newbies. Now let's di-di the hell out of here."

They started to turn, but Rhodes grabbed Akins's arm.

"Listen," he whispered.

From the north came sounds of splashing. Voices mixed in with the water sounds. Then the sound of vehicle engines in the distance. Akins pointed north and took the lead. They moved deeper into the water looking for the edge of the reeds. The sky was beginning to lighten. Dim detail of water and reeds was beginning to show. In chest-high water the reeds thinned and Rhodes could see the river and lights moving on the north shore. Waist deep silhouettes of men were moving through the water toward the south bank. There seemed to be hundreds of lights on the north bank, hand held lights moving toward the water. A company? A battalion? Impossible to tell at that point.

Akins moved close to Pulson and Rhodes. "That's an old elephant ford in the river," he said. "I know exactly where we're at now and I know exactly where those fuckers are too. Let's get back."

Akins took them back to Hood, Shaffer and Doc and they grabbed their packs. He put Doc on point and told him to take them back down the trace left by the Vietnamese during the night. Akins wanted to move fast and get some distance between his team and the mass of soldiers that was coming behind them before he called for a fire mission. The old ford in the river was well known and the grid coordinates were fixed. What he didn't consider in the excitement of planning a fire mission on a mass of NVA was the company of NVA moving south the previous night. They might be moving back north.

Chapter 18

Major Slaughter had been summoned to the Battalion Commander's office. No reason was given, just get there immediately. When he got to the Command complex, the Sergeant Major and Executive Officer were gone. Probably out writing up recons for failing to spit shine their boots while on patrol, he thought. He knocked on the Colonel's door and waited for Colonel Spector to grunt his curt, "Come."

"Reporting as ordered, sir."

"Sit down, Major. Let me finished this damn reply to the G2 and I'll be with you. Get a cup of coffee if you'd like."

Slaughter decided a cup would be good. He'd been working on fitness reports since 0600 and was ready for a break. The Colonel signed his report and ran his eyes over it for a few moments and then set it aside.

"Major Slaughter, I hate dealing with gossip even more than I hate hearing it, but sometimes it has to be done. I wanted to tell you I'm putting Master Gunny Rhodes's commission on hold until I can sort some things out."

"May I ask what the problem is, Colonel?"

"No, you may not . . .Ah hell, If I have to deal with this kind of crap why should you get off the hook? Some questions have been raised about the Master Gunny's integrity and perhaps his fitness as a leader."

"Integrity, sir? That's a damn serious charge. Who the hell is questioning Rhodes's integrity? Rhodes is one of the finest NCO's I've ever worked with. If his integrity is being questioned, then mine is too. He works for me, sir, and I recommended him for his commission. Master Gunny Rhodes is not a liar, Colonel."

"Settle down, Major. I didn't call him a liar and I don't believe he is dishonest, but before we put railroad tracks on his collars I want his reputation sparkling. Sometimes integrity, or its lack thereof, is displayed more by omission than commission. For example, passively taking credit where credit is not due, or failing to give credit where credit is due. Sometimes those two sins of omission go hand in hand. If one of my officers were to do either of those things his next fitness report would kill his career. Questions have been raised about Rhodes's performance on the rescue mission."

"Colonel, I'm confused. Just what is it Master

Gunny Rhodes is supposed to have done or failed to do? I just don't buy it, Colonel."

"Your loyalty to your Master Guns is admirable and perhaps justified. I just don't know at this time."

"Sir, are you saying someone has accused Rhodes of taking credit for something and in doing so failed to give credit to someone who deserved it? On the rescue mission? Colonel, in the debriefing he gave everyone but himself credit for the success of the mission. It was his Marines who told me about Rhodes's leadership. Who's raising these questions, sir?"

"I think that is a confidence I'll keep for now. I just need time to consider it."

"I don't know what's going on, sir, but I don't like it. Dick did an outstanding job on that hill top. I recommended him for a Bronze Star. Colonel, let me pull the debriefings from that mission. Will you read them, sir?"

"Yes. That was my next step anyway. Are they the S2 reports?"

"Yes, sir. Neither I nor Dick had anything to do with drafting them."

"Put your package together, Major . . .and route it directly to me for my eyes only."

Chapter 19

Rhodes was walking tail-end-Charlie trying to keep an eye to the rear and keep from snagging his feet and falling headlong into the brush. The trace created by a company of NVA eight hours earlier wasn't the easy path it had been when Easy Money moved north. Elephant grass is resilient if it is anything. The thick, tall blades, tangled with vines were slowly recovering their vertical positions. Moving along the remaining trace was easier than moving in undisturbed grass, but it was slower than hoped.

He was thinking Akins had to hold up soon and call-in the fire-mission when the first shot rang out from the front. Doc was down. Rhodes bellied forward and pushed Pulson, Shaffer, and Hood ahead of him to get on line and lay down a base of fire. Akins waved them down and to a stop. He bellied forward to check Doc's wounds. No one had seen the shooter. Rhodes took two frag grenades out and straightened the pins. He motioned for the others to do the same thing. This was not the time for rifle fire that would give the NVA a direction and give away the Marine's position.

Two more shots that sounded like AK-47s sounded and the bullets ripped through the grass, close but not on target. Rhodes put his hand on Pulson's rifle and whispered, "No." The gooks were probing and trying to draw fire. Pulson, Shaffer and Hood got the message. Akins began moving backwards dragging Doc with him. Rhodes moved forward and helped him move back. It was lighter now and details of their surroundings began to emerge. When they reached Pulson and Hood, Akins motioned for Shaffer to tend to Doc and pointed at the grenades and held up four fingers.

Akins, Rhodes, Hood, and Pulson pulled the pins on four grenades. Three or four AKs fired putting bullets into the general area. Akins looked at Doc and then Shaffer and raised his eyebrows. Shaffer shook his head no. Doc was gone. He cocked his arm back and nodded. All four launched their grenades in the direction of the rifles and hit the ground. As soon as the grenades exploded, Akins and Rhodes grabbed one of Doc's arms and moved to the west through the grass. They kept moving slowly but as fast as they could in the thick grass as multiple automatic weapons opened in multiple directions. The NVA didn't know exactly where the grenades had come from.

Pulson dove onto tall stands of elephant grass and bent them down so the rest of the team could follow. Hood tossed another grenade and then ran past Pulson and dove on the next layer of grass. Akins and Rhodes carrying Doc moved forward over the crushed grass. Utilities were tearing on the sharp grass and arms and legs were getting cut, but no one hesitated. They repeated the process over and over. With the grenades and bursts of firing from the NVA the team didn't have to worry about noise.

Rhodes figured Doc had stumbled into the sights of an NVA point man who had immediately opened fire. There was a good chance the enemy unit was a point squad or platoon and traveling in column with at least fifteen or twenty meter intervals. The gooks knew good procedure too. Since they were heading back north, it was highly doubtful they were on line presenting a broad front. The main body, if there was one, would be further back. If the team could keep moving west they might be able to flank the enemy unit and get away in the grass.

As soon as the firing from the enemy slowed, the team slowed and moved more quietly. They had moved almost a hundred meters to the west. Akins kept them moving but they had to squirm, push, and snake through the mess now. As soon as the NVA unit behind them moved forward to investigate what their point man had discovered, they would have a well-defined trail to follow behind the Marines and a blood trail from

Doc. They didn't know what they were facing, so hopefully they would move as slowly as the team. Akins needed a harbor to call for artillery and air power. He didn't know it, but the harbor was fifty feet in front of them.

The team struggled through the grass hearing sounds of pursuit behind them. Occasional shots rang out, but none were returned. As the enemy got closer Marines tossed grenades and slowed them down.

Akins and Rhodes suddenly broke through a patch of vines and saw before them just what they needed. They pulled Doc over a berm of dirt and into a large bomb crater. Shaffer, Hood and Pulson followed them and turned to lie against the side of the crater facing their pursuers. Akins immediately broke out his map and took the handset from Hood. He had a good idea of their position but not exact enough to use for artillery. But he knew he was close to a grid square intersection.

Akins called for one marking round on the grid square intersection and waited. When the round screamed in, he adjusted by ear and walked the rounds toward the team's crater. At the same time, he requested extraction and help from any air assets nearby. The Red Horse FO passed the information to the Forward Air Controller. Then Akins began walking the 105s around the crater. The artillery gave him marking points to identify his exact position. Now that Gio Linh had his exact position, he gave the estimated position where Doc had been hit and asked for area saturation. While those rounds were shaking the ground, he called in a new fire mission on the elephant ford on the Ben Hai from the 155mm guns at Gio Linh and the 175mm guns at the Rock Pile and for saturation on both banks of the river near the ford. He called a fire mission on the area of the trace made by the NVA company the previous night. He was like the conductor of a macabre symphony and he knew the score by heart. Akins talked to the FO, the FAC, then he talked to an incoming gunship, then he called another fire mission, all the while keeping watch on his own area. He was very good at what he did, was in his element, and full of excitement. But—in that kind of excitement even experienced and savvy warriors can make mistakes.

While he was calling his missions, and coordinating multiple assets, his mind on many things at once, Akins rose too high above the lip of the crater. Rhodes, seeing what Akins was doing reached to pull him down. Too late. One burst of automatic fire took Akins across the chest. He was knocked to the bottom of the hole. Then automatic weapons opened-up from a broad front that was getting broader quickly. The enemy had gotten it together, got on line, and were doing a sweep of the area.

Automatic fire began hitting the lip of the crater from several positions. The enemy was so close the bullets carried the sound of the rifles with them. Hood and Pulson returned fire on full automatic. Rhodes lowered his bipod and added his M-14 on full auto to the defense. He could see the NVA now. Some were just fifteen or twenty feet away. A chicom landed and exploded in front of the berm. Two more flew over Rhodes's head and landed on the other side of the crater. One exploded the other didn't. He felt the tug of shrapnel on his left trouser leg.

The four remaining team members kept the fire going, slowly burning up their barrels, magazine after magazine. There wasn't any choice with so many enemy so close. They needed to conserve ammunition but they couldn't. Hood and Shaffer alternated throwing their remaining grenades. More chicoms landed in front of them and then they began receiving fire from the flanks. There was no question about it now. They were being surrounded and overrun.

With both Akins and Doc down, Rhodes took over and grabbed the handset. With only four Marines in the crater able to fight and an unknown number of enemy closing on the position, there was no hope of defending themselves until air power arrived on station. The battle was critical right then. He raised his head cautiously to get a quick view so he could decide. He saw human shapes led by muzzle flashes everywhere closing on the crater. No fucking hope at all. The Marines were already fighting back with everything they had and it wasn't making any difference. The NVA were too close, were too many, and closing. Incoming began hitting from behind the Marines. They were surrounded. The crater no longer provided cover.

He knew they had only one chance left and it

was slim and likely to kill the Marines as kill the NVA. He called for saturation fire on his own position while firing his rifle to the rear. Red Horse questioned his call, but Rhodes told him the enemy was right on top of his position and he was being overrun right then. Red Horse replied, "On the way. Good luck."

He seated a new magazine and fired bursts at NVA who were visible now and just feet from the crater. Where the hell was the artillery? He snapped two shots to the left and two more to the right. He needed to keep them out of the crater until the artillery arrived. He loaded a fresh magazine and slapped Shaffer on his pack to turn him around so he could help cover the flanks and rear. Where the hell was the artillery, damn it? Five NVA appeared on the rear lip of the crater. Rhodes slipped the selector to full auto and fired the rest of his magazine across them and realized that had been his last effort. The NVA would be in the hole and on top of them before he could change his magazine again. He pulled his K-bar and prepared to fight them hand to hand.

Then he heard the first ripping sound of incoming and dropped to the bottom of the crater. Their own artillery might wipe them out, and probably would, but it was their only hope now. The NVA were exposed around the crater and the Marines were deep and against the sides of the crater. One round in the hole was all it would take to end it all for the team. Pulson, Hood, and Shaffer pushed close to Rhodes and they covered their ears and curled into tight balls.

The first round hit just fifteen feet from the hole. An avalanche of dirt landed on the Marines and before they recovered from the shock of the concussion a round hit on the east side but fifty feet away and another hit behind them. All four Marines were lifted off the dirt and slammed back down hard. Even in the hole their chests slammed inward with each concussion smacking the air out of their lungs. Before they could get another breath another round slammed into the ground near the crater and emptied their lungs again. More rounds screamed in. Sound became meaningless with ripping sounds of incoming projectiles and explosions pounding ears constantly. Their eyes began aching from the concussions, feeling like they would burst like grapes squeezed until they popped, bloodshot with broken blood vessels behind closed eyelids. None of the four could hear it, but the surrounding grass was filled with screaming, wounded NVA.

He pressed the radio handset against his ear and pressed his other hand over his open ear. He felt like someone was kicking him in the gut and trying to pop his eyeballs out of their sockets with each close round of incoming. His tongue felt like it was filling his mouth and closing off his throat. The other three Marines were lying still on the bottom of the crater, out of it, no longer feeling the horror. Through dazed eyes he watched them lifted and bounced with each round that hit close to the hole. Large jagged pieces of shrapnel screamed across the hole only inches above the Marines. Others angled in to smash into the sides of the crater. Large portions of the crater wall collapsed. His insides felt like they were turning to water. He had to grunt out the words, but he squeezed the talk button and told Gio Linh to keep it coming.

To truly understand the power of an artillery strike you must experience it. Verbal descriptions only touch around the edges of the horror and pain. The noise is so loud and violent it creates instant panic you can't control and causes pain like a physical strike. The shock of the concussion breaks blood vessels in the eyes and they turn red causing blurred, foggy vision. Your senses are taken away and you lose control of your muscles and sphincters. Your nervous system is assaulted so violently nerve impulses are scattered and your brain receives nothing but nervous nonsense. Your heart and lungs are left stunned momentarily without guidance from your brain. Your heart beat goes irregular and you lose consciousness in spurts of blackness only to return quickly to the horror. The physical pain from the concussion is like falling from ten or fifteen feet and hitting concrete. And it won't stop. It just goes on and on and gets worse as you cry, cuss, beg. and pray. Defend yourself? Forget it. Rhodes and his Marines just tried to hold on to life and sanity. After a while they quit trying.

Then suddenly there was just silence. He hadn't called for a halt in the firing, but Gio Linh halted the artillery for their own reasons. It took a few moments for some sense to return, but Rhodes knew someone was screeching in his ear. A few moments later he realized the screeching was coming from the earpiece on the handset. The cord was stretched tight between him and Hood's back. He slid closer to Hood and pushed the talk button.

"Station calling this is Striker Three, over."

"Striker Three this is Avalon. Stay off the net. This is an emergency. "Easy Money, Easy Money, this is Avalon. Over."

"Avalon this is Striker Three. Easy Money Six and Five are down. I command Easy Money. Over."

"Striker three, Avalon, I am above your position. What is your status? Over."

Rhodes bent double and hugged his guts. It felt like they were going to fall out through his asshole and he had a raging headache. He pressed the talk button. Any hope of remembering the codes for encoding his information was gone. It was all he could do to put two thoughts together.

"Avalon, I have two wounded or dead. Three more condition unknown. They are unconscious. I am suffering from concussion. Over."

"Roger, Striker. Help is on the way. Can you move enough to mark your position?"

He didn't bother with call signs now. No one else was on the net.

"I have a red smoke. I am in a crater. I'm tossing smoke now."

Rhodes slid over to Akins and dug in his pack. He found the smoke grenade and moved back to the edge of the crater. Rhodes tossed the smoke just outside of the crater. Hood came-to as Rhodes was sliding back to the radio, but he just sat up and stared around the hole. Rhodes retrieved the handset.

"Avalon, smoke is out."

"Roger, Striker. I've got you."

Rhodes heard the buzzing sound of a small aircraft and looked up. His ears were recovering. The plane was flying to his south. He keyed the radio.

"Avalon, you are to my south. Fly due north."

"Roger. I see your smoke."

"Roger," Rhodes said. "I can hear you. I'll tell you when you're close."

His head was clearing now and he could think again, but not nearly as well as he thought he could. He was hearing Avalon, but he wasn't understanding very well. He wiped his nose and smeared blood across his face. Hood slid up the crater wall next to Rhodes and began watching the grass—or what was left of the grass. He bent double and threw up, but he slid back up the dirt through his own vomit. The low jungle around the crater had become a moonscape of smoking, twisted and torn foliage and artillery craters. The buzzing of the plane got louder.

"You're getting close, Avalon."

"Roger. I see you."

"We are in one of the craters."

Suddenly the plane went directly over the crater.

"You just flew over us. Over."

"Roger, Striker Three, stand-by. I have

movement to your north."

Rhodes was so punchy he didn't even reply. He loaded a fresh magazine in his M-14, his last, and laid out his last grenades. Hood did the same. Pulson woke up and shook his head. He slid across the ground and started shaking Shaffer. When Shaffer sat up, his eyes looked flaky and confused. None of them said a word. Rhodes now had the rest of the team on watch.

"Striker Three this is Avalon. Stay on this net. I have to switch to air control and vector in the shooters. Over."

"Roger, this is Striker Three standing by this channel."

Five tense minutes later Rhodes heard the far-off sound of rotors. The sound grew stronger by the moment. Soon two Marine Huey gunships began circling the position.

"Striker Three this is Grim Reaper six. Over."

"This is Striker Three. Never thought I would be glad to hear the Grim Reaper calling."

The pilot laughed in the mike. "Keep your heads down, Marines. We are about to go to work on your north side. Your chariot is three minutes out."

The sound of rotors moved north and then the sound of explosions began. Reaper was working something over with rockets. Soon the sound of rockets stopped and the mini-guns started. Through the sound of guns Rhodes heard another very welcome sound. Rotors getting close.

"Striker Three this is Reacher three. Request

situation at LZ."

"Reacher three this is Striker Three. Not sure where the LZ is. We're in a crater. Can you find us and then pick an LZ we can move to?" Over."

"Roger. Avalon is vectoring me in. See you in a minute."

The sound of rotors grew loud and then the big beautiful HC-34 was hovering over the crater."

"Striker Three, Reacher Three. I don't see any movement. I have a patch of beat down grass east of your hole that looks clear. Move your team east. I'll tell you when to stop."

"Roger, this is Striker Three, moving east now.

He shook Hood and then pointed to Pulson and Shaffer.

"You two take Doc. Hood and I'll get Akins. Let's move out."

The war birds moved in and worked the area around the crater with their guns. When the guns stopped, the Marines moved.

It took all four of them to lift Doc over the lip and leave him there while they did the same for Akins. The action had been so hot and so fast no one had time to do anything for Akins. It probably didn't matter. The team was taking two bodies back with them. As soon as Akins was out of the hole Rhodes climbed out with Hopkins and took Akins by a shoulder and moved east through still smoking ground and torn NVA bodies. Shaffer and Pulson took Doc between them and followed. While Hood helped him with Akins, Rhodes kept the handset to his ear. He was about at the end of his endurance when the call came.

"Striker Three. You're good. We're on our way."

The bird dropped down, hovered for a moment and touched down on the flattened grass. Rhodes dug deep and found the energy to get Akins to the door. The crew chief helped them inside. Rhodes checked to make sure Shaffer and Pulson were safe inside with Doc, and then he collapsed on the deck of the mercy bird.

Chapter 20

Slaughter and the Battalion CO were waiting when the bird touched down at Dong Ha. Rhodes picked up Akins. The crew chief tried to help, but Rhodes waved him away. Hood and Pulson carried the Doc. They carried them to a waiting ambulance not even seeing Slaughter and the CO. He laid Akins gently inside of the ambulance and a Corpsman immediately started checking him. Hood and Pulson laid Doc next to him.

He looked at the two bodies and then looked closely at the remaining Easy Money team members. Hood and Pulson looked like they had been dead center in an explosion—and had been. Their faces and hands were blackened with explosives smoke. Their eyes were wide and looked strange, just two red orbs staring out of blackened faces. The left pant leg on Shaffer's utility trousers was torn or blown off at the knee with the missing part sagging around his boot, but his leg seemed fine. All of them had patches of blood below their noses and scattered on legs and arms. None of them had covers and their hair was twisted wildly and full of dirt and fragments of burnt leaves and other plant matter. All three Marines looked like they were on the edge of shock. They were a mirror of Rhodes's own condition and appearance.

A corpsman grabbed Rhodes's arm and made him sit on the ground. Another corpsman did the same to Hood, Shaffer, and Pulson.

"Okay look at the sky and keep your eyes open," the corpsman said and started pouring water out of a canteen into the Marine's eyes to flush out the dirt and explosives residue.

"Don't touch your eyes. Let the water drain out naturally."

Rhodes held his head tilted back and did what he was told. The corpsmen continued the treatment until the Marines began blinking naturally.

A hand was placed gently on Rhodes shoulder.

"Can you handle a debriefing right now?" Slaughter said softly.

"Where's Easy Money's platoon leader?"

"He's leading patrols out of a Special Forces camp at Ba To," Slaughter said.

"Give me time to take care of Hood, Shaffer, and Pulson," Rhodes said. "I think we better give them some time with the teams before they face the debriefing."

"Okay. Meet me at the Ops Center when you're done."

He nodded and returned to his team mates. They were watching the ambulance drive away. "Come on," he said. "Let's get a beer."

Rhodes was dealing with Marines, good Recon Marines. He wasn't trying to treat them like kids, but even men who faced what Recons faced every day needed time to deal with death and violence. The best way to do that was with other Recons, not alone in the team hooch or boozing it up alone. He took his three Marines to Boatload's hooch and found Kelly. Kelly knew what had happened and didn't need to be told what needed to be done. His team would be eager to hear what happened and talking it out was probably the best thing for Easy Money right then. Rhodes left what remained of Easy Money with Boatload and went to the water buffalo. He poured water over his head and let it soak his face and utilities.

He knew the shakes would start if he stopped moving around for too long. Too much death. Too many good men gone. He poured another canteen of water over his head. This wasn't his first rodeo, but the moment he had looked over the lip of that crater and saw NVA soldiers not ten feet away was probably the closest he had ever come to total despair. It didn't get easier with practice. Maybe it was easier for the leader afterward. He had to keep functioning. He had responsibilities. He couldn't give in and let it overwhelm him. He walked to the Ops Center holding his sore gut.

Slaughter was waiting with the S2 debriefer. The Colonel sat in.

"Tell it your own way, Master Guns," the Staff Sergeant debriefer said. "Start at the beginning and take us through it."

He began with the hook-up at Con Thien. He took them out the north gate, into the grass, through the drop-off, and through the first night. He described the NVA that were sighted while in day harbor and then described the blunder into the NVA company lines and how they avoided contact. Then he took them to the Ben Hai river and the sighting of NVA crossing the river and the fast movement south to get some distance so they could call in a fire mission. Telling about losing Doc came harder and he had to speculate on some of it since he hadn't seen Doc hit. He explained how they avoided firing and used grenades rather than give their position away with rifle fire. Then he explained crashing through the grass and reaching the crater. Rhodes continued in almost a trance as he described the final moments before calling in artillery on his own position.

The Colonel interrupted and got a glare from the debriefer. "Please go back over your reasons for that drastic decision."

"Do you think it was the wrong decision, sir?" Rhodes asked.

"Not at all," the Colonel said. "The word drastic

wasn't meant to be negative. I just want to make sure I fully understand your decision."

"Yes, sir. It's not really complicated. Akins and Doc were down. I had three men left to fight with. We had limited ammunition and grenades. This was supposed to be a keyhole patrol and we weren't armed like a striker team. There were a lot of NVA and they were in sight and moving forward. Then they flanked us. Chicoms were hitting the hole and the gooks can't throw all that far. They were close and all around us. The hole no longer provided cover. It was the only decision left. We were in a hole. They were in the open. If I didn't do something immediately we were a minute or less from being overrun. I ran out of options and made the call."

The Colonel thought about that for a few moments. The debriefer waited to see if the colonel was done.

"In your opinion, should Staff Sergeant Akins have called for support earlier." The Colonel said.

"No sir. I would have done the same as he did. He was getting his team out of harm's way so he could kill a whole load of gooks. But like most battles, things can snowball on you. Nothing ever goes as planned. Akins was a good combat leader."

"Why did he take the team to the Ben Hai River?"

To baptize a couple of newbies, Rhodes thought and said, "That far north, sir, the tree line along the river is the only real cover in the area. It was the safest place for a day harbor and observation post."

The colonel made a couple of notes and looked up.

"Thank you, Dick," the Colonel said taking the sting out of his questions with a personal touch. "I'll just say this about your decision. I don't know if I would have had the balls to make that call. Carry on, Staff Sergeant. Major Slaughter, may I see you for a few moments?"

"Yes, sir.

The debriefing lasted for another twenty minutes. The S2 Sergeant went back over sightings and land marks and drilled down for more detail. Rhodes was completely spent when it was done.

After the debriefing, Slaughter came back to the room and waved for Rhodes to follow him. They went to the ready room and Slaughter opened two beers and sat with Rhodes.

"You okay, Dick?"

"Yes, sir. Shook up, but I'm okay. I thought I was going to die out there."

"How much combat time do you have now?"

He thought about the question and said, "Just this war or the last one too?"

Slaughter grinned. "This one," he said.

Rhodes counted the months.

"Twenty-one months out of the last twenty-four. Except for the training and leave I've been here since sixty-five."

"Want some time off to get squared away?"

"No, sir. I need to get back to work and sort things out. But Hood, Shaffer, and Pulson should get a couple days down at China Beach. Not right away. They need friends and routine right now. Maybe next week."

"I'll talk to their platoon leader and arrange it. I'm taking you out of the field, Captain Rhodes. You've seen enough now, and it's time for you to learn your new trade."

He tried to cover it, but the sudden drain of tension and stress caused a drop in blood pressure that almost dropped him. If he had been standing, he would have collapsed. After a few moments of deep breathing, he looked at Slaughter through bloodshot eyes.

"Yes, sir. I was wondering if Captain Lang had another patrol laid on for . . .What did you call me?"

"Dick, write this down. New captains should listen closely when their rating officer is talking. Get some rest and get cleaned up. Lay out your best utilities. You'll be spending tomorrow at Division taking care of the paperwork. The Colonel is justifiably impressed with your leadership out there."

He didn't visibility react. He just stared at Slaughter at first. A few hours ago, he was running for his life and hoping for nothing more than just to live another day—and maybe not go over the edge and run around screaming and waving his arms about his head and shoulders. The sudden image of that vision almost made him smile. Now he was safe in camp and being told he would be wearing captain's bars in a couple of days. The moment was becoming surreal. The off and on nature of recon work was screwing with his mind. In the infantry, you could be in the grass for a month or six weeks at a time and often your rest was just shifting to a new patch of grass or taking over security for a fire base. Out of the frying pan into the fire. In recon, you were out for a few days of very scary work and then, presto, you were back in camp and life got almost normal again, for a few days. And then you were a captain. Nothing to get excited about. Just another day in recon.

"I expected surprise, Dick. Jubilation even, is acceptable. Silence, on the other hand . . ."

"Jesus, Major. I'm still trying to process walking away from that fucking artillery. My commission came through? Now? But we just talked about it . . .when? A few days ago."

"Sorry, Dick. I wish the circumstances were better for telling you, but the paper pushers wait for no man. You didn't know it, but we started your paperwork as soon as you signed your waiver to come back to the combat zone while you were still in the states. You had already been selected for Master Gunnery Sergeant. Headquarters wanted candidates in the pipeline. If you had turned me down when we talked, my ass would have been in a sling. The Colonel didn't know I submitted you without your knowledge."

The reality began sinking in and the reality of captain's bars was a whole lot nicer than he thought it was going to be. He looked at Slaughter, grinned, and held his hand out."

"Thank you, sir. I didn't think this was going to happen for a while, and I guess I didn't really think it would happen at all. Me a captain. Damn if that isn't something."

Slaughter grabbed Rhodes hand and shook it hard.

"Shit!" he said. "You had me worried there for a moment. Let's call Lang in here and have a small celebration."

The celebration consisted of some back slapping and two beers each. Rhodes didn't feel like celebrating right then with Akins and Doc still on his mind, and Slaughter and Lang were too busy to get shit faced. Rhodes went back to his hooch to square his gear away, clean his rifle, and get a few hours' rest before reporting to the personnel people at Division Forward Headquarters.

He had just wiped the excess oil from his rifle barrel when someone knocked at the hooch door.

"Come," Rhodes yelled.

"Mr. Striker, can I come in?"

"I said come, numb-nuts. Is your hearing fucked up too?"

He felt a small shot of guilt. His emotions were jumping around between sorrow, anger, joy, and guilt at the joy. Poor Lennon just picked the wrong time to show up.

"I just wanted to check on you," Lennon said as he stepped into the hooch looking like a dog that had just been kicked.

"Check on me for what?"

"To make sure you are okay. Everybody is checking on everybody else, but nobody checked on you, Mr. Striker."

"Lennon, I'm a Master Gunny. I do the checking. I don't need to be checked on."

"You're a person, Mr. Striker and you care. Are you okay?"

He started to explode. The anger shot up into his face and he turned red. He started to scream at Lennon—but shut it down just before his mouth ran away with him and he totally lost it. Lennon was sincere. Christ, it was just the kid's way. The anger went away as fast as it came. He took a deep breath.

"Thank you, Lennon," he said with less drill instructor in his voice. "That was kind of you. Yes, I'm fine. Was there anything else?"

"I just wanted to tell you I wrote my sister in California and told her how good you take care of your men and how much it bothers you when one of them is hurt. She's my big sister and the only real family I have. I just wanted to tell somebody. She's in the Navy and she's an officer."

"Really?" Rhodes said, not really interested in the answer. "What does she do in the Navy?"

"She's a nurse at the hospital in Camp Pendleton. She's a commander."

"That's pretty high up. Well, thanks for the kind words. Anything else?"

"No," Lennon said and turned to leave. "That's it."

"Lennon," Rhodes said gently.

Lennon turned. "Yes, Mister Striker?"

"Stop calling me Mister Striker, numb-nuts!" Rhodes shouted in his best Drill Instructor voice. "Now get the fuck out of here!"

Chapter 21

The admin pogues dragged Rhodes through a stack of paperwork. First, he had to be discharged as a Master Gunnery Sergeant and his pay brought up to date including a payout for his unused leave, mileage pay back to his home of record from San Francisco, uncollected pay on the books, etc., etc. Those transactions came to a nice piece of change. Since he had an allotment for most of his pay to his savings, the finance office made a direct deposit to his Navy Credit Union account for most of it and gave him a stack of MPC notes for the rest. During his record-book close out, Rhodes found out he had a Bronze Star recommendation he wasn't aware of.

The top row of his ribbons, if he ever got to wear them again, would now have a Silver Star, Bronze

Star with gold V for Valor, Navy Commendation Medal with Gold V for combat. the next row would start with the Purple Heart with two clusters. Strangely enough, amidst all that dubious glory, the next ranking ribbon, at the head of the second row, would be the enlisted good conduct ribbon with three clusters, meaning he had served sixteen years without catching the clap. That one would mark him forever as a mustang officer, risen from the ranks. Officers didn't get good conduct ribbons. As chartered gentlemen, their good conduct was assumed.

As far as he was concerned the GCM was a mark of distinction specifically because only enlisted men got it. Later would come the new Combat Action Ribbon when it was issued. Over the years, the pretty pieces of colored ribbon accumulated on your chest—and the scars accumulated on your body, and your spirit. If you were lucky. For some, many, the accumulation stopped abruptly when they were stuffed in a bag and then shipped home in a box. His thinking hadn't recovered from his experience in the crater. It isn't just privates who suffer the after effects of battle.

The paperwork took the entire day and would have taken a lot longer if the Admin officer hadn't been informed by Slaughter well in advance and long before Rhodes even knew his commission was in the works. It was also just a bit uncomfortable. The admin officer was a First Lieutenant sweating out his time and fitness reports until he got his railroad tracks and he wasn't happy about direct commissioning an enlisted man to Captain, even if the man was a Master Gunny. Rhodes had enough sense not to point out that the pogue officer had never commanded a platoon in combat or assisted a company commander with the leadership of his company either. And the pogue never would unless he requested transfer to the infantry. But to be fair, they serve too, those who fight the battles of paper cuts, hemorrhoids, and boredom.

With his discharge papers signed and sealed and his commissioning papers signed and awaiting his oath, Rhodes returned to the recon area. He was scheduled to stand in front of the Colonel and take his oath in the morning. Now he had time to deal with the demons.

Rhodes had two wars behind him with twenty-one months of combat in this one and his own process for purging the demons after a bad action. SNCOs had more practice at covering up emotions, but the demons came the same as they did to Privates. First, he put two cans of beer next to his rack. Then he kicked off his boots, picked up a beer, and lay back on his rack. He raised a beer and began reciting all the good things he could say about Akins. He didn't know Akin well, but he had plenty of time to observe him as a Marine and as a leader. Akins scored high on both counts. With each recitation, he took a slug of beer. The process required that he keep finding good things to say until the last slug of beer. When he shook the can, and estimated just one slug left, he held the can up and said, "Better you than me." and then finished off the can. He did it once more for Doc. Doc was more difficult to get through. He didn't know Doc at all and hadn't had much opportunity to observe him, but Doc was an FMF corpsman so it wasn't hard to find good things to say about him. With the last slug, Rhodes held the can up and once again said, "Better you than me."

The faces and memories didn't magically go away, but having a process and a ritual helped. He'd done it before many times and it did bring a kind of closure. They're gone and I'm still here. I didn't make them disappear and my being here still is okay. In fact, it's a good thing. Sorry Akins and sorry Doc. I wish you were still here, but I'm glad to be alive.

He got two more beers and chugged them. His eyes closed and sleep came.

The commissioning ceremony in the morning was short and sweet. The Battalion Exec, Slaughter, and Lang attended. Slaughter brought subdued Captain's bars and he and Lang pinned them on Rhodes's collar points. The officers shook Rhodes's hand and that was it, except for one little incident he didn't understand.

Right after the Colonel finished the swearing in and Slaughter and Lang shook Rhodes's hand, Major Rockwell slipped out of the door without saying a word. The Colonel went out right behind him. A moment later Rockwell reentered, shook Rhodes's hand and grunted out a curt congratulation. Rhodes was in such a daze he didn't even notice Rockwell's attitude.

Somehow, he felt there should have been more,

like fireworks or something. Maybe a band playing the Marine Corps Hymn. Or at least a record player or something. It isn't every day a Master Gunnery Sergeant gets promoted to Captain. But as he found out, neither was it a very big deal in the scheme of Marine Corps things. Company grade officers were in short supply, especially company grade officers with his combat experience. Fewer college men were volunteering for service with the Marine Corps. The Basic Course and Annapolis couldn't keep up with the losses occurring in Vietnam, and only one in five new officers ended up leading a platoon anyway, and many of them didn't live long enough to become captains. The life expectancy of a new Second Lieutenant in Vietnam was very short. Hence, combat experienced Captains were in short supply and the supply was getting shorter. Solution? Make highly rated senior NCOs in the top two grades with beaucoups combat command experience captains. It was done in WWII, Korea, and now in Vietnam.

By the time Captain Rhodes made it back to the Ops Center, the word had gotten around. Striker was now a captain. Lennon was waiting at the door to the Ops Center. As Rhodes stepped out of the Jeep, Lennon came to attention and snapped a parade ground salute. "Good Morning, Captain."

He had to think before he realized he was required to return the salute. Very little saluting was done in the combat zone because it identified officers and made them targets. But this was sector five in the middle of the Dong Ha Marine base. He snapped a salute in return and replied, "Good morning, Lance Corporal. Haven't you got anything better to do than stand around saluting new captains?"

"I wanted to be the first, sir. No other enlisted men saluted you yet, did they?"

He thought for a moment. He had exchanged salutes with the Colonel, Slaughter, and Captain Lang, but he was saluting and they were returning salutes. Technically he wasn't saluted at the gate. That salute was for Major Slaughter the senior officer. So, it looked like Lennon was the first enlisted man to salute him.

"I guess you have that dubious distinction, Lennon. Congratulations."

"Congratulations to you, sir. And if I may say so, sir, those bars look very good on you."

"Lennon, I don't like ass-kissers. Now get your ass back to whatever work party you're slacking off from."

Lennon came to attention with a big shit eating grin and snapped another salute."

"By your leave, sir."

He had to return the salute. "Get your ass out of here, numb-nuts!"

He was smiling when he entered the Ops Center. That little shit, he thought. He'll go back to Boatload and tell them all about how I fumbled my first salute.

Inside, he found a field desk with giant Captain's bars hanging from the wall behind it. The bars were fabricated from 2x4s painted white and held together with cut-off metal stakes from the perimeter fence. On the desk was a wooden block fashioned into a desktop name plate. Slaughter had hired a Vietnamese carver to produce the plate. On one side, it had a very good replication of the USMC globe and anchor. On the other side, silver captain bars. In the center his name and CAPT. USMCR. The wood appeared to be teak and it was finished beautifully. He put his hand on the name plate and rubbed it gently.

"We all wanted you to have that, Dick," Slaughter said from behind him. "It'll last you a lifetime. After you retire and get a civilian job you can put it on your desk and impress the secretaries."

Rhodes continued to stare at the bars on the wood. "Thank you, sir. I'm still having trouble believing it. All I ever wanted was to make Master Gunnery Sergeant. Did you know Lance Corporal Lennon waited outside until I got back just so he could be the first to salute me?"

"I'd say that's about the finest compliment an officer could receive, Dick. You've already made an impression on the teams. They still call you Striker, don't they?"

"Yes, sir. From my call sign. Well, I'm ready to go to work."

"No doubt in my mind. I'm pairing you with Captain Lang until he leaves. You'll be stepping into his job. Go ahead and get settled in, talk with Lang, and get squared away. Tonight, we wet those bars down at the

O-Club on pogue-side. Look, are you okay for money?"

"Yes, sir. No problem. They had to cash me out. Care to clue me in? What does a wetting down involve?"

"You buy the drinks until everyone is shit-faced."

"That's it?"

"Sure, and, oh yeah, we tell a lot of lies."

"That's a whole lot more civilized than getting your stripes nailed on."

"You are an officer and gentleman now, Captain. You are expected to be civilized."

Slaughter slapped Rhodes on the shoulder. "Welcome aboard, Captain Rhodes. Why don't you get with Lang and then get yourself set up with officer housing and get moved this afternoon? We'll meet back here after chow and head for the O-Club."

He was assigned quarters in a hooch with Lang. A little bigger than a team hooch. Nothing special. And he had to share a hooch now. Two racks, two folding field desks, his own footlocker, and a three-level shelf made of ammo crates. At 1800 the officers of Battalion S3 were joined by S2, three jeeps were wrangled from the First Sergeant, and the party crew drove to the pogue O-club.

No surprise, the pogues had the only O-Club that even looked vaguely like a club inside or had a selection of drinks beyond canned 3.2% beer and rot-gut whiskey. They also had the only collection of NVA war trophies. He spotted an SKS, two AK-47s, an RPG, and an NVA flag hanging on the wall behind the bar. He hoped the pogues had enough sense to make sure the RPG round loaded on the RGP was only a casing.

The party started out slow, but Rhodes spotted the pilot of Reacher Three, the UH-34 that picked up Easy Money. The pilot was invited to join the celebration and brought his co-pilot. They were on a twenty-four-hour mandatory stand-down and were ready to party. The party got loud with several supply and admin type officers joining the fun and sucking down the free booze. He didn't care. He was having fun and had a pocket full of MPC.

At one point an argument broke out between the pilot and one of the supply officers and Slaughter was called in to mediate. He heard Slaughter say, "Well it just so happens we have the foremost expert on arcane Marine Corps lore in the Dong Ha area with us. The amazing, the one and only, and brand new captain who is graciously paying the bar tab, Captain Dick Rhodes. Dick, come over here and settle an argument for us."

By this time, Rhodes was medium brown, the third stage of shit-faced, a condition characterized by drooping eyelids, a dumb, happy expression on the face, and an unshakable belief in one's own wit. "I am at your service, mi major-er-ority," he said and grinned stupidly.

"Okay, here's the deal. This pogue says the term pogue is meaningless and just a stupid sound made up by grunts that don't understand the complexity and demands of the logistics mission. This fearless pilot, on the other hand, who by the way is a pogue only in the very best sense of the term, says the term is an actual word and has a real meaning and probably not something very nice. Oh, master of the arcane, most sublime of seers, enlighten us we beseech thee."

He thought for a moment. After all, he had been a Master Guns until recently and Master Gunnery Sergeants have the answers. That's a given. And if they don't, they make one up. Besides he was a history major and the honor of S3 was at stake.

"Well, I believe there are several speculations on that matter, but I think I can help you out," he said feigning a scholarly expression and stroking a beard that wasn't there. "Our esteemed and much appreciated whirly-bird driver is correct. The term pogue is thought to have come from the British Tommies, the same place we get the term Tommy-gun for the M1 1927 A1 .45 caliber submachine gun which was sent to England to . . ."

"Get on with it, Dick."

"Right. Or possibly from the Aussie Diggers. That's their infantry, by the way. In fact, pogue is an ancient Gaelic word meaning, loosely translated, 'Kiss my arse,' which, strangely enough, are the words grunts hear most frequently from pogues sitting on their fat asses and hoarding all the supplies grunts need to survive. Gentlemen, partake of my wisdom."

"Oh bullshit!" the pogue captain yelled. "That is nothing but a bunch of grunt bullshit pulled straight out of your ass. I laugh at your wisdom. HA! HA! HA!"

"Au Contraire, mi Capy-tan. Look it up."

"How am I going to look up Gaelic words? Huh? You knew there's no way to prove you wrong. Okay, if you're such a big expert, why are Oh-Threes called grunts?" (0300, infantry MOS)

"Ooh, ooh, me, me," Lang said with his hand up and bouncing on his stool. He was almost dark brown, the fourth and final stage of shit-faced.

"The esteemed Captain Lang has the floor," Slaughter said.

"That is an easy one," Lang said with the forced and almost precise diction of stage four inebriation. "It's what the infantry does when they're humping seventy pound packs through the grass. Hence, Grunts."

Everyone nodded sagely and began to agree.

"Not so fast there, Skippy," Rhodes said. "Actually, grunt is an acronym that was used on orders in World War Two."

"Acronym? Bullshit," the pogue captain said. "What's it stand for?"

By this time the pilot was asleep on the bar, and Slaughter was singing to himself and stretching a string of spit from his lip with one finger.

"When men were sent to the pacific in the early part of World War Two straight from recruit training without any infantry training they were turned over to a platoon sergeant for training in infantry tactics and movements. Their orders were stamped GRUNT. General Replacement untrained. You may kiss my ring,"

Rhodes said, holding his hand out to the pogue captain.

"Now that one I can believe," the pogue said. "And you may kiss my ass"

"I rest my case," Rhodes said with an exaggerated bow from which he didn't recover.

Chapter 22

Lang and Rhodes arrived at the Ops Center at 0750 and immediately went to the coffee pot. Rhodes took two APCs (Aspirin with Caffeine) and a cup of black coffee. Lang looked at the coffee and dry heaved. He disappeared through the door.

Slaughter was waiting for them, but he wasn't in any better shape than they were.

With sunken eyes, a pale face, and shaking hands, Slaughter pulled a task order from a folder.

"No rest for the weary or hung-over," he said. "Five Infantry Battalions supported by four Artillery Battalions are preparing for a new sweep. G2 suspects elements of the NVA 324B and 321st divisions are in the AO. We are tasked with final recon of the AO but will primarily support First Battalion, Ninth Marines and Third Battalion, Third Marines who will be operating together. The Operation has been named Prairie Three and begins on the nineteenth, the last day of Prairie Two. It's a multi-company sweep southeast of Con Thien. We haven't got a lot of time so let's get the preliminary planning and assignments done today. You and Lang will attend the G2 briefing tomorrow morning."

"Couldn't you just send me on a one-man recon into North Vietnam, sir? Maybe I'd die."

Slaughter tried a grin, but it came off as a grimace.

"It's going to be a long day for all of us, Captain Rhodes. Try to put on a happy face for the troops."

"Aye, aye, Major, sir. Remind me to stay the hell away from the O-Club in the future."

Later he was going back over the mission concept and Ops Order to be sure he had provided the teams everything that could possibly be provided when Slaughter entered the Ops Center with a tall Army Special Forces (SF) Captain and a civilian in a black jump suit and shiny half Wellington boots.

"Captain Rhodes, please join us in my office."

"Yes, sir."

The four men entered Slaughter's office ahead of Slaughter and Slaughter closed the door when he came in.

"Dick, meet Captain Sullivan and Mr. Coats."

The Army Captain wore tailored tiger stripe utilities and a green beret. His rank was displayed in the blaze on his beret. He looked Rhodes in the eye when he shook his hand, but didn't speak. The civilian sat in one of the only two chairs and didn't offer his hand. Okay, Rhodes thought.

"Change of plans, Dick. The Colonel wants a detachment of recon to work out of a Special Forces camp south of Khe Sanh close to the Laotian border. I want you to command the detachment."

"Aye, aye, sir. How long are we going to be there?"

"Maybe a month, but it's open ended. I'm pulling a First Force team and two teams out of Bravo Company. Third Force Company detachment at Khe Sanh is still up in the air, but we may get another team from them. If we do, you'll have four teams. If we don't you'll have to do what you can with three."

"Yes, sir. May I ask what the mission is?"

The civilian, Mr. Coats, spoke.

"Captain, you and your men will be fully briefed when you get to FOB Three at Khe Sanh. For now, it's enough for you to know you will be working for me. You are being detached to support a mission being conducted out of a new camp at Lang Vei with a Special Forces detachment. Captain Sullivan is with Company C, Fifth Special Forces Group, and Lang Vei's mission and team fall under his operational control."

"And you are, sir?"

"Why, I am Mr. Coats, as your Major told you,

Captain."

"Yes, sir. But *what* are you, sir?"

"Dick, all this will be . . ." Slaughter began but was interrupted by Captain Sullivan.

"Excuse me, sir. Captain Rhodes, Mr. Coats is attached to the MACV Studies and Observation Group. He's a government civilian with an assimilated rank of 06, full colonel. I know this is confusing, but please accept that your superiors including your Division Commander have been briefed and understand the importance of this mission."

Rhodes felt his stubborn rising.

"I'm not questioning that, Captain Sullivan. My boss has already given me my orders. When a Marine is given orders, he says 'aye, aye, sir, and does the best he can to carry out those orders. I'm just trying to understand the reporting structure and what the organization is I'm being attached to. What is it you study and observe, sir?"

"Anything and everything that might help us defeat the North Vietnamese, Captain," Mr. Coats said. "Now, why don't you and Captain Sullivan get together somewhere and discuss the logistics of the move while the Major and I resolve some final scheduling details."

Well, that's obviously an end to the answers, Rhodes thought

"Captain, after you," he said and waved Sullivan through the door.

When the two captains stepped out of the office and

closed the door, Sullivan held out his hand and said, "Let's start over. I'm Marty."

Rhodes took his hand and said, "Dick."

"Yeah, I got that from in there. Do you have someplace we can talk in private?"

"We can go to my hooch. Captain Lang won't be back until after 1700."

"That'll work. You got anything to drink?"

"Beer. It's hot though."

"Let's go by Coat's jeep. I brought some Jack in my bag."

"Came prepared, huh?"

"Always prepared. Anyplace, anytime. Airborne!" Sullivan said, grunting out the Airborne.

Rhodes laughed and said, "I did my time at Benning. Seven jumps at Benning. Ten jumps on Okinawa. I'm not a zealot, but I'm definitely a convert."

Sullivan laughed along and yelled, "Up the hill!"

They picked up Sullivan's bottle, swung by the mess hall and talked the mess sergeant out of a hunk of ice, and hot-footed it to Rhodes's hooch before the ice could melt. He pulled two C-rats cans that served as cups off a shelf and after breaking the ice up, put several pieces in each can. Sullivan poured a couple fingers of Jack in each can.

"Damn, you guys live primitive," Sullivan said. "Believe me, Lang Vei will be better than this."

"Okay, tell me about it."

"Get a slug in you. It'll help," Sullivan said holding out his can.

They touched cans and took a sip.

"Let me give you a little background," Sullivan said. "Fifth Special Forces Group has ten operational detachments deployed around Two-Corps and I-Corps. An A-team manages each detachment. Khe Sanh is a forward operating base for staging not only an A-team but also a South Vietnamese SF team, combat recons, indigenous defense group, and a company of ARVN Rangers."

"How big is the total force?"

"There's thirteen U.S. Special Forces, four companies of CIDG made up of Bru Montagnards and local Vietnamese, all of them understrength and poorly equipped, three platoons of indigenous combat recon, and a Viet SF team who are pretty good, maybe 480 men total, maybe half that trained and dependable fighting men."

"So, you have about a company you can depend on," Rhodes said.

"That's about it, and there's always the chance that any of the Vietnamese can be working for the VC or NVA or will go over to the other side whenever it looks like a good idea to them."

"You're trying to make me feel good, right?"

Sullivan grinned and held his can up in a salute.

"Let me share an old SF saying with you, "It is what it is. Fuck it."

"You probably got that from the Marine Corps infantry," Rhodes said. "So how does Mr. Coats fit in?"

"Ever heard of Civilian Investment Advisors?

No? How about Charity in Action?"

"You're shitting me. CIA?"

"I like to think of them as willing and able investors. Our goals align and they have a lot of money and punch. Think of it as a marriage of convenience where the couple actually like each other."

"And you might or might not get fucked?"

Sullivan laughed. "There is that possibility. Most of them are good operators and spend as much time at the compound as we do. Mind you, to them you are an asset, but they don't like seeing their assets wasted."

"Okay. Not much different than the Corps. How do my recon teams fit in?"

"Right now, Khe Sanh is occupied by my troops including my CIDG, and then there's the marines. We've been informed the Marines have landed and are moving a battalion to the Khe Sanh area. SOG will keep a forward operating base at Khe Sanh, but the A-Team, CIDG and ARVNs are moving down Route Nine to Lang Vei to set up an operational detachment near the border. The Marines don't like CIDG and ARVNs near their perimeter."

"And my teams are going to support the move?" Rhodes asked.

"And take on combat recon patrols until we can reorganize our combat recons. There's a lot of crap going on for us too. Seems things are heating up in the Khe Sanh area. Most of our recon resources are and will be tied up trying to figure out what Charlie is doing in the hills around Khe Sanh. Recon assets are getting scarce and Mr. Coats feels like he is getting short changed by the Army and the Marines. On top of that, Lang Vei is going to be vulnerable as hell until the new compound is built and manned properly. Your job is to see that no major force surprises us while we get set up. Mr. Coats has some interest in things going on just inside of Laos too. We'll be about a klick and a half from the border. Believe me, your plate will be full."

Rhodes took a deeper pull on his Jack.

"How long is this going to go on?"

"I figure about a month until our new compound is established. Marine recon teams will gradually take over the full recon job for Khe Sanh and our platoons will be tasked back to our priorities as the Marines take over that area of operations. The sooner the better. Nobody at Khe Sanh is listening to us anyway. We'll release you back to Third Battalion as we get back on our own tasking."

"Why don't they just put us at Khe Sanh and let you keep . . ."

"I refer you to the previously stated SF old saying," Sullivan interrupted and took another slug from his cup. "You ready for another one?"

Chapter 23

Sullivan and Rhodes worked out the logistics for the move and Coats and Slaughter worked out the schedule. When the Army and CIA left, Slaughter sat down with Rhodes.

"Dick, the Colonel made it clear he didn't want any discussion about this assignment. I don't like it, but he has his reasons. Let's get something clear. I'm sending you as the detachment commander. I want you managing the teams and planning the missions. I don't want you tagging along with the teams. I want documentation when you come back and I don't give a damn what Mr. Coats thinks about that. I want operation orders for every team you send out. Only you will dispatch a Marine recon team. Is that understood?"

"Is there a problem, sir?"

"I hope not. But Coats was just a little too cagey for me. I never did figure out just what the hell he does. In addition to that the colonel isn't telling me much."

"Coats is CIA, Major."

"I know that. It's what he's doing that bothers me and he didn't even attempt to make me more comfortable with what he expects from you."

"I'll run my teams, sir."

"Good. Don't let anyone walk on you. Lang is shifting things around on the new operation and I'm giving you Boatload from Bravo Company. Lang will shift another team to the new Con Thien operation. You've worked with Kelly and seem to have a good relationship with him. You can have your pick from the First Force teams. Lang is picking a team from Echo Company. Talk to the Third Force detachment commander at Khe Sanh and see what he can do. They're in the process of moving back to Phu Bai, but he didn't give me an outright no."

"Aye, aye, sir. I've got the birds laid-on for 0800 Friday morning to take us to Khe Sanh. Captain Sullivan is coordinating the birds to take us to Lang Vei. He's providing logistics for the mission, so the teams will only take a combat issue of ammo and one day of rations and water. Lang is preparing the operations order for the move."

"Okay. Looks like you're crossing the Ts and dotting the Is. You're call sign will remain operational while you're gone, so if you can hit a relay you can get a message to me. Careful out there, Dick. The planning for this thing is just a little too flaky for my taste."

The sudden change in plans didn't upset him as much as he thought it would. He'd be running his own operations and managing the teams from his own operations center. It was going to be hectic without support from experienced recon officers, but he didn't see it as something to be concerned about. Hell, he'd run bigger operations than this one when he was a gunny. Fact was, he was excited about getting out from under the restrictions of the Marine base at Dong Ha and away from the Sergeant Major and the Executive Officer. For some reason, they liked to pick apart everything he was involved in. The change was probably just what he needed to get his nerves settled down. A month of running short duration, close in recon patrols and then back to Dong Ha. Hell, it would be a break for the teams too.

The birds got off on time on Friday morning. They drew four mortar rounds when they landed at Khe Sanh and the teams had to scatter for cover in shallow defensive positions near the runway. Rhodes got a quick headcount from his team leaders when things calmed down and then went looking for Sullivan. He didn't have to look far.

A jeep stopped on a dirt road not far from the runway and Sullivan and an SF Staff Sergeant double-timed to Rhodes's position. Sullivan took Rhodes in the Jeep and the Staff Sergeant stayed with the teams to lead them to their quarters at the SOG Forward Operating Base.

The SF turned out to be good hosts. The teams were assigned bunker hooches next to the Tactical Operations Center (TOC), shown where the water supply was, given free run of the showers, and fed a hot meal, which was a whole lot better than they were treated at Dong Ha by the Marine Corps. Even better, they were told recon patrols were their only duty. No burning shitters and no filling sand bags except for their own needs.

Rhodes was housed in the main command bunker with Sullivan and the A-team. He was given a tour and was stunned by their arsenal. They seemed to have every kind of weapon he had ever heard of.

"Are those Stoners?" he asked.

"The very same," Sullivan said. "Want one?"

"You're shitting me."

"You say that a lot," Sullivan said. "No, I'm not shitting you. I told you our friends have deep pockets."

"I don't want one, but it would be nice to have one in each of the teams. Are they the 63 or 63A?"

"63A."

"Can we have four of them?"

"Consider it done. Take any of the magazines you want too."

"Nice. I like my M-fourteen, but the teams could use a light weight, high-cap SAW."

Because of their high and selective rate of fire

(700 or 900 rounds per minute) the Stoners made an excellent and relatively light weight squad automatic weapon (SAW). The SEALs used them and the Corps had a few in inventory, but not many were made to begin with. At 900 rounds per minute the spacing between rounds even with a fast sweep was close and made the Stoner a great weapon for breaking up an ambush. Just point the hose and spray. And they had a choice of magazines from 20 to 100 rounds. Two Stoners firing at 900 rounds per minute backed up with M-14s and M-16s gives meaning to the term, "overwhelming firepower."

"If you like the M-fourteen," Sullivan said, "I've got something for you too. You won't find them in the supply system. Want some sixty-round drum-mags for the fourteen?"

"Drum magazines? For the M-fourteen? There isn't any such thing."

"That's right," Sullivan said and grinned. "Want some?"

"Show me."

Sullivan opened a locker and took out the strangest looking magazine Rhodes had ever seen. It looked like a standard M-14 magazine with a round drum on both sides. The straight mag in the center fit into the magazine-well just like a standard magazine.

"Are these things reliable?"

"You wouldn't believe the number of rounds that have been fired with them in testing without a failure. You must keep them clean and they are heavy, but they give you a whole lot of fire power in a small package. It's like having an M-sixty without the bulk."

"Hell yes, I'd like to have some for me and the teams. I could set up a Fourteen for each of the teams with an M-76 launcher for Willie-Pete and equip them with these mags for some serious firepower. We could leave the M-sixties home, not that we take them very often anyway, but with these mags, the fourteens become a SAW."

"You got it. Anything else you see in here can be issued too."

"I think the stoners and the drum magazines are all we need. Our best protection is staying out of sight and avoiding a fight. When do we move south?"

"In the morning. We'll be setting up in an old French fort in Lang Vei Village. The TOC is ready, but we still have a lot of perimeter work and housing to do. How soon can you be ready to start patrolling?"

"As soon as we have a mission," Rhodes said.

"You should get that around 1700. Coats will be here then. By the way, let me ask you a question. The Corps does know the hills around here are filled with NVA, don't they? We've tried to tell the base commander, but I think we've been ignored so far."

"Some people know," Rhodes said. "I did a recon patrol on Hill Eight Eighty-One South not long ago. Almost didn't get out. Bravo Company of First Battalion, Ninth Marines is on their way here though, so maybe things are getting better. Know what they call First Battalion of the Ninth Marines?"

"Grunts?" Sullivan said.

"The Walking Dead. That battalion seems to have an inside tract to the worst shit going on wherever they go."

"Thanks for the comforting thought," Sullivan said

Chapter 24

The move went smoothly. Rather than try to move by ground down the nine klicks to Lang Vei Village, Sullivan managed to get Army air assets to move the Americans. The Vietnamese and Bru moved first by truck to Khe Sanh village and then by foot to Lang Vei village. They were ambushed twice south of Khe Sanh village by small VC units. Casualties were light and the SF didn't seem especially concerned by the attacks.

The previous night at 1700, an all-black Huey helicopter without numbers or markings landed at the SF compound and Coats and two other civilians joined Sullivan's party. The first thing they did was break out a whole set of forms that the Marines had to read and sign. Non-disclosure forms. Everything they did, saw, or heard while detached to the CIA was classified and if they ever disclosed what they heard, did, or saw while they were working with the SF and CIA they would suffer unimaginable penalties up to and including castration and loss of three months' pay.

Rhodes signed the forms reluctantly. His Marines signed them with excited whispers to each other. *Can't even talk about what we're going to be doing. Man, this has got to be some good shit.*

After the forms were signed and the CIA men read the penalties for disclosing classified information out loud one more time, one of the new civilians, Jerry Sizemore, briefed Rhodes, Kelly, and the other team leaders on interdiction missions along the Ho Chi Minh trail inside of Laos. He also identified NVA camps and command centers not far from the border and spoke of them as targets. He was very interested in getting current intelligence on those camps and suggested a mission concept for the Marines. Obtaining prisoners was a high priority. Causing hate and discontent along the Ho Chi Minh trail was another.

As Rhodes worked with Kelly and an SF Sergeant to set up communications in the old fort, he wasn't getting any happier about the CIA's idea of a mission concept. It seemed to him the concept amounted to hang the Marines out and cover the CIA's asses. Missions into Laos differed significantly from recon in Vietnam. First, there was only limited previous intelligence, or at least intelligence the CIA and SF were willing to share so far. Instead of filing cabinets full of patrol reports cross referenced for pre-mission planning, aerial photography, interrogation reports, and updated maps, he and his teams would have only verbal briefings from CIA and SF operators. Maps were limited and not very good. Communications across the border were restricted. Worst of all, if you got in trouble in Laos, you were out of luck. You couldn't call for supporting arms to get you out of trouble because there weren't any. The only extraction was by foot until you were back across the border. At least mission planning was simpler. There wasn't a hell of a lot to plan with. His stress level began to rise, not for himself, but for his teams.

He took a break and walked around the village. He just wanted to get away for a few minutes and let his head settle down. He was getting tired and he knew it. Not just physically tired. Tired inside. He was losing his edge. Almost two years of combat was taking its toll. He wondered how the men fighting in World War Two did it. Years of combat. There until hostilities ended. No defined rotation date. But they had something to fight for and were trying to win. That was the problem with this fight, he thought. The Marines were just fighting until somebody back in Washington decided to stop the stupidity or try to win the war. The politicians would run out of balls before they ran out of Marines—hopefully. Problem was, they wouldn't run out of stupid. Kill some more. Die some more. No reason for the killing, just kill some more. It was insanity. No one had even decided what winning was.

He'd have close to three years of constant combat when he rotated back to the states after this tour. He wondered if Slaughter was losing his edge too. Slaughter only had about fifteen months of combat behind him, but it had to be taking its toll. He walked some more and got his nerves settled down and returned to the TOC.

As soon as he had communications up and had checked in with Khe Sanh's fire control center, Rhodes pulled the team leaders in and assigned three recon patrols around the village with artillery coverage from Khe Sanh. Even with his limited S3 experience, he missed the planning resources at Dong Ha. At least he had three good teams, excellent land navigators all, and savvy recon operators. He sent two teams out on five kilometer patrols to the east and south and sent one toward Laos. That day Rhodes was interested in developing better intelligence on trails, native Bru population, and any enemy activity in the area. All patrols were keyhole patrols and told to ignore tempting fire missions. He and the teams needed accurate maps and a firsthand familiarity with the terrain.

With the teams out, he found himself in the unusual position of not having much to do. The teams wouldn't check-in except at status points on their patrol routes, or unless they got in trouble and then the team leaders would work directly with supporting arms.

The CIDG and ARVNs began to arrive and the SF advisors began setting up the camp's perimeter. Rhodes watched trucks of concertina wire being unloaded at points along a line of fighting holes. What looked like a battalion of Bru and Vietnamese mama-sans showed up in black pajamas and straw coolie hats and were put to work filling sandbags and building bunkers—and probably pacing off distances for NVA mortars. SF advisors directed construction of mortar pits and 106mm recoilless rifle positions. A helicopter arrived with a 4.2-inch mortar mounted on a field artillery carriage and it was placed in a fortified firing pit.

Wire was stretched out in deadly coils, stakes driven to keep it in place, tin cans and pieces of metal were attached to the wire as noise alarms. Claymores were set out, bobby-traps set to protect the claymores, and various other kinds of booby-traps were constructed. The camp was divided into an American area and a CIDG/Vietnamese area. Then the CIDG area was divided again because the CIDGs were made up from two Montagnard tribes that didn't get along very well. That bit of news added another few points to Rhodes blood pressure.

By the time the recon teams began arriving back at the camp they had to look for the entrance. In a single day while they were gone, the old fort and surrounding area had become a defendable military operating base. It wasn't done yet, but it was defendable. Rhodes had warned them on the last status checks, but it was still a shock to the teams to see the changes that had occurred while they patrolled.

The last team in was Boatload. Rhodes waited for them at the opening in the wire that served as the gate. It was getting dark and he didn't want a nervous Bru shooting up his team. Boatload moved through the gate quickly. They had plenty of energy left. A seven-hour patrol was just a walk in the sun for them. Lennon was on tail-end-Charlie and carrying one of the Stoners.

"How do you like the Stoner, Lennon?"

"I guess I like it fine, Mr. . . . Captain Rhodes. It did good at Khe Sanh when we played with them, but I haven't got to use it in the grass yet."

"I hope it stays that way," Rhodes said. "Staff Sergeant Kelly, I'll see you in the TOC in thirty minutes."

After debriefing Kelly and updating the master map in the planning center with trails and land marks found by Boatload, Rhodes worked with the other team leaders. Team Easy Times, the First Force team, had the best terrain intelligence, and team Cold Weather had found a complex of enemy bunkers and fighting positions. The complex was abandoned, but it was very well built. The teams reported squad sized NVA sightings within their patrol areas, but no major concentrations of enemy troops and no hostile contact.

The team leaders debriefed each other's team and then Rhodes debriefed the team leaders. He offered Sullivan the opportunity to sit in on the debriefings, but he was busy planning A-team missions.

Sullivan did ask him to set up a night watch list for his Marines and gave Rhodes a list of CIDG defensive positions to be reinforced with Marines. One to a position. Rhodes delegated the task to Kelly.

With the master map updated and patrol reports filed, he decided to take a walk through the camp before it got dark. He wanted to see how the SF deployed their weapons and wanted to get a small level of comfort with the way the perimeter was set up. He was also curious as to how the Marines were mixing with the CIDG. Normally Marines and gooks did not mix well.

He heard Lennon's giggle at the first sandbagged position he came to. He also smelled coffee. Good strong coffee. The fighting position was a hole dug about three feet deep with a double row of sandbags around the lip stacked three high. The bottom was red dirt and sitting in a circle with a small fire in the center were Lennon and three Bru tribesman in green utilities. What the hell did they think it was, a boy scout camp?

Lennon had his Stoner across his lap. Three M2 carbines were leaning against the side of the hole. An open pan of water sat on a rock in the center of the fire. Coffee grounds floated on the surface of the water.

"Everything secure, Lennon?"

Lennon and the three Bru started to jump up.

"Sit!" Rhodes said. "Is that coffee?"

"Yes, sir," Lennon said. "They make really good coffee. You have to hold your teeth together to strain out the grounds though. Want some, sir?"

He found a place in the dirt between two of the Bru and sat down in the dirt.

"Sure. Do you have something I can use for a cup?"

"Use my canteen cup, Captain. If you put one of those cane sticks in it, it's just like adding sugar. The Bru are pretty smart."

"Didn't take you long to get to know them."

"They're pretty nice people, Mr. Striker. Sorry. Captain. They're happy to have me and my rifle here."

One of the Bru next to Rhodes reached over and held Rhodes's hand. Rhodes flinched at first, but remembered holding hands was a common sign of friendship in Vietnam. Everyone did it, men, women, and children. As if reading Rhodes's mind, Lennon spoke.

"They all hold hands," Lennon said. "It doesn't mean anything. That's Coffee holding your hand. The guy on the other side is Milk. And this guy is Tea. I can't say their names so I named them something I can say that sounds like their real name."

Lennon handed Rhodes his canteen cup full of hot coffee. One of the Bru handed him a stick of cane and showed him how to swirl it around in the boiling water to loosen the sugar before putting it in his coffee. When he swirled it in his coffee, he got another surprise. The cane lightened the coffee just like cream does. Steam was swirling from the cup but Rhodes took a careful sip anyway. The coffee was amazing, better than anything the Americans had, especially C-rats instant coffee. He wondered out loud where they got it and spat coffee grounds out.

Lennon said, "All of them used to work on French coffee plantations. They know how to grow and roast their own." Rhodes took another sip of the coffee.

"Lennon, how in the world did you learn all this in the short time we've been here?"

"The SF guys told us a lot back at Khe Sanh and the Bru can speak a lot of English. They know what we're saying now."

Two of the Bru smiled and shook their heads yes.

Handing the empty cup back to Lennon, he said, "Thanks for the coffee. Keep your eyes open Lennon, we could get probed tonight."

"I will, sir. Coffee will keep a good watch when I get some sleep later. He's recon too."

Lennon giggled and the Bru giggled with him.

Rhodes smothered a laugh and got out of there. Sometimes he wasn't sure Lennon wasn't a fairy, but then the kid did some amazing thing in battle and the doubts went away. Hell, it couldn't hurt to have good relations with the Bru guarding the base and they were always laughing or giggling about something. What the hell they had to be so happy about, he didn't know.

The rest of the Marines didn't seem to be as comfortable with the CIDG as Lennon was. Rhodes sensed a little tension in the perimeter positions, both ways. There wasn't much sharing of anything going on.

The next three days went by in a routine of patrols, debriefings, and perimeter watch. They took a few rounds of small arms at night, but nothing serious. The VC/NVA knew they were there but seemed to be feeling the camp out rather than making any serious attempt at hurting them. The patrols added more intelligence to the master map and the intelligence file began to provide some pre-mission intelligence as the teams returned to close-in areas they had visited on previous patrols. Rhodes began to settle down and enjoy his independent command.

On day three he received aerial photos of their patrol areas. On the fourth day, the black helicopter landed and Coats and his two subordinates met Rhodes in the TOC.

"Got something interesting for you," Coats said. "Jerry, brief Captain Rhodes while I spend a few minutes with Captain Sullivan."

Sizemore unloaded a briefcase and spread maps on the table. He brought cups of coffee for Rhodes and himself to the table.

"Here's the recon area of operations," he said tracing an area on the map with his finger. "Sullivan's CIDG will take your team out and drop them near the border. From the drop off point your team will cross the border here and move west into Laos looking for this trail marked in red. Don't try to use the trail because it's heavily traveled by the NVA in both directions and they have camps all along it. But once the trail is found, the team will have a landmark to orient their maps. Okay so far?"

"I'm not sure okay is the word, but I'm following you."

"What's the problem?" Sizemore said. "Laos?"

"Yeah. We don't have authority to conduct combat operations in Laos."

"Then don't get into a fight with anyone, Sizemore said. "The SF operate in Laos all the time. This is just a recon. We want intelligence on a major NVA bivouac and HQ area ten miles inside of Laos. I'm serious here. Your team must stay out of sight and out of trouble and get back with the information they collect."

"So, they're on their own?"

"From the time they enter Laos, until they cross back over the border, they are on their own. If they get in trouble, they must find a way to break contact and di-di back to Vietnam. We can help as soon as they cross into Vietnam, but until then there's no way we can send enough help to pull them out. Air power is out, artillery can't shoot into Laos deliberately, and we can't put a force of combatants across the border big enough to do any good."

He looked at the map for a few moments trying to get a feel for the terrain from the contour lines.

"What's so important about this NVA HQ?" he asked. "There's NVA all over Laos."

"Look at the trail I pointed out. Where does it lead in this direction?"

"Looks like it connects with this. . .is this a road?"

"About as much of a road as you find in this part of Vietnam."

"Then it connects with a road coming . . .right here. "

"Bingo," Sizemore said. "Ten miles west on that trail is the Bivouac and HQ for the NVA 321st division, we think. Aerial photos show it to be a major camp regardless, and it recently got a lot bigger. A significant amount of supplies is leaving the Ho Chi Minh trail and moving that way. It would be nice to know what we're facing and, oh by the way, what the Marines at Khe Sanh are facing besides what we already know to be in the hills around the combat base. And one other thing."

"I don't need one other thing," Rhodes said. "Spying on an enemy division in a country we're not supposed to be in is more than enough."

"Try this on for size. Analysis of the aerial recon photos has indicated the presence of armor at the camp."

"Tanks?"

"They think so. T-thirty-fours or T-fifty-fours. The analysts aren't sure. They are well camouflaged, but the analysts are thinking tanks. We need to know one way or the other. If the NVA are moving tanks down here a whole lot of things need to change."

"Hard to believe though," Rhodes said. "The NVA learned their lesson early on about what happens to their tanks if they bring them under our artillery fan, and they know what our airpower does to them."

"Maybe. Maybe not. They'd present a serious problem for us if they brought them down that trail and they ended up on our wire here. I doubt the Bru have ever seen a tank. They'd be gone in about ten seconds. To the NVA it might be worth losing a few tanks to take out an SF camp sitting so close to the Ho Chi Minh trail."

"Still . . ." Rhodes said.

"In any case, we need to know," Sizemore said

"All right. I need all the intelligence you have on the area. I want two days to plan and put the ops order together."

"No ops order," Sizemore said. "All records of this mission are classified and we will maintain the records."

Well, there it is, Rhodes thought. Now I've got a decision to make. I'm sending my team into Laos, and I won't have any records to show I did it as a valid mission or who gave the order.

Chapter 25

He raised his objections. Sizemore said he understood his reservations about keeping a record of his unit's operations, but then he pulled Rhodes's non-disclosure form from his stack of papers and explained that he no longer worked for Major Slaughter or the Third Recon Battalion. He and everyone in his teams were detached to the CIA until released by Mr. Coats and until that time his operations were CIA operations and classified at a higher level than anyone in Third Recon was cleared for.

"Well, we can go round and round, but I can tell you this right now," Rhodes said. "My Marines are not going out unless I plan this patrol with the team leader."

"No one said you can't plan. You just can't keep

the documentation or share it with anyone but your team leader."

And that kind of painted him into a corner. He would probably be relieved from command if he refused the assignment and that wouldn't help the teams. Somebody else would send them out. But any way he did it, his ass was hanging out if he didn't have an Ops Order giving authority for the mission. This is what Slaughter had warned him about. Well, there didn't seem to be a hell of a lot of choice. He pulled the maps to his side of the table.

"We'll do the planning tomorrow and launch the team the day after tomorrow. What have you got for me in the way of intelligence?"

"Glad you asked that question," Sizemore said, pulling a stack of reports across the table. "Let's start with the aerials of . . ."

He felt like he ought to ask for volunteers, but knew all the teams would volunteer anyway. He decided to give the patrol to Kelly's Boatload team. He trusted Kelly and knew he worked well in an unstructured environment. This one was about as unstructured as it got.

Kelly and Rhodes worked on the patrol plan and route well into the night and the next day. They were almost overwhelmed with the intelligence the CIA provided, an unusual and surprising situation after planning patrols for a week with almost no intelligence. The CIA and SF seemed to have stacks of intelligence on what was happening in Laos, but almost nothing about what was happening within five miles of their own camp.

Because he wasn't completely trusting of the CIA and wasn't sure Kelly would be supported by the SF if he got in trouble in Laos—hell, Rhodes had been told as much straight out—he and Kelly developed their own private shackle sheet between them along with a simple coding method for letters. There wouldn't be any artillery to call, but with their private shackle grid they could encode position coordinates and other number related data such as time and distance and even simple messages. Only he and Kelly would have the key.

Having a way to encode radio transmissions, especially team location data, was critical since the team would be operating where no Americans were supposed to be. The NVA had scanners and monitored American operating frequencies, in fact monitored the entire frequency spectrum of the PRC-25. So, a way to encode messages was necessary.

Their shackle grid consisted of the numbers 1 through 0 across the top. Under each number was a column of letters of different lengths. Because there were ten columns, the twenty-six letters of the alphabet were listed under the numbers unevenly, three letters under one number, one letter under another, five under another, etc. It took two numbers to encode a letter. The first number indicated the column to look in. The second number was the position of the coded letter from the top down in the column. Numbers were encoded with just a letter. Find the column the letter appeared in and read the number at the top. It was a simple system and easy to break if given enough time, but used sparingly, and for only one mission, it was effective. Knowing he had a private way to communicate with the patrol gave Rhodes a small measure of comfort.

Sullivan wanted to assign two CIDG combat recon to the patrol, but Rhodes refused and wouldn't budge on the matter. Kelly was uncomfortable with the offer and everyone on his team but Lennon were uncomfortable around the CIDG. Their first trip across the border was not the time to put strangers on the team, especially gook strangers.

That evening after briefing his team, Kelly found Rhodes walking the perimeter.

"Captain Rhodes, I need to leave Lennon behind."

"What's the problem?"

"He's coming down with something. Sneezes and congestion. Doc said it's just a cold probably, but I can't take the chance of him sneezing at the wrong time on this one."

"No, you can't. I'll pull a volunteer from one of the other teams."

"I'd rather go in light, Captain. Four is easier to hide than five, and one man won't make a lot of difference if we're compromised. Not on this one."

Rhodes wasn't sure about that. If someone was hurt and had to be carried out, having one less man could be a big difference. It was Kelly's team though, and Kelly had a whole lot more experience than he did.

"Not the way I'd do it," he said, "but it's your patrol. I'll keep Lennon in the TOC."

A CIDG patrol with Boatload embedded left the wire in the dark at 0400. An SF Staff Sergeant led the patrol. Kelly checked in at 0600 and using code-words informed Rhodes he was in Laos and moving toward his objective. Rhodes logged the activity and marked Kelly's reported position on the planning map. He also marked a smaller map he kept folded in his thigh pocket and kept to himself.

Rhodes worked on two routine patrol orders between Lang Vei and Khe Sanh and set up two files for the paperwork. He didn't have a lot to do until Kelly checked in or until the teams set out on their patrols so he puttered around and worried about Kelly.

Lennon hadn't shown up at the TOC by 0900 so Rhodes went looking for him. He found Lennon at the other end of the camp with a group of CIDG and it looked like Lennon was giving them instruction in grenade throwing. Rhodes watched for a moment.

Lennon held something in his hand, mimicked pulling the pin, and then tossed the object about fifty feet away and right into a sandpit that was only about three feet across. Next, one of the Bru tried and Lennon corrected his grip and stance. Rhodes heard a voice behind him.

"Morning, Dick," Sullivan said. "I meant to ask

you last night. Can I borrow corporal Lennon from you today?"

"Sure. Kelly had to leave him behind due to sneezing. I haven't got anything for him but make-up work anyhow."

"Thanks. Is he a little funny?"

"How do you mean?" Rhodes said.

"You know—funny," Sullivan said, holding his arm up and letting his hand hang limp.

"No. It's just his way. You should see that kid under fire. He's a good Marine."

"Okay. Whatever it is about him, the Bru like him. Look at them. He's doing better training then my SF troops."

"Well, you got him. I won't need him again until Boatload gets back. Keep him busy."

"Don't worry," Sullivan said. "I'm going to try him with the Bru on weapons maintenance later. Their idea of clean is a little different than ours."

The SF camp had one very nice feature that extended PRC-25 line-of-sight communications with teams in the field. A guard tower fifty feet tall had been constructed before the SF made the move to Lang Vei Village. The SF communications sergeant mounted an R-292 antenna mast on top of the tower with a whip antenna on top raising the effective height of the antenna to ninety-five feet over the base and well above the surrounding canopy. The PRC-25 five-watt signal could hit the SF antenna from well beyond its normal five-mile horizon, and if the transmitting radio were high enough it could reach Lang Vei from as much as twenty miles away. The signal would be weak, but still handy in a pinch. Rhodes checked out the set up and made some notes for his own file of things that worked well. That list was growing. The SF knew their business.

The following day Rhodes sent his two remaining teams to patrol on both sides of Route Nine north of Lang Vei. VC activity had been reported in that area by Combined Action Teams working out of Khe Sanh Village. By 1500, the TOC was getting busy.

Kelly reported he was on high ground and within sight of his objective. The plan called for him to observe the NVA camp for two days before moving his team back to Vietnam. He gave Rhodes shackled coordinates for his position. The signal was weak, but Kelly was understandable. Kelly was receiving Rhodes's signal loud and clear.

Later while Rhodes was stirring a stick of cane in his Bru coffee, team Cold Weather found a bunker complex with what they estimated to be a platoon of NVA dug in. Cold Weather was pinned down and calling in artillery so they could break contact and di-di.

Fifteen minutes after that and before Cold Weather could get free, Team Easy Time reported contact with an unknown sized force. They were attempting to evade and were in a running battle to break contact.

While he was attempting to get gunships and a

slick to extract Easy Time, Boatload called in and gave Rhodes the code-words for contact and compromise and a set of shackled coordinates. When he tried to confirm the coordinates, he couldn't raise Boatload again. He didn't have time to keep trying.

Sullivan, the communications sergeant, and Lennon rushed into the TOC. The Com Sergeant took over on Easy Time and the air/ground net. Sullivan began working with Cold Weather and Lennon became a very busy gofer. Rhodes decoded Boatload's coordinates and marked the master map and updated his pocket map. He tried Boatload again.

Finally, Boatload answered, but only gave the code-word for evading. That code-word had two meanings. First, the team is evading the enemy, and second, don't distract me with more calls. Rhodes put the radio on speaker and began updating the map with positions for Cold Weather and Easy Time and kept one ear listening for Boatload. He grabbed Lennon and sat him next to the radio tuned to Boatload's frequency.

"Listen for Kelly," Rhodes said. "That's your only job. Ignore everything else, and grab me as soon as he calls in. Do you have a pencil?"

"Yes, sir. Are they okay?"

"They're evading. The signal is weak so listen close. Make sure you write his message down." Lennon turned the speaker off and put the handset to his ear.

The Com Sergeant had an OV-10 and two gunships over Easy Time's position and an extraction slick on the way. He knew what he was doing and had it under control. Rhodes checked with Sullivan and was told Khe Sanh's 155mm guns were working the bunker complex over and Cold Weather was moving. He was waiting for the team to find an LZ so he could call in an extraction bird. Rhodes could hear the artillery hitting off in the distance.

He returned to Lennon, but nothing more had been heard from Boatload. The coded coordinates Kelly passed on the radio had him well away from the patrol route they had planned. Kelly was an excellent land navigator though. He could get his team back on course.

The Com Sergeant notified Rhodes that Easy Time had been picked up and they were on their way back to Lang Vei. Ten minutes later Sullivan had an LZ for Cold Weather and an Army slick overhearing the traffic was on the way to pull the team out. Rhodes's stress level went way down. Two of his teams were on the way home.

Then Lennon yelled, "Mr. Striker, Boatload is calling."

"Put it on speaker."

Both Lennon and Rhodes wrote the message down. Using code words and shackle sheet encoding, Kelly told Rhodes he had two wounded and was holed up in a cave and not in immediate danger. He gave the shackled coordinates.

His stress level went way back up. Two wounded out of four. He hoped they were walking wounded. Worse, Kelly had closed with the code-word for evading again, meaning he didn't want to be called.

Rhodes needed more information, but had to wait for Kelly to check in again. He decoded the coordinates and updated first his pocket map and then the master map. The coordinates placed Kelly on the side of a hill with very close contour lines. The hill was very steep. Were Kelly's coordinates correct? How could he get wounded men up that kind of incline?

Chapter 26

With Cold Weather and Easy Time back in camp, Rhodes focused on debriefing and updating maps. The picture of enemy concentrations in the surrounding area evolving from the recon team's sighting wasn't providing much comfort for Sullivan. He decided to fly to Khe Sanh and confer with the Marine's artillery controllers and get a commitment for reinforcements from the Marines if the feces hit the fan. Lang Vei was well within Khe Sanh's artillery fan for both their 105mm and 155mm guns. Sullivan wanted to verify his on-call pre-registered fire missions and get a warm and fuzzy about Khe Sanh's ability to support him. Rhodes spent the night drinking coffee and listening for Boatload.

Kelly finally checked in at 0300. He began with encoded position coordinates. They were the same as his last report. The team hadn't moved. Next, he told Rhodes to shift to their alternate frequency. Kelly was apparently worried about radio direction finders.

He shifted to the alternate frequency and Kelly answered immediately. He read off a message of two-number codes and after Rhodes acknowledged, said he was returning to the primary frequency. Rhodes changed the radio back to the primary frequency and began to decode the message.

The message was not good news. *Two wia unabl tvl. water a rats crit. buku gks. advise.*

Buku gks? Oh, beaucoups gooks. His wounded can't travel. They are almost out of water and rations. They have a large number of NVA around them. How big? Big enough for Kelly to use beaucoups so it's a bunch. Advise?

Number one, he thought, I have a team in trouble.

Number two, SF and CIA said they couldn't help if this happened.

Number three, I am not leaving my team on a hill in Laos.

Number four, it is easier to ask for forgiveness than it is to get permission.

He keyed the handset and told Kelly to remain in place. Help was on the way. Kelly acknowledged.

He met the teams in Easy Time's bunker. He asked for

four volunteers and got sixteen. After picking four men he assigned Staff Sergeant Lutts, team leader of Easy Time, to the TOC and told him to continue running the normal patrol schedule for Easy Time and Cold Weather. Lutts was so adamant about his objection to Rhodes leading the team going after Boatload he had to be ordered to shut up. Rhodes didn't have any reservations about the ability of either team leader to lead the patrol into Laos, but the rescue mission was a rogue mission and he wouldn't put his men in that kind of position. He was going to lead the mission and he was going to take the heat for it.

Of course, Lennon wanted to go, but Rhodes had to deny his request. Lennon still had the sniffles and was still sneezing. Rhodes had the relief team pack light so they could carry extra rations and water for Boatload. They wouldn't need personal items or clothes and he told them to leave their ponchos and liners in camp. The only things they wore on their bodies were jungle utilities, jungle cover, and camo face paint. Their packs contained only extra ammunition, a few pinions for scaling rock, a signal mirror, one claymore each, extra rounds for the M-79s, extra batteries for the radio, flares, and extra LRRP rations.

He carried his M-14 with the big drum magazine and two bandoleers of regular magazines. Two of the volunteers, Corporal Dean and Lance Corporal Bacon carried Stoners, third and fourth, PFC Raleigh and PCF Lavinski carried M-16s. Extra water made up for any weight savings. Considering the steepness of the hill

Kelly was on, he had two men carry fifty foot lengths of climbing rope around their packs.

They couldn't afford to get in an extended firefight in Laos, but he wanted the lighter automatic weapons for breaking contact. The only real defense they had was the "di-di," breaking contact and getting the hell away. Going in, they couldn't afford any contact. They had to reach Boatload without enemy contact or compromise.

As Rhodes was going over his route with Lutts and Lennon one final time in the TOC he heard rotors. Crap! Sullivan was back. He couldn't leave now without Sullivan seeing him leave. He'd just have to face him.

In a few minutes, Sullivan entered the TOC and stopped at the door and looked at Rhodes, Rhodes in face paint and kit with his rifle in his hand.

"Where are *you* going?" Sullivan said with his eyebrows raised.

"I'm taking a patrol out. Staff Sergeant Lutts can brief you."

"What's up?"

Rhodes ground his teeth in frustration. He was a lousy liar. He'd just have to give Sullivan a quick overview and get out regardless of what Sullivan said.

"Our team in Laos is in trouble. Two wounded and unable to move. With only two other team members, they don't have the horsepower to carry them. I'm going in to get them and bring them out."

Sullivan surprised Rhodes. He didn't object to

the mission directly.

"You're a Captain. You've got team leaders for that."

"Not on this one," Rhodes said. "I wouldn't take the few I'm taking if I could carry those guys out myself. Marty, I don't care what Coats wants. I'm crossing the border and I'm bringing my Marines back. I'm taking the heat for this."

"What heat?" I don't know about Coats, but I'd do the same thing. What the hell do you think we are? The only thing Coats will want to know is if the mission is feasible and if you can avoid causing an international incident. He won't want to read about a big battle between NVA and Americans in Laos. How big is the team you're taking in?"

"Four and myself."

"Are you sure you can find them? Show me."

He took Sullivan to the map and pointed out Kelly's position. "I can find them. The problem is going to be getting through the NVA without contact. We're going in light and we're going to avoid any kind of contact if we can. Look, I've got to leave. We've got to get across the border tonight."

"A little trust out of you would have helped," Sullivan said. "I'll do what I can back here to be prepared when you get back to the border. We can't bring a large force into Laos, but we can damn well have one waiting on this side. Stay in contact with us."

"Will do. Lutts, I'll do a radio check at the border."

He tried to get out of the door, but Lennon stopped in the door blocking the exit.

"Captain, take Coffee with you. He knows all about the jungle."

"No time now, Lennon, I'm leaving right now."

"He's right here and he's ready, Mr., I mean Captain.

"Take him," Sullivan said. "He's CIDG combat recon. The Bru know this whole area including the part of Laos you're trying to get through."

He didn't have time to argue. His mind was on two wounded men in a cave in Laos.

"Okay, Okay. Come on, Coffee. Let's di-di."

The relief team finally got out of camp and moved toward Laos around 1400. Getting to Laos before dark shouldn't be a big problem. It was only about three quarters of a mile.

Chapter 27

Moving with stealth through a klick and a half of jungle can be a time-consuming process, but having a Bru along who knew that patch of jungle like the back of his hand cut the time considerably. Bringing Coffee had been a good idea. He took point and seemed to revel in his role.

The team entered Laos well north of the main road with an hour of light left. Coffee found a small hill and led the team through tall elephant grass to an area of low grass at the top. They had a stiff breeze that was getting stronger. A storm was on the way. After bellying to the top, Coffee stretched out in the grass waiting for Rhodes to come forward. Rhodes went prone next to the Bru.

"Map," Coffee said quietly.

Rhodes unfolded the map and Coffee oriented it with compass north. The primitive little guy wasn't so primitive after all. The SF had done some good training. They were lying in grass about three feet high and raised their heads just enough to see the surrounding terrain over the grass. Coffee put his finger on the line marking the border and pointed over his shoulder. He looked at the map and put his finger on a set of contours that indicated a steep sided hill and pointed to the west. Rhodes rose enough to find the hill and nodded. Coffee picked two more landmarks and gave Rhodes the direction so he could find them.

Rhodes put his finger on the mark he had added to indicate Boatload's location.

"This is where the team is," he said. "I want to cross this ridge to here and then move down this valley to here. Understand?"

"Honcho no move in valley. Beaucoups VC. No hide."

Coffee held his hand about two feet above the ground. "Grass," he said.

"Do you know a better way?"

Coffee put his finger on a hill with contour lines indicating a gradual incline.

"Jungle. Hard work. Take longer. VC?" Coffee shrugged.

Rhodes studied the map. Coffee was right. His path would take them a couple of klicks off a direct line to Kelly's hill and over one steep ridge. That ridge had a finger ridge leading to Kelly's hill. Even though longer,

Coffee's way looked better than taking the team across an open area through two-foot-high grass. He traced his finger across the hill and then traced a curve to get to Kelly.

"Like this?" Rhodes said.

Coffee shook his head no and put his finger on the other side of the ridge.

"First, here," he said.

"What do we do then?" Rhodes said.

Coffee traced a path with his finger along the backside of a ridgeline on the map that would put it between the team and Kelly's hill.

"That's pretty steep." Rhodes indicated what he meant with his hand tilted up. "Can we get up that ridge?"

Coffee shrugged.

Rhodes had noticed in camp that the Bru shrugged a lot when talking to Americans. It could mean they didn't understand you, they didn't know, they didn't care, or they hadn't decided yet—or they just didn't feel like answering you. Whatever the case right then, the shrug didn't give him a lot of confidence.

"Well, let's do it your way for now. Lead away, Mr. Coffee."

The Bru giggled like Lennon, and took the point. He seemed tickled at Lennon's name for him.

The breeze had turned into a fifteen mile per hour wind. Clouds were building and the sun was going down. Near the bottom of the hill where they had stopped and in tall elephant grass, Coffee suddenly squatted down close to the ground. Rhodes was in second position and was keeping a close eye on the Bru so he saw the move and raised his right hand in a fist and squatted. Coffee turned his head and put his whole hand over his mouth, the Bru way of saying, *Shhh*. He slowly stretched out prone.

Gradually the sound of grass being pushed and hacked got closer and could be heard over the wind. It reached a point just a few feet away from the team's position before passing by and moving up the hill. Coffee stood and started moving more quickly toward the thick canopied jungle that surrounded the hill. No hand signals, just up and gone. Having figured out the Bru ignored niceties like hand signals and expected others on a patrol to pay attention, Rhodes was ready and signaled the team to move.

Coffee took them into the single canopy and squatted in the thick undergrowth. The rustle of wind driven branches in the canopy was getting louder and blocked out most other sounds. Rhodes brought the team up and knelt next to Coffee. No sense asking. Coffee was listening to the jungle and turning his head to focus his attention. Rhodes kept quiet. Coffee put his hand over his mouth and looked at each of the team members. Each nodded. Coffee pointed to their left and held up five fingers.

He led the team crawling and slowly moving vines and grass away and squirming around bamboo and shrubs. The Bru was so good at leaving the undergrowth undisturbed, Rhodes had to make his own trail. The going was excruciatingly slow, but the team was keeping their noise down below the sounds of the wind driven canopy above them. Coffee stopped again and listened. He stood and began making faster time, pushing at undergrowth, and crushing down elephant grass he couldn't push through.

Thirty minutes later Coffee stopped again. He leaned forward and looked to the left and right. He was on the edge of a narrow trail. Rhodes signaled the team up and spread them out along the trail in the brush. They waited five minutes. Coffee stepped out on the trail and started walking quickly to the west. Rhodes signaled the team out of the brush and set them in ten meter intervals behind Coffee. He hurried up to get in the second position behind Coffee.

As the light went, Rhodes closed the intervals up and stayed close to Coffee. They needed a night harbor, but Coffee didn't seem to be slowing down. The team closed-up more until they could reach out and touch the man in front of them. Suddenly Coffee stopped and got bumped by Rhodes. Coffee squatted down slowly. He took Rhodes's hand and held it. Rhodes waited, trying to hear what had made Coffee stop so abruptly.

Soon, he heard movement in the undergrowth. The sound was subtle and hard to detect in the increasing noise of the canopy. Something big was moving close to the trail. Close to them.

"Con Ho," Coffee whispered and shivered.

Rhodes knew the Vietnamese word Ho. It meant Tiger.

He turned his head and said as quietly as he could, "Tiger."

Four selector switches clicked to full automatic.

"Cool it," Rhodes said. "Move out, Coffee."

"Con Ho hungry."

"Then let's di-di."

"No light," Coffee said.

"Coffee, we can't sit here and talk about it. We have to find a place to stop until morning."

"Stop here."

"We can't stop on the trail. Find us a night camp."

Coffee didn't move right away. Rhodes could just barely see Coffee's head, but coffee was turning it and listening. He wouldn't let go of Rhodes's hand. He figured Coffee wanted him close so the tiger would have a choice and Coffee could get away while the tiger ate Rhodes. That thought caused him to grin and it also caused him to listen hard to the jungle close to the trail.

Finally, hand in hand with Rhodes, Coffee led the team forward. They traveled another thirty minutes, Coffee stopping to listen frequently. The canopy got higher and the undergrowth next to the trail thinned. Coffee let go of Rhodes's hand and led the team off the trail and deeper into the jungle. He stopped suddenly and stood still.

"Con Ho?" Rhodes asked.

"No Con Ho. Camp near. Maybe VC in camp. Wait."

Rhodes put the team into a night wheel as Coffee slipped away in the night. They remained still and waited. Ten minutes passed and then Rhodes heard Coffee's voice.

"Honcho. Come."

"Easy," Rhodes said. "It's Coffee."

Coffee was suddenly next to Rhodes and scared the crap out of him. "Come," he said.

The night had become pitch black and he didn't know how Coffee did it, but he led them to a cleared area with five nicely dug fighting holes in it. The holes weren't typical roughhewn Marine fighting holes. They were cut neatly, square and plumb, with smoothed sides and a flat bottom. They weren't very deep, but at least they provided some cover. The night was all the concealment the Marines needed. He couldn't see anything five feet from the hole. Rhodes would rather have some deep cover in thick jungle and a night wheel for a harbor, but continuing to move in the almost total darkness was a sure prescription for disaster.

He tried to do a radio check but wasn't surprised when he couldn't reach either Kelly on his mountain or Lutts at Lang Vei. They'd need some elevation to contact anyone with the PRC-25. After they ate, he decided to let the Marines get as much rest as possible with only one man on watch. Coffee ate his LRRP ration with gusto and then curled up at the bottom of a hole.

Sleep didn't come after Rhodes ate. He was too keyed up and his left hand was shaking again. He felt the beginning of twitches in his right eye. Got to settle down, he thought. He leaned back in his hole and let the coolness of the dirt relax him.

He thought he heard something in the brush near the edge of the clearing. His eyes strained to see something through the dark, but he couldn't even make out the brush. The twitching of his upper eye lid got worse. He held his breath to hear better, but the pounding of his heart covered any external sounds. Sweat dripped into his eyes and one drop rolled off the end of his nose and dropped onto his lip. A sound of scraping bushes came again. Wind? Or VC slipping up on his position in the dark? He looked to the side to see if the watch was alert, but he couldn't see far enough to tell if the man two holes down was moving.

He forced himself to relax and let the coolness of damp dirt seep into his back. He listened. Nothing. Rhodes spent another hour on edge, but finally fell asleep when no further sounds got his attention. The watch woke him up at 0200 for his one hour watch.

Nothing happened on his watch and Rhodes was beginning to settle down. The twitch in his eye calmed first and then his hand settled into a slow tremor that was so slight he no longer noticed it. He woke his relief up and curled in the hole to get some rest.

He had just drifted off to sleep when he was awakened so abruptly he tasted metal in his mouth from the panicked adrenalin that shot into his blood. The scream he heard was the most frightening thing he had ever heard in his life. It was death. It was all the horrible things that lived in darkness. It was pure panic and horror. Then, after he had just opened his eyes, a rifle fired on full automatic. It was one of the Stoners. Then, just silence and gasping.

"What the hell was it?" Rhodes whispered. "Where, damn it? Give me something here."

"Con Ho," Coffee said.

"Con Ho? What the hell are you talking about?"

All the Marines were in two holes now and close to Rhodes. Lance Corporal Dean was breathing so loud Rhodes was afraid he could be heard a hundred meters away.

"It was that tiger, Captain. Fuck! It was right there. Right in front of my hole."

He started to settle down. They apparently weren't under attack.

"Settle down and tell me what happened." he said as quietly as he could with his own heart beat drumming in his ears.

"The tiger, Captain. It was staring right at me not five feet away.

"Did you shoot it?"

"Shit! I screamed so loud it jumped back ten feet. I think I pissed my pants like a girl."

Rhodes considered his options for a moment. There weren't many. They had to move.

"Okay, mount up. This position is compromised.

Let's move out."

The team moved deeper into the jungle. Each foot of movement through the trees was creepy. Every Marine imagined the tiger stalking them in the dark. Who would it grab?

Coffee found a thick stand of bamboo. They squirmed between the stalks and formed a night wheel deep inside of the stand. With crinkly dried bamboo leaves covering the ground between the bamboo stalks, nothing was going to sneak up on them. Regardless, no one slept for the rest of the night.

As soon as total darkness lightened to a smudge of dawn, Rhodes moved them out but avoided the trail. Coffee understood Rhodes's caution and took them deeper into the jungle before turning to parallel the trail he had followed during the night. They found a decent harbor an hour later and stopped for breakfast. He needed some elevation to establish communications with Kelly and determine his status. He wanted to reach Kelly that day.

Rhodes gripped his rifle tightly to still the tremor in his hand and tried not to look directly at anyone in the team so they wouldn't see his eye twitching. Got to hold it together, he thought, got to hold it together.

Day two of the rescue mission began.

Chapter 28

The team had to cross the ridge they were following to reach a finger ridge on the other side that would take them to Kelly's hill. Rhodes was hot and itching and feeling his age. The rest of the team was coping with the heat and humidity and trying to conserve water. Coffee was taking it all in stride. He was in his natural habitat. Even the war failed to impress him. Vietnam had been at war with someone all his life and all his father and grandfather's lives and the Montagnards were always caught in the middle of whatever the Vietnamese got themselves into.

The morning hike had been a tense one more because of the tiger than fear of compromise by NVA. Everyone had heard of tiger sightings by other recon teams and infantry grunts, but no one on the team had ever actually seen a tiger. Of course, only Dean had seen the thing, but no one doubted his story and each of them was beginning to invent stories about the smell of tiger breath. If they managed to get back, the team would have one hell of a story to tell. And tell it they would. The dire warnings by CIA people not to talk about their patrols would be forgotten. The tiger story was just too damn good not to share. Each teller would own it for himself and make it a little better with each telling. And each listener would do the same.

Coffee remained on point, a place he seemed to like, and kept the team out of trouble. Later that morning they had to find a harbor and wait for an NVA patrol to pass before they started up the ridgeline. That part of Laos was close to the border and it seemed to be crawling with NVA. The NVA patrolled the area just like Marines patrolled around their own bases, and being in Laos and near their own harbor, they were careless and not expecting to find anything. Fortunately, Coffee had spotted the NVA long before the NVA could have spotted the team. He was turning out to be a major asset for the team. He knew of trails the team would never have found, trails that didn't even look like trails and probably weren't even known by the NVA.

From their harbor, Rhodes scanned the side of the ridge with his binoculars looking for a likely route to the top. The ridge was steep and covered with thick low jungle. In a few places, shallow ravines looked inviting, but he knew he had to stay away from them. The team needed cover to conceal their ascent, so he chose the jungle for the climb. He pointed out the route he wanted to take. When Coffee was ready, the team started up the ridge.

It was a steep climb in loose soil and rocks that gave way when pressure was put on them. Trees grew sideways out of the hill and supported massive tangles of vines. They had to climb over or bore through them to make progress. In the vines, insects buzzed, clicked, and looked for blood. The Marines provided a welcome addition to the diets of bugs and leeches used to feasting on wild animals.

Three quarters of the way to the top, Coffee had to take the team back down a few hundred feet to look for another avenue around a wide stand of bamboo that had become so interlaced with thick vines they couldn't even cut their way through. Coffee found a shallow ravine behind a stand of tall trees leading up, but it was blocked with a thirty-foot cliff about half way up. The Marines used ropes and pinions to scale the cliff and one at a time sprawled on the dirt at the top to catch their breath and stretch aching muscles. Rhodes called a halt for chow and tried a radio check.

Lang Vei answered on the second call and he reported his coded coordinates and shut the radio down. They couldn't see Kelly's hill yet so they wouldn't be able to communicate with him until they reached the top.

While they were eating, they heard hard thumps of artillery or a bomb run to the east. It sounded like a fire-mission just inside of Vietnam. Rhodes stopped counting rounds when he got to thirty. Somebody was pounding the hell out of something. As he listened to the power of the explosions, he decided they were bombs. Artillery wasn't that big. Get some, he thought.

With chow done and trash buried, the team began the final climb to the top in crumbling rock with scrub trees for hand holds. Nearing the top and with thinning vegetation, Rhodes moved the team slowly one at a time, keeping in cover as much as possible.

They reached the rounded overgrown crest at 1030. He put the team in harbor watching their ascent route for pursuit and moved to the opposite side of the ridge. He opened his map and got a fix on his position and then on Kelly's reported position. The finger ridge he was looking for was almost a half klick to the west and about three hundred feet lower than the main crest of the ridge he was on. It was going to be a bitch getting down there. He had known the ridge was a steep one from the contour lines, but steepness can't be appreciated until you see it—and have to climb it. From where he sat, the western side of his ridge looked like a cliff. He'd never be able to get wounded men up that incline.

He squeezed the talk button on the handset.

"Boatload, Boatload, this is Striker Three, Striker Three. Over."

Nothing broke squelch. He adjusted the squelch

control until he heard static.

"Boatload, Boatload, this is Striker Three, Striker Three, over."

Nothing interrupted the static.

"Striker Det, Striker Det, this is Striker Three, Striker Three. Over."

Lang Vei answered right away.

"Striker Three this is Striker Det, Read you five by five, over."

"Striker Det, this is Three, do you have commo with Boatload, over."

"Three this is Det, negative, over."

"This is Striker Three, Roger, Out."

He wanted to ask Lutts at Lang Vei when Boatload last checked in, but he knew he had to limit transmissions to avoid radio direction finders. He switched to the alternate frequency and tried Boatload again without success. That wasn't a promising development. He couldn't approach Kelly's hill until he established that Kelly and his team were still alive and his position wasn't compromised. Otherwise, Rhodes could lead his team right into an ambush. He decided to move along the ridge to a point above the finger ridge and try again.

Coffee slid along the ground up to Rhodes's side and pointed at the base of Kelly's hill. It took a few moments for him to see what Coffee was pointing at. Then he saw movement in tall elephant grass, 700 feet below him if the map was right. He broke out his 7x50s.

With the glasses, moving grass resolved into

four men pushing through heavy grass in two pairs, Marines supporting Marines. He couldn't make out faces at that distance, but he knew who it was. Kelly must have decided to make a try for the border. Shit! That was going to make hooking up more difficult.

They were only about a klick away as the crow flies, but that crow would be flying down the hypotenuse of a big right triangle and Rhodes would have to climb down the vertical side and hump along the base to get to Kelly. He tried the radio again. No answer on the radio. Boatload didn't stop or show any sign they had their radio on. He tried to find a man with a radio antenna sticking up from his back to see if the team even had one, but the grass was too thick to tell.

"Coffee, how can we get ahead of them and get down there?"

Coffee shrugged.

"Get Corporal Dean."

Coffee slid backwards through the weeds and returned a few moments later with Dean

"Dean, take the glasses and look down there where I'm pointing. I think it's Boatload."

Dean looked. He scanned for a few moments and then the glasses stopped suddenly.

"Yeah, that's them, Captain. What do you want to do?"

"Get your mirror out."

"Sir? Every gook in ten miles will see it."

"Maybe. Maybe not. It's a risk. But we've got to let Kelly know we're here. He's expecting a team. He'll know what the signal mirror means. Just hit him with it. Get his attention then put it up."

Dean took his mirror out of his pack and looked for the sun angle. "Keep your eye on them, sir, and tell me if they react."

Dean pointed his arm at the place the team occupied in the grass. He put the mirror next to his arm shiny side down. "Watch," he said and flipped the mirror in an up and down sweep and immediately put the mirror surface to his chest. "Anything?"

"No, they didn't even hesitate. Do it again."

Dean flashed the mirror at Boatload again and this time Rhodes saw the two pairs of men fall to the ground. "Here, keep an eye on them," Rhodes said, handing the glasses to Dean.

"Boatload, Boatload, this is Striker Three, over."

Nothing.

"Crap! Their radio must be out. Coffee you've got to find a way down there for us."

"Hokay, Honcho."

"Dean, give them one more flash, up and down so they'll know it's deliberate."

"It might give away our position, sir."

"Yeah, but it won't give away theirs, and we're moving out."

Rhodes marked Boatload's position on his map and gathered his gear.

Dean signaled one more time with a double flash and the team moved south along the ridge on the side opposite the side facing Boatload. Coffee kept them in high grass near the crest and seemed to know where he was going. Fifteen minutes later he found a trail he called a "pig trail" and the team started down the ridge on Kelly's side.

The "trail" was steep and hardly a trail at all, but something had used it regularly and it did move in the right direction. The team used the ropes to get down the steepest sections, sending one man at a time and lowering their equipment separately. By the time the angle of the incline lessened, no one on the team but Coffee had any reserve energy left.

Rhodes put the team in a perimeter and checked his map. He could see the route of their descent and could estimate where he had been when he signaled Kelly. With that estimate he found his current position and made a mark on the map. Setting his compass on the map gave him the course to Kelly's last known position. Kelly may have continued moving, but Rhodes figured he would cut Kelly's trail at the very least. He double checked the course with land marks he had noted before leaving the ridge and moved the team out through eight-foot-high elephant grass.

Twenty minutes later Coffee suddenly squatted and then dropped to prone in the grass. Rhodes, in second position, signaled the team behind him. Coffee raised up to his knees and put his carbine to his shoulder aimed into the grass in front of him. Rhodes moved his selector switch to full auto and signaled the rest of the team forward. He moved up next to Coffee.

Coffee raised one finger and pointed forward. Rhodes nodded and pointed at the ground and then put his hand on Coffee's carbine and shook his head no.

He spread the team out on line facing the threat and waited. Three minutes later Kelly pushed his head through a clump of grass not ten feet in front of Rhodes.

"Kelly," Rhodes said softly hoping Kelly wouldn't panic and start shooting.

Kelly's head snapped toward Rhodes and then he just collapsed in the grass. Rhodes signaled the team in and knelt next to Kelly.

"Where's the rest of Boatload?"

"Have you got water?" Kelly said with a raspy voice through cracked lips. His face was red and scratched up. His utilities were blood covered, ripped, and filthy.

"Yeah, sorry." He handed Kelly a canteen and watched Kelly take a long drink.

"They're in harbor about fifty meters back that way," Kelly said while gasping and wiping his mouth with a filthy sleeve. "After you signaled from the top we spotted you three times on your way down. Tried to intercept you, but my guys couldn't go any further. We need to get some water to my guys and then get the hell out of here. Probably every gook in ten miles saw you, Captain."

"Why didn't you wait for us in your cave?"

"We had to find water. Can we talk about this later, sir? My guys need water."

"Yeah, sorry. Can you lead us back?"

"Give me another drink."

"Here, keep the canteen."

Kelly took another long pull on the canteen and said, "Follow me."

Rhodes figured he had never seen so much relief on so few faces when he crawled into Boatload's harbor. Kelly was already giving water to Masters, one of the wounded. Rhodes's team moved in and handed canteens to each member of Boatload. Doc Anderson put a canteen to Mendes's mouth and when Mendes was done took a long pull on it for himself. As soon as their thirst was under control, Boatload tore into LRRP packets and had their first meal in two days. They were a sorry looking foursome.

Kelly explained that his radio had failed and changing batteries didn't help. When no one on the team could figure out the problem, he decided to smash the parts and bury them and the batteries rather than lug twenty-five pounds of useless weight with him.

Boatload had made a successful recon of the objective and had moved in close to verify the NVA had armor under camouflage nets. He verified the presence of one tank, but couldn't get close enough to say for sure if there were more. On the way out, the team ran into an NVA patrol and two of the team were wounded before they could break contact. Both were leg wounds from shrapnel and bleeding was quickly controlled by Doc Anderson. The wounded men could only move with help and not quickly even then. Worse, two of their canteens had been damaged and lost a lot of their remaining water. What water was left went quickly keeping the wounded men out of shock.

They made it back to the harbor Kelly found on the hill, a safe harbor in a cave that was almost impossible to find if you didn't have land marks, but after two days with no water, he made the decision to try for the border and not wait for help that might be too late. They spent an entire night getting off the hill, and after several hours in the grass, had seen Rhodes's signal. At first Kelly thought his team was being fired at, but when he didn't get any incoming he waited in the grass to see what was going to happen.

When the double signal happened a few minutes later he knew it was a signal and probably from a team coming to help them. He and Doc began scanning the ridgeline for movement with their 7x50s. He was about to give up when he finally saw movement on the side of the ridge a few hundred meters to the south of where he had seen the signal. He watched closely and saw movement two more times. Kelly estimated where the descending team would reach the valley and started moving his team to intercept whatever was coming.

It was a risk, he told Rhodes. But by that time, they were so desperate for water, if the movement wasn't a relief team, they were in more trouble than they could get out of anyway. He finally had to put the team in harbor because Mendes and Masters couldn't keep going even with help. "Then, there you were," he said. "What now, sir?"

Rhodes stood up and got his bearings. He had a good idea of where they were and knew where they had to go.

"There's no way we can get your wounded back up that ridge," he said. "I'm not sure I'm able to make that climb myself. So, we don't have much choice. This valley runs almost to the border, but the last mile is across two-foot-high grass and full of NVA, according to Coffee. We'll rest for an hour and then try to make it through the tall stuff. Then we'll wait for night before crossing the low grass. The only good thing is this is the shortest way back to the border. Take a break while I check in with Lutts."

Chapter 29

With water and food in them, and seven Marines now to share the burden of helping Mendes and Masters, the combined team began making good time to the east. Coffee wasn't happy about crossing the low meadow at the end of the valley and began walking sullenly at the back of the patrol. Rhodes's didn't have time to deal with a Bru attitude problem, so he ignored Coffee. He was beginning to think they had a good chance of avoiding compromise and getting back to the border undetected. But he knew that was only part of the battle. Once at the border, he still had to get through a klick and a half of jungle and enemy with two wounded men to get to Lang Vei.

As the Marines moved forward and dark approached, the elephant grass and vines got lower and thinner. They harbored at the edge of a large open area covered by low grass moving in the wind and lit with a faint glow of moonlight. The meadow went a mile in the direction they wanted to travel and spread out to the north and south onto rolling low hills for klicks and eventually disappeared into the ridge Rhodes and team had skirted on the way in. Copses of trees jutted up at various places and bamboo stands dotted the plane. Tall termite mounds stood up out of the grass like men standing watch. They were the only cover in sight and they were few and far between.

Rhodes kept the team in harbor until full dark. Unfortunately, full dark that night was only partly dark. An eighth-moon rose from behind the eastern hills, from behind their goal, putting them between the moon and anyone watching from behind and illuminating them for anyone watching from their front. It wasn't a lot of illumination, but he felt like a spotlight was on them.

He had the team lie down while he checked in. Lutts was waiting for his call and after receiving the team's approximate coordinates told him help was being assembled by Sullivan. Just a few klicks more to go. They set out across the open field.

The team was almost to what Rhodes estimated to be the mid-point of the low grass when he heard a sound he didn't want to hear. A single rifle shot. A signaling shot. The NVA and VC often used a single shot to signal to other units in the area when they spotted movement in their area. Then Rhodes heard a sound he really didn't want to hear. Tubing. The sound of a mortar round leaving the tube. The team hit the ground and waited, knowing what was coming.

The first round hit a good two hundred meters to their north. The next round hit closer but to their south. The next hit to the north again, but closer. Then another round hit three hundred meters away to the west. He started the men crawling to the east. 82mm mortars continued to hit randomly around the meadow. It was probing fire. It was frightening, but nothing was hitting close enough to put shrapnel on them. Still, it shattered nerves and caused panic. With the rounds hitting randomly no one knew where the next one would come down. They stayed down and continued moving in a crawl.

Half a mile to go, but at the rate they were moving it would take an hour to get to the jungle cover on the east side of the field. Rhodes kept them moving. The NVA obviously didn't know exactly where they were or who they were and maybe weren't entirely sure they were there. Maybe a sentry had seen something, but wasn't sure, so they were doing recon by fire. He kept the team moving and kept them from returning fire.

Hands and knees were getting raw and lacerated. No one complained. The knee in Rhodes's right utility trouser leg was torn out leaving his bare knee scraping along the ground. Masters and Mendes went as far as they could and then Marines had to drag them.

Suddenly Coffee scooted ahead of the team and disappeared into the grass. Rhodes ignored him. The grass was getting lower and he had to go prone to stay below the tops. He heard a "*Psst*" behind him. The team closed-up behind him and Doc Anderson, his rear guard, bellied up next to him.

"Company coming up behind us, Captain." he said in a whisper.

Rhodes took his jungle cover off and eased his head up. The moonlight was now working in his favor. Spread across a wide line behind them was at least a platoon of NVA on line. At that time, they were just bobbing shadows in the dim light. They were moving slowly and cautiously through the grass. Maybe they would find the Marine's trail in the dark or maybe not. If they did it would be just a matter of minutes before they walked right into the Marine's line. The team couldn't run from the NVA and Rhodes couldn't just let the NVA come up behind without any preparation for the fight. He had to take what advantage he could. The only advantage available was surprise.

He signaled Kelly to his side.

"Let's spread them out on line. Ten meter intervals. Stay prone. No one fire until I do. We'll take as many as we can and then di-di. Everything we have all at once. You take the right flank. I'll take the left. Go."

The NVA had screwed up. With their own people in the grass they couldn't use their mortars without risking their own troops. There was no way to tell who was who on that dark field. Rhodes could use the NVA's own favorite tactic and let them get so close supporting arms were useless. He didn't think the NVA would be ruthless enough to sacrifice their own troops just for the chance to get some Americans. It also helped that they couldn't really be sure it was Americans in the grass.

The Marines snaked through the grass and settled into a long line facing the approaching enemy. Mendes and Masters couldn't walk, but they could still shoot. The NVA platoon was still a good hundred meters away and closing slowly, not sure if anyone was really in front of them, looking for shadows, hoping not to find any. They weren't any different than soldiers anywhere. Some of them were hyper-alert. Some of them were bored and tired and just wanted to get back to their sleeping mats. They'd fight, but they'd rather not.

Rhodes settled down on the left flank and double checked his selector switch. Full rock and roll and sixty rounds of 7.62. He'd soon find out just how good Sullivan's magazine contraption was. He doubted he would empty the drum magazine if he fired fast bursts taking one man at a time working from left to right. Kelly carried an M-14 with a standard magazine. The stoners were in the center and could work outward taking as many in the opening seconds as their rate of fire would allow before the NVA recovered from the surprise. The rest of the team had M-16's with double standard magazines taped together. Together they might be able to take out the entire platoon in the first massive blast of automatic fire. They would certainly even the odds and slow down their pursuers. But then the NVA would have no doubts. Their enemy was in front of them.

Rhodes waited and prayed none of the Marines would get antsy and fire before he was ready to spring his ambush. The ambush had to be one massive blast of overwhelming fire power, so shocking and quick the enemy couldn't react. He eased his eyes above the grass to have a quick look. The NVA platoon was still on-line, slightly illuminated by moonlight, and moving forward, but they had shifted somewhat to the left of the Marine's position.

He ducked down. He couldn't take the chance of letting the Team know about the shift or possibly confusing them with hand signals. The NVA patrol was too close and he might be seen moving through the grass. There comes a point in an ambush when you must accept what fate gives you.

He waited until he could hear the NVA's movements in front of him. He estimated just twenty or so feet. It was time. His Marines were watching and waiting for him to fire.

He rose to a sitting position with his rifle to his shoulder. He saw the shadows directly to his front and moved his rifle down the line immediately. It only took a fraction of a second to locate the end of the line and he pressed his trigger in quick bursts, working the tracers up the line. The rest of the Marines were firing before his first short burst was finished. The entire Marine line let loose a burst of automatic fire that crisscrossed the NVA platoon with tracers. It was total surprise. As the Marines ducked back down to load new magazines they hadn't received a single round of return fire.

"Kelly, take the point." he yelled. "Move out."

Kelly, on the right flank, ran bent over toward the far side of the meadow. Two Marines each grabbed the wounded and pulled them between them. Rhodes brought up the rear. The team moved quickly, but not quickly enough. Before Rhodes had traveled fifty feet he started taking incoming small arms from behind. They hadn't gotten all the NVA.

Traveling in column the team presented a narrow target as tracers passed them on both sides. Most of the fire was directed at their old position though. Rhodes took the handset in his hand as he ran and squeezed the talk button.

"Striker Det this is Striker three. We are taking fire and trying to disengage. Over."

"Three this is Det. What is your position?"

"I don't have time. Running for cover. Stand by."

"This is Det, Roger, standing by."

"Keep moving," he yelled as the intervals began to close-up. "Move it. Go for the other side."

They kept running bent over as low as they could get. Blessedly, a cloud covered the moon and gave the Marines a few minutes of complete darkness.

Rhodes could hear Marines breathing and gasping all the way to the rear.

The NVA platoon had been shocked into a defensive mode. They weren't moving forward yet. The firing from the rear let up and became only sporadic sniping as the gap between the NVA and Marines increased. As far as he knew, none of his Marines had been hit. He kept pushing them. The NVA didn't seem to be in a hurry to follow the Marines now.

The grass they were in was getting higher as they approached the jungle and tufts of elephant grass began to appear. He could see the jungle on the other side of the grass as a blur in the night. When they were a half klick out, Rhodes quickened his pace to overtake the team and began pushing the Marines down in the grass as he passed them. When he reached Kelly, he yelled, "Down."

On the ground, he said, "Keep them in line behind me. I want to angle our approach to the north a couple hundred meters. We're on too much of a straight line. Too easy to intercept. Keep them spread out. I'll take the point." He looked up at the moving clouds in the sky. "We move out as soon as another cloud covers the moon."

Doc Anderson moved up and squatted next to Rhodes.

"Captain, we have to get Masters out of here. That last rush opened his wound again and he's bleeding. I got it stopped as much as I could, but he's still bleeding. He isn't going to make it much further."

"Not far now, Doc," Rhodes said. "Do what you can."

Kelly moved off to place the team where he wanted them and Rhodes tried to estimate his position. He knew the course he had taken and they had held the course well, but he couldn't see any land marks and had to guess based on dead reckoning and use his memory of the map. His best guess was the border was two klicks from where the jungle started with one large ridge to cross. The road back to Lang Vei came in from the southeast, turned, and ran west about a mile south of his estimated position. If he turned southeast when they reached the cover of the jungle, he would parallel the road back to Lang Vei or at least back to the border. He keyed the radio. They wouldn't be safe even when they got to Vietnam, but at least they would be legal and could call for artillery and air support.

"Striker Det this is Three, over."

"This is Det, over."

"Det, this is Three, put Beanie Six on." Rhodes knew Sullivan would be in the TOC and Lutts would know who Beanie Six was. SF were called green beanies for their green berets and the Six was the CO.

A new voice called. Striker Three, this is (pause) Beanie Six."

"This is Three. Reference Briefing. Reference planned route. Striker Three team paralleling reference through area two klicks to north of reference. Estimate legal in four hours. May need help. Over"

It took a few moments, but Sullivan finally

acknowledged the message.

Rhodes moved the team on an angle that would intersect the jungle a few hundred meters north of where he would have entered if he had maintained the same course they had followed across the low grass. The grass was chest high now and mixed with elephant grass, vines and thorns. While it provided more concealment, it was also harder to get through, especially for the men helping the wounded. He realized his estimate of time to reach the border was optimistic.

As they approached the jungle, he sent Kelly and Doc ahead to find a safe route into the trees and see if anyone was waiting for them. He put two men watching the rear and two watching forward then made sure the wounded men were still coping and drinking water. Their water was getting low, but they didn't have far to go.

Mendes was doing well. Masters wasn't. Rough handling was causing his wound to bleed more and the Marine was weak and beginning to run a high fever. Doc was doing all he could, but Masters needed a medevac. That wasn't going to happen until they reached the border.

Kelly returned and said it looked like they had a clear path into the jungle. Rhodes moved them out and within minutes was in elephant grass higher than their heads and movement slowed further. Doc stopped Rhodes and told him he had to rig an IV for Masters who had become delirious. Mendes was holding on, but the pain was showing in his face too. None of them had brought ponchos, favoring instead a lighter load, so they had no way to rig a stretcher. Doc rigged the IV. Two Marines carried Masters, and Doc Anderson held the IV above the patient. Six men were tied up getting Masters and Mendes through the undergrowth and the task had them all exhausted. That left only Kelly and Rhodes to break trail and bring up the rear.

They struggled through the grass, the canopy getting closer in the night, more than just a smudge on the sky now. He did what he could to crush a path for the men behind him, but his energy was giving out. He had only a few gulps of water left in his last canteen and knew he had to save that for the wounded.

As they entered the canopy, the struggle lessened in thinning grass and vines. Rhodes called a halt at the last of the thick grass to harbor for a few minutes and let the men carrying the wounded rest. He sent Kelly ahead to see what was south and east of them. He shared the last of his water with Mendes and Masters while he waited for Kelly to return.

Kelly was gone for almost half an hour and Rhodes got worried. The NVA would eventually find the Marine's path through the tall grass and even though they'd do it cautiously and slowly, they would be coming up from behind soon. He sent Dean and Raleigh back along the path a few hundred feet to man a listening post and give a warning if the NVA approached their position.

When Kelly returned, he pulled Rhodes aside.

"Captain, that gook you brought with you is south of here," Kelly said.

"Coffee? Did he wait for us?"

"Yeah, but probably not on purpose. He's dead."

"How'd you find him?"

"You'll see," Kelly said. "We better get moving."

"I'll get these guys up. You go back on the trail and bring Raleigh and Dean in. They're about a hundred meters back."

"Yes, sir. Do you have any water left?"

"No, I gave it to Masters and Mendes. Check with Doc. He might have a little."

"On my way," Kelly said. "Let's get the hell out of here."

Chapter 30

Kelly retrieved Dean and Raleigh and the team moved out on a south-easterly course. Kelly took point. They moved deeper into double and triple canopy jungle with the undergrowth thinning more almost every foot. Soon Kelly led them to a trail and the team's struggles lessened. After fifteen minutes he stopped the team and signaled for Rhodes to come forward. Rhodes moved up to Kelly's side and squatted next to him.

"What's up?" he whispered.

"Look, right there," Kelly said with his hand extended.

Rhodes looked in the direction Kelly was indicating, but all he could see was the dark outline of trees.

"What?" he said.

"Hanging on that tree," Kelly said, pointing again.

Rhodes concentrated and tried to see what had Kelly's attention. He squinted and thought he saw something on a tree truck that didn't belong there.

"What is it?"

"Coffee, your gook," Kelly said.

"Jesus! What'd they do to him?"

"Nailed him to a tree. mutilated him. Want a closer look?"

"You sure he's dead?" Rhodes said.

"Yeah, and missing parts."

He thought for a moment. Marines didn't leave Marines behind. Coffee wasn't a Marine, but he had been part of the team. Still, they didn't have enough Marines left to carry him. Shit!

"We'll have to leave him and come back for him later. Can you find this place again?"

"Maybe with a company of Marines."

That's not going to happen. We still have a klick and a half to the border. I have a pretty good estimate of where we entered the canopy. We'll have to estimate from that."

"Should we pull him down, Captain?"

"Do you think he cares?"

"No."

"Let's di-di." Rhodes said.

Moving along the trail under the canopy was much easier than moving in the grass even on the small ridges they were crossing. Then on the upslope of the final ridge about a klick from where Rhodes estimated the border should be, Kelly stopped the team. Rhodes moved up to see what the holdup was. He knelt next to Kelly.

"What's the problem?"

"That," Kelly said while pointing.

Rhodes squinted to focus on what was ahead. At first all he could see was more dark and outlines of trees. Then he noticed the difference. In one area ahead of them, light was getting through from above and the trees were more distinct than any of the surrounding trees.

"There's light getting through the canopy," he said in a whisper.

"Looks like it," Kelly said. "Should we see what's up there?"

"I don't like surprises. Let's get the team in some kind of harbor and you and I can check it out."

There were a few outcroppings and downed trees on the ridge side, so Rhodes got the team under as much cover as the surroundings provided and started forward with Kelly. They moved close to the ground and from tree to tree. The closer they got the brighter the area in question got. Moonlight. They bellied the last hundred feet to the edge of a clearing. Each foot closer to the clearing brought a stronger stench until finally it was all they could do to keep from retching.

The jungle stopped abruptly and ahead of them was a stretch of churned and plowed ground with broken tree trunks strewn around as though some giant had ripped them up and snapped them in two before tossing them around randomly. The canopy was gone and clear sky could be seen above. The cleared stretch was ragged and about a hundred meters wide. It ran in a straight line the length of three football fields right up the slope. Massive craters pock-marked the ground surrounded by large piles of scattered dirt. The stench was overpowering. Rhodes covered his mouth and nose with his sleeve and crawled into the eerie moonscape.

What he had thought were broken branches of trees sticking out of the ground were human body parts. Arms and legs. He knew what he was looking at. From the size of the craters he figured they had been made by big bombs, maybe a mixture of 750s, 1000, and 2000 pound bombs. The Air Force had been just a smidge off on their navigation and bombed half a klick inside of Laos. Probably the noise they heard that morning. The smell of decaying flesh filled the air. Body parts poked up out of the earth surreally in the moonlight like a scene from a B-grade horror movie. The earth itself carried the stink of corruption and death. The bodies had cooked in the sun all day and bloated and burst during the night.

He signaled Kelly to move back. Then he had a thought. He stared at the churned-up earth for a moment counting the putrefying flesh and bone markers of shallow graves. A large group of people, or soldiers were partially buried in that mess. Seemed like a strange coincidence that a mistake in navigation put the bombs right on top of a . . .what? . . .company of NVA? Why didn't the NVA come for their dead? They were as good about not leaving their dead behind as Marines were. They would come in the dark of the night. Like when it was as dark as it was right then.

"Let's move," Rhodes said when he reached Kelly. "We've got to get around this mess and get over the ridge."

They discussed how they wanted to skirt the bombed area and moved back to the team and organized them to move out. Both the wounded were holding on, but Masters was getting worse. He was moaning softly.

Kelly took point and led the team to the north to skirt the bombed area, but staying close to its edges to keep from going too much off their course. Every hundred feet off course meant another hundred feet carrying the wounded back to the course.

As they reached the mid-point where the slope leveled out for a hundred or so feet, they still had about a football field's length of bombed area to get around. The slope got steeper on the other side of the level stretch they were on and with the weight of the wounded men the team would be getting slower. Kelly called a halt before crossing the level area where the trees thinned and cover was sparse. After listening and watching the deep shadows for a few seconds he rose slowly and started into the relatively open area. Two steps. Bent over. Keeping a low profile. Another step and it happened.

At first it was just a rustle in the low undergrowth to the front and right. Then behind them also to the right. Then directly to their right. The sounds of moving men under the canopy grew closer and extended further to their front and rear. Nowhere to go but to the left. Right into the bombed-out patch of destroyed jungle.

Kelly led the team into the broken timber and craters looking for concealment and cover. He hoped to lead them through and to the other side, but the sounds had been too close. With the moon and opening in the canopy they wouldn't make it across before whatever was coming would spot them. They had to hide. On an extended flat plateau running almost to the jungle cover on the other side, Kelly chose a crater. If they had to run for it the flat area would give them a chance. He led the team in.

Masters and Mendes were sheltered near the bottom of the hole against the ragged side. The rest of the team checked weapons and ammunition and prayed whatever was coming wouldn't come looking for them. By the sounds, it was more than a platoon spread out on line with good intervals. Rhodes wanted his team spread out in more than one hole, but no other holes were close enough to keep the team together and it was too late now in any case. And the place stank. The buzz of blue-tailed flies was almost constant. He saw Raleigh gag. Control it, boy, he thought. Rhodes slid down to the bottom of the hole.

"Kelly, help me cover the light."

Kelly reached in Rhodes's pack and took out his air panel. Rhodes went prone on the dirt with his map in his hand and Kelly covered him. The red flashlight cap worked fine for what Rhodes wanted. Red light was hard to see in the dark and the little that would escape from under the panel on the bottom of the crater couldn't be seen from the edge of the bombed area. He estimated their position as near as he could and squeezed the talk button on the handset.

"Striker Det this is Striker Three, Over."

Lang Vei answered right away.

"Three this is Det, over."

"This is Three. Status. Team has two bingo walking. Harbored at the following location."

Rhodes read off the shackled coordinates.

"Enemy in sight. Estimate a platoon plus. No way to evade. Will attempt to remain concealed. Over."

"Three this is Det. Roger. Are you in immediate danger of compromise? Over."

"This is Three. Not compromised yet, but that could happen within minutes."

"Three this Det. Keep Beanie Six informed. Over."

"This is Three. Roger out."

Rhodes turned the flashlight off and slid out from under the panel.

"Fold it back up," he whispered. "If we're lucky they won't look too closely at this hole. Most of the bodies seem to be concentrated on the lower half of the area. I *hope* that's all they're looking for."

He had a quiet word with each team member and then settled against the crater side. He didn't want to fight unless they absolutely had to. Their water was gone and their ammunition wouldn't last long. He watched the jungle and figured the odds may have caught up with him this time. He watched some more. No movement from under the canopy yet.

A whisper from the radio handset. Rhodes grasped it and squeezed the talk button. There was a hint of movement in the trees.

"Say again," he said quietly into the handset.

"Three this is Det. what is your status?"

"This is Three. No change. Over"

"Roger. Beanie Six is working on something. Hold on as long as you can. Over"

"This is Three, Roger, out."

The hint of movement in the trees became outlines of men in the dark. First, one man stepped out of the trees into the relative openness of the broken ground. The small amount of light on the scene suddenly dimmed as clouds moved across the moon. Just before the dark was total, Rhodes felt a chill as silhouettes appeared out of the trees all along the length of the bombed-out area. Maybe fifty. Maybe sixty. No way to tell now that the light was gone.

The clouds thickened over the night sky reducing visibility to almost zero. The clouds were high and wouldn't be bringing any rain so they weren't really much help or hindrance. Kelly slid in next to Rhodes.

"Knives?" he whispered.

Rhodes understood the question. If the NVA kept spread out to search the area for bodies, maybe only one or two would come close enough to the Marine's hole to spot the Marines in the dark. They'd almost have to climb down in the hole to tell. It was worth a try to silence them without giving away the Marine's presence. One or two might not be missed in the dark with all the digging and carrying off bodies, at least for a while. Maybe long enough.

"Yeah," he whispered. "Maybe we'll look like gook bodies in the dark. It's got to be quick and quiet. Make sure somebody is right next to Mendes and Masters."

"Got it," Kelly said.

The handset whispered from Rhodes's shoulder.

"Three this is Beanie Six, over."

"Three."

"Can you evade to east and find an LZ? Over."

"Negative, Six. Bandits in sight. Over."

"This is Six, roger, out."

Chapter 31

As Kelly moved from one Marine to the next, Rhodes heard the faint sliding sound of K-bars being pulled from scabbards. He doubted any of the team had ever had to kill in that kind of up-close and personal fashion, getting blood on your hands. Few Marines did. Knife work was only necessary when a unit is being overrun and hand-to-hand combat ensues. Would they hesitate? No. They were Marines . . . and they wanted to live.

It took a while for the first searcher to approach the Marine's crater. Soft sign-song Vietnamese could be heard from several points around the Marines. The searchers were moving all over the bombed-out area and several had moved to the east of the team. Although the NVA didn't know it, they had surrounded the recon teams and now Rhodes had no avenue of retreat.

He heard the *fluka-fluka* sound of a helicopter off to the east. Over Vietnam. Close to the border by the sound of it. Just a klick away, a short half mile, on the other side of the ridge. Might as well be a thousand miles away. No help there. A rock dislodged and rolled through rubble just a few feet from the crater. The Marines froze against the side of the crater. Shuffling steps in the rubble getting close to the lip of the crater. Slow steps. Cautious steps.

Rhodes saw movement to his left, but heard no sound. Kelly moved soundlessly against the side of the crater to a spot directly under the approaching footfalls. He pushed up the wall flat against the dirt and waited. Then dirt broke free from the lip and fell on Kelly.

It happened so fast, Rhodes almost missed it. Hardly a sound. One moment Kelly was motionless. The next moment he reached up, grabbed an ankle and jerked the NVA soldier down so fast the soldier didn't even have time to yell. Kelly was on him and had him silenced with only a few scuffle sounds. Even with the smell of putrefying bodies filling his nostrils Rhodes smelt the coppery smell of fresh blood. He slid up the side of the crater to the lip and took a cautious look around.

He couldn't make out details, but he could see motion. The NVA were scattered all over the broken ground. There seemed to be more of them than he saw in the brief moment of light when they stepped out of the canopy. Motion and sounds of movement in all directions. No opening. No way to evade. If they were discovered, they'd have to fight their way to the east giving up their cover.

Damn, that helicopter sounds like it's getting closer, he thought. The sound of rotors was getting louder and sounded like it was coming from just above the top of the ridge. He looked hard, but there was nothing but dark up there. And then he forgot all about helicopters.

A voice was calling in Vietnamese from just a few feet away. Rhodes ducked down and pressed against the dirt. The voice got closer. The Vietnamese words sounded slightly different than he was used to from his time in the CAG, but the gook was calling for his friend, probably the friend lying on the bottom of the crater bleeding out. And then the dumb fuck walked right over the lip of the crater.

As he fell, the NVA soldier not only screamed but managed to fire his AK on full automatic. Kelly was on the soldier and had his K-bar through the soldier's throat before he realized what happened. Rhodes thanked God for Kelly, a hell of a thing to do, considering.

Several NVA fired in the direction of the sounds. It was crazy firing out of fear and shock. Shooting at phantoms. Striking back at the fear and dark. Suddenly a whistle sounded from the south, another sounded from the east, and the panicked firing ceased quickly. Scattered quiet voices became command voices, and scattered random movement became organized.

Rhodes hurriedly checked to see that his Marines had formed a perimeter around the crater. Kelly was on the job. The perimeter was formed about as well as six Marines could manage. Masters couldn't get to the lip of the crater and had to curl up near the bottom. The rest knew what to do.

NVA soldiers were moving in the direction of the shooting they had heard. They were organized and on edge, but they weren't quite sure of the source and it had been AK47 fire, a sound they were familiar with. There had been no answer to the AK47 so they couldn't be sure if anyone but their own troops was there. Maybe just someone firing at shadows. All those things would go through the commanders' minds.

Cautious footsteps and occasional stumbling. Rocks kicked and sounds of disrupted clutter traced the progress of the advancing line. More commands in the night. The Marines remained quiet. They had targets, but they also had concealment for the time being.

The first probes reached the area of the crater a few moments later. A round came from the east, the tracer a few feet above the hole. Then another shot in the dark. Then another. Recon by fire, trying to draw fire, trying to locate the Marines. The Marines knew what was happening and held their fire. The radio whispered from Rhodes's handset.

"Striker Three this is Shadow One, Over."

Who the hell is Shadow One? Rhodes thought.

"Shadow One this is Striker Three, Over," he whispered into the handset.

"This is Shadow One, what is your status? Over."

"I'm being probed. Taking small arms incoming. Over."

"Are you the tracers, half way down the ridge?"

"That's them, but we're in that area, Over"

"This is Shadow. Roger that. Can you mark your position? Over."

"Shadow One this is Three. Where and what the hell are you? Over"

At that instant one of the Marines got nervous and fired at a shadow out in the churned earth. The Marine's luck had turned bad. The round was a tracer. That one red tracer was all it took. Automatic weapons opened-up on the crater from every side. Green tracers flew just inches from the lip and bounced off rocks.

"Grenades," Rhodes yelled.

Marines began pulling pins and tossing grenades to all points of the compass. Returning fire with rifles and tracers would further pin-point their position. Grenades falling out of the air with no idea where they were coming from would cause panic and confusion. The Marines needed both right then. Incoming increased as the NVA commanders brought up more troops, but the scattered nature of their tracer pattern indicated the NVA company still wasn't sure where the Marines were.

"Striker Three this is Shadow One. I'm your chariot. I see the tracers. Mark you position.

Screw it, Rhodes thought. The gooks are going

to find us now anyway. He turned on his flashlight and put it on the lip of the crater with the red light shining up at the sky. He couldn't take the chance the NVA might be listening in on the transmission and hear him describe his marker. They could then duplicate the marker somewhere else and confuse the pilot.

"Marker out," he said into the handset. "Tell me what you see."

"Roger. Stand by."

He heard the rotors getting louder but still couldn't see the helicopter.

"Striker Three, I see a red steady light."

"That's us," Rhodes said into the handset.

"Roger. Get your heads down."

Suddenly he heard the whirring, burping sound of a mini-gun. The churned-up earth around the crater began to erupt in geysers of dirt. The gun worked its way around the circumference of the crater and then worked its way outward from the hole.

"Striker three, have you got anything that even looks like a usable LZ down there?"

"Roger, Shadow One. Directly to the east of my position is a flat area. Maybe forty feet long with a slight slope to the south, over"

With the sound of rotors in the sky the enemy shifted some of their fire at the sound, but plenty was still hitting the lip of the crater.

"Roger," Shadow One said. "Let me check it out. You've got incoming from everywhere. Can you put some smoke out to give me a little cover?"

"Smoke on the way," Rhodes said.

"Kelly, use the Blooper and put smoke all around us about fifty feet out. Everybody else start putting down a base of fire. Now! let's do it."

Kelly began loading smoke rounds in the M-79 and blooping them high, working his way around the circumference of the crater. The rest of the Marines began firing bursts of automatic fire into the dark. The incoming small arms slowed as the NVA got their heads down. The sound of rotors got loud just to the east of the hole.

"Close your eyes," the voice on the radio said. "I'm going to light it up."

"Cover your eyes," Rhodes yelled.

Then a blinding floodlight lit up the whole hillside. It was only on for a second or two, but even through closed eyelids it left a green spot in everyone's eyes. It probably blinded the NVA not expecting it.

"Striker Three this is Shadow One. Mount up and get your people to the LZ. I'm coming in. I can take seven. Over"

"Roger, roger, roger. Mounting up now."

"Get Mendes and Masters. Kelly, lead them out to the chopper. I'll bring up the rear and give you some cover."

Kelly waved his hand and the Marines moved quickly. Two men pushed Mendes over the lip and followed him. Doc and another Marine pushed Masters over the lip and they followed. Kelly led them forward as the all black CIA helicopter appeared out of the dark sky like a dark ghost and began to hover. The CIA and SF had come through after all and risked their own asses, and probably careers as well, to get the Marines out of Laos. CIA stock went way up in Rhodes's emotional portfolio. He fired bursts to all points of the compass hoping to keep the NVA down for just a few seconds, just long enough to get his Marines on the bird.

The helicopter dropped and hovered just a foot off the ground. The Marines with help in sight got a charge of energy and got the wounded to the helicopter through the dust storm being kicked up by the rotors. They got the wounded loaded and Kelly helped the others up to the door. NVA incoming began again and increased. Shadow's door gunners fired at every direction they could reach in long sustained blasts. Rhodes crawled over the lip of the crater and ran bent over toward the chopper.

Kelly was on the ground returning fire. Incoming tracers flew through the dust and clanked against and through the skin of the helicopter. Rhodes ran to the chopper and yelled and waved for them to leave. He dropped next to Kelly and added his fire to the cacophony of rotors, flying dust, incoming, and machinegun fire from the bird.

The rotors beat harder and the bird began to ascend creating a stinging maelstrom of flying dust and ear splitting noise. In the dust cloud raised by the rotors, Rhodes grabbed Kelly's shirt and pulled him up and to the east through the blinding dust. Incoming rounds were piercing the dust cloud from all directions, but at least the NVA couldn't get sights on the two Marines.

The pilots must have seen what they were doing and moved east with them keeping them in the dust cloud. The chopper began drawing all the incoming, so Kelly and Rhodes could sprint hard toward the canopy on the east side of the bombed-out area. Their mouths, noses and eyes were full of dust and they had to trust to luck to keep from running right into the NVA.

Finally, the dust cloud began to thin and the pelting of downdraft from the rotors lessened. Rhodes saw the shadow of a mound of dirt and led Kelly behind it. The Helicopter lifted and the sound of rotors diminished to just the distant *fluka-fluka* of the departing bird.

"We've got to keep moving," he whispered.

"Flat on the ground. They'll figure everyone got out on the bird. I'll take point," Kelly whispered back.

The firing from the NVA was continuing but it all seemed to be focused on where they had been. As they crawled away the firing dropped off to just probes and individual sniping.

"Striker Three this is Shadow One. Over."

"Not now!" Rhodes hissed into the handset and hooked it back on his shoulder.

They stayed prone all the way to the canopy and then ran bent over into the tree-line. Kelly turned up-hill and they moved toward the crest of the ridge and the border on the other side. Rhodes's throat was dry and breathing was difficult. Kelly was no better off. When they reached an outcropping just a few meters from the crest, Rhodes called a halt for a rest in the rocks.

They slid up on a rock overlooking the area they had just left and watched the activity, but their recon was disappointing. Other than a few hints of movement in the dark they couldn't see anything.

"Striker Three this is Shadow One. Over."

"Shadow One this is Three. Go ahead."

"Roger. Goods delivered. No further damage. Over."

"Shadow One this is Striker Three. Let me buy you a case of beer sometime. We are evading and moving to that magic line."

"Roger that. Find an LZ and check in."

"This is Striker Three. Roger. Out."

"It's going to be light soon, Captain" Kelly said. "Want to harbor for a while or keep moving?"

"Let's keep going. We need some water."

"Yeah and when it gets hot we're going to really need it," Kelly said.

"Let's get down this ridge at least before light. You want me to take the point?"

"Yes, sir." Kelly said. "That would be just fine."

After a long struggle down the ridge and shedding anything they didn't need, Rhodes stopped them in a patch of jungle.

"Help me get the radio off my pack. I should

have gotten rid of the pack when you did."

After he had the pack off, he stuffed a few things in his pockets and carried the radio in one hand. He wondered how long the batteries were going to last. He had no spares now. He put the map and shackle sheet on the ground and composed a message. He put the handset to his ear and squeezed the talk button.

"Striker Det this is Striker Three. Over."

"Striker Three this is Striker Det. Reading you weak but readable, over."

"This is Three. Standby to copy. Message follows. 01, 83, 24, 61, . . . "

In shackle code, Rhodes gave his current estimated coordinates, the course he was taking into Vietnam, and his expected border crossing coordinates. He added he was bingo on water, food and ammo. A very weak reply came back.

"Striker Three, roger your message. Stand by to . . . "

"Striker Det this is Three, say again your last transmission, over."

This time Striker's transmission was broken up and garbled.

"Striker Det. You are weak and garbled. Say again. Over."

Rhodes turned the squelch all the way off so everything would reach the handset. He only got loud static.

"Shit!" he said. "I don't know if it's their radio or ours. At least they acknowledged the message. We'll try again when we get across the border."

"Same course?" Kelly said.

"Have to. I gave them our position and our route home. If they send help it will be along that route."

"Better find some water soon, Captain."

Chapter 32

Dong Ha
3rd Recon Battalion

Major Slaughter looked up when he heard someone enter his office.

"Major, I'm getting a run around from those SF people in Lang Vei," Captain Lang said. "They keep saying Captain Rhodes is unavailable."

"Did they say why?"

"No, sir. I can't get any sense out of them. They keep telling me something new every time I call them. They said try again tomorrow on my last call."

"How about Kelly? He and Rhodes are tight. He ought to know what's going on."

"I thought of that. Same story. He's not available. Try again tomorrow."

"Well, who the hell is available? Somebody has to be available."

"Seems like the whole detachment is on patrol," Lang said.

"That's bullshit. Rhodes wouldn't have the whole damn unit out on patrol at one time. Someone must be standing down, as a reserve if nothing else. Get in touch with whoever is the senior man at Lang Vei and let me talk to him."

"I'll try, Major, but I haven't been able to get past the Communications Sergeant so far."

"Do what you can. The colonel said to get Rhodes back here today even if we have to send a bird down there to get him."

"What's the hurry, sir? Coats is going to release the teams back to us in a few days anyway."

"Don't let this get around, but admin screwed up on Dick's commissioning paperwork and the Exec is trying to claim Dick isn't even an officer. Don't ask. Whatever it is has put a twist in the admin officer's panties. He's screaming to the Colonel that Dick's status is in limbo. His commission can't become final until he signs some damn form and swears to a half dozen things. I think the exec is using it to try to embarrass the Colonel. I wish someone would tell those pogue son of a bitches we're trying to fight a damn war here."

"So, he's still a master guns?"

"That's the problem right there. No. He was

discharged to accept a commission. That paperwork was done correctly. Officially, no one knows exactly what his status is. Hell, maybe he's a civilian until he signs the damn form and swears to whatever it is that's so important. In effect, we potentially have a civilian commanding a detachment of Marines. Get Lieutenant Marks ready to leave for Lang Vei to relieve Dick so we can get him back here to sign the damn form and make everything official. Christ, I hope nothing happens before we get that done."

"I'll try Lang Vei again, Sir. Do we have a bird to get Marks down there yet?"

"I'm working on it. Get things moving."

Chapter 33

Kelly did find a small pool of scummy water and they both had a mouthful or two. When they reached the point where Rhodes felt like they had finally entered Vietnam, what little help the water had provided was gone. If anything, their thirst was worse than before. The jungle was so dense Rhodes angled them southeast to try to intersect with the road. They had made only a small amount of progress when they heard artillery off in the distance—from the direction of Lang Vei.

The sounds of battle grew. Apparently, Lang Vei, or something nearby, was taking a pounding. The explosions didn't sound like big artillery, more like mortars, but there were a lot of them. They pushed on, but began to wonder what they were pushing on towards. If Lang Vei was getting hit, then NVA/VC were between them and Lang Vei. After an hour had passed, Rhodes tried the radio again.

"Striker Det this is Striker Three, over."

"Striker Det this is Striker Three, over."

Nothing.

"Well," Kelly said. "That's that, I guess."

"Yeah. I better save whatever juice we have left. Let's di-di."

"Wait," Kelly said. "What the hell was that?"

They stopped and listened. The sound of small arms came again.

"That's Ak-47s. There's a lot of them. Listen."

The distinctive sound of the AKs came again and then a different weapon. A very fast automatic weapon. Rhodes knew the sound from the Special Forces camp.

"That's a Stoner. Do the NVA or VC have Stoners?"

Then came a smaller cracking sound on full automatic.

"Carbine," Kelly said. "Who the hell is out there?"

"Let's go find out."

"Captain, those guys are in a fire fight."

"Yeah and one side is American or ARVNs. They probably have water and ammo. Let's go.

They came in on the fire fight from the right flank. There were a whole lot of Ak-47s and maybe a few SKSs on one side and just a few, maybe only a Stoner and a few Carbines on the other. Grenades were crumping on both sides.

"How much ammo do you have?" Rhodes asked.

"Most of one Magazine. One more full."

"Crap! I'd like to enfilade them, but that's out. Let's circle and come up behind the good guys."

"They might blow us away before we can identify ourselves."

"You got a better idea?"

"Yes, sir, Captain Rhodes, sir. Di-di the fuck out of here."

"Ain't gonna happen, Kelly. You want point?"

"I wouldn't deprive you of the honor, sir. You just go right ahead, Captain Rhodes, sir."

"Fuck you very much, Kelly."

"We're both fucked. Let's go."

Rhodes took the point and moved away from the fight and then turned back to come up behind the sound of the Stoner. He didn't know who they were, but the AK-47s were shooting at them. That was good enough for him. There weren't any good guys in that neck of the woods with AKs. They bellied through brush for the last fifty feet. Rounds passing over the American's position shattered branches over their heads. He was sure there had to be at least one American up there because of the Stoner. When they were very close to the Stoner, a chicom grenade landed fifteen feet away and took most of Rhodes's hearing away, but the shrapnel went over them. He started talking.

"Americans coming in. Americans coming in.

Hold your fire. Americans coming in."

"Mr. Striker! Don't shoot at them. Stop! It's Mr. Striker."

Rhodes poked his head through a thick bush and there in front of him were Lennon and two Bru. He pushed his way into the small clearing they were occupying behind a vine covered basalt rock outcropping.

"Lennon, give me your canteen."

Kelly crawled into the clearing and one of the Bru pulled his canteen out and handed it to Kelly. The each gulped half a canteen and then handed the canteens back, gasping with water running down their chins.

"What's out there, Lennon?"

"A whole lot of Vietnamese, Mr. Striker. The camp has been getting hit hard with a bunch of mortars and they wouldn't let the teams come out to find you. There's Vietnamese everywhere. Me and Tea and Milk got out anyway and came to . . ."

Several rifles on automatic opened-up on the outcropping and two chicoms exploded against the rock. A fewer number, but more troublesome, opened-up from in front but out to each side. The Bru each emptied a magazine at the flankers.

"You can tell me later. What's in those bandoleers?"

Lennon and his Bru all had several bandoleers of ammunition slung across their chests and stuffed in their packs. The only things they brought with them was ammo and water and their personal weapons.

"Most of its seven point six two," Lennon said. "Your message said you were out of ammunition. We brought you some."

"Kelly, get a couple bandoleers. Give me two, Lennon. How many grenades do you have?"

"A bunch," Lennon said and patted his pack over his shoulder."

"Everyone take three grenades. Now!"

They all straightened pins and waited for Rhodes's orders.

Rhodes made an Arc with his hands and mimicked tossing the grenades. Everyone pulled a pin.

"Now." Rhodes said.

They each tossed grenades across an arc in front of the rock. He pointed to Kelly and the left flank. They both tossed a grenade deep on each flank. The others continued tossing until all the grenades in front of them were gone.

"Let's get out of here. They're going to get around us. Kelly, take the point."

Three Marines and two Bru moved back the way Rhodes came in. They only went about fifty feet when the Bru moved up and took the point together. Rhodes didn't object. The Brus' asses were on the line too, and they knew it.

The small group evaded Charlie for the rest of the day. Lennon and the Bru brought plenty of ammo and plenty of water. That's all they brought and they brought as much as they could carry. It was going to get hungry, but at least they had water and they could shoot back.

They harbored several times in thick jungle and moved away from help. At least that's how Rhodes saw it, but he decided to trust the Bru. They were obviously afraid and he figured it was like being a passenger on an airplane. The pilot doesn't want to crash any more than you do. And they were in the Brus' backyard. He let them decide where to go.

At one point he suspected they were back in Laos and by dark he was sure of it. The last land marks he found before the sun went down confirmed his suspicion. Well, at least they were alive. The Bru took them north in the dark and then led them into a jungled ravine on a ridgeline. Half way up the ravine the Bru stopped and waited for Rhodes to catch up.

"Honcho sleep here," Tea said.

Rhodes pulled the team in and set up a night wheel. After listening for sounds of pursuit and hearing none he took a spot next to Lennon.

"Lennon, how did you know where to find us?"

"I didn't, Mr. Striker. You found us."

"But you were close. How'd you do it?"

Lennon took a map out of his utility pocket and shook it at Rhodes.

"What's that?"

"It's the map, Captain. The Army Captain plotted your messages on the big map in the TOC. I copied everything down. I had a good idea of where you should be and my Bru buddies said they could find you.

We only had to go about a mile. Then we got found by the Vietnamese."

"So, you just saddled up and came out to find us?"

"Yes, sir. They wouldn't let the teams out of the base. Staff Sergeant Lutts was really pissed-off."

Rhodes stared out into the dark for a moment.

"I don't know if I should recommend you for a medal or a court-martial," he said. "In any case, thank you. Do you think your buddies can get us back to Lang Vei?"

"Yes, sir. They'll get us back."

"Okay. Get some sleep. We have a long hike in the morning."

Rhodes took the first watch. The whole team was exhausted, including the Bru. The silence of the night closed in and a dense fog settled over the ridge and into the ravine. He relaxed slightly. Nothing that didn't have the senses of an animal could find them in the thick milky fog the French called crachin, or cracking, or some frog word like that. All he knew was the white crap was thick, thicker than any fog he had ever seen. He had marked his map when they entered the ravine so he had a good idea of where they were, but without a working radio there wasn't much value in pinpointing his location. He pulled the useless radio close and picked up the handset. He should have dropped the damn thing and put a bullet through it to save the weight, but he'd kept hold of it. The battery still had a little juice in it.

He put the handset to his ear and turned the power on.

Static. He turned the squelch until the static stopped, but kept the handset to his ear. Maybe he could pick up a little chatter from Lang Vei. He started to yawn and froze.

"Striker Three this is Cold Weather, over."

He was so shocked he didn't answer.

"Striker Three this is Cold Weather, over."

"Easy Time this is Cold Weather. Negative contact. His radio is probably dead. over."

The signal was strong. The teams had to be nearby. Rhodes pressed the talk button.

"Cold Weather, Cold Weather, this is Striker Three, Striker Three, how do you read, over."

The voice that answered was excited and loud.

"Striker Three this is Cold Weather. Read you weak but readable. Stand by."

"Easy Time this is Cold Weather. Contact. I say again. Contact with Striker Three, Over."

"This is Easy Time. Roger. Striker Three this is Easy Time. Over."

Easy Time this is Striker Three. Loud and clear. Over."

Everyone in Rhodes's team woke up and squirmed close to him.

"Striker Three, Easy Time. You are weak but readable. What is your Status? Over."

"This is Three. In harbor. No casualties. Have

Boatload pitcher and two Mountain men along for the ride. Do you have striker three shackle with you? Over."

"Three this is Easy time. That is affirmative. Request shackle meet. Over."

"This is Three. Three directs Easy Time and Cold Weather to harbor. Contact first light. Acknowledge."

"This is Easy Time. Roger, out.

"This is Cold Weather. Roger, out."

Rhodes immediately turned the radio off to save power. He just needed it to last for one more transmission. He talked quietly with his team.

"The teams came out. They're out there and I think they're close. At first light, I'll encode the coordinates for a rendezvous. Now get some sleep."

He stretched out on the stones and tried to let go, but couldn't. He needed rest. He now had his teams together, almost. The excitement of finally having friendlies close was too much and his eyes remained wide open. He looked around the wheel and his eyes stopped on Lennon. That little shit, he thought. Unbelievable.

Chapter 34

It was a hungry awakening for Rhodes's team in the morning. Their backs were coated with a film of dew and every one of them was stiff with cramping muscles. He made sure they all drank some water and kept them in harbor waiting for the fog to lift. By 0800 the fog had thinned and he took Kelly and climbed up the ravine to try to get some land marks to fix his position. Two hundred feet up the ridge he was out of the fog and could see enough of the hill tops around him to get a good estimate of the Ravine's coordinates. After encoding his current coordinates Rhodes studied the map with Kelly and picked a rendezvous point inside of Vietnam and not too far from his current location. He turned the radio on.

"Easy Time, Easy time, this is Striker Three,

Striker Three, over."

Easy time must have been waiting for his call because he answered immediately.

"Striker Three this is Easy time. Authenticate Bravo, over."

Rhodes ran his finger across his shackle sheet, found bravo, and picked a letter in the same column.

"Easy Time this is Three. I authenticate Charlie. Stand by to copy. Message follows . . ."

He read off his encoded coordinates and the coordinates for the rendezvous. Then he read the numbers for the short, encoded message telling Easy Time and Cold Weather to meet Striker Three at those coordinates. Easy Time told him to stand by.

Easy Time took a few minutes to decode the message and encode his own message. When Rhodes was sure he had Easy Time's message he told them to stand by while he decoded their message. It turned out that Easy Time and Cold Weather were harbored within a hundred meters of each other and only a half klick from his position. He changed his plan

"Easy Time this is Striker Three. Cancel my last. Remain in place. Striker Three is proceeding your location. Acknowledge. Over."

"This is Easy Time. Copy remain in place. Striker Three moving to our location. Be advised. Your signal is very weak but you are still readable. over."

"This is Striker Three. Roger, out."

Rhodes turned the radio off and pointed down the ravine.

"Let's di-di," he said. "We'll get a compass fix on the teams when we get back to harbor."

Kelly took point and the Bru didn't try to interfere. Coffee had been the only map expert apparently. These guys knew the terrain, but they couldn't read a map. The team moved down the ravine carefully. The rocky, brush covered ground was difficult to move over on a down slant. The rocks were large and the brush filled all the space between them.

They were spread out with ten meter intervals. Lennon brought up the rear and kept his Bru in front of him. Rhodes was in front of the Bru and Kelly walked point fifteen meters in front of the team. They picked their way slowly to the bottom of the ravine. Kelly stopped in elephant grass that bordered the beginning of single canopy jungle and waited for the rest of the team to exit the rocks. Rhodes closed-up on Kelly to about five meters and the Bru moved up close to Rhodes and squatted together holding hands. Lennon sat down on the last of the big rocks to slide over it instead of trying to push through the brush around it. In doing so he was exposed momentarily to the surrounding jungle. That's all it took.

Unknown to the team, they had been followed the previous night and a platoon of NVA were waiting and watching. The NVA had been unwilling to follow them into the ravine at night and set up their own harbor just inside of the canopy fifty meters from the mouth of the ravine. As Lennon paused on top of the rock preparing to slide down to the ground, one shot sounded from a tree in the canopy. Lennon was knocked backwards over the rock and didn't make a sound.

The Bru were the first to reach Lennon, sliding around the rock like snakes and disappearing. Several other shots sounded from the canopy and Rhodes and Kelly had their hands full returning fire. Rhodes tried to move back to Lennon, but was pinned down by automatic weapons fire. Kelly was in grass with good concealment, but no real cover. Small arms rounds pierced the grass around him and all he could do was hope.

Rhodes called to Kelly and told him to move back under covering fire. He immediately switched to full automatic and swept a full magazine across the canopy with his M-14. They made it back to the rocks before the NVA got their heads back up, but they were pinned down again before they could get to the rock Lennon was behind. Rhodes grasped the handset and squeezed the talk button.

"Easy Time this is Striker Three. I am pinned down near my previous coordinates and can't move. Can you reach my location? Over."

"Striker this is Easy Time. We hear the noise and are on our way. Echo Tango Alpha fifteen minutes. Over."

"This is Striker. Estimate a platoon of regulars. Easy Time and Cold Weather take the flanks. Over."

"This is Easy Time. Roger."

"Captain, the gooks probably have reinforcements moving up too," Kelly said.

"Can't help that. See if you can get around to Lennon. We need his Stoner."

"Give me some cover."

"Go!"

Rhodes fired bursts into the trees at grass top level. He emptied a magazine and quickly loaded a fresh one. As soon as he started firing again, Kelly wormed his way through the brush around Lennon's rock. Rhodes eased up. He was beginning to worry about their ammo supply. Lennon and the Bru had brought a lot, but they were going through a lot also.

"It's a head wound," Kelly called. Rhodes felt a sudden bleakness and sense of loss. Then Kelly continued. "It's not serious. It just cut the hell out of his scalp. Bloody as hell. Maybe a concussion. He's still out, but I think he'll be okay."

"Get the Bru up here with their weapons. I need cover."

"The assholes bugged out. They're gone."

"Cover me with the Stoner."

"Okay, tell me when."

"Now!" Rhodes yelled.

Kelly cut loose with the stoner and Rhodes dove toward the rock with incoming hitting around him. He pushed and squirmed through the crushed brush left by Kelly and the Bru. As soon as he got behind the rock he went straight to Lennon. He lifted the bandage on Lennon's head.

The slice across Lennon's scalp started at the crown of his head and ran partially down the back of his scalp. He must have been looking down when he was hit. His scalp was laid open all the way to the bone. Either the Bru or Kelly had used the bandage in Lennon's med-kit on his cartridge belt to slow the bleeding. Rhodes pressed the bandage back on the wound and retied the gauze under Lennon's chin.

"Movement in the grass," Kelly said.

"Wondered how long it would take for them to move forward." He looked around. "It's going to take some time for them to flank us. They can't do it in the ravine so they have to go up both sides and come down from above us. Hope Lutts gets the teams here pretty soon."

"They've stopped shooting. What do you think they're doing?"

"Maneuvering. Hand me a grenade."

Kelly opened Lennon's pack and pulled out two M-26 frags. The kid had brought half a ruck full.

"Keep one and toss it when I do," Rhodes said. "You throw right. Not too far out."

"Hold on. Let me get two more out. Maybe we'll scare up a target."

Kelly handed Rhodes another grenade and they both pulled the pins on the grenades they had ready.

"Twenty, twenty-five feet," Rhodes said. "Then get ready to do it again. Ready?"

"Yeah," Kelly said.

"Now!"

They tossed their grenades and ducked down close to the ground behind the rock and grabbed their second grenade. The first two exploded and Rhodes heard a scream from the left.

"Again," he said. "Both to the Left. Further out. Now!"

Two more grenades sailed up in an arc and landed maybe forty feet out from the rock. Ak-47s opened-up from the grass and Rhodes held Kelly down near the ground.

"Ready with the Stoner?" he said. Scatter a magazine your side."

Kelly nodded. Rhodes checked his M-14 and wished he still had the big drum magazine. But maybe not. They were going through a lot of ammo. He looked at Kelly and mouthed, "Now."

They both raised up enough to get their muzzles over the rock and fired into the grass at waist height. Neither of them emptied a magazine before they had to drop down to avoid a fusillade of automatic weapons fire. Incoming rounds struck their cover and ricocheted into other rocks ricocheting back into their small hide. Rhodes could feel the shock of rounds hitting the dirt near his feet. There was nothing they could do but hunker down and hope nothing hit them.

The NVA or VC, whatever they were, seemed to have a goodly supply of ammo. The incoming continued for ten minutes almost uninterrupted. They returned fire in short bursts whenever they could and kept the enemy away from the rocks, but they were getting closer.

Then a new sound added to the cacophony of incoming AK-47s on full automatic. A Stoner from the left joined by the sharp sound of M-16s on full automatic. Then an M-14 on the right and the *crump* of M-26 grenades out further in the grass. Marines on the right and left shouted a war cry and suddenly the NVA found themselves in the same position they had recently put Kelly and Rhodes in. They were flanked and getting slammed with automatic weapons.

The incoming stopped hitting their rock and the sound of AK-47s began getting further away and changed to single fire. More grenades exploded probably a hundred meters away near the canopy. Then a voice on the radio.

"Striker this is Easy Money. Hold your fire. We're coming in, Over."

"Easy Money this is Striker. Roger. Holding fire. Make a lot of noise."

"Roger. We're fifty feet in front of you and on your left. Moving in now."

"This is Striker Three, roger."

Lutts brought his team in at ten meter intervals. Each recon Marine in Easy Money found a place in the rocks and formed a perimeter. When he reached Rhodes, Lutts called Cold Weather and brought them in talking to them all the way. When the last of Cold Weather reached the rocks, Rhodes had eighteen Marines with him and only one wounded.

Cold Weather's corpsman went straight to

Lennon.

"Why didn't you bandage his leg?" The corpsman asked.

"He just has a scalp wound," Kelly said.

"Not any more. He must have taken another in his leg during the fight. He needs a medevac right now."

Rhodes took over.

"You and you. Carry Lennon. Lutts I want you in the middle of the column. Kelly bring up the rear and don't let them straggle. Ten meter intervals. Let's move out. We've got to get back to Vietnam and call a medevac."

The column moved out through the grass and reached the canopy without any contact. Inside the canopy, Rhodes stopped the column and called Kelly and Lutz forward. They compared maps and agreed on their current position. They were close to the border and Lutts knew of a clearing from one of his recon patrols where one slick could get in to medevac Lennon. The column moved out again.

Chapter 35

Lennon had lost a lot of blood and had never regained consciousness from his head wound, but Rhodes was still hopeful. If they could just protect the kid and get him on a slick, he had a chance. Doc said he needed to get Lennon out as soon as possible. Rhodes moved the column along as quickly as he could, knowing he had enemy in the area and the teams were risking an ambush. He had lost so many good men over his twenty-one months of combat and every one of those losses weighed on him. He was *not* going to lose Lennon!

Lutts took them to the clearing and used his radio to call for a medevac. The teams made sure the perimeter was clear of enemy and moved back to Rhodes. He wanted UH-34s for an extraction, but he had to make sure Lennon got out first. The kid was looking bad and Doc was worried. Don't you dare die on me, Rhodes screamed inside his head.

Rhodes, Lutts, and Kelly deployed their Marines in a perimeter to protect the Evac slick and waited. The slick had to be deployed from Camp Carroll and the FAC gave Lutts a fifteen-minute ETA. As Lutts was talking to Lang Vei to give Sullivan a status, Lennon's Bru buddies ran out of the brush in the trees and almost got wiped out.

Rhodes spotted them as soon as they broke cover and had to shout to keep them from getting slaughtered by the Marines. They ran straight to Rhodes.

"Beaucoups VC, Honcho."

"Where?"

The Bru who was talking pointed with his hand and circled the whole perimeter.

"Beaucoups," the Bru said.

"How close?"

The Bru shrugged.

"Kelly, Lutts, come here," Rhodes shouted.

"The Bru say the VC are all around us. Lutts, work out an on-call 360 pattern and call it into Khe Sanh right now. Kelly make sure the Bloopers are positioned to cover the full circle. Get the Stoners and fourteens set up in place of machine guns. Distribute all of Lennon's grenades and ammo. I'll talk to the gunships. Go."

They each got their tasks done and the Marines

tried to dig in with whatever they had, mostly K-bars, but two Marines had entrenching tools, one in each team. Nobody wasted time on getting deep. They just tried to scrape out a place to get below ground level lying down.

"Three minutes," Lutts shouted. "Get down. The gunships are going to work the surrounding jungle. Throwing yellow smoke now."

The Marines laid in their shallow cover and waited for the Huey's to rock and roll. Yellow smoke marked the LZ. Then it came. Two Gunships came in. One hovered over the clearing and worked the jungle with his guns.

"One minute," Lutts shouted.

The gunships hadn't drawn a response from the VC supposedly in the jungle around them. Rhodes began to hope they could get Lennon out of there and start moving to Lang Vei or a larger LZ without a fight. Then the flutter of rotors was over them again. It was the slick this time.

The pilot talked to Lutts to get a status on the LZ and then started descending into the clearing when he was told the LZ was quiet. Doc and two Marines carried Lennon closer to the center of the clearing and waited for the slick to get low enough to load. The slick hovered about ten feet off the ground, his door gunners ready on their guns. The pilot turned the tail away from the men holding Lennon and settled to the ground.

As soon as the helicopter touched down, Doc and his helpers loaded Lennon, and Doc climbed on board with him. Rhodes hated to lose a Doc, but Lennon had lost so much blood he wanted the Doc with him until he reached Charlie Med at Khe Sanh. The slick began lifting off as soon as Doc was on board. Oh God, yes, Rhodes thought. The kid is safe. Go! Go! Get him out of here.

And that is what the VC/NVA had waited for. The Bru had been right. The VC were out there, but they were interested in more than the Marines. As soon the slick was above the thirty-foot canopy automatic weapons opened-up from a couple hundred meters away. The gooks wanted a helicopter more than they wanted the Marines. You didn't get anything but praise for wiping out Marines, but a helicopter was special. POWs had told about the rewards for getting a helicopter. At least a visit home. Sometimes even a cash reward. They had slipped in quietly and waited without revealing themselves, knowing the helicopters would come.

The VC gunners were dialed in on the airspace above the LZ with enough distance to see the slick clearly. They waited for the slick to lift slowly and pause before dipping his nose to pick up speed. The VC nailed him when he paused. They poured it on. Multiple automatic weapons. Rhodes could hear the slugs from automatic weapons ripping the skin of the chopper and shattering the cockpit glass. Louder clanks and bangs rang out when a slug hit the rotors or the engines. He saw the cockpit windshield shatter and the sparkle of windshield falling from the slick.

Then a smoke trail rose from the jungle and traced a wobbling path toward the wounded slick. Oh Jesus, no, Rhodes screamed.

At first it was just a flash of light, but then one of the rotors collapsed and the smoking hulk of what had been a Huey slick slammed back down into the LZ and parts flew in all directions. Rhodes, overcome with the sudden change in events, ran toward the wreck. He made it about ten steps before the small arms from the perimeter started. The shock of a glancing round that hit his side spun him around once and caused his feet to tangle in the undergrowth. He went down hard.

The Marines opened-up on the flashes in the undergrowth along the tree line. Rhodes tried to stand and get to the helicopter, but he tripped again and stayed prone as incoming zipped over his head. The VC were so close the sounds of firing couldn't be distinguished from the sonic pops of the rounds passing by. His side was stinging, but he didn't feel anything seriously wrong.

He began crawling, his eyes locked on the smoking wreckage. He was only about thirty feet away when the slick exploded. A wall of flame and intense heat rolled across the brush and grass and engulfed him. Instinctively, just before the fire hit him, he curled into a ball, turned his head, and covered his eyes. The puff of flame was only on him for an instant before it dissipated, but that was long enough to burn the exposed side of his face, ignite his hair, and start his utilities smoldering.

The pain on his face and hands started immediately. He wanted to scream. He wanted to jump up and run. He wanted to escape his pain and torment, but he could only curl up and try to endure the pain. Then he felt tugging at his feet. He was pulled backwards through the burning grass and brush, his face and hands rubbing along the dirt and grass. He screamed and kept screaming. Then Kelly was squatting next to him and swatting at his utilities. Kelly took off his utility shirt and smothered Rhodes's smoldering hair with it.

Incoming was still saturating the LZ and the teams were responding as hard as they could, but the VC were spread out around the LZ and there were a lot of them. Incoming small arms were hitting all around Kelly and Rhodes. Then, considering the volume of fire, the inevitable happened. As Kelly bent over trying to cover Rhodes's face with a large bandage, a round found Kelly. A round tore through Kelly's throat and he fell across Rhodes, his fatal wound bleeding across Rhodes's blistered face.

The VC began moving in on the Marines in the LZ. Lutts pulled his circle in, closing-up his perimeter as each of the Marines were picked off by VC marksmen. Lutts tried to work artillery and gunships in, but the VC had done exactly what they had planned. They were now so close the gunships couldn't engage the VC without endangering the Marines.

A 60mm mortar exploded within ten feet of Rhodes and Kelly, but Kelly's body absorbed the low shrapnel that reached them. The concussion from the round knocked Rhodes out.

Sullivan and a company of CIDG had set out from Lang Vei as soon as Lutts reported the teams moving toward the LZ. By the time they reached the Marines, and put pressure on the VC from the rear, Lutts had lost eight Marines KIA and all the remaining Marines were wounded at least once, but they had held out. The disciplined fire of ten Marines beat back rush after rush by the VC. The VC tried, but they were trying to take a squad of Marines with more than fifty feet of open ground on all sides. Ten disciplined marksmen piled up VC bodies in a large circle around their perimeter. Before the VC could deplete the Marines' ammo, Sullivan showed up with his CIDG and began attacking the VC from the rear. With the tables turned on them, the VC began slipping away into the jungle. It would be a happy night in the VC camp. They had got their chopper and slaughtered some Marines to cap their day.

Chapter 36

"Jesus!" Sullivan said when he and Lutts finally found Rhodes and Kelly. "Both of them got blown away."

"Help me pull Kelly off the Captain," Lutts said.

They lifted Kelly and Rhodes groaned. His eyes opened and he tried to sit up.

"The Captain's alive," Lutts said. "Just lie still, Striker. Let us see what's wrong with you."

"Face. . .hands. . .burn," Rhodes said.

"Okay, sir. Don't move. Corpsman! Corpsman up!"

The corpsman arrived and did a quick exam. He only had to look at Kelly and feel his neck. Rhodes seemed to be breathing okay, so Doc wasn't worried about his airways. He cut Rhodes's utility shirt off and found the grove across his ribs on his right side. Doc decided that wound could wait and began examining Rhodes's hands and face. He poured some water on his face and scalp and gently blotted the blood away from the skin. The blisters could be seen through the blood, but now the burns could be seen. Doc estimated second degree burns, partial thickness, but was afraid there could be third degree damage. Not the emergency confirmed third degree burns would be, but still extremely dangerous because of infection from the filth that covered them. And burns had a way of progressing in severity over the first two days.

Rhodes held up his hands. Doc looked at them and pushed them back down. He cleaned the burns as much as he could with water. He found the ointment he wanted in his unit-one and covered the burns as much as he could until Rhodes couldn't handle the pain any longer. Then he cleaned the burns on his hands. While Lutts called for another medevac, Doc bandaged Rhodes's burns and side wound.

"Do I have to go out on a slick, doc?" Rhodes said. "I think I can walk."

"Yes, sir, you're going out. Here, take these. They'll help with the pain." Doc gave Rhodes two big Motrin pills and held the canteen for him. "Your wounds aren't dangerous yet. But the burns are going to get infected if you don't get proper burn care immediately. You're going out on the bird, sir."

"How bad are the burns?"

"Don't worry about it. You're good, sir. The surgeon can do a better assessment than I can."

Doc covered Rhodes's burns with a sterile dressing and finished bandaging his side wound.

"Just stay still till the slick gets here, Captain," Lutts said. "They're three minutes out."

Rhodes was taken first to Charlie Med at Khe Sanh and then transferred to NSA Hospital at Marble Mountain in Danang. Everything happened fast at Charlie Med. They were treating casualties from operations in the hills around Khe Sanh and didn't have time or resources to deal with border line severe burns. At Charlie Med, the surgeon confirmed the diagnosis of second degree partial-thickness burns to the face and hands. While the burns didn't cover a significant amount of body area, they were in critical areas. The surgeon wasn't a burn surgeon and didn't want to diagnose burn depth or decide if the burns needed excising and grafting to promote healing and prevent contractures. IVs were started for fluid replacement and a catheter inserted to monitor fluid loss. The burns were further cleaned and the surgeon applied antibiotic ointments and decided Rhodes had to be moved to a sterile environment and provided a higher level of care than the field hospital could provide. Since Rhodes wasn't experiencing shock he was given morphine for pain and sent out on the next medevac flight that left Khe Sanh.

Things happened ever faster at Danang. There was a window of just a few days to make decisions about burns and surgery. At Danang the surgeons and burn specialists felt Rhodes's hands were safe and would heal without contracture in about two weeks. He would have some scarring, but hand function was safe. His face and partial scalp wounds bothered them though. The upper part of the left side of his face, left ear, and the left side of his scalp above his ear had second degree burns that had blistered. Based on the blistering, color of the dermis, and moistness of the wound, they felt reasonably sure the burns were shallow enough to recover without surgery with only minor scarring and didn't want to excise any of the burn bringing about the need for skin grafts. But the location bothered them. If they were wrong, Rhodes could end up with contractures on his face and severe scarring.

The surgeons decided to medevac Rhodes to the states for further evaluation while there was still time to make decisions. Rhodes went out on a medevac to the Naval hospital in San Diego the following day. Low doses of morphine were controlling the pain, he was recovering his strength, and was ready to mutiny against the restrictions being placed on his movements—until the doctor held a mirror so Rhodes could see his burns. After that he did what he was told. Only two days and part of the day he was wounded had elapsed when he found himself over the pacific and on his way to Norton Air Force Base in San Bernardino, California. The whirlwind transitions were overwhelming. His Marines were still in Lang Vei and so was his mind.

Once on the ground in California, Rhodes was transferred to San Diego by ambulance. Three days after he was hit, he was in the burn unit at San Diego Naval Hospital. San Diego not only had a good burn unit, but they also had access to all the burn specialists in the area.

He was seen by a lot of people, but he had one visit that left him shaken and wondering what to do next.

"Morning, Captain. Mind if I look at your wounds?"

The nurse smiling at him wore Lieutenant Commander gold oak leaves on her collar.

"Might as well," Rhodes said. "I seem to be an interesting specimen by the number of people lifting my bandages."

She had a pleasant smile, but it was the smile of a professional doing her job.

"I'm sure it feels that way, but we want to make sure you have the best possible care. I'm Commander Lennon from the hospital at Pendleton. We're expecting you to spend some time with us when San Diego gets done with you. I just need to get a look at you to see what we need to plan for. How are you feeling?"

"Like a pin cushion," Rhodes said. "So, this isn't my last stop before I can get back to my unit?"

"Are you in a hurry? Enjoy the break. You won't be going back until your wounds are healed."

"How long will that be?" Rhodes said.

"Let's take a look."

Nurse Lennon lifted his bandages and studied his burns for a few moments. She replaced the bandages and pulled a chair up next to his bed.

"Well, you'll be here for a while. Can't say how long right now, but figure on a month at least. Infection is the biggest danger at this point. Let me look at your chart."

She skimmed through the doctor notes on his chart and then returned to the top page again. She read for a few moments.

"Your doctor has requested consults from local burn specialists, but he seems to feel you are on the mend. Why don't you wait and see what he says? From the looks of your burns and your chart I'd say we'll be seeing you at Pendleton in about a month."

"Thanks for that much anyway," Rhodes said. "Will you be checking on me?"

"No. I think I have all I need. Hopefully, I'll see you in about a month."

He watched her as she walked out of the room. Not bad, he thought. A little plain, but not bad. No rings, but probably married to the Navy. He put those thoughts away. The last thing he was interested in right then was a female's rear end—well, maybe not the last thing, but close.

He was still groggy from jet lag and battle fatigue and wasn't thinking clearly yet. After about an hour, with a nagging memory trying to rise to his conscious mind, it hit him—Commander Lennon! From the hospital at Camp Pendleton! Lennon's big sister? Could there be two Commander Lennons at Pendleton hospital? Oh Jesus. She didn't know. How long would it take for a notification team to find her? Should he try to get in touch with her and tell . . .No! The Corps had its own process for notification. They knew how to do it right. But he had to be sure.

He was seen by five burn specialists before his doctors decided surgery wasn't necessary. They did keep him for a month, his burns healing and looking better every day, his psychological state getting worse. As his wounds healed and concern for his own health decreased, memories of Lennon and Doc Anderson began haunting his mind. Concerns for Lennon's sister and what he would say to her took away what little peace he had found.

The crashing, burning helicopter flashed in his mind over and over. Part of it was the event itself. Much of it was the accumulated effects of twenty-two months of combat. The sudden change from the desperate fight for his life to a safe and clean hospital bed ten thousand miles away and complete separation from his Marines had an effect he didn't expect. He was thrown into an agitated depression full of guilt. The looming meeting with Lennon's sister deepened his guilt. He knew he had to face it.

He didn't expect the depression, but his doctors did. Noticing his deteriorating emotional state, his primary physician called in a clinical psychologist. After two meetings with Rhodes and hearing Commander Lennon's name mentioned several times along with Rhodes's expectation of being moved to the Marine base at Pendleton, the psychologist requested nurse Lennon visit with Rhodes again and just try to get him to talk out his concerns. She sounded reluctant, explained to the doctor that she was dealing with a personal tragedy of her own, but finally agreed to do what she could.

Early one morning Commander Lennon surprised Rhodes by wheeling in his breakfast tray.

"Well, Captain Rhodes, it seems you will be joining us at Pendleton before long. How's your appetite?"

He was shocked out of speech. He had just been thinking about her and how he should handle telling her about her brother. He stared at her. She looked haggard and tired, but she also looked professional in the detached way of nurses. Did she know? Was he wrong? Was there another Commander Lennon? He covered his shock and blustered through the uncomfortable silence.

"I . . .I could eat a bear. I thought I wouldn't see you again until I got to Pendleton."

"Don't sound so shocked. It's my job." she said. "Your move is getting close and I wanted one more check to be sure we're ready for you. Everything going okay?"

"Seems to be," Rhodes said and pulled the tray stand close to cover his nervousness. "The Doc said I'm healing well. What's going to happen at Pendleton?"

"Not much really. You'll finish recovering and the Marine Corps will decide what's next on your schedule. Still anxious to get back to your unit?"

He opened his fruit cup and lifted the cover off his breakfast plate. He took the napkin and put it across his chest. What could he say?

"Not anxious," he said. "But I'll be glad to get out of the hospital. Tell me something . . ."

"Yes?" she said.

He couldn't hold it back any longer. "Did you have a little brother in the Marine Corps in Vietnam?" he blurted.

Commander Lennon's face blanched and she stumbled and had to grab the breakfast cart to keep from falling. She managed to regain her balance and straightened up quickly. It took a moment for her to regain her composure and she stared at Rhodes with a slack look on her face the whole time. Finally, color returned to her face and she used her hands to straighten her uniform to gain some time. She took several deep breaths and then pushed the cart back over Rhodes and straightened up the food tray. With nothing left for her hands to do, she stood with her head bowed for a few moments.

"Did you know Terry?" Her words were almost a whisper.

I didn't even know his first name, Rhodes thought, and said, "Lance Corporal Lennon worked for me. I was there when he . . .when he . . ." the grief he had been suppressing suddenly rose up and overwhelmed him. His throat tightened and cut off his words. His eyes moistened and he choked back a sob.

Rhodes went rigid fighting the grief down and trying to regain his composure, but all he could do was clamp his jaw shut and shake.

"Oh God!" Commander Lennon cried. "Captain Rhodes. How did I miss that? You're Mr. Striker. You're him. Terry idolized you."

Then she noticed what was happening to Rhodes. The grieving sister subsided and the nurse took over. She moved to his side and put her hand on his face.

"Okay, Captain. Come on, take a deep breath for me. Good. Another now. Deeper. Hold it. Now let it out slowly. That's it. Now breathe in for three and out for three. Ready? One, two, three. Now out. One, two, three. Let's do it again . . ."

His heart began to settle down. The color in his face turned from pale to normal. His breathing slowed and the quick catch of emotion in each breath disappeared. He took a few more deep breaths while she watched him. Finally, he felt like he could talk again.

"I'm so damn sorry," he said. "I didn't put the name together with what Lennon told me about you until after you left, and I didn't know if you had been notified yet. I was going to call you. I really was."

"It's okay, Captain. Settle down now. Let me pull a chair up. God, my behavior was so unprofessional. So, Terry told you about me? How'd that happen?"

"It was just once. He mentioned he had written you about me. He said you were his only real family. I guess that's why it took so long for it to come to me when I first got here."

"You two were close?" she said.

"No. Well, maybe."

"Which is it? No or maybe?"

"Commander, I was a Master Gunnery Sergeant at the time, and Lennon was one of my Marines. You try not to get close to the troops you lead, but Lennon was one of the better ones. I guess we were close in the sense that I tried to look out for him. He always seemed so damn vulnerable . . . but he was a tough little son of a . . .I mean he was a good Marine."

"Terry? It's hard for me to think of him as being tough, but you're right about the vulnerable part. He was vulnerable, especially in the Marine Corps. Why in the world he joined, I'll never understand. I probably should have stopped him."

"Why?" Rhodes said. "He was a little swishy in his manner and that caused him some trouble, but under fire he was as cool as any Marine in the teams."

Commander Lennon watched his face for a few moments. Rhodes could see the sadness there and something else. Curiosity maybe.

"You obviously didn't know," she said.

"What?"

She watched him a few moments longer with a small smile on her lips.

"Nothing, Captain. I like the way you remember him. I think I'll make your memories of Terry mine. I received the notification of his death two days after I visited you. I didn't even make the connection with your name until just now. If you think you can talk about it, what can you tell me about his life over there?

Nurse Lennon spent three hours with Rhodes that morning. They talked about Terry Lennon and a lot about other things, but he didn't share anything about himself or his career. She tried to get him to tell her about his experience in Vietnam, but he spoke only in generalities. She wasn't sure how much good she had done for him, but Rhodes was smiling a lot more by the time she left. She was sure he had brought her a measure of closure. At least Terry had had a friend in Vietnam. Her grief was still raw, but talking with someone who had cared about her brother and was with him in his last hours helped. Commander Lennon related her visit with Rhodes to the psychologist who had asked her to make the visit and then she returned to Pendleton.

At the end of his month stay in the burn unit Rhodes was transferred to the hospital at Camp Pendleton for final recovery, evaluation, and transfer back to an active unit. The Docs were pleased with the way his burns were healing, but they were worried about his mind. They'd leave it to the Marine Corps to decide if he needed help the burn docs weren't qualified to provide. As far as they were concerned, you had to be half crazy to be a Marine in the first place.

By the time he arrived at Pendleton, he no longer needed to keep the wounds covered. His facial burns were now recovering with red and pink skin. There was some scarring on his cheek and on the side of his head, but it wasn't nearly as noticeable as he thought it was. His ear was an angry red mess, but his hair was beginning to grow back in. He thought he looked like a freak, but it didn't take a lot to convince him he was a lucky man. Two faces visited him each night to let him know he had gotten off easy.

He was moved out from Lang Vei so quickly and then moved again to Danang and then San Diego, he never did find out how the battle at the LZ had turned out. He was anxious to get back to his unit and find out what the toll on his teams had been. He knew he had lost Doc Anderson, and Lennon, but he didn't know about the rest of the teams. He wondered if Kelly had gotten the teams back to Lang Vei. He had to find out. When the Marine Corps Psychologist visited him to decide if he could go back to his unit he knew he had to play the game right.

Playing the game for the psychologist was easy for Rhodes. He played the game regularly in the war zone. Every leader did. No matter how bad you felt, you didn't let it show. You were the man your team was looking to for strength. If you let down your guard and showed your feelings your whole team suffered whether it be a company, platoon, or recon team. You were always "on". You had it under control no matter how bad it looked. You were the guy who knew what to do. Always. You knew what came next. You were the guy who held it all together even if you were dying inside. And when you lost a man, well, that was war. You counseled others to move on. One pogue psychologist was nothing.

The visit with the psychologist went well and things began to move along quickly. He hadn't seen nurse Lennon and wondered why. After convincing the psychologist he was just tired but stable he had a visitor from Admin.

"Captain Rhodes?"

"Yes, sir," Rhodes said to the Major holding a folder at the foot of his bed.

"I'm Major Tucker. I have some paperwork that needs to be filled out and some decisions I have to get from you. First of all, two additional clusters for your purple heart have been approved. That leads us to the second item. You now have four awards of the purple heart. Policy is to transfer a man out of the combat zone after three wounds. As an officer, you may choose to finish out your tour if you prefer. That's the first decision I need from you."

At first Rhodes felt a wild exhilaration and hope, but as quickly as his spirits rose he felt a shot of guilt. His Marines were still back in Lang Vei and he was lying on his ass on clean sheets.

"You mean I have an option?" he said to gain some time.

"Yes. If you wish to exercise your right to be moved out of combat, I'll begin processing new orders for you. If you choose to stay with your unit, I'll begin processing transportation back to Dong Ha. Would you like a couple of days to think about it?"

"If I choose to return, can I get a few days leave to get some uniforms. I only have utilities right now."

"I'm sure that can be arranged. I'm authorized to approve up to a week delay in reporting."

He thought about it for a moment, but no longer. What the hell did he have to keep him in the states anyway? Everything that mattered to him was in Vietnam.

"I don't need any time to think about it. Get me back to my unit."

"You're sure? You don't have to decide right now. Take a couple days and think it through."

"No, sir. I want to get back to Third Recon Battalion. Let me have a week to buy my uniforms and I'm ready."

"Well, that takes care of that. Saves a lot of paperwork too. You are being released from the hospital tomorrow. I'll set you up for a flight sometime after Monday a week. Now, if I can get your signature on something that's a little unusual. Captain Rhodes, do you remember signing this form when you did the paperwork for your commission?"

The major looked very hard into Rhodes's eyes as if trying to tell him something. Rhodes caught the caution in the major's voice.

"Is it important, sir?"

"It's very important that you remember, Captain."

"Let me see, sir. I signed a lot of forms."

"Sometimes important forms, forms that could cause a lot of administrative problems and have an impact on your commission if they were lost, can get lost," the major said handing the form to Rhodes."

Rhodes looked the form over. It was just one more piece of administrative bullshit as far as he was concerned. He had to swear by signing that he had never done a lot of things or belonged to any of a list of organizations. Somebody had screwed up, but the major said it was important that he remember. A hint?"

"Yes, sir. I remember this form clearly because of the list of all those organizations. I signed the form."

The major relaxed slightly.

"Things happen," he said. "That one is predated to the day you did your paperwork. If you're sure you signed it before, could you just sign it again? I'll see that it gets in your file."

He signed the form and handed it to the Major.

"Thank you, Captain. That saves me a lot of grief. Have a nice leave."

Rhodes had to get a Navy Corpsman to make a run to the officers clothing store for him. After the Major left he realized he didn't even have utilities. His were cut off him in the field and he hadn't been in a uniform since. The corpsman got a new set of utilities with rank, boots, socks, and underwear for him and even went to the PX to buy and stock a shaving kit. The little kit the hospital issued was about shot.

He checked out of the hospital in the morning and checked into the transient BOQ on Pendleton. His face was still tender and he had to apply ointment four times a day. His side wound was healed and the scabs had fallen off. Otherwise he felt good physically. He spent the day lying down in the BOQ.

For some reason, he was reluctant to go outside and walk around on a safe and secure Marine base. He put off going out for several hours and thought about the trip back to Vietnam. Around 1700 his stomach started rumbling with hunger. He dressed slowly and stared at the door a lot.

He started to go out and stopped. He sat down on the bed. Suddenly he felt like his life was rushing out of control toward something unpleasant, unreal. So many changes were taking place so fast he couldn't catch up. He felt like if he went out that door and everything was normal and routine, the sun was shining, America was right there, he'd come apart. He stared at the door for another fifteen minutes breathing deeply, getting his nerves under control.

Finally, he stood up and checked his uniform. Good to go.

Chapter 37

Utilities turned out to be acceptable for one section of the club. The base was conducting training operations twenty-four hours a day and officers had to eat. Rhodes ordered the steak special with French fries and a long neck Bud. Now that he was out of the hospital, out of his room, and the world paid no attention to him, and Marine Corps routine continued regardless of his presence, he began to absorb the familiar sights and sounds and began to shed his stress. This was his world. He cut the steak slowly, savoring the sight and anticipating the taste. He picked up one French fry and took a bite. He closed his eyes and let the taste fill his mouth. God, that's good, he thought. Vietnam receded in his mind as he let the almost forgotten sounds in, sounds of normal people going about their normal routines. He didn't want to open his eyes.

"You look like you're having sex, Captain Rhodes. I can't believe a French fry is that good."

The voice was female and familiar with a little laugh hiding behind the words.

Without opening his eyes Rhodes said, "How would you know what I look like having sex?"

He opened his eyes and looked into a pair of green eyes on an amused face, an amused Navy Lieutenant Commander's face. She was a nurse, in whites, and her shoulder boards said she outranked him a full grade. A Navy Lieutenant commander, even in the nurse's corps, is equivalent to a Major in the Marine Corps. Well, equivalent in a technical sense. Commander Lennon smiled at him. He hadn't noticed the eyes before. He must be getting better. She was still sort of a plain Jane, even off duty. No makeup.

"I'm guessing about the sex," she said. "But if you keep making love to that potato, people will talk."

"Commander, I spent the last five weeks eating hospital food and nothing but LURPs and C-rats for three months before that. I haven't had a decent meal in four months. Right now, I'd take a French fry over a French kiss. Will you join me?"

She watched him for a moment with a tiny smile on her lips. She was a neat looking woman, sturdy in the way of career nurses, a little heavier than he liked, not gorgeous in any sense, but for him, pleasant to look at. Probably a late thirties spinster married to her job.

"I might," she said. "As long as you are planning to stick with French *fries*."

He laughed and stood to hold a chair out for her.

"In any case," he said, "the company of a lovely officer of the Naval service is very welcome tonight."

"Ah. An officer and a gentleman. And a risk taker too. Flirting with a superior officer could have dire consequences, you know."

"Yes, ma'am. I suppose it could. By the way, my first name is Dick."

"Welcome back to the Corps, Dick Rhodes. I'm Marjorie, but you may call me Commander, Captain Rhodes." She smiled and winked. "Or just Marge in private, Dick."

"Thanks, Marge. I hope you won't mind if I pay the French fries a proper amount of attention. I'm feeling faint."

"Go right ahead. I'm going for the buffet. It's probably the same thing they're serving in the mess hall, but its wholesome. We can talk when you feel your energy returning."

He dug in, stuffing his mouth alternately with French fries and steak. Surprisingly, a sudden memory of Lennon didn't bring any sadness and he turned his thoughts to Lennon's sister. Marge hadn't said anything about his face and hands, but she had looked. Maybe it didn't look as bad as he thought it did. He managed to get a swallow of Bud in between bites but the movement was so smooth it was hardly noticed. Normalcy was engulfing him and he was happy to let go of his morbid thoughts and sink into it. The soft sounds of a woman's voice had helped also. She was pleasant to talk with. Marge ate more slowly and watched him with a fascinated look on her face.

"I've seen starving men eat with less gusto," she said. "You are definitely recovering.

"A month ago, I *was* a starving man. Only one meal in almost four days. You know what? I thought less about food then than I do now after a month with you medicos."

"Fascinating," Marge said. "Tell me about it."

"Can't. It's classified." Rhodes stuffed his last piece of steak in his mouth and chewed it with a satisfied look on his face."

"And I do look so much like a spy," Marge said." Believe me. It was tough getting on this big Marine base and stealing a commander's uniform."

He grinned and took a long pull on his Bud.

"Damn, it's good to drink cold beer again. That's not just bullshit, Commander. I was threatened with everything up to and including castration if I got diarrhea of the mouth. Do you know what time the exchange closes?"

She looked at her watch.

"In about twenty-five minutes. We can still make it if we hurry."

"We?"

"You just got back. You obviously don't have a

car. I do. I don't mind."

"Thanks. I really appreciate it. I have to get some civvies so I can get off base."

"Why not just wear your uniform?" she said.

"Let's talk on the way. I really need some clothes."

In the car, he explained his predicament and how short a time he had been a commissioned officer. It turned out that Marge could relate very well. She had been a Navy corpsman before getting her nursing degree and returning to the navy as an officer. She also knew exactly where to go to get custom uniforms with fast delivery near the base and offered to take the day off and take him there the next day.

Marge went in the exchange with him and talked while he shopped. She asked him about the tremor in his left hand. "Is your hand bothering you?"

"No," he said. "It's just something that comes and goes. Probably just a pulled muscle. Look, I don't know much about the west coast. Are you doing anything tonight? Want to show me around some?"

Marge blushed. Rhodes thought that was kind of cute. He hadn't met many women lately who could still blush.

"Why, Captain Rhodes. Are you asking a superior officer for a date?"

"Damn right I am," he said. "How about it?"

"Well . . .it is a slow night on base. Want to go into San Diego? I know a nice place with no cover charge."

"Can I wear jeans?"

"I'm sure you can. I see men in jeans there all the time."

"Let me check out and we are on our way."

With new jeans, shirts, and loafers in hand, he rode back to the BOQ with Marge so he could change and then get off base for a couple of hours. His previous fear of a normal world was gone. Now he just wanted to be around normal people, raise a little hell, and drink away the smell of Vietnam from his mental nose. Marge was off duty, willing to party, and knew a good place to do it. He couldn't think of a better combination. They returned to her quarters so she could change and then drove into San Diego to raise a little hell.

For the first time in months he was feeling good without getting shit-faced. The stress that usually marked each of his days and nights seemed to have slipped away. Marge in civilian clothes changed. She got kind of shy and blushed more. She was still a plain Jane, but she had a new glow about her. He wondered what that was all about.

The specter of her brother's death hung over them, but it seemed to pull them together rather than the opposite. They shared something important in both of their lives and the sharing eliminated those first uncomfortable minutes or hours that usually begin a new relationship. A friendly woman, a night on the town, cold beer, that's all he needed, he told himself.

They talked some more about Lennon on the way to San Diego. It wasn't morbid talk, more like filling in the blanks for Marge and somehow Marge always managed to turn the conversation from her brother to Rhodes. She seemed to have made her peace with her brother's death. Soon, they were talking about each other. Soon after that the idea in both of their minds bloomed.

The innuendo started after the first dance. It was one-way at first and Marge blushed as though she had just realized what Rhodes's intentions were. The likelihood of Marge just realizing Rhodes wanted her in bed was slight. She was thirty-five, single, and although not undesirable, she wasn't exactly beating admirers off with a stick either. The blushes were a reaction to the realization that Rhodes wanted her and with a shock she knew she was willing.

The first kiss happened on the dance floor two drinks and three dances into the night. The dancing got closer and more intimate.

"I'd use the old May West line about you having a pen knife in your pocket," Marge said. "But it's probably not a joking matter for you, is it?"

Rhodes nuzzled her ear.

"No, it is not," he said.

"Umm, do that again."

He nuzzled her ear again. "Hope you're not one of those don't do it on the first date ladies."

"I was afraid I was going to be one of those don't do it at all ladies." She laughed nervously. "Let's

379

get something straight before we go any further. I'm not a quickie and I'm too old for the back seat."

"How about making this night last until 0600? We're in civvies. We can find a place. What are you thinking?"

Marge squeezed him tighter. "I'm thinking that would be nice," she said.

They found a motel on the way back to base. The natural chemistry between two lonely, healthy, and reasonably attractive thirty-somethings, unattached and willing, and with a bond strangely rooted in grief, progressed to a satisfactory conclusion. Rhodes was smart enough to pick a nice motel to avoid any hint of cheapness. Marge, while not a beauty queen, was still a very special person, a person he felt like he wanted to know, and not just in the biblical sense. The room was nice, the bed big, and the mini-bar provided all the refreshment they wanted. They relaxed on the bed.

"Don't plan on getting off the base before noon," Marge said in a sleepy voice with her cheek on his chest.

"Are you sure you can get off?"

"Oh sure. I hardly ever take off. I've got too much leave on the books anyway. If I don't use some, I'll lose it. I might even take a week off."

"If you want someone to spend it with, I'm here for a week." Rhodes said.

"Why do you think I mentioned it? Of course, we'll spend it together. Have you got anything else to do besides get your uniforms?"

"Just check in with Admin. I should be free for a week after that.

"That shouldn't take long. Want to get a place on the beach in San Diego? Sun, sex, and booze?"

He agreed and they lay together quietly for a few moments.

"You don't own a liquor store, do you?" he asked.

Marge laughed. "No, we have to buy our booze, I guess."

"Damn. You came that close to being the perfect woman."

In the morning, Marge helped him put the ointment on his healing skin. She told him about a certain brand of moisturizing soap and body lotion that would help the new skin stay soft.

They checked out of the motel at 0600 and Marge dropped him off at the BOQ at 0645. He got some chow, took care of some business at the Navy Credit Union, checked in with Admin, and met Marge at the MCX at 1100. She had a suitcase in the back of the car and a smile on her face. Getting him fitted for uniforms didn't take long, and they were on their way to find a place on the beach after a quick lunch.

They found a room on Coronado Island across the strand from the beach and checked-in at two in the afternoon. Marge took over the duty of applying the ointment to his face after cleansing it with the soap she brought. One thing led to another and they didn't get unpacked until after five. They managed to get to the beach at six that evening. After buying him the stupidest hat he had ever seen, a long walk on the beach, and very nice meal in a small sidewalk cafe, they returned to the hotel.

The rest of the night didn't turn out the way he planned. The spirit was willing, but the body was weak, weaker than he thought. He lay down on the bed to wait for Marge to come out of the shower and closed his eyes for a few minutes—he thought. When he woke up at 0700, the sun was shining in his eyes and Marge was nowhere to be seen.

Fifteen minutes later he heard the key in the lock and Marge opened the door carrying two large coffees.

"Back with the living, I see," she said. "You went out like a light last night."

"Sorry," he said. "I guess I still have some recovering to do."

"We'll make up for it tonight. Trauma is like that when you're recovering. It can catch up with you at the worst times. How are you feeling today?"

"Like a bull. But I better get some coffee in me before I commit to anything."

Marge laughed. It was a nice sound.

"Get some coffee in you and then get a shower. I found a cute little place for breakfast."

Chapter 38

It was a beautiful, sunny day in San Diego. The beach on Coronado Island reminded Rhodes of the sand at China Beach in Danang. He watched a bunch of Navy SEAL trainees run past on the wet sand in boots and utes. They looked like zombies as they struggled through their five-mile run in the sand. Two SEALs struggling along behind the pack reminded him of how the recons looked coming back from a five-day patrol. That memory led to more mental pictures and then to Doc Anderson and Lennon and then to the artillery crashing down around the crater.

Lying on a towel on the beach while Marge was walking in the wash from breaking waves, Rhodes felt the first touches of panic, a panic that came out of nowhere. His life was going well right then and there was absolutely no reason to freak out, no one reason, but many reasons, all of them dead, except in his head. Suddenly pain laced across his chest and he went into a total panic. His heart began pounding increasing his panic. His breathing became shallower and faster. His skin tingled. His eyes dilated as though he was drugged.

Rhodes sat up and put his hand on his chest. He started huffing air feeling like he was suffocating. He looked around wildly for Marge. Heart attack, he thought. Oh, Jesus, I'm having a heart attack. He spotted Marge walking slowly across the sand toward him and waved wildly. She started running to him. He was getting dizzy. He couldn't get his breath and the pain increased. His whole chest felt like it was gripped in a vice.

As Marge got closer and saw what was happening she ran harder and started waving at the life guard. She slammed to her knees and slid in the sand next to him.

"What? What's happening, Dick?"

"Heart," he said. "Pain in my chest. Can't breathe."

"Lie down. Quickly now. Calm down, let me get your pulse. Where does it hurt?"

Rhodes made a fist with his hand and put it against the middle of his chest.

"It feels like something's crushing me."

He had broken out in a sweat and the beads were popping out on his forehead. His pulse was irregular and fast. The life guard ran to the blanket and knelt.

"I'm a nurse," Marge said. "Call an ambulance now." She returned her attention to Rhodes. "Dick, calm down. We're getting help. I'm right here with you. Take a deep breath for me."

He tried to get his panic under control. He'd been in worse situations than this. He was a Marine. He forced his breathing to a slower and deeper pace. It seemed to help. He heard the sirens. Marge wiped his head with her towel. "Don't worry about the pain," she said. 'We can give you something for that. Try to relax. The ambulance is here.

A county ambulance was stationed at the beach with EMTs. They responded to the call from the life guard's radio almost immediately and pulled up on the strand not 200 feet from where Rhodes lay on the towel. They got to him with a stretcher in less than a minute of arriving and had him back to the ambulance in another minute. Marge entered the ambulance with Rhodes and told the EMTs she was a trauma care nurse. They didn't argue with her.

"Give me the leads," she directed and stuck the ECG leads on Rhodes's chest. "Okay, run a strip.

She looked at the strip while the lead EMT talked to the hospital on the radio. He informed the emergency room a trauma nurse was present while the other EMT took Rhodes vitals.

"Pulse one-ten, pressure one-forty over ninety-seven, temperature ninety-seven."

The other EMT transmitted the strip to the

emergency physician. Marge had already seen it and felt better.

"Dick, you can calm down. You're going to be okay. Just relax for me now, okay?"

"Feeling a little better," he said. "Still dizzy, but I don't hurt as bad."

The emergency room physician told the EMTs to start a Ringers IV and transport.

Later Marge pulled the curtain back from his bed in the emergency room and stepped close to the bed.

"Hey, Marine. Looking for a good time?"

She was in green scrubs and smiling. He thought she was about the prettiest sight he had ever seen. The doctor had already been in with the results from his tests. There was absolutely nothing wrong with his heart. It had settled down into a text book normal pattern. They wanted to keep him for a couple of hours for observation, but had quit worrying about his heart. The doctor suspected a panic attack and acute stress. He explained what a panic attack was and asked Rhodes if anything was going on that might cause the kind of stress that could cause that kind of attack. He asked the doctor if he could think about it for a while.

"Where'd you run off to?" he said.

"I might be a nurse, but not in this hospital. The duty Doc chewed me out for interfering. Besides, I needed something to cover this gorgeous body. We came in bathing suits, remember?"

"Good point," he said. "How am I going to get

back to the motel?"

"You should be worrying about when. What happened out there?"

"Christ, I don't know. I thought I was having a heart attack. The Doc thinks it was a panic attack, but, hell, there wasn't anything on the beach to panic about. You were safe. I was safe."

"Dick, that kind of attack can happen from residual stress and you should take it as a wake-up call. Some horrible event in the past can rear up its ugly head when you least expect it. I know some of what you went through with Terry. Want to talk to me about what's going on behind that big, tough Marine mask you wear?"

"How much in the past?" he said.

"Depends a lot on how you deal with unpleasant things. Last week. Last month. Maybe years ago. It's only been, what, a month, six weeks since you were wounded and Terry died?"

"Yeah. But hell, it's what I do. Lennon was just the latest."

"Latest? How many more like Terry are you carrying around in your head?"

He closed his eyes for a few moments. He really didn't want to talk about it.

"A few," he said. "Look, can we get out of here. We only have a few days and I don't want to waste them in another hospital."

She watched him for a few moments. She started to say something, but stopped before she could form the words. Then she decided not to push it.

"They want to observe you for a couple more hours. Tell you what. You rest and I'll take a cab back to the motel and pick up the car and some clothes for you. By the time I get back, they should be about ready to let you go."

"Great!" he said with a little too much exuberance. "Now that sounds like a plan."

Marge watched his face for a few moments, smiled, and patted his arm with her hand.

"Dick, when we get back to the motel, we're going to talk."

"Yeah, sure," he said. "Whatever you say."

After a dinner at the Hotel Del Coronado they walked the beach for a while and returned to the room. Marge had picked up a bottle of Gin and a bottle of tonic for night caps and made them a drink while he took a shower. He knew she wasn't going to let it go. Their evening had been uncomfortably quiet at times, almost as though she was looking for the right time to bring something up. He knew what she wanted to bring up and he didn't really want to get into a long discussion about what was going on inside his head. He wrapped a towel around his waist and opened the bathroom door.

"Did you fix me one? he said.

"Yep. It's there by the TV. Take a good slug. It's time to talk."

"Marge, do we have to do this?"

Marge didn't answer right away and let his

words hang. Then she looked up with a serious look on her face.

"Am I more than just a piece of ass to you?"

"Yes, of course you are."

"After just a couple of days?"

"Yes, damn it. And you know it."

"Then we have to talk. The kind of attack you had on the beach can happen again. I want to know what's behind it. I want to know more about you."

He took a drink of his gin and tonic. What the hell. What harm can it do? He was full of stress and heart sick from the loss of Anderson and Lennon, especially Lennon. The kid was so damn vulnerable. And Marge cared. That was obvious. Or maybe he just needed somebody to talk to.

"Okay. I'll tell you what I can. What do you want to know?"

Marge patted the bed next to her.

"Com'ere. This will work better if I'm rubbing your back," she said. "First, thanks for trusting me. How long have you been over there?"

"A little over two years."

"Two years?" she said raising her voice. "How long do you have left on your tour this time?"

"Another eight months. You see, I extended my first tour for six months and then at the end of the extension my boss talked me into coming back after some leave and training."

"Has all of that been in combat?"

"Yeah. All the time in-country. I did get a four-month break for leave and training."

"What kind of training?"

"Parachute, jungle warfare, Recon."

"That's stressful, isn't it?"

"You bet."

She rolled over and took a drink of her gin and tonic. She looked very good rolling over. Hell, I can't be that messed up, he thought.

"Dick, are you telling me you've been in combat for two years and still have eight months to go?"

"Sounds about right."

She rubbed his shoulders and didn't say anything for a few moments.

"Tell me about when you got the burns. When Terry died."

"That will take all night."

"You got anything else to do?"

"Well, now that you mention it . . ."

"Umm, yeah," she said. "We'll have to take break later. How'd you get the burns?"

"Jeeze. Okay, I was sent down to Lang Vei . . ."

The talking went on for most of the night. When sunlight peaked in through the curtains he was rung out emotionally and physically. They didn't make love. The bottle was close to empty. He opened one eye and pulled Marge close to him so they fit like spoons. In one night, they had grown closer than he had been with his ex-wife after four years.

Marge was a good listener and showed her

interest with good questions, but she let him talk. And talk he did. It came hard at first, but with her encouragement and his need, he was soon telling her things about his feeling he wasn't even aware he felt. The isolation had been strong as an NCO, but it was almost total as an officer. You simply didn't discuss your personal life with anyone, especially anything that might be seen as weakness or instability. It simply wasn't done. You couldn't talk to your subordinates because it could break down discipline. You couldn't talk to your peers because it might be a sign of weakness and they depended on you. You couldn't talk to your superiors because they rated you and controlled your future. Marine NCOs and officers weren't supposed to have feelings. They had discipline. Once he decided to trust Marge, and that surprised him, he opened the flood gates. By morning he was drained and Marge owned a part of him.

After getting some rest and a good meal at noon, they spent the rest of the day walking the beach and talking. Marge began to open-up to him and shared her fears and told him a little about Terry Lennon. Rejected by his father, the kid had had a hard time. When he asked why the father had rejected his son, Marge evaded and got Rhodes talking about his parents. By that night, they had gotten through family and pasts. They knew the time was short and they wanted to cram as much of getting to know each other into the few days left as they could.

Marge asked him about turning down orders and asking to go back to his unit. She tried to talk him into reconsidering, but she didn't push it. She asked him about his unit and got his address so she could write. She asked him about his commanding officer and got his name. They enjoyed every minute of the time they had left together.

The following Monday, Marge went with him to the San Diego airport. They had had a great week together on the beach and she waited with him for his flight to San Francisco so he could catch his flight out of Travis Air Force Base to Okinawa. She wasn't as good at hiding her feeling as he was. She clung to his arm until he finally had to cross the tarmac and board his plane. They were in uniform and didn't have the option for an outward display of affection, so a final kiss was out. The look in each other's eyes they shared made up for it.

On the plane to San Francisco he thought about his situation. Marge was going to write and he had promised to come to where ever she was stationed when his tour in Vietnam was up. He wasn't alone anymore. Maybe it wasn't something that would last a lifetime, that was still to be determined, but both wanted to find out. He now had something to come back to. That would make eight months seem a lot longer.

Chapter 39

Rhodes had a lot of practice shutting down his emotions. Vietnam did that to you. Problem is, you can shut them down on the surface, but they don't go away. For him, the flight across the pacific could only be called numb. He spent two days at Camp Schwab feeling no motivation what so ever, and caught a C-130 back to Danang and then a slick going north to Dong Ha. The transition he was going through was brutal.

When the slick dropped him off at the air strip, Dong Ha was taking a pounding. He jumped to the pad and a crewman threw his bags out behind him as the slick was lifting off. He grabbed everything and ran for a sandbagged CP at the edge of the LZ. The base was taking both mortars and rockets. The mortars were hitting along the runway and the rockets were hitting deeper in the camp. There's nothing like getting you right back in the mood.

The smell of explosives was heavy in the air as he crouched behind the sandbag walls of the CP. The Marines there went about their business as though the incoming was an everyday affair. With a shock, he realized it was an everyday affair and was going to stay that way until he rotated out again. He was back and had to get his act together. He looked like a pogue cowering in the corner of a bunker in his brand new, custom, ripstop, tailored jungle utilities.

One of the CP Marines elbowed his buddy, indicated Rhodes with tilted head, and grinned. Rhodes saw it from the corner of his eye but found himself unable to get up and move around. His heart was pounding and his breath was coming in shallow, quick pants. Oh, Christ, he thought. I will not have an attack, damn it.

A mortar hit close to the bunker and even the Marines dropped to the dirt. Rhodes pushed his back into the sandbag corner and curled up. Got to move. Get out of this corner. Act like an officer. His hands began shaking and his heart pounded harder. Okay, I know what's happening. No need for panic. Get it together Rhodes.

Finally, the strength came. He pushed up off the sand and stood for a moment. Good, he thought. Legs are steady. It's just a mortar attack. You've been through a hundred of them. Unless one lands right smack on the CP overhead, it's just noise, and if it does it won't matter. Move around. He forced himself to walk over to the forward edge of the bunker and look out through the observation port. Smoke was still rising from a small crater near the landing pad.

"All right, numb nuts, get your asses back to work," he said. "It was just an eighty-two."

He was pleased that his voice was steady. He didn't feel steady.

The Marines all resumed their activities. Rhodes asked one of them to call Third Recon and get a jeep sent out for him.

"Your first tour in-country, sir?" the corporal asked.

"Yeah," Rhodes said. "It started in sixty-five. How long have you been here, Corporal?"

Damn, that was a cheap shot, Rhodes thought. He couldn't blame the Marines in the bunker. Hell, he looked like a newbie pogue in his new utilities.

"Too damn long, Captain," the corporal said. "Where'd you get the new camo utes?"

"Pendleton. Had them made up while I was in the hospital. If you were wondering, no, it is not good to be back."

The Marine grinned. "Is it as screwed up back in the world as they say it is?"

"Wish I could tell you. I didn't get a lot of time to see much of anything but the hospital. I need to get some air. Hang in there corporal."

"Yes, sir. Not much choice."

He went outside and took a deep breath of

smoke laden air. The attack seemed to be over. Sharp explosives smells cut at his throat. I don't want to be here, he thought. Why the hell didn't I let them give me orders?

The Jeep arrived with Staff Sergeant Lutts driving. Slaughter was in the passenger seat. Rhodes started to pick up his bags.

"I got'em, Striker." Lutts said. "Jump in the back, sir."

He shook hands with Slaughter before getting in.

"The face looks pretty good," Slaughter said. "The reports I got ranged from you only had a charcoal lump left for a head to minor burns. Glad to see it was closer to the latter. I was surprised when I got the message that you were returning. How are you feeling?"

"Good to go, sir. Ready to get my head back into something besides trying to get out of the medico's hands."

"Turn around here," Slaughter said. "Let me see the burns."

He complied.

"Your ear looks nasty. Will there be any scarring?"

"Maybe the ear," he said. "The Doc didn't think the rest was too bad. I got stuff from Marge to rub into the skin every day. It's supposed to help."

"Marge?"

"Lieutenant Commander Marge Lennon," Rhodes said. "Navy nurse."

"Ah ha. You have a letter just arrived today. Smells very nice, too. Am I correct in assuming Marge is a little more than just your nurse?"

Rhodes grinned. "You are a major and may assume anything you like, sir. I, on the other hand, do not kiss and tell."

"So, there was a kiss involved. This is getting interesting. Wounded warrior. Navy nurse. Lonely nights on the ward . . ."

"Let's not get carried away, sir." he said, his grin getting bigger. "I was only there a month."

Lutts was grinning along with the officers. Wisely he kept his mouth shut.

"Are my teams back from Lang Vei?" Rhodes said. "How's Kelly doing?"

Both Slaughter and Lutts snapped their heads around and looked at Rhodes. From the expressions on their faces he didn't need any words.

"He didn't make it?" he said.

"You were out cold," Lutts said. "I forgot. Sorry Striker. Kelly was hit at the LZ. He was dead when we found him."

Rhodes stared straight ahead. Christ, Kelly too, he thought.

"Sorry, Dick," Slaughter said. "I didn't even think you couldn't have known. Captain Lang rotated out, by the way. I'll brief you when we get to the Ops Center. Go ahead and get checked in and draw your gear. I'll get with you at 1600."

Unknown to Rhodes, two letters from LCDR Lennon had arrived at Dong Ha. One for him and one for Major Slaughter. The difference was her name did not appear in the return address box of her letter to Slaughter and the letter itself sounded a whole lot more official than the one Rhodes got. Slaughter had to read between the lines to get the gist of the nurse's purpose, but a couple of close readings revealed two subtle but important pieces of information. LCDR Lennon was interested in Rhodes as more than just a patient on the personal side, and on the professional side she thought allowing him to return to Vietnam was risky and stupid.

At first he got pissed. What the hell was some split-tail nurse doing interfering in Marine Corps business? What the hell did she know about Vietnam, or command, or Marine Corps officers for that matter? After reading the whole letter again, he got over his anger. She obviously cared for Rhodes, tried to keep the letter professional, and made her points very subtly. Nothing in the letter could hurt Rhodes. Once he accepted that LCDR Lennon wasn't trying to interfere in his command he could read further between the lines and begin thinking about Rhodes as Marge had hoped he would.

Slaughter was feeling the effects of eighteen-months in the combat zone himself and wondered what twenty-four months was going to be like. He was already thinking way too much about getting the hell out of Vietnam. Rhodes was already there and was facing another eight months and facing those months carrying fresh wounds. Why the hell had he come back? He didn't need more combat time for his career. Was that it? Did he want a company? Slaughter decided to observe Rhodes more closely and try to make some decisions about keeping him.

Lutts stayed with Rhodes to take him around the camp to check in and draw his 782 gear. Rhodes got an update on the teams and a briefing on what happened after he was medevac'd out from the LZ near Lang Vei. The teams had lost eight KIA besides the losses on the crashed helicopter and everyone else had at least one wound. Lutts was lucky and only took a glancing hit across one calf. He stayed with the teams and led them back to Lang Vei with the SF and CIDG. The Marines had been pulled back to Dong Ha the following week.

Rhodes dropped his gear off at his hooch and Lutts dropped him off at the Ops Center. Slaughter was working with a captain Rhodes hadn't seen before. They had a large map spread open on a table.

"Slide in here, Dick. Meet Charlie Townsend. Charlie, this is Dick Rhodes."

Townsend smiled and offered his hand, but didn't say anything. Rhodes did the same.

"No rest for the weary, Dick. While you were gone Con Thien was hit by the NVA and One-Four lost forty-four men. Gio Linh, Dong Ha, Camp Carroll, Cam Lo and Khe Sanh were also hit. The NVA are using the southern DMZ as a staging area and Division wants to clean them out. Four operations are laid on concurrently. On eighteen May, Two-Twenty-six and Two-nine will move north with armor into the DMZ from positions near Con Thien. That's Operation Hickory. Concurrently, Three-Four will land in the DMZ by helicopter and provide a blocking force near the river. At the same time, the ARVNs will be conducting Operation Lam Song east of Hickory and two Marine SLFs, Alpha and Bravo, will be conducting Operation Beau Charger and Belt Tight east of them in the DMZ. We will be supporting the operations with eight teams spread across the TAOR two days prior to the start of the operation to provide fresh intelligence. We can expect a lot of enemy movement in the area. Dick, I want you to plan the insertions for Hickory and Lam Song. Charlie will plan the insertions for Belt Tight and Beau Charger. Let's go over the task order."

Although it was a large combined operation, the recon operations were straight forward. Two days of observing, avoid enemy contact, verify intelligence already developed. Slaughter reviewed the tactical area of operations and terrain features and latest intelligence including suspected enemy units in the area. After time for discussion he turned Rhodes and Townsend loose to start the planning. They only had two days to plan and launch the teams. Most of the work was already done and Rhodes only had to concentrate on the Operations Orders.

As Townsend and Rhodes started to leave to

find a place to work—Townsend was occupying Rhodes's desk—Slaughter stopped Rhodes.

"Dick, could I see you for a minute?"

"Yes, sir. Charlie, I'll get with you when I get done here."

"You know where to find me," Townsend said.

Rhodes sat down next to Slaughter's desk. He looked nervous. Slaughter watched him closely for a moment.

"Dick, I'm sorry things are so disorganized. This multi-battalion operation was dropped on us three days ago, and we've been scrambling ever since. Look, we didn't know you were coming back and I had to bring Charlie in to fill in for you. He's been doing a good job and I have to make a decision about keeping him."

"Well, I'm back, sir. What's to decide?"

"Look, I'm just saying, you've got four purple hearts and you've been in the combat zone for over two years. Why the hell did you come back? You didn't have to."

"I've still got half my tour left, Major."

"What's the shaking in you left hand all about?" Slaughter said, deliberately staring at Rhodes's shaking hand.

Rhodes pulled his hand off Slaughter's desk quickly.

"Probably just a pulled muscle," he said. "What's that got to do with anything? Major, I've got eight months left on my tour and I'm going to finish it. Our Marines don't get to bug out half way through their tour just because they get scratched up a little."

Slaughter remained silent for a few moments and watched Rhodes. Rhodes's hand had a definite and regular tremor in it. Why hadn't he noticed it before? Why had it taken a letter from a nurse who knew Rhodes less than a fraction of the time Slaughter knew him? Because I needed him here, that's why. As Slaughter looked, Rhodes became visibly uncomfortable. Slaughter reached a decision and tried to speak as gently as he knew how.

"No, Dick. You *had* eight months left. You are rotating out as soon as I can get orders for you. Are you going to give me any trouble on this?"

"Major, what the hell is going on? Did I screw up?"

"No, damn it. You'll leave here with an outstanding fitness report. Dick, this mess isn't going to be over any time soon. You'll be back and you'll get your company. Don't fight me on this. Take a year or two back in the states."

He looked at his lap and put his right hand over his shaking left hand to still it.

"Christ, Major, I don't know what to say. Has everyone gone crazy? I'm in Vietnam, then I'm in the states, then I'm back in Vietnam, and now you're telling me to go back to the states. I'm having trouble catching up with me."

"I'll tell you what to say. Repeat after me. Aye aye, sir."

He didn't answer right away. He held his

shaking hand and tried not to hope. He wasn't at all happy with the relief and joy Slaughter's words brought.

"Think I can get a west coast assignment?"

Slaughter smiled. Rhodes wasn't going to cause trouble.

"Would this have anything to do with a Lieutenant Commander in the Nurses Corps?"

Rhodes blushed. He could feel it.

"Probably," he said.

"I'll do what I can. They need combat experienced officers in the training command at Pendleton. It would be a good assignment for you."

Rhodes tried to smother the hope he felt. Slaughter had no idea how much relief his words brought. He had no idea how much Rhodes was regretting having turned down a chance for new orders in the hospital.

"I won't try to fight it, Major."

"You won't be running to the Admin office and signing wavers as soon as you get to the states, will you?"

"No, sir. I don't figure I will."

Chapter 40

The hooch no longer had Lang's stuff in it. Rhodes figured the new stuff in the book case and on the other field desk was Townsend's. He reached behind the book case and felt around for his case of warm beer. It was still there. He pulled six cans out.

The cans were corroded, but looked okay. The beer ought to be good—well, wet anyway. He opened one and took a long pull on the suds saturated beer. Hot beer. Damn, that sucked after a month of drinking cold beer. He took another long pull, emptied the can and opened another. He was feeling better than he had in a long time. Maybe just a few days, he thought. Slaughter was well respected and liked. He had friends everywhere. If Admin got off their asses, he could have orders in just a few days and be on the freedom bird back to California.

He reclined back on his rack. I've got to write Marge, he thought. Don't know where I'm going, but where ever it is I'll get thirty days leave and I'll take it in California. If I'm lucky I'll get orders to a training slot at Pendleton. Man, wouldn't that be great?

He chugged another warm beer getting mellow as the alcohol hit his blood stream. The sudsy stuff was getting better. He dug in his foot locker for a pen and some writing paper and then thought, screw it, I'll write in the morning. Then he didn't want to be alone. Maybe Lutts wanted to drink a few beers with him. He started to get up and put his boots on when it occurred to him he couldn't sit around and get shit-faced with the enlisted men, and getting shit-faced was on his schedule for that night. He opened another beer and sat on his rack. Wonder where Townsend is. Probably ought to get to know him.

He heard the alert siren go off, but thought, Screw it. Probably rockets and they'll hit somewhere out by the runway. Why bother? He took another long pull on his beer. He reached for another beer, but his hand didn't make it to the fresh can next to his rack.

Rhodes was blown completely off his rack and the roof of the hooch came down on top of him. Fortunately, his rack was blown across the room with him and slammed into the sandbag wall and ended up on top of him. Fortunately, because the next and almost immediate effect of the 122mm rocket that hit two hooches down from his hooch was the impact of a hot, concussive wall of fire and burning debris.

Unfortunately, a large, twisted, razor sharp piece of shrapnel came with the debris ball and hit Rhodes just below the knee of his left leg. He didn't know about it and didn't feel it. He was twisted and unconscious against a stack of torn and leaking sandbags.

The reaction team arrived minutes after the blast. They came at a run and stopped suddenly and just stared at the wreckage of officer's country. Eight hooches were destroyed or heavily damaged. It only took them a moment to regain their composure and start searching for survivors. Marines began calling out for survivors and moving wreckage. It was still daylight and hopefully the hooches were empty, but they had to be sure.

Two Marines found Rhodes under the wreckage of the hooch overhead and his mattress and didn't try to move him. They lifted the mattress off him and lifted sandbags away from his legs. One of the Marines turned away and retched at the sight of Rhodes's almost severed lower leg. His partner yelled for the corpsman. Other Marines answered the call and began putting out the small fires that remained. A Marine checked Rhodes's neck for a pulse and felt a weak and fluttery movement under his finger. He called for the corpsman and pulled off his utility shirt and used it to slow the bleeding from Rhodes's leg. The Marine with him gripped Rhodes's leg as hard as he could manage just above the knee trying to cut the blood flow.

The corpsman examined Rhodes quickly and applied a tourniquet above the knee. He applied a proper bandage to the wound and debated whether to sever the strip of flesh that was holding the lower part of Rhodes's leg on. He decided not to. He had a lot of leeway in the field, but performing an amputation was not within his discretion. Even severing the useless strip of flesh would be considered an amputation. He loaded Rhodes and his lower left leg onto a stretcher and transported him to Delta Med on base.

The surgeon at Delta Med typed Rhodes's blood and started IVs. He performed the amputation and disposed of the leg. He cut flaps and put the sutures in. Slaughter showed up as Rhodes was being moved to a bed to await medevac to Danang and then Japan where the surgeons would do whatever else was necessary to dress the wound and save the rest of his leg.

"How's he doing?" Slaughter asked the surgeon.

"He'll live. He lost a lot of blood, but we got to the wound quickly enough so he shouldn't have any complications. Of course, there's no guarantees, but I'd say he'll recover and do well with a prosthesis."

"I haven't got a lot of information here, doctor. How much of his leg did he lose?"

"Lower left, below the knee. If you have to lose one that's the way to do it. He won't play football again, but with therapy he'll do well."

"How soon are you moving him out?"

"He'll be going to Danang as soon as he is stable

and can make the trip. Not sure how long he'll be there. Depends on how he responds to treatment. As soon as the surgeons down there feel he is stabilized, they'll ship him out to Japan and then back to the states."

"Any idea where in the states?"

"Usually San Diego initially. Hard to tell after that."

"Thanks, Doc. I've got to get a letter off to his . . .his people."

Slaughter found the letter from LCDR Lennon and wrote her a quick letter describing Rhodes's wound and assuring her Rhodes was safe and being well taken care of. He promised to give her more information as soon as he got it.

Ah Christ, Dick, Slaughter thought. Why the hell did you go and do that for? What are you going to do now? All you had was the Corps, and now you lost that. I hope they treat you okay. He gave his friend those few words and a moment of thought and then he had to get back to the war.

By morning Rhodes looked like he'd been beat with a sledge hammer. Both eyes were black, red and purple, lips swelled and cracking, and his nasal airways were swelling closed. His body was a mass of bruises and contusions. He didn't have any broken bones, but every muscle in his body was bruised from the explosion. Had the mattress not covered him he would have been flash burned also. At least he had that much to be thankful for.

He had regained consciousness during the night, but the surgeon sedated him to assist his body in the recovery. As soon as his vitals were stable he was loaded on a slick and transported to Danang.

The surgeons at Danang gave him a complete exam and double checked the stump. They gave him more whole blood and began a regimen of antibiotics. Danang is where Rhodes regained full consciousness and discovered he had lost his leg. He was surprised at how little it mattered to him at the time. Maybe he was just numb inside.

It was summer and beautiful in Yokosuka, Japan when he arrived at the U.S. Naval Hospital. Officers were segregated from enlisted even in the hospital overseas. Rhodes was put in a semi-private room with a Marine First Lieutenant who had also lost a leg. The Lieutenant's wound was a transfemoral (above the knee) amputation and he was ready to return to the U.S.

"Dick Rhodes," Rhodes said from his bed after the corpsman pulled the curtain back so Rhodes could see his roommate. "Been here long?"

"Too damn long," the Lieutenant said. "I'm Charlie Mitchel. Where'd you come in from, Dick?"

"Dong Ha. Third Recon Battalion. How about you?"

"Phu Bai. Three-four."

"No shit. That my old battalion. What

Company? We probably know some people."

"Charlie Company. Hell, I didn't even get to know anyone. I got this two days after I reported in."

"Booby-trap?"

"Mortar," Mitchel said. "How about you?"

"Rocket. Shit, I was in my hooch thinking about California. I only had a few days left."

"Damn! That's some hard shit to take. So, you finished your year?"

"Actually, I was finishing up twenty-four months and still had eight months to go."

"I though you said you only had a few days left."

"Yeah, I did," Rhodes said. "But I just got back from the hospital for my fourth wound and my boss wanted me out of Vietnam. Looks like the NVA took care of it for him."

"Damn if they didn't. What are you going to do now?"

Rhodes leaned back against the pillow and closed his eyes. He still ached all over but the bruises were slowly turning yellow and some had already cleared.

"I haven't thought about it too much," he said. "The Corps is all I know. I have a girlfriend in California. I guess I'll see how she handles this and then see what's out in civilian life."

"You're older than most captains. You a mustang?"

"Yes. I just got commissioned three months ago." Rhodes thought for a moment. "I think it was three months ago," he said.

"What were you before your commission?"

"Master Gunnery Sergeant. Infantry. Only need four more years to get my twenty. I guess that's out now."

"Are you sure? Your wound is below the knee. You might be able to retrain and stay in. Probably not in the infantry, but hell, you ought to check into it. We had a light colonel back at Quantico with half of his foot missing. They kept him."

"Big difference between a half foot and a half leg," Rhodes said.

"Maybe not as much as you think. Have they fitted you for a leg yet?"

"No, I just got here. Can't you tell? How about you?"

"I've tried it out with the units they have here. I can get around a lot better than I thought. They won't fit me for my permanent leg until I get home. I'm telling you, if you want to stay in you ought to check it out. What can you lose?"

"I guess you're right. I hate to get my hopes up for nothing though. Maybe it's better to focus on getting on with my life."

Mitchel relaxed back on his pillow and didn't say anything for a few moments. Then he turned his head and smiled.

"Well," he said, "you've got a good attitude about it. It took me a lot longer to accept I was out of the Corps and had to figure out what to do with the rest

411

of my life."

"What did you decide?"

Mitchel thought for a moment and put his hands behind his head.

"I'm thinking of teaching. My degree is in history. You don't need two whole legs to teach history."

"Hey, I'm a history major too. I hadn't even thought about teaching. Have you looked into it?"

"Sure. I just need to get about thirty hours of education credits and do my student teaching. Shoot, with my GI Bill and disability pension I could get a master's in education and then start teaching. It's really helped to have something to look forward to."

They didn't talk for a few moments. Rhodes turned Mitchel's words over in his mind. Teaching. He hadn't even thought about that.

"Thanks, Charlie. At least it's something to consider."

He was kept in Japan for three weeks. his bruises and contusions began to heal and fade. He didn't know it, but his roommate had been chosen specifically because of his attitude. Charlie had overcome depression early in his recovery and began planning for his future as soon as he could get around in a wheel chair. His positive attitude impressed the doctors, especially the clinical psychologists, so much they began using him to help with other amputees not doing so well. When Rhodes checked in, his almost numb emotional state worried his psychologist. They arranged for Rhodes to room with Charlie. It was a brilliant move.

Charlie's positive attitude was infectious and Rhodes began taking part in his own recovery. Having a couple of options to consider gave him something to occupy his mind and something to hope for. Still, he was a Marine, damn it, and he wanted to remain in the Corps. But, each day he thought less about his missing leg and more about what he was still capable of.

At the end of his second week five letters from Marge caught up with him. He had written every day, but the topics they each wrote about were two weeks apart in his recovery. He decided to try to get a call through to her quarters so he could bring her up to date—and get a real feel for how she was dealing with his new gimp status.

Yokosuka is sixteen hours ahead of San Diego. So, if he called at noon it would be 2000 the previous night in San Diego, date wise at least. 8pm was a good time to catch her in quarters if she wasn't on duty. He had to take the chance. He could get a regular long distance call through from Japan and not have to worry about using a MARS radio hookups. It would be expensive, but he only planned to call once to get them both on the same page. Hopefully, he would be in the states before too long.

Chapter 41

He put the call through person to person the following day.

"Bachelor Officer's quarters, Corporal Janson speaking, sir."

"I have a person to person call from Japan for Lieutenant Commander Marjorie Lennon."

"One moment, please. I'll ring her room."

The phone rang five times making Rhodes very nervous. Then,

"Commander Lennon."

"This is the overseas operator. I have a person to person call for Lieutenant Commander Marjorie Lennon."

"This is she."

"Go ahead, sir. Your party is on the line."

"Marge? This is Dick. I was so afraid you'd be on duty."

"Dick! Oh, God, I've been so worried. How are you? How is your leg?"

"Better. A lot better. The doctor says everything is healing just the way it should. It's still kind of oozing, but even that's healing. Look, I think they're going to ship me back to the states in about a week. I'll be at Naval Hospital San Diego. Can you come see me?"

"You just try to keep me away. Can you. . .can you get around okay?"

"Well, I won't be playing soccer any time soon, but yeah, I'm doing pretty good. I think we'll have to skip the dancing until I get my new leg, though."

"God, it's good to hear you talking like that. I was so worried. You didn't hurt anything else, did you? You know, like . . .uh. . .like important things?"

He laughed his first real laugh in a month. Marge was okay with the leg.

"No," he said. "No damage, but maybe a little rusty from lack of use. God, it's good to hear your voice."

"You let me know where and when you are coming in and I'm going to be there."

"Okay. As soon as they have a flight for me I'll send you a telegram. Are you sure you want to hang out with a gimp?"

Marge was quiet for a moment and he knew he had screwed up.

"Captain Rhodes, if you ever say anything like

that again I will slap the living shit out of you. Are we on the same page now?"

"Yes, ma'am," he said. "Sorry, Marge. I'm still a little shaky about . . .well, about everything. It's getting better though. I've been considering some alternatives for the future. I'll write you a long letter tonight and tell you about it. Tell me what you think."

"That's better. I'll look forward to your letter. Dick, this is costing you a fortune. We better get off here. Don't forget the telegram. I'm serious. I want to be there when you get in."

"I'll do it. Can't wait to see you."

"Oh, don't worry. You're going to see me, all right. And don't be worrying. Just get well. Bye for now."

"Bye."

By the time Rhodes got back to his room, his face had a relaxed look and he was smiling.

"I take it the previously willing nurse is still willing," Charlie said.

"You take it right. Well, we'll see how it works out. How about you? Any word yet?"

"Yep. Leaving in the morning," Mitchel said, but without much enthusiasm. "I am attached to a medical holding company and assigned to the VA hospital just five miles from my hometown pending rehab and discharge. So far, no willing nurse though."

"You don't sound all that excited about it. What's up?"

Mitchel didn't answer right away. He relaxed on his pillow and closed his eyes.

"Thinking about the future is one thing," he said. "Actually, facing it with this stump is another. In about three days I've got to face the looks on people's faces. People who knew me all my life. It was easier to face here in the hospital."

They were both quiet for a few moments. Mitchel pulled his stump up to a more comfortable position and grunted with the effort.

"Yeah," Rhodes said. "That brings me back to earth too. I keep wondering how Marge is going to react the first time we undress together. It kind of looks like the ass-end of a giant worm, doesn't it?"

"Or a sausage. Do you get phantom pain in the missing part yet?"

"No," Rhodes said. "The stump still hurts and itches and the doctor said I wouldn't get much of the phantom pain until the pain goes away in the stump."

"Sometimes my missing foot itches," Mitchel said. "Let's find something else to talk about."

"War stories?"

"Sure. Believe it or not, I only have one and it's only two days long. Isn't that some shit?"

"They'll love you at the VFW. I had this kid who worked for me in recon. First time I ever saw him I thought he was a fairy. . ."

Later that day he wheeled himself to the general ward to visit with some Marines. It was nice to have a semi-private room, but being stuck there with the same person day after day was getting on his nerves. One of the corpsmen suggested he visit with some of the wounded Marines.

The ward had thirty-six beds and the maladies ranged from intestinal parasites to lost limbs. As he passed through the door a Marine passed him on crutches with an artificial leg tucked under one arm. The Marine looked at Rhodes's stump and nodded. He didn't say anything, just nodded. Rhodes was finding out that stumps aren't great conversation pieces.

He rolled into the ward. On his right was a young Marine missing an arm almost at the shoulder. He was weeping quietly. He didn't look like he wanted company so Rhode's moved on. On his left was a black older Marine, probably an NCO. He was missing a leg below the knee and an arm below the elbow. He was sitting up on his bed and playing solitaire one-handed. Rhode's wheeled himself up to the bed. The chart said SSGT Lucius Macon.

"Staff Sergeant, how's it going?"

Macon looked up slowly. He didn't smile.

"How the fuck does it look like it's going? Did you lose an eye too?"

Rhodes's started to get pissed, but then couldn't find the energy to care.

"Na, just part of my leg. You look like you're healing well."

"Muthafucker! You be the fuckin chaplain now or the fuckin doctor? Why don't you go find some white boy needs your bullshit?"

Rhodes felt the stubborn streak in him flare up. Okay, I can play your game too.

"Going to be hard eating watermelon with one arm," he said.

"Going to be harder finding watermelon in Detroit," Macon said. "That supposed to be some kind of whitey bullshit to make the poor dumb nigger feel better? What the fuck are you anyway? You too old to be a grunt. You a Gunny?"

"Was at one time," Rhodes said. "I'm a captain now. Minus a leg."

"Yeah? That supposed to impress me? I'd stand at attention and salute, but, oops, sorry, Captain, I seem to be missing a leg to stand on and a hand to salute with. Fuck it. It don't mean nothin. Go find somebody want's your honky bullshit."

Fuck it, Rhodes thought. I'm too tired for this shit. What the hell do you say to a guy who lost and arm and a leg. Have a nice day? Shit. This was a dumb idea. He wheeled through the ward getting more depressed the further he went. Finally, he just looked straight ahead and wheeled through the doors at the other end.

The corpsman wheeled Mitchel out of the room at 0600 in the morning. Rhodes promised to look him up when he got back to the states, but knew he wouldn't. A new roommate was wheeled in that afternoon. This one was not good company at all. He was burned on over seventy percent of his body and covered in bandages from head to foot. He wasn't expected to last the week out and was on a permanent morphine drip. Three days later and feeling lower than at any time since he had arrived in Japan, Rhodes watched the corpsman roll the bed with a sheet covering the body out of the room. He felt guilty at the relief, but he was glad the kid had finally died. It was the only way he would ever get out of the medico's hands.

That afternoon he got the news he was waiting for. After examining his stump the doctor told Rhodes he was leaving for San Diego in two days. He talked the corpsman into getting the flight information with ETA in the states and got a telegram off to Marge through the Red Cross. Two days later they wheeled his chair to a lifting machine next to a C-141 and loaded him on the medevac flight. Fifteen hours later after a non-stop flight, he landed at Norton Air Force base and was put in an ambulance for the ride to San Diego.

It was 0300 when they arrived at San Diego Naval Hospital, so he figured he'd see Marge the following day. He was wrong.

Chapter 42

As they pushed Rhodes through the swinging doors at receiving, a nurse in green scrubs and surgical mask detached from a group of doctors and nurses and approached Rhodes. She squatted down next him.

"Hi there, Marine," Marge said and pulled her mask down. "Looking for a good time?"

He reached out and put his hand gently on her face. He looked into her eyes for several moments as his eyes got moist. He couldn't talk.

"Okay," Marge said quietly. "Go easy now. Let's get you in your room and then we can talk all we want."

He nodded his agreement and swallowed hard to get his emotions under control. Crap, he thought, I'm a Marine Captain not some little girl. Marge waved a corpsman away and got behind his wheelchair. She took him to his room and helped him into the bed.

Marge closed the door and sat on the bed next to him.

"Okay now?" she said.

"Yeah, everything's okay now. Do I get a kiss?"

"Just a quick one. Remember, this is a military hospital and I'm on duty."

Well, that didn't work out. The "quick" one turned into a long and involved embrace that anywhere else would have turned into something much more. Finally, Marge put her head on his chest

"Oh, God, I glad you're finally back," she said. "Let me go. I've got to do nurse stuff. Come on, let go."

"Do I have to?" he said. "Why don't you throw the lock on that door?"

"Every wounded Marine's dream, right? Bag a nurse in your room. Not going to happen, Dick. Get your libido under control. Come on, let me go. I've got to get your vitals and look at that leg."

"Well, if I must. One more quick one though."

Marge gave him a quick kiss and managed to dodge his arms before he could pull her back down. "All right, that's enough of that. Did the trip cause you any pain?"

"No. It's healed up pretty good now."

"Let's take a look."

She uncovered his leg and removed the protective covering from the stump.

"Can you feel this?" she said and she probed the scars.

"I can feel it, but it doesn't hurt."

"Good. Dick, they did a nice job closing the wound. I think you're going to have an easy time adjusting to a prosthesis. Now, let me look at that ear. You hardly had time to recover from your burns."

"I've been using the soap you gave me and keeping the ointment on it."

"It looks pretty good, considering. You were lucky."

"Well, I don't think I would use that word. Maybe I wasn't as unlucky as I could have been."

She patted his leg. "Whatever. You're back and that's all that matters. Now you're going to get some rest. I'll be back tomorrow. The Hospital released your bags to me, so I'm going to put all your uniforms in the cleaners. When the corpsman brings the release form for you to sign, don't give him any trouble. Need anything else?"

He raised his eyebrows.

"Besides that," Marge said with a smile.

"About twenty hours of sleep. Thanks, Marge. Come back as soon as you can. I need you."

She touched his cheek. "Don't you worry. I will. Get some sleep now."

The following week was a whirlwind of doctor visits, therapist visits, nurses, corpsmen, administrators, chaplains, Red Cross girls, a boy scout troop, and, of course, Marge. Whenever he thought he was going come apart and start screaming, Marge would magically show up and the pace of life would slow down as she took charge. Of course, it wasn't magic. She had friends who called her whenever he showed signs of becoming overwhelmed by the never-ending process of hospital routine and well-meaning but tediously encouraging supporters.

At the end of the second week at San Diego, he was transferred to the medical holding company at Camp Pendleton for initial prosthesis fitting, therapy, and rehab. Marge could then visit him anytime day or night and she did, often spending the entire evening in his room. Since his was a private room outside of the hospital and he was ambulatory, he was not on the routine lab and pharmacy schedule and locked doors were not a problem.

After another month of healing, mundane routine, and therapy, he was fitted for a lower leg. It was one of the new titanium legs with an articulating ankle joint. He found it to be extremely uncomfortable and clumsy at first. But each time the prosthetist adjusted the socket his stump reacted better. He had to use crutches with it for two more weeks, but with determination he was finally able to wear it and walk without crutches for thirty minutes at a time.

He began wearing his service bravos during the duty day and feeling like a Marine again. He had lost a lot of weight, but his weight was increasing again with a steady diet of good food, physical therapy exercise, and Marge. His uniforms no longer hung loosely on him. At the end of his rehab he was allowed to check out of the holding company for the weekend. He and Marge drove to the beach.

Marge and Rhodes grew closer each day. Life was so good he couldn't help but wonder when the other shoe would fall. He had been knocked down so many times recently expecting another disaster just came naturally, but the days went along and life just seemed to get better.

Rhodes was notified his records had been passed to the medical review board. His doctors and therapists were ready to release him back to duty. The board would evaluate his recovery and give him a disability rating. The future of his career depended on that rating. He requested a face to face interview with the board and put his request to remain on active duty in writing.

While he waited for the administrative wheels of the Corps to grind on, Marge decided not to just wait for whatever happened. She talked him into meeting with an advisor at San Diego State University. Rhodes wanted to remain on active duty, but recognized that his chances of that were slim. He took a day and met with an advisor in the education department. He knew high school teachers didn't make a lot of money, but then, neither did anyone in the military.

The following Monday he parked Marge's car in the visitor slot in front of the administration building on campus and almost left without even going in. Twenty-five or thirty long-hairs in bell bottom jeans, beads around their necks, and angry looks on their faces were blocking the entrance to the building. He doubted peace and love were on their minds. Their anti-war signs made it clear he was in the wrong place at the wrong time.

He was in service alphas, not yet having replenished his civvies inventory. If he went in, he'd probably cause an incident. He grew agitated while he waited to see if they would leave. Why the fuck was he wasting *his* time waiting. All those numb-nuts put together weren't worth one good Marine. He turned the car off and opened the door. He guided his left leg through the door with his hands and got out when he was sure the foot was solidly on the ground. He reached back in for his barracks cover and squared it on his head. With one final pull on his blouse to square away his appearance, he strode directly at the crowd of hippies. If they gave him any shit, he was ready to . . .

"Make way for the General," the long-haired kid in front of Rhodes yelled.

The crowd parted so quickly he was caught by surprise and pulled up short. He had a clear path to the entrance lined with laughing and smiling kids. That's what they were, just kids. Kids like Lennon. Well, not exactly like Lennon, but kids his age. His anger receded slowly.

A pretty, barefoot girl with flowers in her hair stepped out of the crowd and looked his uniform up and down.

"Darn if you aren't the prettiest thing I have seen all morning, General," she said. She pulled a flower out of her hair and reached up to put the stem behind his ribbons. "We award you the order of the wilted petunia. Go and sin no more."

He tried not to, but the smile came anyway. He reached up and tucked the flower stem in until it was secure and then he did the most impulsive thing he had ever done. With his hands around her waist he bent forward and kissed her on both cheeks.

"Love and peace," he said and straightened up. As he hurried into the building, he heard the gang of kids laughing and clapping. Maybe they weren't all assholes after all.

Chapter 43

Life just seemed to keep rushing at him. Not just mundane things, major life changing events. He had to catch his breath, mentally at least. On the way back to Pendleton, he had to admit to himself that maybe there was more to life than the Marine Corps. Dr. Allison had advised him that, yes, he could get his certification by completing thirty-six hours of education professional credits and his student teaching, but she also asked him to consider enrolling in graduate school and working on a joint masters in history and education. She told him a master's degree in his major would go a long way with recruiters from the better schools and it would be a lot easier to get it done now than later when he would have to carry a full teaching load and get his advanced education at night.

With alternatives for his future settled, or at least laid out, he allowed his thoughts to shift to the big issue he had been thinking about since he arrived in Japan and faced the odds that he would be separated from the Corps—Marge. Life wasn't going to settle down until he dealt with that issue. He had something to offer now, one way or the other. He wouldn't be just a gimp and a burden. Maybe not a Marine Officer, but if not, a high school history teacher. Maybe she would consider . . .

He discussed the advisor's advice with Marge that night and she told him to get with his disability counselor to determine what training benefits he could expect if they discharged him with a service related disability. With that topic out of the way, he decided to see where she stood on the other issue, the big one.

"Marge, I'm not sure what the hell is going to happen now. Maybe I get to stay on active duty, maybe they discharge me. Either way it looks like I'll have something to look forward to. Now, I'm not sure where you're at, but I've been thinking that we make a pretty good team. I'd kind of like to get your take on it."

Marge just looked at him for a few moments. Then she smiled.

"It?" she said. "My take on it? Team? Are we talking about starting a business or something else?"

"Well, hell, you know I'm not talking about a business. Us, damn it. I'm talking about us and our future."

"Oh. Did I hear the word love in that speech somewhere?"

"I guess not, but yeah, I'm talking about love. Hell, you know that."

"So, this is a proposal?"

"Well, I was wondering about where your thinking was on it?"

"Dick Rhodes, if you are asking me to marry you this is about the most round about proposal I've ever heard of. Say what you mean."

"Ah hell, Marge. I know I'm not much of a catch now, but yeah, will you marry me?"

She just stared at him shaking her head back and forth. He felt a chill of disappointment. He couldn't know she was shaking her head in wonder not denial.

"Did you really think . . .Never mind. Of course, I'll marry you, you silly ass. What did you think? When?"

"You will? You'll marry me?"

"I said yes. When?"

"I guess as soon as you're ready. Tomorrow is good for me."

"No. You've got to meet my family and they have to have time to make plans. Soon though. Are you going to kiss me or what?"

He grinned real big. He knew the answer to that one.

The story of Striker should have a nice tidy ending, something final to close with. But life isn't like that. There just aren't a lot of tidy endings in real life—until you die—and sometimes that's not real tidy. Service in Vietnam wasn't like that either. There are very few tidy endings that came out of that conflict. For most, most that survived, it ended quickly, overnight really, a plane ride across the Pacific. Some put it behind them as soon as they could, and they got on with life the best they could. Others had a hard time putting it behind them, but eventually found a way to live with the memories. Some never did get over their experience, never were entirely sane again. Striker's war was over when he checked in at the medical holding company. The rest of it was someone else's war.

The Marine Corps did retire Rhodes with a combat related disability. The VA gave him a 40% disability rating with a monthly check, medical benefits, and retraining benefits. He and Marge were married a month after this story closed. He finished his master's degree with the GI bill and VA benefits and took a job teaching history in a good high school until Marge got orders to another station. He moved with her until she retired.

He told Marge later, after he retired, that he liked to think he had a chance to teach his students some of the truth about Vietnam, about the fighting men in Vietnam. Hollywood put out so much pure crap about his war, about the people who fought it, but they weren't alone in those distortions. The news media failed miserably in their reporting. They simply didn't give an accurate view of the war fighter, preferring instead to focus on the more fashionable and sensational stories of race and drugs. Sure, there were plenty of drugs and plenty of racial incidents. After all, an armed force is just a microcosm of the society it is drawn from. GIGO works for the armed forces as well as computers. Garbage in, garbage out. But those things weren't nearly as widespread as Hollywood and novelists would like you to believe. The media, and worse, historians, failed the majority of soldiers, Marines, sailors and airmen that served honorably in a very nasty and unwanted conflict. The media and historians still fail them today.

By the way. If you were wondering, yes, Terry Lennon was gay. Flaming, I think they call it. Marge told me about it eventually. Of course, we called them homosexuals or queers in those days. And sadly, a lot of other things too. The term "Gay" didn't become popular until much later. Strangely, the knowledge of Lennon's sexual orientation didn't change my feelings about him. I remember him just as different, a good kid. He had one hell of a grenade arm. I remember his death as a stinking, useless loss.

Marge put her twenty in and retired a full commander, equivalent to a light colonel in the Corps. I'm very proud of her. My missing foot still itches sometimes, but mostly I don't think about it. I guess life has been good to us and we've enjoyed a measure of success.

Don't get me wrong. I love Marge and the kids and teaching, but I still wonder what life would have been like if I had turned Slaughter down and instead remained a Master Gunnery Sergeant. Top of the heap. It's all I ever really wanted.

END

ABOUT THE AUTHOR

Raymond Hunter Pyle is a two tour Vietnam Veteran. Both tours in Vietnam were served in I-Corps. Today he spends his time in Florida enjoying life with his wife of fifty years and writing tales of war and adventure.

Made in the USA
Monee, IL
24 July 2020